THREE DOG KNIGHT

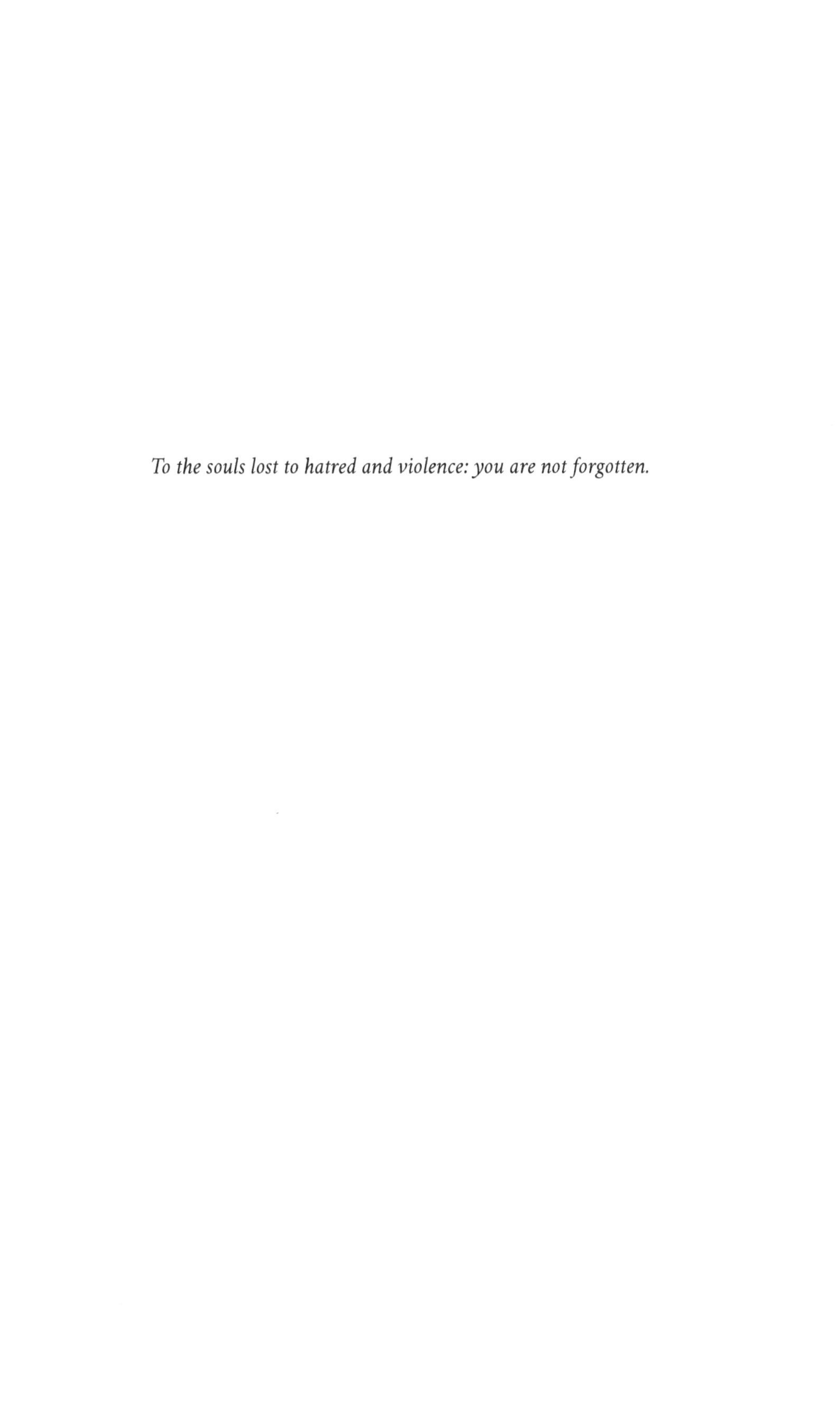

To the souls lost to hatred and violence: you are not forgotten.

1

____

While waiting in line, James Coldstone called the wolf to move closer so he could hear the vocalist, only to be met with someone clearing their throat. The ground outside the Fillmore was already thrumming from the sound of the music. The low, rapid, and rhythmic thunder of the bass drum sounded less like music and more like construction equipment, thanks to the block walls and steel, allowing a small percentage of the noise through the open doors and into the evening air.

The wolf lay on its stomach in his mind, its paws over its head to shut out the noise. James glanced sidelong at Phillip. "I always enjoy the Line Ride feature to every one of these we go to."

"Hey, this group is popular," Phillip said.

James nodded. "It would help if he could be understood."

"That band is female-fronted."

"She may need to consider getting that looked at by a professional."

"It's a vocal technique."

"I thought it might be smoker's lung."

Phillip laughed, prompting James to join in. In truth, James enjoyed a good heavy metal band. The fast-paced tempo, the complex chords and melodies, all combined with unforgiving lyrics, made for an entertaining ride. Phillip Brown's mother often joked, referring to her son as "Musically Bi-Polar." James remembered combing through Phillip's CD wallet in college, noting the Bone Thugs-N-Harmony and 2-Pac CDs were seated next to the Iron Maiden and Cradle of Filth CDs. Phillip tended to keep his Johnny Cash and Muddy Waters CDs near his Mozart collection. "I'm still struggling to wrap my mind around the concept of a concert combined with a comicon."

"You're just uncultured," Phillip said as the line moved, drawing them closer to the two guards charged with searching each concertgoer before they entered the building. "Hey, if you didn't like these shows, you wouldn't come. I've met you."

"Then you know that I would come regardless," James said. Phillip had an affinity for comic books and fan conventions as well as concerts and other types of live performances and events. James, on the other hand, preferred his own company and rarely went out on his own beyond a beer at the bar near his home. Large crowds and social situations made both him and the wolf uneasy. Far too many smells, noises, and tastes. Too much stimulation.

But he also knew Phillip enjoyed the events more when he had someone to go with. That, alone, outweighed James's preference for quiet and solitude.

Phillip shrugged. "Hey, beats sitting around and not hearing from yet another girl in your life."

"Molly is different from Lacy," James said.

Molly had upended James's habitual cave dwelling since they'd met at James's regular bar. James knocked out her loser of a date, a guy unsurprisingly named "Chad" who'd decided to get a little too handsy and abusive in the parking lot when she'd tried to leave.

Phillip snorted. "No shit. Ones got a badass job that makes her travel on occasion, and one is a literal man-eater." He looked at James. "She still coming?"

"She said she'd be here after her shift is over," James said. "She may be looking for a parking spot right now."

They stepped up to the guards, both people wearing Charlotte-Mecklenburg Police uniforms. The younger one, a black man looking in his late twenties, approached Phillip, his face twitching slightly as if holding back a burst of laughter. "Arms out, please."

Phillip huffed, squaring his shoulders and puffing out his chest. "This 'cause I'm black, isn't it?"

James watched as both men burst into laughter and clasped hands before hugging each other and clapping one another's backs. "Good to see you, man," the cop said. "Been a while! You still with RHPD?"

"Nah, went contract work," Phillip said as he pulled away.

The cop turned to James and offered his hand. "Clint Gordon," he said. "Me and Phillip here went to the academy together."

"James," James said as he shook Clint's hand. "I work with Phillip."

"Nice," Clint said. He cleared his throat. "Okay, let's keep this movin', guys." He motioned to Phillip, who held his arms out while Clint searched him.

James heard someone in the line behind them grunt. "Watch 'em be cousins or something." He pushed the growling wolf back in his mind as he spread his arms out to consent to the search from the female cop working with Clint, keeping his own face stoic at the man's remark as he spoke over his shoulder. "I see no resemblance."

The guy in line blinked, then looked away and started chatting up his date.

Phillip shook hands with Clint again before catching up to James. "What'd that dude say to you? You looked pissed."

"Nothing that matters," James said as he approached the entrance. "Contract work?"

Phillip shrugged. "Beats explaining that I help your sorry ass hunt down shit that would send most people on a grippy-sock vacation at the silly ward."

"This is fair."

The music thundered inside the Fillmore as the local band on stage played on, the female lead singer belting out the lyrics to a song James had never heard before, her low growls obscuring any words he may have understood otherwise. He felt himself nodding along, finding the repeated guitar riff keeping time with the drums catching. Phillip was already at the merch table perusing shirts and CDs for the headliner and opening acts. James looked at the back of the event room and noticed a slew of vendors selling a variety of toys, games, and other geeky treasures, as well as an author trying to sell books during a live rock show. He watched as the author signed book after book while the woman at the table with him collected payments and chatted up other showgoers. One woman yelled and clapped her hands at seeing him, immediately pulling down her shirt to expose enough of her breasts for the author to sign one with a Sharpie before taking a photo with her.

The wolf grunted, giving off an air of respect. *Writers have all the fun, I suppose,* James thought to the beast, a smirk forming on his face.

A booth in the corner caught his eye, the wire racks and tables lined with leather goods normally found at a Renaissance festival. A set of bracers caught his attention, the wolf reacting to the design pressed into the leather. A small, aetheric woman with short blond hair and large, energetic eyes was helping a middle-aged woman with red hair and even brighter red lipstick try on a leather breastplate. The petite woman was adorned head-to-toe in armor pieces that looked less battle-ready and more leather bikini. "The chest is a little small," the older woman was saying as James approached.

"Oh, we can take it out easily," the armor-clad girl replied. "I can get your info and ship it to you when we get it done. Just need your size!"

"Do you ship to Alaska? We're moving there in a few weeks."

"Sure! We'll talk shipping."

James continued to move closer to a particular set of bracers, the wolf chuffing and lowering its head inside his mind as if in deference. The insignia was a wolf encircled in an ornate ring, the detail on the beast's features sharp as if the piece had originally been carved in stone before being turned into a press for leather goods. The wolf was fierce; its mouth slightly open as if overcome with the rush of battle. Smells of sweat, food, and beer mixed with the aroma of leather from the large booth gave him a calmness in the surrounding storm of people shouting over the intensely loud heavy metal music.

Another scent moved in, faint but growing stronger by the second. James barely noticed Phillip step up beside him as he focused on the smell, identifying it as cedarwood. With the number of cedars on the Coldstone Keep grounds, it smelled of home and captivity.

"Holy shit, man," Phillip shouted over the music as he held a DVD case up for James to see. The cover had an alien on the front with a gray, wrinkled face resembling a death's head skull. It wore sunglasses and a business suit, the film title scrawled across the top of the cover. "It's a damn director's cut of *They Live!* We're watching this as soon as we get home!"

"I'm going to bed as soon as we get home," James replied.

"You know that's your problem, right?" Phillip said. "You're an old man."

"I'm thirty-five."

"Your brain is ninety." Phillip held the movie up again. "This is a piece of timeless cinema, and likely one of the most important films ever made. Appreciate what you are in the presence of."

James nodded. "Fair point." He pointed at the bracers. "What symbol is that?"

Phillip studied the bracers. "Fenrir. He's the Wolf God in Norse Mythology." He looked back up at James. "I'm surprised you didn't recognize it."

"Just because I am one does not mean I am fully aware of every aspect of wolf lore," James said.

"Oh, but you were somehow drawn to that symbol in particular?" Phillip laughed. "Way to feed the stereotype."

The wolf growled inside as the cedarwood scent swelled suddenly, overpowering the leather, the sweat, the food and drinks. It filled his senses, not wholly the natural scent of the wood but mixed with a musk he didn't recognize. On edge, James looked beyond the wire rack, catching a figure behind them staring at him intensely before the man turned around and blended in with the swell of people moving through the aisles.

James felt a hand touch his arm gently. He looked down at the girl who'd gotten his attention. She was of medium height, her bright purple hair cut into a bob just below her ears with the bangs left long to frame her angular and delicate face all the way past her chin. She wore a band shirt with the sleeves removed exposing her tattooed shoulders, and James caught a glimpse of another tattoo peeking out from the large tear in the front thigh of her jeans. The scent of cotton candy wafted from her, and James envisioned himself walking through a carnival. The wolf flashed him an image from the Scott Pilgrim movie Phillip had made him watch a few nights back.

"Excuse me," a voice said in his head, calm and soft. Far too soft for what should have been audible over the music. The girl stared at him intently, and he heard her speak again despite her lips not moving. "You're James Coldstone?"

James nodded.

"I need you to take me to the bar." She indicated the bar in the back corner. "And take me over there like I'm your date. I need to order an Angel Shot."

He knew the term. Women ordered an Angel Shot when they needed help because of a man at the bar who was a problem to the point of being a threat. James saw an empty spot near the end.

He looked over his shoulder and found Phillip a few booths away playing a video game with a kid no older than twelve. Phillip whooped and pumped his fist in the air. The kid groaned and rolled his eyes, obviously having lost to Phillip on whatever game they were playing.

James turned his attention back to Ramona Flowers. He put his hand on her shoulder, felt her reach up and put her hand over his as they walked through the crowd to the empty spot at the bar. The bartender approached them. The girl waved her hand, and the bartender stopped in his tracks, blinked a few times as if he'd forgotten what he was doing, then turned away and began making a mixed drink. He finished quickly, then poured a beer and brought both over to James and his new date, setting the drinks down without a word before moving down the bar to tend to other customers.

"I'm called Ginger," Ramona Flowers said, shouting to be heard over the music. The shift from telepathy was more jarring than the telepathy itself.

"You already know who I am," James said while he thought to himself. *So much for meeting Scott Pilgrim.*

"That's because you don't protect your name like you should," Ginger replied with a smile. "Spirit world clucks like hens all the time. Hell, we don't even need cell phones in a pinch."

"I gather you are a witch."

"You gather correctly."

"I believe you wanted a particular drink."

Ginger nodded, the smile faltering slightly. She touched his shoulder in a flirtatious gesture as she leaned in, speaking without moving her lips again. "You're the only one here who can serve me an Angel Shot, James." She motioned back toward the leather outfitter's booth they'd just come from. The red-headed woman attempted to try on another piece while the booth owner chatted up another customer. The petite woman was a small child in comparison to the man's height. He kept his back to James, the position seeming purposeful to keep his face hidden. He wore an untucked dark beige button-down shirt with the sleeves rolled up and blue jeans. James felt the hairs on his own neck rise in response to the wolf's hackles going up in his mind, the beast emitting a low growl as it stepped forward, enhancing his sense of smell. He caught the scent of cedarwood again.

It was coming from Ginger's problem person.

"He's been following me since I left the house," she said.

James turned his attention back to Ginger. "My friend, Phillip, is around as well. You are more than welcome to join us."

Ginger smiled. "Thanks, but I don't think it's going to matter."

James looked back at the leather goods booth again to see the petite woman talking to a man in a cowboy hat who was also wearing some leather armor. The Alaska woman was finishing up her purchases.

The guy Ginger was hiding from was gone.

James scanned the room with his eyes, the wolf coming forward enough to help him see inside the venue that was otherwise dark besides the colored light show from the stage. He saw Phillip looking around before he spotted James and came walking toward him.

"Oh shit," Ginger said, panicked. "Where the fuck is he?!"

"Hey, check this out," Phillip said as he approached, pulling a comic book from the bag he carried. "Who's this?"

"This is Ginger," James said, the hairs on his neck still upright. "And we need to leave. Now."

Phillip's expression switched to serious in an instant. "Who am I looking for?"

James caught the loud popping a split second before his beer cup was blown off the bar. More pops, sharp and rapid. People screamed, the music onstage stopping as the lead singer shouted one word into the microphone. "*Gun!*"

The crowd turned into a swarm of mayhem and panic as people flooded the doors in a desperate attempt to escape. Phillip took cover behind the bar, and James moved to pull Ginger down to cover with him, only to find her barstool empty. He crouched as more bullets sprayed the area. The man who'd been following her headed down the back hallway where they served food, walking with determination in a sea of people trying to escape. The gunfire stopped briefly. He caught the telltale sound of someone reloading and saw Phillip's friend Clint holding what looked like an assault rifle. His face was calm, focused, as he slapped the new clip into place. James saw a large group rush him before he could start firing again. Clint vanished in a swirl of bodies, the gun taken from him and tossed to the side.

Well, that's one issue resolved, James thought. He moved from his cover, barely hearing Phillip's protests and shouts of "Where the fuck are you going?!" as he made his way toward the corridor he'd seen Ginger's stalker move down. He could smell the faint traces of cotton candy overlaid by the cedarwood, both fading quickly. James tried to pick up the pace, but the crowd was in pandemonium. He shoved through, finding himself in the cool night air before he realized that he'd stepped through the back door, people running to the street desperately trying to escape despite the shooter, Clint, being stopped. They screamed in terror and panic, some shouting for help while others released the tension with a wordless noise.

One scream stood out from the rest, more a cry of pain. A death shrill. It came from the overpass nearby, at least a quarter mile from the Fillmore.

To hell with it, he thought. *Panic makes an effective smoke screen.*

James shifted, his clothes shredding away as Ginger's scream echoed in the night and was cut short. He loped in the direction it came from, crossing the street and ending up underneath the overpass. He stopped, looked around as he breathed in all the scents, the stench of urine and garbage mixed with gasoline and asphalt.

Cotton candy. Cedarwood. Blood.

Something moved in the dark. James crouched low, waiting to pounce on the thing as it shifted around. It sat up, and James watched the zipper on the sleeping bag open as an older man stared out at him, his eyes wide with terror. He pointed off to the right, his hand trembling with fear. James heard growling and grunting, tearing flesh and breaking bone. He saw a large fur-covered form crouched low in the dark corner where a column met a concrete wall. The thing peered over its shoulder, its eyes yellow and glowing as it chewed hungrily, greedily, tendrils of meat dangling from its blood-soaked maw.

James charged, snarling and gnashing his teeth, the wolf inside mimicking the attack. The other werewolf reacted quickly, rushing back at him. The impact caught him by surprise, knocked the wind out of him. The other was stronger, faster. It slammed its hand into the side of James's head, clapped his ear. James felt his footing shift off balance. The werewolf used his own momentum against him, sending him face-first into a column. James fell to the side, rolled up onto all fours, ready to counter. His breathing was heavy, fast, his heart pounding as he scanned the dark area to see which way his enemy had fled. He heard no sound, saw no trace of the other werewolf outside of the trail of blood on the concrete to Ginger's poor, broken body.

He moved closer to her, his chest heavy with grief and frustration. Her eyes were still open, staring at nothing. Her throat had been torn out, her chest ripped open like a set of double doors. James gnashed his teeth in rage as he backed away from her, fighting back the urge to howl for fear he would hurt the homeless old man. A scent in the air stood out ahead of the other smells of the city night as sirens screamed in the distance, the noise approaching closer with every second.

Cedarwood. He smelled cedarwood.

Another scent layered in, smelling more like cologne. James turned to see Phillip standing several yards away, staring at Ginger, his eyes wide in horror. "Oh, fuck." He looked at James. "What the hell happened here?"

The sirens grew louder, now accompanied by the sounds of police cars pulling up to the Fillmore. James barked, motioned from Phillip to Ginger, and back again.

Phillip cursed, pulled James's phone from his pocket, and tossed it over. James caught it in his mouth, holding it gently to not crack the screen. "James, get the fuck out of here. I'll meet you later. Go!"

James took one last glance at what was left of Ginger, the girl soaking in a pool of her own gore. The images of the other werewolf eating her as he approached replayed in his mind over and over. He shook his head and ran off into the night.

2

James stayed in his wolfen form, sticking to the shadows as he slowed his pace from his wolfen speed and used the nearby alley-ways to keep the cover of darkness. Despite his size, he was able to move much more quietly and deftly in his wolf form, and his fur kept the cold air from making his joints stiff.

It was difficult to see the stars at night due to the typical light pollution found in major cities, and Charlotte was no exception. Dark areas abounded for someone to hide if they chose, and the homeless tended to stick to those places. James did the same, moving from an alleyway to one of the underpasses below the John Belk Freeway. The underpass was ripe with the stench of stale urine, the pillars and walls on either side covered in graffiti. Several homeless people in sleeping bags lay around the area, most of them completely covered up in an effort to ward off autumn's nighttime chill in contrast to the days ruled by summer's heat. Two towers stood a block down from him, the buildings separated by a small parking deck. The compound was across from a coffee shop, the place was closed, and the parking lot was full of cars. One or two had a boot on the wheel, indicating the individual had not paid for parking.

He crouched low, the sound of traffic on the freeway overhead loud and constant. He pulled the phone out of his mouth carefully and checked the front screen to see if he had any messages from Molly or Phillip. The screen showed a missed call from Molly, but that was it. The time stamp had come through a few minutes before the shooting. He couldn't use the touch screen because of the large pads on his fingers, so opening the phone and trying to contact Lacy, Molly, or Phillip wouldn't work unless he shifted.

Clothes, he thought, looking down the street leading into Uptown Proper. He didn't know what clothing stores would be open, but he did know he couldn't parade around the city as an eight-foot werewolf.

He flinched at the sudden sound of sirens as four cop cars blew through the underpass, followed by a transport with the Charlotte-Mecklenburg Police Department SWAT logo on the side of the black vehicle. The transport stopped under the bridge, and two team members disembarked. Both were in full gear, their assault rifles in their hands and readied. They began shouting, approaching the sleeping bags and ordering the occupants to show their faces. Some of the homeless cried out in fear, others froze up and did not come out of their cover until they were forced out via kicking and threats of being shot. As each one emerged, hands up and eyes wide in terror, the officers called out to one another that the people they'd awakened and threatened were not suspects.

"This area's clear," one said.

The second one pulled off his mask and spoke loudly to the homeless community around them. "All of you are to vacate this area immediately. There is an active shooter on the loose." He paused as the people voiced fearful protests, then belted out again. "*Move!*"

The homeless began packing up their camp and leaving. The two officers didn't shoulder their weapons until the last straggler wandered off into the night.

"Fuckin' place smells like piss," the first one said as he put a cigarette in his mouth and lit it.

"Clint, man," said the other. "Who the hell would've thought?"

"Right?" the first one said as he blew a cloud of smoke into the air. "Good dude. Great to have a beer with."

"What about that girl they found?"

"Gut shot. She's in bad shape. Four people dead, twelve injured. She might end up making it five dead."

The second officer shook his head. "Nah, man. I mean the one they found under the bridge."

The first officer nodded. "Yeah, that was pretty fucked up."

"What the hell does that? Some kind of animal?"

"Remember that Wolf-Man Killer thing that happened in Rock Hill?"

The second officer shrugged. "Before my time, but yeah."

"Reminds me of that," said the first. "Same shit. Girl was torn open. M.E. saw she was missing her heart before he even bagged and tagged."

James's phone vibrated in his paw. He looked down and saw a text message from Phillip. *Get over to the stadium. Back lot.*

James shifted into human form and replied to the text.

Stuck under a bridge.

Phillip texted back. *Where?*

James looked around, then shook his head. *Not sure. Can see coffee shop bagel logo pink bridge smells like pee.*

Stay put, I know where you are.

James sent Molly a text message, hoping she was still tied up in traffic and nowhere near the Fillmore.

Stay away. Active shooter.

James shifted back into wolf form. There wasn't going to be a good way to get out of there without getting the attention of the two SWAT officers chatting on the sidewalk. He would have to be fast, take them down without killing them.

He stepped out from behind the large column. The wolf started to come forward in his mind and assume its position to take over for what James had been calling his Sonic Howl. James pushed it back. *We cannot afford to carry the blame for blowing the eardrums out of two human police officers. We have a rather full schedule.*

The wolf gave an indignant chuff and settled back into its place, leaving James in control as one of the cops turned around and startled. *"Jesus, fuck!"*

James charged as both cops opened fire, the sound deafening in the underpass. He dodged, putting a slight zigzag into his assault to avoid as many of the rounds as possible as he closed the gap between him and the officers before going low. He collided with both, the impact barely registering as the officers flipped head over heels into the air, their guns and other accessories flying in different directions before they landed hard on the asphalt. James spun on his heel and readied for another assault. One of them lay still, though James could see the cloud of steam coming from his mouth, indicating he was still breathing. The other tried to stand. James placed the phone down on the ground, stepped up to him, grabbed him by the chest armor, and lifted him off the ground. The officer had to be over two hundred pounds, which was child's play for James. The officer's eyes widened, his face stricken with terror as James bared his teeth and widened his eyes, snarling as he put his face inches from the human in his grasp.

The officer fainted immediately before the smell of shit permeated the man's armor. James dropped him, then reached down and yanked the body camera off the man and crushed it in his large palm. He did the same with the other cop before he looked around the area, his yellowed night vision showing he was the only one still there.

He held up a hand to block the headlights shining in the underpass as a small blue 2021 Honda Civic SI pulled up to him. The window rolled down, and Phillip leaned out of the driver's side. "Let's go!"

James shifted to human form, retrieved his phone, and got in, barely closing the passenger side door before Phillip pulled off and took a left. James reached in the back and grabbed the backpack from the backseat where Phillip kept a spare change of clothes for instances where James had to shift and couldn't strip first. He started to dress as Phillip pulled onto the freeway. "Your timing is excellent."

"What the hell happened?" Phillip said as he merged into traffic.

"The officers were in my way, and I needed to move," James said as he pulled his jeans on. "They are just unconscious. And one of them may need new pants."

"I mean at the Fillmore, dummy," Phillip said. "I dove behind the bar the minute the shooting started because I don't have *my* goddamn gun, the gunman gets rushed, and I find you under a bridge with what used to be the girl you were talking to at the bar."

"It was another werewolf," James said. "She came to me for help. He was stalking her."

"God *damn*."

"How did you manage to leave?" James asked.

"I went after you once the shooter got tackled."

James pulled his shirt on then began tying his shoes. "Clint."

"What about Clint?"

"Clint was the shooter."

"Bullshit."

James looked at Phillip, his expression stoic. Phillip glanced at him, then back at the road. He shook his head. "No way. Clint wouldn't do that."

"And yet, he did," James said, returning to tying the laces on his tennis shoes. "I saw him before he was rushed."

Phillip shook his head again. "Doesn't make sense. Clint is one of the most level-headed guys I know."

"Either way, he is now on the run." James finished with his shoes and sat back in the passenger seat, buckling his seatbelt as he spoke. "I overheard the two officers I knocked out say that there is a citywide manhunt."

"A manhunt for a cop who lost his shit?" Phillip said. "Damn, this ain't gonna be pretty."

"I'm more concerned about the other wolf," James said.

Phillip nodded. "Makes sense. The cops can handle finding Clint. They won't know to go looking for a werewolf."

Phillip pulled off the freeway onto the interstate heading south toward Rock Hill, South Carolina. James replayed the events in his mind, straining to remember anything that stood out other than the scent of cedarwood. He'd only gotten a brief glimpse of the man Ginger indicated was after her, but he'd disappeared a few seconds before Clint had opened fire. It had happened so quickly; all he could recall was the basics: white male, tall, dark hair.

Which narrowed it down to roughly half of the U.S. population, and he'd already ruled himself out as a suspect.

Ginger had been a witch. She used her abilities to track James down specifically. He remembered being warned by Agatha, the necromancer he'd met and subsequently killed in Savannah a month ago, that giving his real name left him open to the spirit world. Hoyt had confirmed later, also noting there was no turning back from it. The spirit world knew who and what James Coldstone was. But why come to him? The Supernatural Crimes Unit was no secret to the supernatural world; the outfit only being unknown to James because he never got out much before getting swept up in his hunt for a vampire group of human traffickers. She could have gone to Agent Smith, filed a report, and had herself placed under their protection.

She could have also gone to the Council of Night, the vampire council that ran the Southeast.

She went to him instead, and he'd failed her.

"Cedarwood," James said.

"What about it?" asked Phillip.

"The werewolf smelled like cedarwood."

Phillip nodded. "Okay, that's a start. Next thing is going to be–" The artificial ringing sound from the car speakers cut him off.

Phillip answered the call by pressing the answer icon on the dashboard screen. "Lotta shit going on, Hoyt. What's up?"

"No shit, you got a lot of shit going on," Hoyt said over the car speakers. "A mass shooting and a werewolf attack in one night? You guys don't stay bored long, do you?"

"We do enjoy a game of chess every now and then," James said.

"Well," Hoyt continued. "You guys aren't gonna have time to set up for your next game."

"This is why you're calling us on your encrypted line?" Phillip asked.

"Yup. Smith's got the SCU hunting you two down. Manhunt is just as big for you as it is for the shooter."

Phillip snorted. "They fired our asses. Probably don't even know what kind of car I drive anymore."

James heard the sound of a button clicking on a computer mouse just before Hoyt spoke again. "2021 blue Honda Civic SI?"

Phillip sighed. "Well, fuck."

"I was calling you guys to see how soon you could get to me," Hoyt said. "Didn't know you were going out."

"Is everything okay?"

"Not sure I'd call it okay, man. Got a couple of victims here in the shop you might wanna take a look at. And the chatter I'm hearing is telling me I have another one incoming as soon as Smith takes over jurisdiction."

"Lovely," James said. "I am going to guess that they all were mauled and missing their hearts?"

"Good guess," Hoyt said. There was a pause, then he said: "Oh, shit. James, man."

"What is it?" James asked, the hairs on his neck rising up as the wolf bristled inside, sending him a feeling of dread.

"They…they just identified Molly as one of the injured. Gut shot."

James felt as if someone had punched him in the chest as he slumped back in the passenger seat. He'd never seen her show up, had no idea she was even there. He stared at his phone at the missed call from her. She likely called him to let him know she was there. He felt sick as the images of how things may have played out in her mind, fought back his mind showing her small body being torn to shreds by the wave of bullets from Clint's gun. Had she been close to Clint when he had opened fire? Did she ever have a chance of not getting shot?

Would she have been saved had James answered his phone and not been focused on helping Ginger?

He barely heard Phillip's response of "Oh, shit. How bad is it?"

"She's in critical condition," Hoyt said as a few more clicks sounded over the speaker. "Looks like they're hauling her into emergency surgery as soon as her ambulance gets there. Presbyterian in Uptown." He sighed. "James, I'm sorry, man. I'm hacked into their system now. I'll keep you updated."

"Ain't a whole lot we can do about it if the SCU is all over our asses," Phillip said.

"Best thing you guys can do is lay low," Hoyt said. "Give me time to see if I can clear you. Venues like that all have security cameras; I'm sure I can find something."

"Right," Phillip said. "Just let us know, Hoyt."

"Will do. Later." Three loud beeps indicated the call was over.

"I should've answered my phone," James said, feeling his stomach churn, his chest still aching. He felt hollow and heavy at the same time; the thought of her being hauled away by the paramedics as she bled out made him feel sick to his stomach.

"You didn't get Molly shot," Phillip said as he pulled off the interstate onto Arrowood Road. "There's no way you could've known something like this was gonna happen. Hell, it happens so damn much nowadays it's become the norm." They rode in silence for a few minutes as Phillip took a right and drove until they arrived at the parking lot at the Light Rail Arrowood train station. Phillip parked at the back corner of the lot and killed the headlights, leaving the car running. "She's gonna be okay, man."

James stared out the window at the lonely-looking train station. Only a few people wandered on the boarding platform, a couple of them huddled together near the vending machines and covered by a single blanket.

All he could hear in his mind was gunfire. The wolf was unable to stop the mental image of Molly clutching her stomach as blood flowed from between her fingers and under her hands, soaking her shirt and pants. She dropped to her knees and then fell forward. More gunfire. Screaming.

"You need to talk, man?" Phillip asked. "James? You need to talk?"

James shook his head, clearing the mental movie from his immediate thoughts as he looked at Phillip. The wolf sent him images of the sun setting over the trees, one of his favorite views from the balcony at Coldstone Keep. "No, I'm fine."

"You don't look fine," Phillip said. "Hell, you witnessed a mass shooting and saw a girl get torn to shreds by another werewolf. I'd be worried if you were fine."

"We need to get to Molly," James said.

"We need to get off Smith's shit list first," Phillip said. "We're not gonna do her or Clint any good if we've got the SCU up our asses."

James felt a sudden swell of anger. The wolf growled low in its throat, its hackles rising only slightly. "I have to ask why I would have any interest in helping the man who shot over a dozen people, including my girlfriend."

"We won't know what made him snap if we don't take him alive," Phillip said, his face a mixture of concern and confusion.

"Whether or not he is taken alive is irrelevant," James shot back. "He killed people tonight and scarred everyone else who was there for the rest of their lives. I am more concerned with the werewolf running around killing people than I am a psychopath who decided to murder a building full of people."

Phillip closed his eyes and gave a large, controlled sigh in what he often referred to as one of his "Woo-sah" moments before he opened them again and spoke in the tone James had heard him use with crime victims in the past. "Look, man. I get it. You've got every right to be angry. Lot of people died tonight, a lot more got hurt, and Molly's one of them. She needs you calm and cool. Right now, there's a dude I've known since my cadet days runnin' around Charlotte who has lost his shit completely, and he needs our help just as much as these girls Clifford the Big Ugly Asshole killed need our help. We don't help him, he'll do it again, and more people will get hurt. Be angry but be rational."

James nodded, letting some of his anger go. The wolf padded around inside his head, sending him images of steak dinners and mauled deer. *There is more to life and happiness than food*, he thought to the animal.

The images changed to at least thirty people engaged in an orgy. James rolled his eyes and sighed. *You're an idiot.* "Clifford the Big Ugly Asshole?" he said to Phillip.

"Catchy, ain't it?" Phillip said. "Maybe I'll write a children's book or something." Both of them laughed at the joke, but the laughter was grim and weighed down by the night's events. Phillip let his laughter die as he stared out the front windshield. "I don't get it, man. We *saw* him just before it all happened. He was fine. I didn't see anything that indicated he was on the verge of…*this*. It makes no fucking sense."

James's phone chimed in his pocket. He pulled it out and paused at the name on the notification banner.

Lacy Faulkner.

> Meet me at Epicenter. We need to talk. Bring Bacon. I'm already there.

3

J ames and Phillip took the train, opting to leave the car at Arrowood rather than park in Uptown.

Despite its name, Epicenter was not the dead center of Charlotte, North Carolina. It was, however, one of the more active areas of the city. Shops and restaurants populated the outdoor, two-story strip center, and it served as a stop on the Light Rail train system that ran all the way to Concord and back. A large hotel connected the area, the rooms priced well outside the grasp of someone making less than half a million a year. People strolled from one destination to another or gathered at the railing on the second level in front of the bar that took up several store spaces and hosted live music.

"Brazilian steakhouse?" Phillip said, reading the sign at the door of a nearby restaurant as they walked past it and a candy store. "Fifteen different cuts of meat? That sounds pretty damn good."

James barely heard him, searching the area with his wolfen senses. The wolf chuffed in his mind, pressed its paw slightly harder against his consciousness, enabling him to take in more scents his human form would not otherwise detect. The smell of cooking food was intense, strong, mixing with perfume from a woman who walked by him, her head down as she texted furiously on her phone. James heard another woman call out, saw a teenage girl help her mother with the stroller while the mortified mom chased after her toddler son, who had wandered over to a potted plant and proceeded to pee into it. Several couples milled in and out of the bars and diners, and James could also see men and women in suits talking on their phones as they moved with purpose toward the banks and businesses nearby.

"Damn, this place is crowded," Phillip said as a lively Led Zeppelin cover played in the upstairs bar.

James nodded. "Given the events of this evening, coupled with an ongoing manhunt, I'm surprised the police haven't cleared this area and locked the city down."

"They don't want to cause a panic," Phillip said. "The Pro-Gun versus Gun Reform crowds have already started going nuts on social media, and the damned shooting was an hour ago. Looks like a lot of these people are headed to the train station anyway. Besides, they'll have sectioned off the blocks nearest Music Boulevard. No one gets in or out." He paused, then spoke again. "She didn't say anything else?"

"She did not," James said, still searching around. "Just told me to meet her here."

"Epicenter is a big fuckin' place, James," Phillip said as they stopped in the middle of the square. "You expect to find one five-foot-five vampire chick in this?"

"She does have a particular scent," James said, taking in the smells again.

"Right," Phillip said. "Forgot. Vanilla. And *blood*. Damn, man. What the hell is it with you and women who eat people?"

"It's a kink."

"Yeah, I'll bet," Phillip said. "What do you think she wants?"

James pushed the wolf back to give himself a break and glanced at Phillip. "I have no idea. This is the first time I've heard from her since we came back from Savannah."

"Dude, look at the obvious," Phillip said. "Shit went down, and here she is again. That's her MO. Shit went down in Charleston, she showed up. Shit went down in Savannah, guess who came running?"

"It does seem suspicious," James said.

"Suspicious, my black ass," Phillip said with a grunt. "She's involved with something. Gotta be. And tonight? Big damn werewolf that isn't you on a killing spree? I'm surprised she's stayed away this long."

"*Hey, dorks!*"

James instinctively fought down the urge to spin on his heel, instead turning casually around to face the direction they heard Lacy's shout. She waved at them, smiling as the breeze coming through the open shopper's courtyard made a lock of her long chocolate waves move into her face. She brushed it away gracefully as she walked toward them. James watched her as she approached, her trademark denim shorts replaced with a dark blue pair of Levi's. She wore a black leather jacket that likely would have cost someone, not him, a full paycheck. It was open in the front to reveal her favorite pink Hello Kitty shirt. James could hear the sound of her boots clopping on the ground as she drew nearer and dialed his hearing back as she stopped in front of him.

"Lacy," James started.

Lacy reached up and hugged him, not an embrace but the kind of hug one gets when they see a friend or relative for the first time in a while. "It's so good to see you, Jimmy!" She let go of him and turned to Phillip. "You have to get another facial expression for me besides a disapproving scowl, Bacon. Still cute, though!" She hugged Phillip, who kept his arms by his sides and his hands in his jacket pockets. Lacy pulled away from Phillip and looked back and forth between them. Despite her warm welcome, James sensed unease in her demeanor. Something was wrong.

"What is this about?" James asked. "In case you haven't seen the news, tonight has been rather eventful."

"Yeah, I heard all about that," Lacy said. "I figured you guys might've been there."

"You tailin' us now?" Phillip said.

"No," Lacy said. "It was a combination concert and nerd show. Why wouldn't you be there?" She winked at him. "Nerd."

"I'm certain you also heard about the girl who was mauled while that was happening," James said.

Lacy nodded. "Yeah, that's what I wanted to talk to you about. Jimmy, it's bad. Smith is after you hard. Word is he's got the SCU under strict orders to bring you in."

"How would *you* know?" Phillip asked.

She shrugged. "I'm pretty and charming. People tell me things." She looked at James. "And I'm telling you that Smith thinks you've gone serial killer."

"I'm sure," James said as he pulled his phone out and brought up her text message to him. "Does this pertain to this text message?" He showed her the screen.

"Kind of." Lacy glanced around, then focused on him again. "Look, it's gonna be easier if you just listen and cooperate."

James put the phone back in his pocket. "Cooperate? With what?" He felt his ear twitch as the wolf heightened his senses, the small noise the creature had likely heard louder. No longer a background murmur. Someone talking, the voice tinny as if inside a can.

Or over a small speaker.

"She's talking to them now."

James tensed his body but kept his stance the same as he spoke in a low tone. "Do not react. Lacy, I believe you were tailed."

Lacy's eyes widened. "Shit."

"Goddamn knew this was gonna happen," Phillip muttered, also keeping his reaction stoic. "Got an idea on how many?"

James nodded slowly, still glaring at Lacy as he shifted his weight casually, making sure his feet were subtly positioned for him to react to whatever might come. "I only heard one. On a radio."

"That's helpful," Phillip said. "No telling how many, then."

Lacy tilted her head, then ran her hands through her hair and sighed again, blowing outward. James saw her glance around. He did the same, looking away from her as he turned his eyes up at the bar where the crowd was gathered. A couple leaning up against the railing chatting closely stood out to him. They reminded him of Phillip's description of "Karen and Chad." Chad stared down at him, then turned his attention back to Karen as he leaned close to her as if they were sharing an intimate moment. "He's suspicious. Go, Plan B."

"Phillip," James muttered. "Balcony. Karen and Chad."

"Got 'em," Phillip responded. "Twelve o'clock. Fucker talking into his watch. Real subtle, dumbass."

"James, don't do anything stupid," Lacy said. "This could go bad. We need to split up."

James started to speak when she spun on her heel and walked the other way, stalking off as if she'd had enough. She pulled her phone from her pocket and called someone, speaking hurriedly as she left. Phillip cursed and tapped James on the arm. "Fuck it, man. Let's roll. She's right. We're going this way. Light rail station."

They started toward the station, moving past a group of recently disembarked passengers. James could hear someone playing an acoustic guitar ahead and moaning some religious-themed song as the train left the station, making virtually no noise other than a pre-recorded train horn sound effect that came from a speaker somewhere on the front. He listened for Lacy, but she was too far away and the crowd noise too heavy.

A large, burly man in a suit stepped in front of them. He was a head taller than James's six-foot-four, and his broad shoulders made him wide enough to have to turn sideways to fit through the door frame of the restroom he emerged from. His muscles threatened to tear through the suit, and the fabric strained and stretched across his frame. The sunglasses he wore reminded James of one of those bald henchmen from the movie *Flash Gordon*, the glasses more like puny goggles on the man's face. His jaw was squared and matched the stone-chiseled appearance of the rest of his visage. James caught his scent, the cologne akin to the stuff Phillip wore on occasion. Acidic and rancid, mixed with sickly sweet, the artificial fragrance mingled with some kind of body oil he couldn't place.

James and Phillip stopped in their tracks as the wannabe wrestler stared them down.

"Well then," James said. "May we help you?"

"James," Phillip said, nudging James's arm. "That's a *big* bitch."

"Nonsense, I'm at least a foot taller if I shift. Certainly heavier."

"You can't out here. Too many people."

"You're no fun."

The man worked his impressive jaw a bit, puffing his chest out as he spoke. "You two need to come with me."

James blinked, taking a second to appreciate that the high-pitched, helium-like voice had come from the giant in front of them. James and Phillip looked at each other, back at the man, and burst into hysterical laughter.

"I'm sorry, man," Phillip said, gasping for air. "Just...*damn!*"

"SCU," the giant said, his helium-voice harsh with irritation as he flipped open an ID booklet, flashing his badge. "You're under arrest. Both of you start walking." He pulled a giant revolver from his coat and pointed it at them. In James's hands, it would've been Phillip's favorite nickname for large guns: a "God Damned Hand-Cannon."

In this guy's hand, it resembled a Derringer made for a lady's purse.

"This is loaded with silver, I'm sure," James said, calming his laughter and turning his gaze steely as he focused on the big agent.

"We've been briefed on you," the squeaky giant snapped. "We aren't stupid,"

"I feel the need to disagree."

"Get fucking moving."

"I do apologize," James said, keeping his tone casual. "But I'm afraid I cannot take you seriously with that voice."

"James," Phillip said, his laughter gone and his tone serious. "That is a Colt Python .45 caliber God Damned Hand-Cannon he is basically holding between his thumb and forefinger. *You* might not mind bullets, but I'm kinda allergic."

Called it, James thought to the wolf. The beast chuffed with laughter. "I am aware." James kept his stare on Agent Cliché, his mouth turning up into a smirk. "I am also aware that the report that gun will give off will be just as bad, if not worse, than me shifting in such a public area." The giant's face twitched as James spoke. "Especially during a citywide manhunt only a few hours after a mass shooting."

"Hell yeah," Phillip said with a grin as he turned to the massive agent. "You're right. Hell, this climate? People will take some big-assed werewolf runnin' around over a damned gun going off any damn day of the week."

"And twice on Sundays, I'm sure." James stepped forward, looking up slightly at the agent as he grinned. "I believe we'll be going."

James felt the wind leave his lungs and his feet leave the ground a split second before the pain from the agent slamming his open hand into James's chest registered. James heard people shout and move out of the way as he flew backwards and hit the ground at a backwards roll before sprawling onto his front. He forced air into his lungs as he made himself get up in time to see the agent grab Phillip by the throat and lift him off the ground as people cleared away from the scene, gasping and shouting. Some had phones out and were recording as the suit looked around. "Stay back, people," he squeaked. "This is Federal business!"

Phillip kicked and punched at his captor with no luck. James got to his feet as he pushed the wolf back to stop it from rushing in. *No,* he thought at it. *Too dangerous. We could cause a panic and hurt Phillip.* The wolf chuffed in irritation, moving back with some reluctance as James charged at Cliché. He crashed into the agent, the blow knocking the big man sideways. The agent released Phillip as he fell, his grunt sounding like James had squeezed the largest squeaky toy ever made.

"*Go!*" James shouted as he helped Phillip to his feet. They took off back toward the open courtyard area, the crowds scrambling out of the way as three more suited agents pushed their way through. He glanced over his shoulder and saw a few more heading down the escalator, shoving people aside as they made their way down. James nudged Phillip on the shoulder. "This way."

Phillip looked in the same direction as James and blinked. "You kidding? Those fuckers are gonna be just as armed as Agent Squeaky Toy is."

"I like it," James said quickly. "He is now Agent Squeaky Toy."

"You two hold it," Agent Squeaky Toy shrilled as he made his way toward them, his revolver aimed. "You're coming with us!"

James felt the wolf push forward again. His muscles tensed but didn't shift. His body seemed lighter. His legs were more powerful, his arms swelled slightly along with his chest and shoulders, but not enough to make his clothes feel tight. His vision yellowed, and a low growl came from his human throat as he charged the two oncoming agents on the moving stairways.

He collided with the first one and sent the suit over the side. The other agent pulled a gun, but James smacked the firearm away. The agent came at him. James sidestepped him and sent him rolling down the escalator, made it to the top, and slapped the large red Emergency Stop button with his hand. The machine jerked to a halt, and James saw Phillip kick a stumbling agent to the side before running up the steps.

"Nice move," Phillip said once he reached the top.

James nodded. "Super Wolf saves the day."

"That shit again?" Phillip said. "Why can't you just say: 'I'm a *bad* motherfucker?' Something that doesn't make you sound like a dipshit?"

More of Agent Squeaky Toy's people started up the locked escalator after them. James looked to his right and saw Lacy duck around a corner at the end of the long corridor. Phillip shouted for him to run, then took off in the other direction. James went after Lacy, panicked shoppers moving aside as he closed the gap between him and where Lacy had disappeared. The wolf stayed forward, giving him just enough to move a bit faster than his human form could manage, and his muscles were showing no signs of fatigue. James slowed when he reached the spot, following the scent of vanilla and blood as he turned the corner and saw Lacy standing there. She stared at him, her jaw set and her fists clenched by her sides, her ice blue eyes seeming to glow brighter from where her perfect, long brown curls framed her delicate face. Her stare was hard, business-like.

And sad.

James started to speak when she cut him off. "Stay right there, James."

James blinked. "What?" He heard scuffling behind him, along with Phillip's favorite insult of "punk motherfuckers," and turned to see Phillip being dragged around the corner by two suited men with Agent Squeaky Toy following close behind.

Phillip stopped struggling against the agents holding his arms and glared at James. "Ya' girl screwed us. *Again.*"

James turned back to Lacy to find her closer, locked in a well-trained shooter's stance, and pointing a black handgun at him. She moved her thumb, and James heard the telltale clicking sound of a safety being disengaged. Her stare was all business, but James could see the hint of wetness in the corner of her eye as she spoke. Even though he heard the reluctance in her voice, her words still cut him.

"I need you to come with us, Jimmy."

4

James sat at the table with his arms crossed in front of him, staring off as he pieced the evening together. It had been a month since he'd set foot in the SCU offices in the Bleachery building of Downtown Rock Hill. He and Phillip were in Savannah when Smith fired them for arresting Noble Jones, and they'd even been put on a death notice as per SCU policy when it came to those it ended employment with. There was never a solid explanation of why Smith called the SCU SWAT off, though James assumed that Noble Jones had something to do with it after James and Phillip had killed Agatha, the necromancer who had used Jones to massacre the Abercorn witch coven.

And here they were in the interrogation room, hauled in by possibly the most confusing person James had ever met.

How long had Lacy been working for the SCU? Had she been a plant all along? It explained why she kept showing up then disappearing afterward without so much as a text or a middle finger. The only text he'd gotten from her since Savannah was her cryptic warning.

It's bigger than we thought.

He wasn't unaccustomed to Lacy not being the most forward person when it came to information. But he could see some reasoning in her constant back and forth. It also explained how the SCU got involved so quickly when he and Phillip were working to rescue Mindy. Then again,

Phillip had also lied about being brought on by the SCU, leading to a major falling out between them until Phillip confessed.

Lacy had apparently held strong with her lie the entire time.

She'd let her guard down when it looked like she and James were about to be intimate. In fact, he remembered more than once where her feelings seemed genuine.

He sighed as the wolf lay down in his mind, resting its chin on its paws and staring up at him. He sensed confusion from it as well, felt the same sense of bewilderment. *It doesn't make sense,* he thought to the animal. *And yet, it makes complete sense.*

Another thought hit him, made his chest feel tight as he saw himself and Lacy kissing in the cabin on Westenra Island, pulling at each other's clothes as they grew more passionate. Lacy stopping him, locking herself in the bathroom as the sunlight began to peer into the windows.

His mind continuously flip-flopped back and forth, once again going from Lacy back to Molly. She'd been hurt. She was in emergency surgery, and James couldn't go to her even if he wasn't sitting in an interrogation room. The hospital would be crawling with police looking for Clint or anyone who may have been a witness to the shooting while detectives waited for Molly to wake up so they could get a statement from her. His family name was far too well-known for him to simply waltz into an ER and inquire about his very recently shot girlfriend.

His mind flipped again. Ginger had been actively pursued. She grew desperate enough to recruit James as a bodyguard. A random witch who knew who he was and knew she had a chance if he could help her. James being there hadn't deterred her stalker. In fact, the stranger acted as if he'd expected James. The other werewolf had countered him easily, had been stronger and faster, so his being older than James was a given. Male, obviously, the musk of testosterone gave the cedarwood an edge. He worked on remembering more about the other wolf's fur color and facial features, but it had all happened too quickly. He kicked himself for rushing in, not thinking. If he hadn't been so quick to fight, he might have gotten some more useful information other than "He smells like cedarwood."

The wolf chuffed inside when James bounced back to Molly, pushing back with its own thoughts of Ginger's killer. *Interesting,* James thought to the beast. *You seem to be all business this evening.*

The wolf growled at the image of the murderer werewolf, ending the sound with another more aggressive chuff.

"Here we go again with this fuckin' place," Phillip muttered, grumbling as he paced around the room. He shook his head at James and crossed his arms, copying his body language. "You and that thousand-yard stare."

"I feel I've earned it," James said, breaking his stare and looking up at Phillip. "All things considered."

"I told you to leave that girl alone," Phillip said.

"It seemed important," James said.

Phillip nodded. "Yeah, tracking your flea-bitten ass down and putting us both in handcuffs was probably pretty-damn important."

"I just wanted to be helpful."

"You fucked up," Phillip said, sitting down across from him. "Ain't the first time, won't be the last."

"Fair point," James said. "I believe this is where you tell me that we all fuck up."

Phillip shook his head. "Nah, just you. I don't fuck up."

"I appreciate your encouragement."

"Thanks for coming to my TED Talk."

James raised an eyebrow. "You forgot something."

"Dumbass."

"Much better."

Both of them chuckled, James feeling some weight lift from the banter. More often than not, it was James egging Phillip on. Sometimes he enjoyed it when Phillip turned the tables and gave him a hard time. "We gotta be able to give each other a ration of shit now and then," Phillip had said once. "Otherwise, shit would just drive us nuts."

James smiled. "I seem to remember the last ration of shit I gave you."

Phillip's eyes narrowed at him. "I owe you for that one, nasty-ass."

The door to the room opened. Both of them straightened up as Agent Smith walked into the room with Lacy close behind, carrying paperwork. Lacy glanced at James, then looked away as if she heard the wolf inside him growling at her. Smith made a hand gesture at the large plate-glass two-way mirror in the room, then stood facing them with his back to the window. "Well," he said in his thick and proper British accent, smiling at James. "Here we go again, Mr. Coldstone."

"Copycat," Phillip muttered.

"Dogs and cats do not generally get along," James said.

Phillip looked at him. "What about that werecat? Angel?"

"She was much more attractive than Agent Smith," James said. "She got a pass."

"She tried to kill you."

"So did he, and she was still more attractive."

"I'll give you that."

"He's boring."

"And not as entertaining as he thinks he is."

"Good point."

Smith clenched his jaw and spoke through gritted teeth. "That is quite enough stupidity from both of you." He snatched the file out of Lacy's hand and opened it, looking it over as he paced around the room. He pulled a photo out and dropped it onto the table in front of James. James studied it, recognizing himself and Ginger at the bar at the Fillmore. "Is this you?"

"I assume so," James said. "Otherwise, he's simply a devilishly handsome metal fan with an affinity for comic books."

"Cool it, Jimmy," Lacy said, her tone unusually authoritative. "Just answer the question."

"Yes," James said immediately. "It is me."

"Very good," Smith said, waving his hand. "We now have confirmation on record."

"Of what?"

"That you are not the Wolf-Man Killer." Smith kept his eyes focused on James, watching him as if waiting to see what the reaction would be.

James didn't give him the satisfaction, though internally he was trying not to explode. There had been one Wolf-Man Killer. *One.* David Coldstone. His own father. And the man had died at the hands of James's mother, Layla Coldstone. James was not one, in general, to hate anyone. But he harbored a seething hatred for his father, so much so that the billions he'd inherited still sat in accounts mostly untouched outside of James's basic needs of food and utilities. James had never worked a day in his life, not out of laziness, but because his family name carried so much vitriol in Rock Hill. He had no desire to face public abuse because of his father's insanity. The city had done well to keep the incident out of the national headlines thanks to an unwillingness to bring Dark Tourism to Rock Hill, but people knew werewolves were real. Fortunately, the Southern instinct to be well-mannered and "just not talk about it" was strong, and the subject was left largely unmentioned.

James liked to think his habitual solitude over the years contributed to that.

"You are not as adept at what one would call a 'Poker Face' as you would like to think, Mr. Coldstone," Smith said.

"I disagree," James said without moving or changing his expression. "I like to think I'm quite good at stoicism."

Smith gave a small chuckle. "Your eyes betray you at every turn."

"What the hell is this about, Smith?" Phillip asked, his voice elevated in an effort to break the tension between Smith and James. "We've had a shitty night, and being here ain't helping."

"I am aware of the events of your evening," Smith said as he opened the manila envelope again. He dropped several photos onto the table and gestured at them. "Please, gentlemen."

Phillip grunted and began to look through the photos, but James sat in place, still staring at Smith. He needed the focal point. The mention of his father, given what he'd seen under the bypass, had rocked him. It wasn't David Coldstone, that was for sure. David was dead and buried. So, who was the other werewolf? His first thought was Clint. It made more sense. Clint had been swarmed as soon as there was an opportunity. It made sense that he could've escaped by shifting and taking off at supernatural speed before the humans in the room were aware of what was happening. It meant the two events were connected.

But, if Clint was the werewolf who had killed Ginger, then who was the man James had seen her seemingly trying to avoid before Clint opened fire inside the Fillmore?

"Are you not interested, Mr. Coldstone?" Smith said, interrupting his thoughts.

"I was there," James said with equal disdain. "And I've seen crime scene photos before, Agent Smith."

"Yeah, he ain't wrong," Phillip said as he went over the photos. "There's nothing to see here that stands out."

"Exactly," Smith said. "Which means the SCU is not concerned with Officer Gordon's apparent mental breakdown. That is a crime for the local police to deal with and is outside of our purview. Our focus is on this copycat killer who has decided that Mr. Coldstone's father's crimes are the perfect model." He picked up a small stack of photos held together by a paperclip, separated them, and laid them out on the table. Ginger's poor, broken body was the subject of almost every photo, her throat torn out and her chest opened wide to reveal mauled lungs and shredded meat where her heart had been devoured. "I must ask the significance of the heart," Smith said.

Phillip looked up from the photos. "Oy," he said, speaking in a mocking Cockney accent. "Fuck you, you right nutty wanker." He dropped the accent as he continued. "You fucking arrested us and hauled us in like a couple of felons, and this is *after* you force us to work for you and then fire us for arresting a politician. And you want our help?"

"I agree," James said. "I will not cooperate without an explanation."

Smith bristled, his smirk fading as he kept his eyes locked on James. James leaned forward, now wearing his own knowing smile. "I am going to fathom a guess that you are not used to people pushing back against you, Agent Smith. You find it easier if the sheep just follow orders without question. You are highly intelligent, and you are very good at your job. However, I am no sheep."

Phillip turned to James. "What about me, asshole?"

James didn't break his stare from Smith. "You have your moments."

Phillip started to argue, then stopped himself and shrugged. "Yeah, I was a cop. You got a point. *Baa!*"

Lacy shook her head and muttered under her breath. "Why do I hang out with these two morons?"

"Fine," Smith said, his tone clipped. "The Wolf-Man copycat has been at large for quite some time. Even before your little field trip down the East Coast looking for Mindy Robertson's kidnappers, though, he was not as busy as he has been these past few days. We had already gathered intelligence on you and Mr. Brown's activities. We had agents in every city you visited watching you. While you were off galivanting around like two television stars in a classic American car, the copycat killed three more women. All of them witches. The unsub then went dark until your trip to Savannah."

"Who killed the agents on Westenra Island?" James asked.

"We suspected a necromancer, which was why Agatha Bonny became such a priority despite her more genocidal intentions."

"She had a real beef with House Tepes," Phillip said. "She said something about it right before she died."

"Most magic users do," Smith said. "Tensions between vampires and witches date back centuries. As House Tepes is the head of the Council of Night, I am not at all surprised that she would carry a specific ire for Tepes."

James scrutinized Lacy as he spoke to Smith. "I am to guess these killings are why you had Lacy meet us in Charleston?"

"She insisted," Smith said. "As her great, great grandniece was one of Count Wangenheim's victims."

James kept his stare hard, meeting Lacy's eyes with his own. She appeared stoic, defiant. But he could also see some regret as she stared back at him. "Why did you blackmail me into working for you?"

"Because I knew you would refuse," Smith said. "You became a valuable asset."

"And why fire us?"

"You arrested a member of the Council of Night. I had to show some sort of action to save face."

"You tried to kill us."

"Protocol," Smith said with a shrug. "Nothing personal, I assure you."

"Nothin' personal, my ass," Phillip said.

"I cannot bring you back in," Smith said. "The council would see it as a disrespect, given your inept arrest of Noble Jones."

"So you do have good news," James said. "I'm sure I will move on from my upset at being ostracized from your organization."

"Sarcasm?" Smith said. "Entertaining, but you're assuming that I would want you back here. As Agent Kimble has so eloquently stated on more than one occasion: you are a couple of dumbasses." He sighed. "And yet, you are still useful. Agent Brown has his proficiency for profiling. You, Mr. Coldstone, do have a talent for detective work. However crude that talent may be." He raised an eyebrow. "The matter of the heart, if you please?"

James glanced at Lacy again, the wolf growling at her inside, distrusting. "Fine," he said. "The heart is the most flavorful part of the kill. It houses the most blood in the body, making it particularly rich."

"So there is no other reason to specifically go for the heart?" Smith said. "Leaving the rest of the victim?"

"No," James said. "Not without eating the rest of what was killed. The legends about werewolves exclusively consuming the heart or doing so out of some idea that it carries any significance other than flavor are simply that: legends."

Smith turned to Phillip. "I suppose you have questions that require answers before you cooperate?"

Phillip stared at the photos again, and James could tell from his facial expression that he was already putting a profile together. Phillip had once wanted to be part of the Behavioral Analysis Unit of the FBI, a branch dedicated to hunting down criminals based on building a psychological profile. It became his passion, and he was extremely proficient. The only thing that stopped him was being pulled into the SCU as their own profiler. He looked up from the photos and sucked his teeth at Smith. "That's rich. You want me to help you after you sat here and grilled my best friend. You tried to kill us." He dropped the photos back onto the table. "Fuck you."

The door to the room opened, and Kimble stepped in. She glanced between James and Phillip, rolled her eyes, and then turned to Smith. "The shooter from the Fillmore, Clint Gordon, has been spotted." James saw Phillip tense up, his expression shifting from angry and defiant to haunted.

"Officer Gordon is not our concern," Smith said. "Though do continue to track his whereabouts and deliver anonymous tips to the Charlotte-Mecklenburg Police and local Federal agents."

"Will do. Also, another Wolf-Man victim was discovered," Kimble said without missing a beat. "The killer was long gone, but the body is in the same condition. Mauled, heart missing."

"A witch, I presume?"

"Yes, sir."

"Thank you. Please deploy agents to the location." He spoke to Lacy over his shoulder. "Agent Faulkner, you will take the lead."

James stood. "As you can see, I am not a serial killer. And this conversation is over."

"Indeed," Smith said, also standing. "I expect that you will stay out of this affair now that you have been cleared."

"Bullshit," Phillip said, also standing. "If this guy is running around, James is gonna just end up as a suspect again at some point. We need to take him down. James already has a scent on him."

"You will not operate outside of the law, Mr. Brown," Smith said. "If you and Mr. Coldstone pursue this, I will arrest you for interfering with an ongoing Federal investigation, and you will spend time in prison." He looked at James. "I promise you that we have adequate means of containing you despite your...affliction."

"What about Clint?" Phillip asked.

Smith shrugged. "What about him? He is not our concern. He is yet another mass shooter in a long, long list of those who choose to commit such an atrocity. The police can handle one man with a gun."

"Ginger came to me for help," James said. "This other werewolf was after her for a reason."

"And that reason is for us to discover," Smith said, his tone suddenly sharp and assertive. "Not you. You will remain at Coldstone Keep until this matter is resolved, or you will rot in a cell made of silver and decorated with enough wolf's bane to make every one of your kind in the area gag on their own vomit. Do I make myself clear, gentlemen?"

"Punk ass," Phillip muttered as he turned down the long driveway stretching across the front pastures of Coldstone Keep. "About the only good goddamned thing coming out of this hellscape of a night is you being cleared of a shitload of murders you didn't even know were happening."

James's phone chimed with a text notification. He checked the screen and saw Lacy's short message. *Hey, just wanted you to know that Molly is out of surgery. She's unconscious, but she's stable. She's going to be okay. Figured you'd want to know.*

"I need to go see Molly," James said, putting the phone down.

Phillip shook his head and sighed, his tone calm and understanding as he spoke. "Dude, it is damn near three in the morning, and she's in the ICU. There's no way they'll let you in. Besides, we both need some sleep. I'll take you in the morning, no problem. I think visiting hours start at eight or nine." He paused, then spoke again. "You good?"

James stared at him. "I've witnessed a mass shooting where my girl-friend was shot and almost killed, and I failed to save an innocent girl from being mauled by an insane werewolf who kicked my ass soundly afterwards. I was subsequently arrested and interrogated by another female with whom I have an extremely complicated situationship and threatened by a government agent for whom she works in what may or may not be a sham organization, and I've been told to take my ball and go home." He shrugged. "All-in-all, I think I'm doing quite well."

Phillip nodded. "Yeah, must be Tuesday." He pulled the car up to the front of the house, put it in park, and turned to James. "Look, man. It's a lot. But you know I've got your back, right? You need anything, just say something."

"Thank you," James said. "At the moment, I believe I would like to go to bed. We need to be up early to get to Molly when they open visitation."

"Yeah, we do," Phillip said. "You need to get your driver's license."

Both of their phones chimed at the same time. Phillip still had his phone connected to the car's Bluetooth. He pulled the text up on the screen on the dash. Hoyt had sent them a message in their group chat. James felt his stomach sink a little, not at what the message might entail, but at the fact that he would not be getting much sleep, if any, before going to see Molly.

Need you two to come see me ASAP.

5

Hoyt's lab was in the basement of the medical examiner's office and looked like every morgue James had ever seen on television. He also had an office upstairs in the main public building, but that room was completely empty because he preferred his workspace in one location. There was also little-to-no space in his office for his computer setup as he was pulling double duty as both M.E. and computer forensics. He'd been doing the same thing for the FBI when James and Phillip met him in Savannah, but Hoyt also had skill with some Native American Magic taught to him by his shaman grandfather. Because of a lifetime of being fed lore of the supernatural world while harboring and growing an interest in science, Hoyt had an extensive knowledge of both the supernatural and was top of his class in med school and in his computer studies at M.I.T.

Life wasn't mundane for anyone with an IQ of a hundred and ninety-five.

James could hear heavy metal music blasting from the lab long before he opened the doors and entered with Phillip next to him. Strident electric guitars accompanied by thunderous drums vibrated through the tiled floors. All six of the large screen monitors on the left wall where Hoyt's desk was flashed with images of fire billowing and shooting on the screens to the rhythm of the furious shredding accompaniment. The chemicals on the lab table in the corner rippled inside the various vials and beakers. James saw the microphone stand in the middle of the room before the lights went out, and the monitors were the only lighting in the room. The music faded, and a spotlight shone on the microphone from out of nowhere as Hoyt stepped into the light, his lab coat absent in favor of black jeans and a black t-shirt with the logo of one of his favorite Indigenous metal bands splashed across the front. The music swelled again as he started growling unintelligibly into the microphone, the roaring guttural vocals occasionally broken by a higher-pitched rasped scream. He slung his long black hair in between vocals, then pulled the mic close to his mouth, and released a horrific low, blood-curdling demon's scream that made James's vocal cords hurt listening to it.

Hoyt let the scream fade with the music, then looked at them and waved. "Oh, hi, guys!" He tapped the microphone stand. "Band's new song. What'd you think? It's called 'I Really Want Some Fry-Bread.'"

"I think it sounds like lawnmowers in the bowels of hell being accompanied by Satan," Phillip said humorlessly.

Hoyt grinned and held his fist up with his pinky and index fingers extended like horns. "Hey, thanks, man!" He pulled his phone out and tapped on the screen. The lights in the morgue came back up, the makeshift concert venue turning back into a sterile medical facility. He put his phone in his pocket, walked over to his computers, and started typing as he continued speaking. "You guys must have been on the way already. I didn't think you'd get here so quickly." The monitors flickered, the spinning colors replaced with data sheets, websites, code, and a desktop with at least a hundred folders. Hoyt clicked on a few folders, and the dossiers of each victim appeared on the largest screen, all seven presented in a tile layout. "Lacy said you two were done with interrogation, so I went ahead and got everything ready to show you."

James suppressed a growl the wolf tried to force through his own throat. He pushed Lacy from his mind. He'd deal with her later. "It has been an eventful evening."

Hoyt gave a bitter chuckle, still working on his computer as he spoke. "No shit. I was actually gonna head to that show before I got another Wolf-Man victim in. The showrunner was interested in having some Rez-Metal at the next event and wanted to meet up." He hit the Enter button, and one of the monitors displayed a photo of a young woman with strawberry red hair, hazel-colored eyes, and high cheekbones. She grinned as if she were in mid-laughter, and James could see someone's arm draped around her shoulders. The other individual had obviously been cut out to focus on the girl. Hoyt picked up a tablet and held it out. Phillip took it, and Hoyt began talking immediately. "Anastasia Benson, friends called her Ana. Twenty-three years old, just graduated from Winthrop University with a double-major in Chemistry and Religion. They brought her in about an hour before I was gonna leave for the Fillmore, so sometime around seven."

"James and I were at the beer garden next door getting dinner," Phillip said. "We'd just stepped out to get in line to go into the show." He looked down at the tablet and scrolled. "Says here she was mauled, heart missing."

"Same with every other victim," Hoyt said with a nod. "I've got six and a half girls in here with the same injuries. More or less."

James raised an eyebrow. "More or less?"

Phillip blinked. "Six and a half?"

"She almost got away, ended up taking a fall off the overpass over Cherry Road, and hit a cable on the way down."

"Damn."

Hoyt shrugged. "Got clipped in half with a cable. Doesn't count, but I still gotta note it."

"That's fucked up, man," Phillip said, eyeing Hoyt.

Hoyt shrugged again. "Hey, I gotta keep things detailed. Besides, you try doing this shit on almost no sleep and no dark sense of humor."

"This is fair," James said.

Phillip shook his head and went back to the tablet as he grumbled under his breath. "Y'all need Jesus."

Hoyt continued. "Each one was reported missing to the SCU by a coven here in the Charlotte area. The Daughters of Baba Yaga is their local council."

"All from the same coven?" Phillip said. "That narrows it down."

"One would think that a city the size of Charlotte has more than one group," James said.

"Each city has one main council," Hoyt explained. "And then there are covens that are subsects of that council. The Abercorn Witches in Savannah, for example. But you still have a regional council that governs the whole. Not a whole lot different from the Council of Night, honestly. A coven is usually thirteen women. You have twelve followers and a leader, or Prime." He looked at another computer screen with a Word document pulled up. "The Geechee are the main coven in Savannah. They're a South African group that's been there since they were brought over during the slave trade. They run with a mix of African witchcraft with Christianity."

"Okay, it doesn't narrow down a damn thing," Phillip muttered. "Great."

"Wish it did, man," Hoyt said. "And the murders are pretty much straightforward. The victims were mauled, and their hearts were eaten."

"James already gave the rundown as to why werewolves go after the heart," Phillip said.

"It's an old werewolf myth," Hoyt said. "Werewolves eat the hearts of their victims for various reasons."

James raised an eyebrow. "As the resident werewolf in the room, I can confirm that this truly is a myth. It literally is because of the flavor. It's the same as eating the premium cut of beef from a cow."

"I kinda figured as much," Hoyt said. "The injuries aren't consistent with any type of ritualistic killing or methodology. Serial Killers aren't always picky. Even werewolves."

"Indeed," James said. "However, this werewolf is only killing witches."

"Which means he's got a plan," Phillip said. James recognized the tenor in his voice. Phillip already had a profile. "He's smart, calculating. This unsub knows exactly what he's doing, and he's working toward something. But he's also angry. He's got a lot of rage against women, particularly witches. He could just take the heart and move on, but he takes the time to destroy the bodies. He's patient and cunning, but he doesn't mind letting loose once he knows he's got his victim dead to rights." He looked up from the tablet and at James. "He's not gonna stop until he's wiped out every witch he can find. And not being a witch isn't going to make any woman in his way any safer. He's a textbook serial killer."

"And if it's Clint?" James said.

Phillip shook his head. "Then it means he's also confused, panicked, and psychotic, which doesn't line up. We can add mass shooter to the list. Also, it doesn't line up. A mass shooter isn't looking to kill a particular victim in the room. They're usually trying to take down as many people as possible in the shortest amount of time possible. It's why they tend to use assault weapons. If he'd been after Ginger, he would've been more calculating, and he'd have made a little more effort to target women when he opened fire. He wouldn't have mowed down a room full of people. It doesn't line up with the profile. Serial killers are specific. Even the ones who seem to kill randomly have a pattern."

James replayed his introduction to Clint in his mind. The wolf pushed on his senses, allowing him to experience the memories with smells, sounds, and tastes. He smelled Phillip's body wash, cologne, and aftershave. The rich aroma of fryer grease and hops emanated from the restaurant next door and mixed in with the collage of different scents from the hundreds of other people in line. He caught the slight tinge of cedarwood, but it was gone as quickly as he'd picked it up. James looked around in his memory, trying to spot Ginger's stalker, but he was stopped by Clint for his search. Phillip and Clint spoke to each other, bantering back and forth. James could still smell Phillip's scent. Only Phillip's scent. He decided to separate the other scents in the air again, picking up on each individual smell and identifying its source.

None of them pointed to Clint.

"Clint had no scent," James said, coming out of his thoughts.

Hoyt grinned. "Hey, that's pretty good, man. Poet and don't know it."

"I am aware," James said. "It gave me a bit of a scare."

Phillip stepped in between them. "*Hell* no. Don't you two get started."

Hoyt shrugged. "If I don't get these bodies prepped, it'll smell like a zombie farted."

"I hate both of you."

James nodded. "It does seem like we're in a zoo."

Phillip shot him a glare. "You said Clint didn't smell like anything?"

"I said he had no scent," James said, dropping the rhyme. "Everyone smells like something. In his case, I could smell the material of his police uniform. But the scent is different. It's there whether you are clean or not, clothed or not, and it's underlying and part of every other fragrance on you. Clint had none of that."

"There was also a shitload of people out there," Phillip said. "You might have just not picked it up in the sea of damn smells. Hell, the dude in front of us smelled like B.O. so bad I had to hold my breath whenever Pits McGee put his arms up."

James shook his head. "I was able to identify every other scent out there. Including Pits McGee and the beeswax and peppermint of the female officer. For whatever reason, I could not identify Clint's scent."

"There's another possibility," Hoyt said. "Forensically speaking, it's not impossible to cover up your scent. Hunters typically use deer piss to both attract other deer out of hiding during rutting season and to cover up their scent. Scents carry pheromones, and instinct makes those pheromones give the scent more potency and attraction. That's why antihunting activists piss in areas where hunters have already primed it to bait their kill. It contaminates the setup."

"There you go," Phillip said to James, motioning at Hoyt. "Clint might've covered his scent up without even realizing it."

James couldn't resist. "Insinuating, then, that someone peed on Clint?"

Phillip flipped him off.

"I gotta agree with Smith on this one," Hoyt said, giving Phillip a solemn look. "You guys and the SCU need to focus on Clifford and let the cops handle Clint. I hate it, man. But he's just gonna be a distraction for you while the Wolf-Man is doing his thing."

"Yeah," Phillip said, setting the tablet down. "Except Smith wants us to sit this out, period."

Hoyt waved it off. "He's blowing smoke. He knows you two can get places he can't."

"If there are seven victims now," James said. "That means that we have six more before the coven is wiped out."

"Even small towns have a coven," Hoyt said. "These girls aren't all part of the same group."

Phillip blinked. "But you said they all belonged to the Daughters of Baba Yaga a minute ago."

"Nope," Hoyt said as he made his way over to the cadaver storage cabinets. "I said the Daughters *reported* these girls missing. While it's not uncommon for covens to look out for each other, the Daughters are a council, not a coven. And they're the witch council in the area, so they look out for everyone."

Phillip picked the tablet up again and scrolled through the report. "Says here every missing person's report filed so far has come from the same contact. Doesn't say who, which is odd."

"Someone is already ahead of us," James said.

"Yup," Hoyt said as he opened a cabinet and rolled a cadaver out. The body was covered in a sheet, the form small and delicate. Feminine.

"We need to find out who is making these reports," James said. "They may be able to point us closer to stopping Clifford."

"Clifford? Okay, good name. Got one more thing for you," Hoyt said as he pulled the sheet back and folded it to reveal the girl's face and shoulders without exposing her further. Her body was a pale bluish color, her eyes closed and her facial features relaxed and peaceful. She'd dyed her hair pink at some point. James could see the holes in her upper lip where she'd had a snakebite piercing, and noticed her earlobes hanging in loose loops where she'd once had gauges. "She's an alt girl, no idea who she is or where she's from."

"Jane Doe?" Phillip said. "Smith didn't say anything about an unidentified victim."

"Because he doesn't want to cause a snag in the investigation," Hoyt said. "If he lets out that we have three Jane Does in here, the SCU will end up under pressure from both the vampire and witch nations to identify the bodies, and that'll hold up any progress he could make on tracking down the killer."

"Smith keepin' secrets," Phillip grunted. "What else is new?"

"This one isn't the most recent," Hoyt said. "They found her in Fort Mill, maybe two miles outside of Pineville." He motioned at her neck. "I don't recognize that mark, either. But they found her on the Southbound side of the interstate."

"She was running," Phillip said.

"That was my guess too," Hoyt said as he pulled the sheet back over Jane Doe.

"We should go to the scene of Ginger's murder," James said.

Phillip looked at him. "And this evening's award for 'Bad Ideas' goes to Scooby-Doo. Are you crazy? Smith already said he'd lock us up if we go anywhere near this thing. We shouldn't even *be* here."

"I am aware."

"Oh, then I don't have to remind you that your girlfriend is in the hospital right now, thanks to a gunshot wound. You aren't gonna be able to check on her if you're locked up." Phillip paused, his expression showing the realization of what he had just said. "Shit. James, I'm sorry, man. I…I got nothing. I'm sorry."

James stood still, staring at him without blinking as the image of Molly passed through his mind. His chest ached slightly from the reminder that someone special to him was fighting for her life, and there was nothing he could do for her. He couldn't go to her, couldn't wait in the hospital until the doctors had news of her condition. He would be a sitting target for Clifford. He had to wait until things cooled off.

"We cannot just sit this out," he said, keeping his tone even. "Agent Smith's tendency to play a long game could result in more deaths before Clifford decides to move on." He paused. "*If* Clifford decides to move on. And if he does, we may lose our chance to stop him before he starts another killing spree in another city. As you said, he is not going to stop."

Phillip shook his head. "Damn," he muttered as he rubbed his face. *"Damn."*

6

I t took some convincing on Phillip's part to get James to go home and rest up. "You aren't gonna do her any good if you go there," he'd said. "Dude, she just got out of emergency surgery for a gut shot. She's probably asleep, and it's outside of visiting hours. All you'd be doing is sitting in the waiting room and worrying." Phillip promised that he would take James as soon as Molly was able to have visitors. Dawn was already approaching by the time they got back to Coldstone Keep, and James could feel the exhaustion setting in, some physical but most of it from his concern about Molly. Phillip was ashen from sleep deprivation, driving carefully and with the windows down to keep himself awake behind the wheel.

Before they left. Hoyt had approached James. "She's gonna pull through, man."

James looked at him. "I hope so."

"I know so," Hoyt said without pause. "I checked in on her as soon as it hit the police network. Right before I texted you guys." James nodded. Hoyt had learned a few things under the guidance of his grandfather, one of them being astral projection. He couldn't physically interact, but he could be seen or not seen depending on his preference, and he could communicate. "Gunshot to the abdomen is serious shit, but the guy working on her is a guy I went to school with. He's good at what he does. She's gonna be okay."

James wanted to be hopeful, but he'd seen too much already over the years. Some of what he'd seen in this year alone fell into the "Horrific" category. Phillip was concerned it was getting to James, and James didn't disagree. He knew he was more withdrawn and moodier since his trip down the East Coast to save a little girl from an evil he never wanted to be near again. Fighting a necromancer in Savannah had been a relief of sorts, as if someone had turned the dial on the Tragic Situation Machine down from an eight to a four.

Or a three. It depended on the day.

He slept fitfully, waking about every hour or two from the same recurring nightmare of being outside, standing next to Molly when she'd been shot. He wanted to help her, wanted to step in front of her and take the bullet instead. James could shift and heal from it. Being shot was nothing new to him. But he stood there watching every time as she fell to the ground and lay still in a growing pool of blood, stared at her stupidly, watched her die. He hadn't seen it happen, but his imagination ran wild and caused him physical pain every time he saw her drop to the ground.

James gave up on sleeping and went outside onto the upper balcony overlooking the front pastures of Coldstone Keep. He sat in his Adirondack chair and stared beyond the grass into the woods, trying to find some peace. He checked his phone and saw a text message Lacy had sent two minutes before sunrise.

> I know you're angry. But we need to talk. I'm on your side, I promise.

He heard the sound of Phillip's voice as the door to the balcony opened and shut behind him. "At least you're consistent."

"I'm not entirely sure what you mean," James said, keeping his gaze out over the fields.

Phillip sat down next to him and set the coffee carafe on the table between them, along with two mugs. He talked as he poured himself a cup. "You come out here whenever you want to brood." He poured a second cup and pushed it over to James. "You know most superheroes stand on a tower overlooking the city."

"You finally accept the reality that is Super Wolf."

Phillip snorted. "I accept that you're a goofy bitch." He took a sip of his coffee. "But it made you crack a joke, so I'll take it."

"I'm worried about Molly," James said. "That's all."

"I'd be worried if you weren't," Phillip said. "And hell no, that ain't all. You've been goofier than usual ever since Lacy showed back up."

"I will not let her complicate things with me again," James said flatly. "I have other concerns."

"Like a goddamn serial killer werewolf on the loose," Phillip said. "I know that's been messing with you bad."

"Am I that transparent?"

"You got daddy issues."

"I do not have 'daddy issues.' I have issues with my father."

"Same shit." Phillip pulled his phone out and checked the time. "It'll be dark in about an hour. Might wanna get going."

The drive back to Charlotte took twice as long thanks to evening traffic. Phillip pulled off the 277 bypass into a parking lot next to one of the ubiquitous coffee shops, this one had a green logo. He motioned at the map on the dash display. "Looks like we can take about a ten-minute walk and get to that spot under the bridge where you found Ginger," he said.

James took in the night air as they got out of the car, discerning the different scents and smells in the air. Fried food, coffee, gasoline, tire rubber. Nothing out of the ordinary. He followed Phillip over to the kiosk. As Phillip paid for the parking spot, he saw a figure jogging toward them, a man shirtless and wearing tennis shoes. His pace was slow, his gait giving away a level of exhaustion as he pressed on. Sweat beaded on his dark skin despite the air carrying the welcome nip of a cold front moving through, the sharpness made only mildly cooler by the breeze created by the multitude of buildings populating Uptown Charlotte.

"Damn," Phillip said, also seeing the man. "Little cold for shorts. That's a dedicated man."

James paused, watching the man as he drew closer. "I do not believe those are shorts."

Phillip kept watching, his face falling from suspicion to disbelief. He spoke slowly. "What. The. *Fuck?*"

The jogger was soon close enough for James to see every grisly detail. He was shirtless, said shirt instead wrapped around his waist and barely covered his nude lower extremities. What James had thought initially to be running shoes were white athletic socks. He reeked of sweat and cologne combined with the sweet smell of women's body wash and pheromones. The guy nodded to them as he jogged by, giving them a look of both curiosity and embarrassment at the same time. James stepped aside to let him by as the man spoke. "S'cuse me, fellas. Got me a bit of a situation."

James and Phillip watched him as he kept on down the road and disappeared around the corner. "Okay," Phillip said. "What the hell just happened?"

"I believe he said he has a bit of a situation," James said.

"No shit, he does," Phillip said. "Not the first Walk of Shame I've seen. Let's go." He started across the street once the traffic was clear. James followed, his eyes falling on the parking deck between the two apartment buildings where the jogger had vanished. Something had been different about the jogger. He hadn't been a vampire. Their scent was far too obvious, too strong to hide under the other scents they carried. Even Lacy carried the blood scent, though hers was unique in that the vanilla was more forward, and the blood side carried no smell of rot like other vampires.

"I wasn't aware that you could also smell him," he said to Phillip as they stepped up onto the sidewalk.

Phillip looked up at James. "What? Hell, no. I just know what the Walk of Shame looks like."

James gave Phillip an appraising stare. "Interesting. I once claimed to know everything about you, and yet I learn something new."

"How's that?" Phillip asked.

"When did you do the Walk of Shame?"

Phillip narrowed his eyes at James. "Don't worry about it."

"I'm curious."

"You're ignorant."

"At least give me the year."

"Nineteen mind-your-fuckin'-business."

James caught another scent in the air; sage mixed with soil and the sweet smell of pipe tobacco. He glanced around, the wolf growling inside and sending the hairs on his neck up in alarm. *He smells like cedarwood,* James thought to it. *Not tobacco. Definitely not sage or dirt.* "I smell something."

"Your upper lip."

James pointed at the parking deck. "It's coming from there."

Phillip nodded and checked the 9mm Beretta he carried in the holster underneath his coat. "Alright, let's take a quick side quest."

Scents of motor oil and tire rubber met James as he and Phillip walked down the sidewalk alongside the high-rise, turned the corner, and made their way to the parking deck. The strange scents were slightly stronger here, allowing him to focus on them and ignore the more common scents a person or canine might pick up inside a parking garage. He attempted to narrow down a direction, and find a path where the scent would grow stronger. It was as if whoever, or whatever, was putting off the scent was changing direction constantly. He also smelled the last remnants of the Jogger of Shame, but those scents faded almost immediately upon entering the deck as he had continued beyond the building on his journey.

The structure was solid concrete with electrical and plumbing pipes surface-mounted and leading to different areas for lighting, and what little water was needed for the occasion when the owner might hire someone to pressure wash the oil drips off the floor. Bright lights burned a cool white, and arrows pointed drivers in the direction of their desired spots. Underneath were posted signs saying "One Way." James caught the tobacco scent coming from the ramp leading to the basement level of the garage. The way was blocked by multiple runs of yellow police tape warning the curious not to cross. The tape was accompanied by a row of orange road barrels in the drive, weighed down by sandbags.

"I believe that is where we need to be looking," James said.

Phillip grunted. "That's good detective work, James. How'd you guess?"

"The scent," James said.

Phillip dropped his sarcastic demeanor, reached into his coat, his tone instantly became all business. "Shit. Clifford?"

"No," James said. "It's tobacco and sage. Not cedarwood. I would still recommend caution." The wolf stepped forward in his mind, enhancing his senses beyond his human ability. One more step would start the change.

"Take point," Phillip said, drawing his 9mm from the holster. "I'll cover us from the rear."

James grinned. "We've been friends a while, but this is truly sudden."

Phillip glared at him and chambered a round. "Ever seen *Old Yeller?*"

James chucked, turned, and started toward the closed ramp. He stopped at the corner and peered around, sniffing the air as his eyesight yellowed slightly, making everything clearer. He could see the small dust particles falling from the pipes and fixtures above, could see the specs of dirt on the concrete. The scent filled the air again, the new faint aroma of dried blood mixed in. He moved onto the ramp and made his way down, keeping to the curvature of the right wall as he went and keeping his voice low as he spoke over his shoulder. "I'm not sure that it was the best release of that year."

"*The Curse of Frankenstein,*" Phillip said automatically.

James snorted. "Seriously? I would have guessed *Plan 9 from Outer Space.*"

"Wasn't officially released until '59. Plus, you can't beat Hammer Horror, and it was Hammer's first color horror movie," Phillip said. "*Plan 9* is a classic, though. Even got the remake."

James paused and looked over his shoulder at Phillip. "There is a remake of that movie?"

Phillip nodded. "Goddamn right there is." He set his jaw and spoke through gritted teeth in a harsh whisper. "*Pay. Attention.*"

James continued forward, coming to the end of the ramp and into the lower parking area. The lighting was dimmer, and some of the overhead fixtures were either out or broken entirely. The security gate had been torn down. Three cars were still parked in their spots, though two of them were smashed. The third had had the front windshield caved in. All three were covered in blood, and a large patch of dried blood painted the concrete around them. James saw scorch marks on the walls and columns, the concrete blackened and cracked in the center of each one as if they'd been hit by some kind of blast. There were scratches in the concrete as well, rows of what had to have been made by huge claws being wielded with furious strength.

"This looks more like a showdown than a crime scene," Phillip said, moving closer to one of the rows of claw marks that ended in a chunk of concrete missing from the wall. "Jesus, what the hell did this?"

"Clifford," James said. "It may be safe to say that she put up a fight."

Another voice spoke from the shadows.

"You're damn right, she put up a fight."

Phillip whipped around; his gun aimed in the direction of the voice. The wolf pressed harder against James's human mind, sending a crawling sensation under his skin as his wolfen form readied itself. Phillip barked orders, his tone sharp and authoritative. "Hands where I can see them!"

James felt himself already starting to ease, the wolf cautiously stepping back in his mind with a wary mewl. He saw Phillip's stance waver, but the gun stayed pointed at the elderly black woman leaning against the column near the remains of the security gate. Her skin was wrinkled and leathery, her small form wrapped in an orange, brown, and yellow wool shawl that gave her a moth-like appearance. She wore blue jeans, the flared bottoms barely revealing the sensible black dress shoes she wore. Her silvered hair was combed straight in a style James figured could only be achieved by daily trips to the salon. Her lips were full, and she wore a small amount of makeup. She looked at Phillip, her expression unimpressed as she took a casual puff off the cigarillo she was smoking. She gave a dismissive grunt, then blew the smoke out in a series of rings with no more effort than someone simply releasing a typical cloud of cigarette smoke. The sage and soil scents from earlier were immediately strong, mixed with lavender and, what James could recognize as cocoa butter lotion.

Not pipe tobacco, James thought. *I was close.*

The wolf suddenly gave him the urge to hug her, offer her coffee, and call her "Amma."

"You ain't the first one to point a gun at this old lady, sugar," the woman said with a smirk. "I'm pretty sure you ain't gonna be the last. Put that thing away before you hurt yourself."

Phillip lowered the gun. "Who are you?"

"You can call me Ruby," the woman said as she stood from the column and started casually toward them. "It's nice to meet you boys, finally."

"Finally?" James asked.

She looked at him and smiled. "James Coldstone, you've been on my radar for a good bit." She motioned at Phillip. "You and Phillip have been busy boys."

"How do you know our names?" Phillip asked.

"Because you two were stupid enough to give them freely to a necromancer in Savannah, Georgia who called herself Agatha." She waved her hand in the air. "The spirits haven't shut up about you since. Little annoyin' at times, not gonna lie."

"But you just told us your name," James said.

Ruby shook her head. "I told you what you may call me."

Phillip put his gun away. "Okay, Ruby. You know who we are. I guess that means you know why we're here."

"Nope, that's just a guess." She shrugged. "Considering you boys have a habit of bumbling your way into trouble, I'm pretty confident you're here for the same reason I am." She looked at James. "Only thing I know is what you are, James Coldstone. I would know that even without your name."

"How do you know that?" James asked, the wolf inside giving a low grumble.

Ruby gave a knowing smile. "In due time, honey. Got more important things to worry about." She walked past them and stood facing the wreckage of the crime scene. She took a long pull off her cigarillo and blew a massive cloud of smoke into the air, settling over the scene like a dense fog. Shapes formed in the cloud, featureless shadows at war. A girl hurled blasts at something large before another cloud formed into a giant creature and picked her up. It slammed her against the remains of the car over and over again, then made motions as if tearing her chest open. The scene dissolved into nothing as the smoke monster began to move as if eating the girl, and Ruby let out a long and shuddering sigh. "Good girl, baby," she said in a quiet voice. "Fight like hell."

James tried to process what he'd seen. Clifford had chased this victim into the parking deck, but she'd fought him back. "It would seem that her fighting like hell only enraged Clifford more." He looked at Phillip, who stood staring at the wreckage where the smoke had given its performance, his eyes wide in amazement. "Phillip?"

"That shit was cool as *hell*," Phillip mumbled.

"You've seen magic before."

"Still cool as hell."

"This, coming from someone who associates with a man who turns into a werewolf."

Phillip blinked at James. "Can you imagine what we could do with something like that? We could solve cases in minutes!" He turned to Ruby. "Can you do it again? With more detail?"

Ruby gave a derisive grunt and took a puff on her cigarillo. "It's smoke, honey. Not an HDTV. You get what you get."

"Fuck," Phillip muttered before looking back at James. "Yeah, I got that too. She fought him back, and he got real pissed off. That girl was what? Just over five feet tall and probably weighed a hundred pounds fully clothed and soaking wet? She was dead when he slammed her against the car the first time."

"Indeed," James said. "He took the time to use her to smash a car in before harvesting her heart."

"What is his issue with women?" Phillip said. "It has to be some kind of childhood trauma."

"Not just women," Ruby said. "Warlocks as well, though male witches are exceedingly rare. The Daughters of Baba Yaga received reports of male witches being killed in the same fashion, nearly to the point of extinction, as far back as the nineteen twenties." She motioned at the car. "This werewolf you two call Clifford has probably been around for a while."

"It makes sense," James said. "We live for quite a while."

"It means the profile is off," Phillip said. "Damn."

Ruby smiled at him. "We all make mistakes, honey. But you two need to figure this out before…" She trailed off, her expression going from casual to alarmed.

James caught the scent of cedarwood only a few seconds before Clifford plowed through the wrecked car and barreled down on Ruby. James shifted immediately and charged, collided with Clifford as he closed in on the old witch. They grappled and rolled, teeth gnashing and claws raking over fur and flesh. James planted his feet, grabbed Clifford by the head, and slammed him into the nearby column hard enough to crack it and make some of the concrete crumble. He heard Phillip shouting. "Ruby, get back! James, *move!* I don't have a goddamn shot!"

Clifford recovered and stood, his yellow eyes wide with wild hatred and fury. He snarled at James, challenging him. James returned the snarl, his teeth bared. He saw Ruby step in between them. She stared Clifford down, her shoulders back and her chin out. "We're not done here." Ruby took a long draw off her cigarillo, the cherry bright red and crackling as it turned into a long cylinder of ash. She tossed it away and blew the smoke out, the flow growing in thickness as the area was flooded with a thick fog of sweet-smelling tobacco smoke.

James could still see Clifford in front of him, the smoke seeming to have little effect on him. Clifford looked around in confusion, dropped down onto all fours, and sniffed the air.

Now, James thought to the wolf. *We can end this now.*

The wolf pushed back against him, flashing a mental image of Clint shooting the Fillmore up.

Clifford charged blindly; his guess was more accurate than it should have been as he closed in on Phillip. James tackled Clifford to the ground, and Clifford rolled him into another bout of snapping jaws. James kicked him off, and Clifford hit the ground running, taking off into the smoke in the direction of the ramp.

"Go," Phillip shouted. "Don't let him get away!"

James loped up the ramp and out of the parking deck and onto the street. He saw a glimpse of his quarry as Clifford climbed the bridge up onto the parkway with ease. James followed at his wolfen speed and was on the overpass in seconds. Cars swerved and horns blared as he raced down the crowded interstate. Clifford dodged traffic just as deftly, not looking back to see if James was on his tail as he cut down the exit ramp on the left. James did the same, finding himself on Independence Boulevard. He pushed harder as Clifford plowed through traffic, the motorists often crashing into each other or the guardrails in an attempt to avoid the large thing moving through at insane speeds. Clifford darted right, hopped a twelve-foot fence with a simple jump, and disappeared into the parking lot at the coliseum. James kept up easily, raced through the rows of cars as he watched Clifford duck into a loading area at the back of the building. James did the same, stopping at the sight of a legion of black tour buses parked behind the building.

And no sign of Clifford.

He went low, moving slowly on all fours as he trailed Clifford's scent to a set of doors on the loading dock. The security guards who were supposed to be watching the place lay sprawled on the ground, both knocked unconscious.

He's not making this difficult, James thought. The wolf chuffed in a similar tone as James pushed the door open and entered the long corridor. The scent was faint, almost gone. He stood tall, looking around the dim area, his wolfen vision unaffected by the low lighting.

The wolf growled inside, his body tensing at the sound of the voice behind him.

"What the *entire* fuck?!"

7

A door opened, and a small man with a bouffant haircut, sunglasses, and a jacket studded with loads of glittering fake gems stepped outside. His bedazzled jacket contrasted against his plain dark blue jeans, though the tacky cowboy boots completed an aesthetic the man was obviously going for. He resembled a bad Elvis Pressley impersonator, right down to the large sideburns.

He tensed visibly when he saw James and started talking rapidly before James could react to him, the sharp Brooklyn accent jarring in comparison to what James had expected Elvis to sound like.

"Are you fuckin' kiddin' me, right now?" Discount Elvis waved his hands around as he spoke, his tone manic and high energy. "Kid, what the fuck are you *doin'* to me?! I been lookin' all over the place for you! Jerry said he saw you runnin' through the parkin' lot like a goddamn criminal a minute ago!" He looked James up and down. "Shit, that costume's a helluva lot better than the one I got for you. The fuck you get it?" He shook his head as he moved toward James and grabbed his arm. "Fuhgeddaboudit, we gotta get you in there, your match is up next."

He came through here? James thought. He could smell the traces of cedarwood in the air. The wolf grumbled inside, gave a low bark in his mind. *You're right,* James thought. *Better play along.* He stood to full height and shrugged. Discount Elvis seemed unfazed as he yanked James's arm toward the open door. He allowed himself to be pulled along as the wolf made an inquisitive noise while Discount Elvis kept chatting like he had corner the market on energy drinks, saying things like "You gotta keep your head in this, kid" and "You're fuckin' *killin'* me right now" as he was led through a locker room and down a corridor in the underbelly of the coliseum. The concrete tunnel was busy with wrestlers either interviewing with reporters and recording their bits for television or doing meet-and-greets with fans for photo ops and autographs. A few heads turned at the sight of a short, loudmouthed Elvis impersonator leading an eight-foot-tall werewolf through, and James even heard a few comments as he went.

"Damn, look at that outfit!"

"I heard there was a new guy in the amateur match tonight."

"Shit, that's branding from hell!"

"He got stilts in that suit?!"

The chatter faded as James and Discount Elvis made their way to the end of the corridor. The lighting was down to almost nothing, the only light coming from a couple of people on either side of a curtained opening holding small flashlights over the clipboards in their hands as they spoke into their headsets. James could hear the tinny voice coming from the tech nearest to him as the guy spoke, marking furiously on his clipboard.

"Got the wolf guy in place. Effects check?"

"About damn time. Effects check good. Ready in twenty seconds."

"Thank you, twenty."

Discount Elvis clapped James on the back. "Okay, kid. Remember: we're throwing the match tonight. Gotta get the setup going for next week's rumble."

James heard someone shouting from outside the dark area, and heard the sound of a crowd cheering as the man spoke. *"I heard we got a dog problem!"* The crowd cheered again as the man continued. "Yeah! Guess he got scared off!"

Another voice boomed over the PA system. "I don't blame him. Ain't no ugly, furry, foul-smellin' fleabag got the—" he paused as the crowd shouted *"Stones!"* before he continued. "To go up against the Van *Hell*-sings!" He stretched "hell" out for a few seconds as the crowd roared with approval.

Discount Elvis slapped James on the rump. "You're on, kid! Get out there!"

James stepped out from the backdrop as a pipe organ played a low, melodic, gothic symphony. He saw a small glowing piece of tape on the floor, saw the large open arena in his yellowed wolfen vision only seconds before his senses were overloaded with the bright flash of pyrotechnics and the roaring crowd, the pipe organ transitioning into an explosive and epic dirge. The wolf cut a backflip in his mind, panting excitedly as Discount Elvis shouted from backstage. "The fuck is wrong wit' you, kid?! *Howl*, goddammit!"

He didn't smell the cedarwood anymore. *Shit*, he thought. *This isn't good. I need to get out of here.* James readied himself to bolt, then reality hit him as he recognized where he was standing. He looked around the loud and packed arena, any doubts about the place being able to fit over eight thousand people gone. There were a multitude of cameras everywhere, and large screens above the arena and over each section of seating showed his image as clearly as any high-definition television could. Animated graphics flashed a name at the bottom of the screen.

The Big Bad Wolf.

The wolf urged him to howl. *I can't,* James thought to it. *I'm on national television, and they think it's fake. We need to keep them thinking that.*

The crowd noise started to waver, a few boos coming through as he stood there while Discount Elvis screamed at him from backstage. He saw two men standing in the ring, both dressed as Victorian gentlemen, though the sleeves on their buttoned shirts had been removed to reveal their heavily muscled arms. They resembled two long-haired, bearded Vikings in what passed for what Phillip called "Steampunk" outfits. One of them grinned as he held his mic up, his voice loud in the arena. *"Looks like Scooby-Doo forgot his Scooby Snacks, brother!"*

While James had an appreciation of different media properties, Phillip was by far the biggest wrestling fan James knew. He knew more about the wrestlers and their stories than anyone James had ever met, though they'd never been to a live show together. Usually, either Phillip had been working during his time at the Rock Hill Police Department, or they were both off trying not to get themselves killed by whatever new supernatural thing had decided to be a criminal. Above all the action and stunts in the ring, James had one favorite aspect of the entire platform. One thing that always stood out to him as the most entertaining part of professional wrestling.

He felt his mouth turn up in a large, toothy, canine grin. *Shouty words.*

Sometimes, when they were in the midst of doing things around Coldstone Keep, James and Phillip would pass the time by having their work-based conversation in the same style the wrestlers used to "talk smack" to each other. It wasn't unusual to hear the back and forth between them devolve into shouting even the most basic things as a challenge.

"James, did you get the kitchen cleaned?"

"*I got that kitchen so clean you can eat off the floor, brother!*"

"*You better not have forgotten to unload the dishwasher, fleabag! Or Imma* make *you unload it with your* face!"

"*Come get some of this detergent, flatfoot!*"

James didn't need the ability to speak in order to level a challenge at these two fellow giants. He reared his head back, opened his arms, and released a howl that made the crowd immediately stop booing and cheer even harder. His heart pounded with excitement, his blood pumping as he looked back at the two startled wrestlers in the ring and snarled at them, contorting his face into his well-practiced "Psycho Wolf" expression. He started down the ramp as the organ music continued, blaring and dark, the flame throwers on either side spewing fire into the air. He heard the telltale voices of the announcers at their table off to the side as they spoke rapidly to each other.

"Whoa! What the hell?! Do you see this, K.D.?!"

"I'm seein' it, Bobby! That is a *hell* of a costume! This kid is ready for tonight's Monster Mash!"

"Happy friggin' Halloween, folks! I can't believe that howl!"

"Looks like he's working alone tonight, K.D. A real ballsey choice going into a tag match solo."

"He definitely has his stuff together tonight, or thinks he does, Bobby, because his teammate is nowhere to be found. The question is: can he *solo* the Van Helsings?"

James reached the ring and climbed in, going over the ropes and stopping to raise his arm and howl again, the fans cheering him along. *I have to play this up to get out of here,* he thought, trying to map a way out in his mind. He staggered slightly at the unfamiliar way the mat felt under his immense weight as he approached the two wrestlers. He towered over them despite their own considerable size and height. The one on his right nudged the other one and muttered under his breath. "Go easy on this kid, Dave, he's new. He's supposed to throw it anyway."

The other one rolled his eyes. "Yeah, Tom, I know. I read the script too." Dave turned his attention to James. "You got balls, kid. You were supposed to have a partner." He gave a sly grin. "Got us a real showman here, Tom."

Tom grinned. "Let's do this."

Dave and Tom each had a grip on James's arms a second after the bell rang. They heaved—

And James stood there perplexed as the two strained and kicked to force James to take a step like two toddlers pulling their parent into a toy store. The wolf barked in James's mind.

What? he thought. The wolf sent him an image. *Oh, right.* James relaxed, following the momentum the Van Helsings were pushing as he ran out of their grasp, hit the ropes on the opposite side of the ring, and intentionally grounded himself and rushed back as if the ropes had actually slingshot him across the ring. The Van Helsings parted and lifted their arms in time to catch James in the chest, but he burst through and hit the ropes on the other side of the ring, going back in again and going low. He spread his arms and caught both wrestlers by the shins, swept their legs out from under them, and caused them both to hit the mat. James felt his insides vibrate with the explosive bass from the arena speakers. He took a step, hearing the sound in the speakers that would be inaudible were he in human form.

He grinned at the same time the wolf began to pant happily. *Oh, hell yes.*

One of the Van Helsings, Tom, was already up. He charged, shouting as he rushed in. James grabbed him by the chest and slammed him down, pulling back on his strength in an effort to keep himself from hurting the man. The bass thundered again, filling him with adrenaline.

"Looks like the Van Helsings have their hands full tonight, K.D.," James heard Bobby say from their table.

"You ain't wrong, Bobby," K.D. replied with equal intensity. "Dave 'Wall Meat' Van Helsing is already trying to come in to help his brother with this one." James saw Dave arguing with the ref as the smaller man kept directing him to step out of the ring, both of them pantomiming angrily at each other as Dave conceded and stepped out. Tom rushed in again, this time leaping at James. James caught him by the arms and slung him against the ropes hard enough to literally catapult the man off his feet and back at James. *Shit, too much,* he thought in the split second it took him to relax and let Tom collide with him and send him to the mat. He heard Tom speak low in his ear.

Or at least where his ear would be in human form.

"Damn good show, kid. Just remember the script. *Shit,* you're strong!" Tom sat up and raised a fist as the crowd cheered.

James heard Lacy's voice, turned his head, and saw her in the front row. "Jimmy, what the hell are you doing?" She was back in her favorite pink Hello Kitty shirt and denim shorts. Lacy jumped the fence and was in the ring before security could catch her. James barely heard the announcers over the roaring crowd as she ran at Tom. Dave came at her from the right, sweeping her legs out from underneath her. She hit the mat. Dave made a big show of laughing out loud, then spoke in his wrestler voice. "Aw, ain't that sweet? Baby Girl likes it doggy style!"

Lacy got up and punched him in the chest, sending him flying into the ropes. He slid from the ring, and James bucked Tom. Tom recovered and went at him, jumping on his back and trying to pull him down. *These two are strong for humans,* James thought. The wolf gave an annoyed huff in agreement. He reared back and sent Tom to the mat. *And what the hell is she doing here?*

The crowd roared as another wave of thunder shook the stadium. James took a split second to look around and saw someone in the crowd who stood out. The wolf growled inside, and James realized who he was seeing. Who was standing in the front row staring at him with murderous intent.

Clint stood stock still as the people around him jumped and cheered at the show they were getting. He wore a long trench coat, one large enough to hide whatever weapon he'd likely brought in with him. James braced himself for Clint to pull the gun out and start shooting the place up, felt the panic churning in his gut. *So many people,* he thought to the wolf. *If he opens fire here, the chaos alone would kill just as many people as bullets would.* Clint began to undo his trench coat, staring hard at James as he reached inside.

We need to stop this. Just keep it mild.

Wolf stepped forward, the James stepped back. Too many innocent humans. Had to call Fenrir carefully, pick its call wisely. Wolf reared its head back, faced the man-lights as the call welled, its maw opening to release enough to back the two big loud humans away, shake their weak floor. The call came.

And was halted as something kicked the back of its leg, dropping it to one knee.

Wolf rounded on the loud human, the one the James called "Tom," anger rising in its chest. The James shouted in protest, but Wolf ignored it as it grabbed the Tom by the neck, picked it up, and slammed it down on the soft floor. Floor gave, collapsed, and dragged some of the white cover with it. The thunder was loud, the high-pitched cracking of man-made wood sharp in the air, painful to Wolf's ears. The Tom lay in the hole whimpering as the two humans from the table shouted to each other in unfettered excitement while the sea of humans all barked and howled at once.

"Holy shit, Bobby! Did you see that?!"

"I damn sure did, K.D.! The Big Bad Wolf just sent Tom 'Bloody Tears' Van Helsing straight to Hell! I can't believe it!"

"It's gonna take time to fix the arena, Bobby, and Tom might need medical attention! Get the goddamn paramedics down here! It's all over, ladies and gentlemen! *The Big Bad Wolf takes the match! I don't believe it!*"

Then James forced his way to the forefront, shoving Wolf back into the mind. *What part of "careful" did you misunderstand?*

The wolf mewled and hung its head in remorse.

Lacy moved in front of James, already talking. "James, what the hell are you doing here?! *Go!*"

The crowd's roar was deafening. James turned to where he'd seen Clint, but the space was empty. He searched around the audience, finally seeing Clint's back as he stepped through a doorway and disappeared into the lobby area outside the arena. There was a grunt, and James looked over his shoulder to see Dave walk up to the hole and look down at his partner, then back up at James in both awe and anger. "Fuck, kid, do you know what throwing the match actually means?!"

James ignored him, jumping out of the ring and running up the ramp he'd entered on and backstage, where Discount Elvis was screaming into a cell phone and waving his hands. "Are you fuckin' nuts?! That was amazing! No, I don't give a shit about a damn script! The crowd loved it! Look at the fuckin' ratings!" He glanced up at James. "Kid, that was top goddamn notch!"

James hit all fours and moved down the corridor, people stepping to the side as he went. He blew through the doors and into the night, then ran at wolfen speed to the center of the parking lot. He stopped and stood to his full height, scanning the lot and sniffing the air, trying to find any scent leading him to Clint.

Asphalt. Gasoline. Motor oil. Fried food. Overflowing garbage bins.

Cedarwood, already faded to the point of being impossible to pinpoint, just before his senses were flooded with blood and vanilla.

Lacy zipped up next to him, shouted at him to follow her. He obeyed, keeping her in sight as he bolted after her. She turned down Independence Boulevard and ran along the side of the road, bypassing traffic. James followed suit, keeping pace with her as best as he could, thankful the human eye wouldn't see much when he hauled ass at that clip.

They stopped once they reached Lacy's car in the empty parking lot behind a derelict shopping center. She opened the door to the Mini Cooper and looked at James. "C'mon, Jimmy. Got your spare clothes in the back. You can shift here. No cameras."

James shifted into human form and quickly got into the passenger seat. He reached for the bag in the backseat and immediately started to dress in the cargo pants and black tee she'd brought him. "Thanks."

"Jesus *Christ* eating a *cupcake*," Lacy spat. "What in the actual *fuck* are you doing here, Jimmy? Are you *trying* to piss Smith off?"

James stared at her, already primed to tell her everything and fill her in on what was going on. See what she knew. Combine forces and take down the bad guys. Super Wolf and his sidekicks. The dynamic trio.

Just like old times.

Then he remembered he was pissed at her.

"Phillip and I came to Uptown for dinner," he said, keeping the urgency out of his tone. "We saw Clifford try to attack someone, and I chased him."

Lacy narrowed her eyes at him and cocked her head to the side. "Jimmy, no offense, but you suck at lying. That's more my thing. Try again."

James stared back at her without blinking, his expression stoic. "We ran into Clifford at a murder scene, and I chased him."

Lacy straightened up and nodded. "Okay," she said, her tone still full of doubt. "That one I believe more."

"Same question," James said. "How did you know where I was?"

"I was assigned to tail you two morons," Lacy said. "But then Clint Gordon showed up on camera near the stadium."

James's heart sped up slightly, the wolf wagging its tail in anticipation inside. "When?"

"When what?"

"When did you see Clint?"

"I didn't see shit. I got the report. It was about five minutes before you made your big entrance." She shook her head. "God, you're a ham, Jimmy."

James looked away from her and out the car window as the pieces fell into place. "Then that settles things."

"Settles what?"

He turned back to her. "Clint is Clifford the Big Ugly Asshole."

Lacy blinked, then sat back in the driver's seat and let out a long breath. "Okay. Well. That complicates things." She rolled her eyes. "More."

"I need to get back to Phillip," James said.

Lacy pulled her phone out, cranked the car, and connected the phone to the vehicle. She pulled Phillip's number up on the large screen on her dash and hit "Call." It rang once before Phillip answered. "I wouldn't pick up otherwise," he said. "But I'm taking a guess you ran across a stray I know?"

"I'll take care of him," Lacy said. "Honest."

"I am paper-trained," James chimed in.

"You're a dumbass," Phillip shot back. "Where the hell did you end up?"

James sat forward. "It's an interesting story. But I believe I've figured out who Clifford is."

"I'll bite," Phillip said. He came back almost immediately with "Hang on, Hoyt's calling me." The line went silent for a moment before he came back. "Where are you two?"

"Old shopping center about a mile or so from the coliseum," Lacy said. "What's up?"

"Visiting hours are almost over. Might wanna get over to the hospital in the next five minutes."

8

It took Lacy nine minutes to drive from the parking lot on Independence to the hospital. Both the security guard at the front desk and the nurses in the Intensive Care Unit tried to stop James from seeing Molly since visiting hours had just ended. Lacy used her vampiric influence on them to change their minds, a trick she'd referred to before as a "mindjob." A quick suggestion from her, and James was certainly welcome anytime.

"Don't worry," she said as they rode the elevator up. "They'll still be able to do their jobs just fine. I'm giving them a suggestion, not a prime directive."

"I seem to remember a man dubbed 'Cookie' from Westenra Island," James said, raising an eyebrow.

Lacy shrugged. "Prime directive. And I fixed him before we left." She paused. "I think. It all happened so fast."

James sighed. "I'm sure there are ways to turn any food into some variation of a chocolate chip cookie."

The elevator door opened to another sterile beige elevator lobby with doors on either side. James's senses were assaulted by the smells of cleaning chemicals permeating the hallways. A sign pointed them through the set of doors that led to the nurses' station, where they could check in. Lacy went ahead, and James was able to check in and find out where Molly's room was just before a doctor came out of one of the offices and nodded to James. He saw Lacy leave the doctor's office in nothing more than a split-second blink as she continued her psychic attack on the entirety of the staff.

The doctor approached James. He carried a tablet in his left hand and offered his right for a handshake. James recognized the slight dullness in his eyes immediately. "Mr. Coldstone? I'm Doctor Allen. It's nice to meet you."

James shook his hand. "How is she?"

Dr. Allen broke the handshake and motioned for James to walk with him. "Her room is this way," he said as James fell into step alongside him. Allen held up the tablet and opened a file folder on the screen. James didn't put much effort into trying to see what was on the screen. He was worried, but he also respected Molly's privacy. "She's stable," he said before he started reading over the file. "The surgery went pretty well."

"Then why is she still in the ICU?" James asked.

"Because she is still in need of intensive care," Allen replied without hesitation, his tone casual but not impolite. "The surgery went well, but she's in bad shape. They were able to stop the internal bleeding, which is fantastic news. They repaired her large intestine, which had been nicked upon entry, but she lost some of her small intestine since the round perforated the abdomen as it traveled. It missed her spinal column by millimeters, which is lucky because she would likely be paralyzed if it had connected. Her liver was also damaged, but they were able to repair it with minimal tissue removal."

James sighed, his chest heavy. "One bullet," he mumbled.

"The round passed through the door before making contact with Miss Akter. That change of trajectory and speed caused a lot more damage. A slower bullet tends to bounce around inside the target and makes a bad mess." He looked up from the tablet at James. "She's extremely lucky, Mr. Coldstone. She was bleeding internally and in the early stages of sepsis by the time the paramedics got to her. She lost a substantial amount of blood, and the trauma sent her system into shock."

James nodded. "What happens now?"

Dr. Allen lowered the tablet to his side and shrugged. "All we can do is wait. We're monitoring her vital signs closely, and so far, things are on an upswing. But the healing process for an injury like this is slow. She was in severe shock when we got to her, and she's in a coma at the moment. We're confident that she will recover, but she may be here for a month or two." He gestured ahead, and James saw that they'd come to a room.

Through the closed door, he could hear the soft rhythmic beeping from the equipment. Allen cleared his throat. His eyes dulled even more, revealing some of Lacy's vampire handiwork in play as he spoke. "I'm saying this between us, Mr. Coldstone. As friends. And off the record. Considering the state she was in and the amount of blood lost, Miss Akter should have died. It's a medical miracle that she's alive."

James stared at the door as he spoke to the doctor. "Please note that all medical expenses for Miss Akter are to be forwarded to me."

Allen blinked. "I mean, that's very generous, Mr. Coldstone, We're billing her insurance company, but—"

"I will pay for all expenses up front and as they are incurred," James said, his eyes still on the door, his tone firm. "The insurance company can send any reimbursements directly to her. I do not want to chance any portion of her care not being fully covered by her insurance, nor do I want any of her care choices to be less than optimal because of insurance considerations and limitations." He turned his head slightly, meeting Dr. Allen's look of surprise. "Please get me the contact information for whom I need to speak to in order to set this up."

"Sure," Dr. Allen said after a small stammer. "Of course."

James motioned at the door. "May I?"

Allen checked the time on his watch, then shrugged. "Visiting hours are over," he said, his tone casual and conversational again, as if nothing had happened. "But it's not a problem."

James opened the door, instinctively trying to be as quiet as possible. He'd been in a hospital before. He knew that a nuclear explosion would not disturb Molly due to the amount of drugs she was being given on top of being in a coma.

His past experience and knowledge were useless in protecting him from the figurative punch to his chest when he entered the room.

Molly laid on her back in the bed, the low rhythmic beeping of the electrocardiograph next to her monitoring her heart beating steadily. A long plastic tube hung out of her mouth, feeding her oxygen and causing her chest to rise and fall artificially as if she were some sort of animatronic puppet, the sound of air moving in and out just as mechanical as one of the figures he'd seen on various attractions at amusement parks as a kid. An IV tube ran from her arm to a bag hanging on the EKG stand, the bag still nearly full as the fluid dripped methodically into the chamber where the tube connected. Multiple pads were stuck to her in various spots, the wires going back to the EKG. The screen showed a multitude of data, lines reflecting her heartbeat and numbers indicating her oxygen levels and blood pressure.

Life support, James thought to himself as her chest rose and fell mechanically, the machine doing the work for her. *Why is she on life support?*

"Oh, James. I didn't know you'd be here."

James looked over at the far corner of the room to find Hoyt sitting in a chair. "I didn't know you would be here, either."

"I'm not," Hoyt said. "I'm still in my lab. Just checking in on her. Saw you on TV. Good match. Need to work on your form, but hey."

James shook his head. "I will worry about the fallout from that later." He motioned at Molly. "Why is she on life support? Dr. Allen said they are confident she will recover."

"Oh," Hoyt said. "That's normal after a major surgery and for anyone in critical condition. Think of it like they're retraining her body to start working again. It doesn't mean she's on the brink of death or anything. This is what they mean when they say she's in critical condition, but she's stable."

James nodded. "That does make me feel better."

"Good," Hoyt said. "Listen, I gotta run. I'll hit you up when I have something new."

"Thanks."

Hoyt gave a thumbs up as he faded away. James looked back at Molly, his jaw clenched as he sorted out the mixture of grief, guilt, and rage swirling inside him. He breathed out slowly, his breath shaking as he fought back tears.

He had done this. Not just by insisting she meet them at the concert. By meeting her in the first place. He had brought her into his life, put her in danger by knowing him. Being involved with him. He knew trouble followed him, seemed to always know where he was at any given time. What would happen if they continued to see each other? Phillip was a human, like her. But he was trained in firearms and self-defense. Molly was what Phillip called a "normie." She was an air-traffic controller. She'd told James once she'd never in her life fired a real gun, had never gotten into a fight.

And now, she was fighting for her life because of her interest in James Coldstone, a werewolf in constant conflict with the rest of the supernatural world.

James blinked, the wetness flooding his eyes, running down his face as he took a deep and shuddering breath. His emotions were running wild before he'd come into the room, before he'd seen Molly in her hospital bed. The panic, uncertainty, and worry were dulled by both Dr. Allen's and Hoyt's explanations of her current state.

She was going to be okay.

And all of James's emotions began to solidify, grew hot inside him as he replayed the shooting again, replayed his encounters with Clifford. He felt his jaw clench as he grit his teeth, his muscles tightening as he glared at the result of Clint's actions. He clenched his fists at his sides, his nails digging into his palms. His sadness, his regret, his panic, none of it was going away. They combined, becoming one singular emotion he was all too familiar with.

Rage.

"You can't lose your temper right now, James," Lacy said from behind him. "She needs you to stay calm more than she needs revenge."

James looked over his shoulder at Lacy. She stood in the doorway, leaning up against the frame with her arms crossed in front of her. "Am I that transparent?" he asked.

Lacy nodded. "Your scent changes with your emotions. You of all people should know how that works."

James grunted and turned back to Molly. "And what do I smell like?"

"Cedarwood." She paused. "Not the same cedarwood scent Clifford has; his is a little different. Should already know that too."

James turned away from Molly, and Lacy moved aside as he left the room. He heard her behind him as she closed the door. "Where are you going?"

"To find Clint and kill him," James said, his tone as casual as if he were telling her he was going to the grocery store for some eggs and milk.

"Jimmy, wait," Lacy called behind him as he rounded the corner and stalked toward the double doors leading to the elevator area. "Hold up!"

He spoke over his shoulder. "I don't have time for this."

"James, stop," Lacy said, moving in front of him and barring his path. "This isn't going to help her, and you know it."

"Get out of my way," James said, his voice a low growl. The wolf growled as well, adding a deep rumble in his chest and throat as his vision flashed yellow. He towered over Lacy, looking down on her like a predator over its prey.

Lacy stood her ground, her hands on her hips. "James Coldstone, we already talked about you looming over me once."

James responded, almost cutting her off. "I feel this particular situation warrants it."

Lacy's already ice-blue eyes glowed an even more brilliant blue. Her fangs elongated, making a small clicking noise like a pair of switchblades. Her skin grew paler, her features darkened as she dropped her fists by her sides and managed to put her face closer to James's despite her solid twelve-inch deficit in height compared to his six-foot-four. "You listen to me, you son of a bitch: you don't scare me. You don't intimidate me. And you fucking *damn* sure don't take your bullshit out on me. I'm not your fucking punching bag." She paused, glaring at him, then spoke again through gritted teeth. "Back. The fuck. *Up.* Or I will kick your ass all over this hospital."

The wolf snarled hard enough for the sound to be heard from James's own mouth as he stared back into her eyes. He could see her wild fury, could smell her vanilla and blood scent intensify tenfold. There was something else there in her wide-eyed glare, something that caught him off guard, gave him pause.

Pain. Hurt.

The tear rolling down her cheek made him push the wolf back into its place in his mind. He took a few steps back, still staring at her as he nodded, conceding despite the wolf's anger at his choice to back away from a challenge. Her body was trembling despite her vampiric nature being on full display, her lower lip quivering.

"You don't know me, James Coldstone," Lacy said, her voice shaking. "You don't know what I've been through, you don't know where I came from. One man has *ever* intimidated me, and I killed the *shit* out of him the moment I was turned." She sighed, wiping the tears from her face. "Fuck, James. I need you to trust me."

"Then fill me in," James said with an exasperated shrug. "Be honest with me for a change."

Lacy's eyes faded back to their normal blue, her fangs retracted, and her skin returned to its more human tone. "Fine."

"Why did the SCU want me specifically?"

"Because of your dad," Lacy said. "When Smith heard about what happened with Wade Anderson, and heard you were involved, he knew that you being who you are would cause a shit-show with the council unless you were under some kind of control. I volunteered to go when I found out Marianne was taken at around the same time they took Mindy."

"How long have you been with them?"

"About a year before I met you."

"Why does Smith want me and Phillip to stay away from Clifford?"

"Classified," Lacy said immediately.

"You sent me a text a while back that said this was bigger than we thought," James said. "What did that mean?"

"Classified," Lacy said again.

James sighed. "You're not being helpful."

"I'm being far more helpful than you think," Lacy said. "Jimmy, there's definitely something big going on. But if I read you in, it could bury this case for us. If we mess this up, we could lose any opportunity we have to stop what's going on. Again: shit show." She rubbed her face and released a long sigh of frustration. "Look, I'm on your side. I promise. I'm not trying to blow smoke up your ass."

"Then help me," James said. "Help me and Phillip take Clint down before he shoots up another public area or mauls another witch."

Lacy shook her head. "I can't. Not directly. That's how delicate this thing is. Our adventure down the East Coast rocked a hell of a boat, and we discovered some real trouble that's been brewing right under our noses." She crossed her arms in front of her. "I left the first time because I got orders to get back to the SCU and look over the new findings. I left the second time because the Wolf-Man Murders had ramped back up. Now, it's about finding whoever is masterminding this whole thing."

"What whole thing?" James asked. "What is going on?"

Lacy shook her head. "That, we still don't know. We have our theories, but none of them are really panning out." She looked him directly in the eyes. "That's the truth. I swear."

James closed his eyes and breathed out slowly, imagining himself blowing his stress out in the form of a fire that had started in his chest. Phillip had taught him the calming technique back in their college days when James had less control of his temper. He rubbed his face. Woo-sah.

He pulled his hands away and looked at Lacy, guilt mixing in with his subsiding anger.

Lacy pulled her cell phone out. "I'm gonna shoot Kimble a text now and put in a request for a security detail for Molly. Then we gotta get back to Phillip."

"Who was he?"

Lacy stopped and stared up at him. "Who?"

"The man you mentioned earlier."

He could see her bristle slightly before she answered. "Dead. That's what he is."

James nodded. "Fair enough."

She held her phone up, studying her screen with some confusion. "Huh."

"What is it?"

"You sent me a text message about five minutes ago."

James shook his head. "I don't have my phone. I dropped it in the parking deck when I shifted and chased after Clint." He paused. "Phillip."

"Looks like he's okay," she said. "But he's also wondering why he just got hauled into Epicenter by—" She looked closer, then back up at James. "Agent Squeaky Toy? Really? That's mean."

"Yet funny."

"He has a speech impediment."

"I would be more inclined to be nice had he not aimed a large handgun at my face."

Lacy paused. "Okay, yeah: I'll give you that one. They probably picked Phillip up because of your new career as a pro-wrestler. Smith might actually press charges this time, Jimmy."

James's nose tingled with the coppery scent of blood filling the hallway, the sweetness of rot behind it clashing with Lacy's bloody vanilla scent and the cleaning chemical smells of the hospital. James saw a younger man wearing scrubs and holding a clipboard approaching them. The wolf growled inside, his own hairs raising along with the animal's hackles. Lacy's eyes began to glow blue again. The nurse smiled politely. "Excuse me, Mr. Coldstone?"

"I am," James said, keeping his glare locked on the vampire. The suckhead was close enough to see the details on his badge. *Hakeem Jackson, Hematology.*

Classic, James thought. The wolf chuffed in agreement.

The vampire's smile turned into a grin as he glanced over the clipboard. He looked up again, his grin even more boyish. "Okay, I'm supposed to read this decree to you. But, *dude!* I watched that match while I was on break. You were *awesome!*"

"I try," James replied.

Jackson pulled a small notepad from his pocket. "Hey, can I have an autograph? I'm in a pinch, so I can read this while you sign it, if that's okay." Jackson tensed excitedly. "*Man,* you got a fan! The way you sent that one guy to Hell with just a choke-slam? Fucking *epic!*"

James's tension shifted from *En Garde* to bewilderment as Jackson held the pen and pad out. He took them, still cautious. "To Hakeem, I assume?"

"Oh, you'll personalize it?!" Jackson pumped his fist in the air. "Man, that's awesome!"

"Jackson," Lacy said while James signed the pad. "We can smell you from a block away. What the hell is a vampire doing in a hospital? And working in Hematology?" She crossed her arms in front of her and gave him an unimpressed look. "Real subtle, jackass."

Jackson shrugged. "Hey, even us bloodsuckers gotta pay bills. Besides, I don't eat at work. Shit's too expensive." He held up a thermos and tapped it. "I bring my lunch. And this puppy keeps it nice and warm for my whole shift."

"You mentioned reading me something?" James handed the pad back.

Jackson smacked himself on the forehead. "Oh, yeah. My bad." He held up the clipboard and began reading. "*The Council of Night hereby summons one James Eriksson Coldstone, son of David Bjornson Coldstone, to present himself before the council on this night within an hour of being presented this decree and no later than one hour past the reading of this decree, to testify to the council on charges of blatant and purposeful exposure to unapproved individuals in the form of media presentation.*" He handed James the clipboard. "Oh, and you gotta sign this, too. Just acknowledging that I read it to you." Jackson shrugged again. "Formalities, you know."

9

It was midnight by the time James and Lacy arrived at Epicenter. The place was still bustling, the bars and restaurants open to the Charlotte nightlife. The music coming from the different venues mixed in the open center court area where James and Phillip had engaged in their brief skirmish with the SCU. James noticed right away that there was no noticeable trace of the fight from the night before.

"The SCU has a hell of a clean-up crew," Lacy said as if reading his thoughts as they walked past the now closed candy shop and into the courtyard.

"I can tell," James said.

She led James through the crowd and into a large building with the name of a bank on the doors. The interior was all marble and tile, the ceiling at least twenty feet in the air and braced by ornate columns. An older man in a black suit stood behind the desk near the elevator watching the security monitor in front of him. He looked up at them, nodded, and motioned to the elevator. The doors and framework were brass-colored and polished to a mirror finish. "The council is expecting you."

"Thank you," Lacy said with a nod.

"It is nice to be expected," James said.

Lacy rolled her eyes. "Shut up, James." She boarded the elevator with James close behind. The doors closed, and the elevator began its ascent without Lacy pushing any buttons. It only took him a second to realize there were no controls on the wall panel other than an emergency stop and a keyed fireman's access control. "You're about to meet the most powerful vampires in the country. This council controls the entirety of the Southeast, but its influence goes all the way to the Federal government."

James raised an eyebrow. "I suddenly feel much more important."

"If they're summoning you like this, that means you've rattled a nest of hornets," Lacy said. "They don't bring people in for casual visits, Jimmy. This is bad. *Real* bad."

"I'm not sure as to what nest of hornets they would be referring to," James said. "The wrestling match makes sense, but I thought I pulled that off surprisingly well."

Lacy looked at him sidelong. "You choke-slammed a three-hundred-pound man *through* the ring."

James nodded. "Indeed."

She rolled her eyes and shook her head. "My god, you can be *so* dense."

"They also do not strike me as wrestling fans," he continued. "At least Noble Jones and Montoya do not."

Lacy shrugged. "Maybe? Who knows? They don't always exactly detail *why* they want you front and center. They call, you show up."

"And if I had refused?"

Lacy shuddered. "Yeah," she said. "Don't do that."

"We need to call Phillip," James said.

"I tried earlier," Lacy said. "Went straight to voicemail."

James turned to her. "That is not normal. Phillip never turns his phone off."

"I'm sure he's fine. If he's already here, his phone is turned off. It's one of the rules of the chamber."

"Does the council know about Clint?"

"I'm sure they do," Lacy said. "They keep in contact with Agent Smith on the regular. They're the biggest reason the SCU even exists. Supernaturals are just as capable of crime as humans. The big difference is that supernaturals can cause a lot more damage and carnage than human law enforcement can deal with. Pile that on top of trying to make sure that the humans still see us as Halloween costumes and characters in weird erotica stories, and you end up with a need for a group to keep things under control."

Thus, the funding from Tepes to the SCU, James thought, remembering

Phillip and Hoyt's findings while they were in Savannah. James and Phillip had just been fired from their very short stint with the SCU for arresting Noble Jones. Phillip and Hoyt uncovered records showing transfers of money from what they assumed was House Tepes to the SCU, and no funding from any government agency. It was proof that the SCU was an independent dark organization masquerading as a branch of the FBI. Even their office was in the FBI headquarters in Rock Hill alongside the Behavioral Analysis Unit. He turned away from her, both of them standing side by side in the elevator staring at the doors as they waited for the inevitability of the doors opening to a meeting James wished could be an email.

He saw her reflection next to his. Seeing her standing beside him reminded him of how tiny she was by comparison, his six-foot-four frame hulking over her five-foot and change. By looking at her, it was easy to see how unbelievable the idea of her being able to match him in a fight could be. The memory of kissing her on Westenra Island played in his mind again. His want to feel her lips on his again, to run his fingers through her thick chocolate curls and feel her body pressed against him, clashed with his anger and mistrust. She'd lied to him. He couldn't argue against her reasoning, but he knew he couldn't trust her, either. He'd felt some guilt over his first night with Molly, his relationship with her. The guilt quelled after he'd decided he was done trusting Lacy. He wanted nothing to do with her lies.

And yet, here he was with her again. Like everything was just fine.

"Do you hate me?"

The question caught James off guard, interrupted his thoughts. He saw her reflection staring at him. It sent his mind into a new spiral of thoughts.

The wolf mewled in his mind and lay down, covering its eyes with its paws.

"No," he said instantly. "I don't."

Her mouth turned up slightly. "You don't trust me."

"No. I do not."

She nodded. "I can live with that."

The doors opened to a vast and extravagant lobby area with polished hardwood floors that James could see his reflection in, and walls of cold concrete with a glossed finish that caught the reflection of the firelight from the mounted candelabras lining either side of the room and led to the large oak doors at the far end. The painted ceiling was high enough to be mostly masked in shadow. James could make out what looked like angels cowering in terror as a legion of vampires charged them, all of them commanded by a dark figure sitting high on a coach pulled by horses with smoke rising from the fires serving as their eyes. Two werewolves stood on either side of the coach, and James could see the leashes on either neck leading up to the dark man's clenched fist.

"I've always hated that painting," Lacy said as she fell into step with James. She shuddered. "Fucking creepy."

"What is it?" he asked.

Phillip's voice echoed in the room, the sound coming from multiple directions as it bounced mercilessly off the walls and floor. "It's about goddamn time."

James stopped as Phillip stood up from one of the many red cushioned chairs stationed outside the door. "You run off and leave me in the damn parking deck, and I get pulled over a half hour later by the SCU and dragged in here."

"I'm glad you're alright," James said. "We tried to call you on Lacy's phone."

"They made me turn the phones off." Phillip looked at Lacy. "You do know she's the reason we're in this mess, right?"

"Sorry, Bacon," Lacy said. "Not me this time. I had no idea we'd end up here."

Phillip grunted. "Yeah, right."

"I believe her," James said. "Considering I was served the summons from a vampire nurse named Jackson, who works in Hematology."

Phillip snorted. "Way to feed the stereotype, Jackson." He handed James his phone. "Dropped this, by the way. I texted Lacy with it because she wasn't responding to mine. And where the hell have you been?"

James decided against going into the events of the wrestling match. That would be a conversation for later. "I lost Clifford somewhere on Independence Boulevard." He turned to Lacy. "I'm guessing we can expect Robert's Rules of Order to be in play?"

"Vampires love their old traditions," Lacy said with a snort. "Henry Martyn Robert was a vampire who knew how shitty people can be without some kind of rules in place. Just don't be a dork and you'll be fine."

"You're asking too much," Phillip said.

The doors opened before James could answer, the sound low and booming as the heavy oak doors swung to the side. A young girl stood in the center of the doorway, her straight blond hair framing her face and stopping at her shoulders. Her outfit was a flowered dress, and she wore a large pink bow on her head. She smiled at James, her eyes hard and piercing despite the innocence her face conveyed.

Her fangs reached down to her lower lip.

"Mr. Coldstone, a pleasure," she said, her voice light and airy despite what her age may have been. "The council will see you now." She stepped to the side and held her arm out into the dark corridor. "If you would, please?"

James nodded and walked into the room. Phillip and Lacy fell into step on either side of him. Phillip bristled. "That was not cool. A little girl vampire?"

"We don't get to choose when we get turned," Lacy said. James glanced at her, saw her features grow haunted, her lower lip shuddering as she spoke. "And, a lot of the time, it's someone we know."

"She couldn't have been more than ten, man," Phillip said.

They all stopped at the entryway as a low, rasped growl filled the room they found themselves in. "She is over two hundred years old."

James saw the speaker sitting at a large, round oak table in the middle of a room that looked too much like a concrete vault for his liking. The red curtains and warm glow from the candelabras did nothing to assuage his feeling of the walls closing in.

He blamed the wolf for his claustrophobia. Animals were never meant to be in cages.

The speaker stood from his high-backed chair at the table. Though the man wasn't as tall as James, he had a broad build of solid muscle as if his full-time job was weightlifting and he pulled overtime most weeks. He had thick and straight black hair down to his elbows, the deep ebony offsetting his deathly pale skin. He wore crimson-red robes with a large and vaguely familiar crest stitched into the front. Three other figures sat at the table, all of them wearing similar robes with their hoods up and their faces shrouded in shadow.

"We're fucked," Phillip breathed next to James.

"They seem friendly," James said in a deliberately nonchalant tone as he gestured to the speaker. "See? He's even welcoming us."

Phillip leaned in close to James and spoke in a harsh whisper. "That is Vlad. Fucking. *Tepes.* That dude was...*is* about as friendly as a scorpion."

Tepes leveled an intense, humorless stare directly at James as he raised his hand and pointed a finger with a long, sharp nail to a seat at the table. "Please."

The wolf tensed and growled inside him, sending the hairs on the back of his neck and on his arms stiff as the beast radiated a vicious want to attack the vampire with everything it had. James mentally braced against the creature. *We are heavily outnumbered.*

The beast chuffed in frustration and backed down only slightly, keeping its senses on high alert.

James sat, Phillip and Lacy choosing seats on either side of him. Tepes motioned to the others, who pushed their hoods back to reveal themselves. Noble Jones nodded to James in somber acknowledgement.

James couldn't blame him. The last time they'd met, Jones had been controlled by a necromancer while his home was under siege by an army of the dead.

"*Hola, mi amigos,*" Eduardo Montoya said from his seat next to Jones. He smiled at Lacy. "It's been too long, *mi amore.*"

A woman James didn't recognize sat on the opposite side of the speaker from Jones and Montoya. Her raven-black hair was perfectly styled, wavy and flowing and long. The deep red of her robes made her impossibly white skin seem even more porcelain. Of the five vampires in the room, she reeked the most of blood, the rich coppery scent creating a razor's edge between his human side's nausea and his wolfen side's feral euphoria. She sat perfectly still, her red eyes locked on him, her expression admiring and…hungry. "I sense tension in you, werewolf," she said in a rich, silken Hungarian accent. "Not fear?"

The wolf grew more agitated at the woman, forcing James to swallow the snarl building in his throat.

The woman smiled. "Ah. There it is."

"Fuck," Phillip breathed next to James, stretching the word out for a second. "Why do they have to be creepy?"

"We don't mean you any harm," Noble Jones said. "It is against our laws to commit violence in this chamber unless under direct attack."

The woman's smile grew into a fang-revealing grin. Her eyes glowed red. "If you behave, we will behave."

"We take our laws seriously, Jimmy," Lacy said.

James felt the wolf ease in begrudging acknowledgement. "Very well," he said, still eyeing the woman. Something about her was unsettling the wolf, the creature whimpering as it recoiled. He'd never felt actual nervousness from it before, and it made his own nerves stand on end.

"We will begin," Tepes said as he picked up a tablet and read the screen. "This is an emergency meeting of the Council of Night to discuss the actions tonight that have potentially compromised the safety and security of the supernatural world." He glared at James. "Those responsible shall be held accountable."

Noble Jones gave Tepes a look, rolled his eyes, and stood. "Noble Jones of House Wormsloe, present and accounted for."

Montoya stood as Jones took his seat. "Eduardo Velazquez-Montoya of House Diabolito, present and accounted for."

The woman stood, still staring at James as she spoke. "Elizabet Bathory of House Bathory, present and accounted for."

James sensed Phillip tense up next to him. "Holy shit," Phillip muttered under his breath. "No goddamn way."

The woman took her seat. Every movement she made was an essay in elegance, effortlessly calculated and controlled. The wolf bristled inside again, and James urged it to remain calm and vigilant. "Vlad Tepes, of House Tepes. Presiding." Tepes nodded. "So begins this session of the Council of Night." He sat down. "You have been brought before the council to address the accusation of blatantly and willfully jeopardizing the security of the supernatural nation. How do you plead?"

Phillip turned to James. "What the hell is he talking about?"

Tepes waved his hand. James saw a screen lower in the back of the room and looked up to see a projector mounted on the ceiling directly above the table. "Please play the footage taken this evening."

James saw the television footage of his wrestling match from earlier, though no audio was playing. He felt his stomach drop slightly, and his chest tightened as his video counterpart picked up one of the Van Helsings and slammed him to the mat hard enough to collapse the ring. Digital graphics splayed across the screen calling the victory to "The Big Bad Wolf" as Wrestling James raised his arms in triumph to the crowd. The video paused, and Tepes turned his stare to Phillip and James.

"Oh my god," Phillip breathed as he covered his face in his hands. "You have got to be fucking kidding me."

Tepes nodded. "Does this answer your question, Agent Brown?"

"It does," Phillip said from behind his hands. "Thank you."

James needed levity. He nudged Phillip, unable to help himself. "I'm on TV."

Phillip grunted, his hands still over his face. "I hate you."

Noble Jones sighed and stood. "Master Tepes. I formally move to disregard Robert's Rules of Order this evening in an effort to simplify our conversation for those who are less cognizant of the substance of our dialogue." He motioned at James. "In layman's terms: we should consider shorter words and sentences given the defendant's handicap."

"I will not have disorder in this chamber," Tepes growled, glaring at Jones.

"I agree with Master Jones," Bathory said as she reached out and touched Tepes gently on the arm. "I find these formalities exhausting. For the love of God, Vlad. It's been over four hundred years. Some ease would be most welcome." She addressed James. "What handicap does he refer to, may I ask?"

"Ah, this I can answer, *mi amore.*" Montoya motioned casually to both James and Phillip. "They are idiots."

Jones raised his hand. "I can confirm this."

Vlad looked at Lacy, who turned to Phillip and James. "Sorry, guys. At least I *look* human in that video."

The tall, dark, somber vampire master pursed his lips and waved his hand dismissively. "Fine." He muttered what sounded like a Romanian profanity. "We require an explanation for the footage we have just shown you."

Phillip turned to James. "I'd like to hear that one, myself."

James nodded, pushing back the urge to make a joke about how cameras and broadcasting worked. "I was in pursuit of the Wolf-Man copycat killer."

Bathory leaned forward. "Interesting," she purred. "I was under the impression that you were released from the SCU for your misguided arrest of Master Jones."

"Indeed," James said. "Though I was brought on at the SCU under penalty of exposure should I choose to decline. Which makes no sense to me."

"Many of Agent Smith's actions make little sense to those not inside his head," Montoya commented. "The man remains an enigma."

Noble Jones turned his attention to James. "If you aren't with the SCU, then why are you after the Wolf-Man copycat?"

"Because I was suspected of being the copycat," James said. "He and I apparently share a similar scent."

"Meaningless," Montoya said with a wave. "Many people share a scent. Someone may smell like red roses; another will smell of white roses. But, to the untrained nose, a rose is a rose."

James spoke before he could stop himself. "Another poet. Do you know it?"

"*James*," Lacy hissed.

Phillip turned to James. "Why? Just...*why*? Do you *want* us to get killed? Most people just save the effort and jump off a building."

Bathory looked at Montoya. "I see that you were not being hyperbolic earlier when proposing a simpler level of communication."

Montoya nodded somberly. "*Si, señora. Idiotas.*"

Bathory turned her attention to Phillip and grinned. "At least Mr. Coldstone was kind enough to provide refreshments for later."

Phillip's complexion went ashen. He muttered "This is how it ends," and then began to pray under his breath.

"I jest," Bathory said with a laugh. She turned her attention to James. "Have you been able to discern the identity of this new Wolf-Man Killer?"

"Clint Gordon," James said without pause.

"Are you kidding?" Phillip asked, rounding on James. "What the hell?"

Jones turned to the rest of the council. "The officer who shot up the Fillmore. There's a citywide manhunt for him."

Tepes sat back in his chair, his eyes fixed on James as he clasped his hands together in front of him in a casual gesture. "You will both be pleased to learn that the event this evening was themed. Mr. Coldstone's performance is being seen as a central showcase, and any who suspect are being seen as conspiracists. Agent Smith has been ordered to ensure that all SCU resources are in place to prevent this from growing into some-thing more." He leaned forward, his tone harsher. "This does not mean you are...'off the hook,' as one would say." His scowl turned into a knowing smile. "I can assure you that you now have our full attention. *My* full attention."

James raised an eyebrow. The wolf growled. "I'm not sure that is having the effect on me you are looking for."

Tepes's smirk grew, his gaze becoming more reptilian. "I cannot deny your wit, Mr. Coldstone."

"I like to think of it as my most charming attribute."

Tepes nodded in agreement. "And yet, with that wit, comes your inability to keep your mouth shut. Much like your father."

James gritted his teeth but remained calm. "Why am I not surprised that you knew my father?"

"Knew him?" Bathory said. "So much more than that, Mr. Coldstone. You are seated in the very place at this table that he once occupied."

A wave of cold washed over James, the chair instantly uncomfortable. He clenched his teeth harder, fighting the urge to speak. He had always known David Coldstone was connected, having spent a large majority of his time overseas in Europe. But Elizabet Bathory's comment made him realize one thing he'd never given much thought to. What had his father done for a living? How had he amassed such a fortune meaning James and his mother never had to work, never had to worry about having the money available? James paid cash upfront for college, for his books, everything. He had no credit cards, no loans, no debt. Nothing more than normal monthly recurring bills.

"Nothing?" Tepes said. "No witty comments or jokes?"

James stood, squaring his shoulders as he addressed the council. "I feel the need to point out that, per my understanding, this council is what serves as the ruling body of the vampire nation." He directed his attention to Tepes in particular, ignoring the rest of the council. "I find it difficult to believe that you would allow a werewolf to serve as your equal."

Tepes stood and began walking around the table slowly as he spoke. "David Coldstone did not serve on the council as our equal. He was our weapon to use in times of disruption, when an incident occurred in the supernatural nation that would disturb the treaty that the Council of Night and the Daughters of Baba Yaga have worked so hard to achieve." He paused, standing next to Noble Jones's seat. "Before the Supernatural Crimes Unit, we had the Knightwolf."

"Wait," Phillip said. "Lemme make sure I have this straight. David Coldstone, the billionaire Wolf-Man Killer, was hired muscle?"

"In a sense," Bathory said from her seat at the table. "He sat with us, dined with us, was present for all decisions made. He would also act as liaison to other countries and vampire house communities."

"And he killed when necessary," Tepes said. It was only then that James realized the vampire master was standing close enough to him for the cold breath reeking of blood and rot to hit the skin on his face.

James looked at him sidelong, staring back into the vampire master's crimson eyes and refusing to blink. The wolf growled inside him, low and warning. The growl was underlying in James's voice as he spoke. "On that, I must disagree. He killed indiscriminately and without remorse."

"David Coldstone was insane," Phillip said. "He killed over a dozen people that we know of."

"It is true, *señor*," Montoya said as Tepes backed away from James, still engaged in the staring contest. "There did come a time when we no longer had control over the Knightwolf. *Señor* Coldstone was a madman. But you are not."

"In fact," Bathory said, amusement lacing her words, "you are quite noble."

James looked at her. "On this, I also disagree." He motioned at Jones. "*That* is Noble."

"Our time runs short," Tepes said in an irritated and clipped tone, keeping his eyes on James as he spoke. "We will notify Agent Smith of your findings and inform him you are not charged for interfering as this new development is most helpful."

"What does that mean?" Phillip asked.

"It is simple, Agent Brown," Bathory said. James glanced at her, saw her mouth twitch as if she were fighting back a hungry grin. "The copycat killer must be destroyed at any and all costs."

James looked back into Tepes's icy, unblinking stare. Tepes spoke, his stare and his tone unwavering. "A decision has been made. This meeting of the Council of Night is adjourned."

10

James turned on his heel and headed for the chamber doors. He glanced down at Phillip as he passed, saw his best friend's bitter and icy glare. Phillip lived in a perpetual state of "annoyed." But James also knew this look all too well. Phillip was angry. Legitimately angry.

He kept moving, passing by Lacy as she put her hand on her forehead and closed her eyes, muttering under her breath. "Fucking *shit*, James."

He could hear the council murmuring behind him, responding back and forth to each other. Chairs moved. Bathory said something in Romanian, and Tepes responded in like. Montoya took a phone call, speaking rapid Spanish to the caller. Jones started talking to Lacy and Phillip.

James barely reached the door before Tepes whipped in front of him at vampiric speed, blocking his exit. Apprehension took him immediately, his body tensing even more as the wolf inside him growled and prepared to attack. His vision yellowed, and he felt his canines grow. Tepes's scent was overwhelming, the coppery tinge of blood and rot also carrying the heavy musk of soil. "It isn't polite to cage animals," James warned. "Particularly wolves."

"I see you also carry your father's temperament," Tepes said. "There are some of us who surmise that his sanity was the price to pay for his constant anger."

"The fewer similarities I learn about David Coldstone, the better it is for those who are trying to educate me," James said. "Please step aside."

"You have a gift, James Coldstone," Tepes said, stepping closer to him. "You have a drive that the SCU lacks, the willingness to do whatever it takes to right the injustices that you see. And a natural gift most investigators would kill to have."

"And yet, I am no Sherlock Holmes."

"You hunted down and destroyed a vampire master who was running a sex trafficking operation and managed to also bring down a vampire house smuggling unheard of amounts of cocaine, and you somehow killed two mythical monsters working for Master Wangenheim along the way. All because a young girl you barely knew was taken from her family to be sold."

"I can only hope the experience does not cause me to view all waitresses as a threat."

"You are noble. You carry a sense of justice about you."

"I also make an excellent deer roast," James said through gritted teeth. "And my French toast is a masterpiece in culinary arts. Get the hell out of my way."

"Your place is here," Tepes said, moving even closer until his face was inches from James's. "It is your birthright. *La fel ca tatăl, la fel şi fiul.*"

James didn't speak any other languages, though he knew enough from his Spanish classes to ask where the bathroom was and where he could get some cheese if he happened to be in Spain. But the wolf knew. It sent him back the translation, the words coming to him as if he were just as fluent in Romanian as he was in English.

Like father, so too, the son.

"You want me to be the new Knightwolf."

"It is your birthright," Tepes said. "Once a family is brought into the council as a functioning member at any capacity, that family's bloodline is bound to serve. Ergo, you already are."

James made a show of looking himself over, scrunching his face slightly as if in deep concentration. He stopped and shook his head. "I don't feel any different. Am I missing something?"

Tepes glowered at him. James saw the vampire's eyes begin to glow deep crimson, saw his fangs grow. "You believe mocking me will make a difference in your obligation to this council?"

James stood his ground, the wolf inside him giving a warning growl as it pressed dangerously close to causing him to shift. "I can assure you that

I have no obligation of any kind to the Council of Night. Mocking you is simply for my own amusement." His vision yellowed more as he held Tepes's glowing red stare inches from his own face. "*Ergo*, I believe you can go fuck yourself." He pushed past Tepes and headed toward the doors. The little vampire girl opened them, gesturing much more elegantly than a child appearing her age normally would.

Tepes chuckled behind him. "How interesting. You are just as stubborn as your father." James stopped, fighting to ignore the familiar gut punch he felt every time he was compared to his father. He looked over his shoulder. Tepes eyed him as he retracted his fangs. The glow faded in his eyes, but they still carried a deep red hue. "David Coldstone joined us eventually. You will be no different."

Phillip barely avoided bumping into the vampire master as he entered the lobby. He stepped aside, stopping as Tepes nodded to him. Phillip raised an eyebrow at him, cleared his throat, and spoke in his most professional tone. "Can I help you, sir?"

"Not tonight," Tepes purred. "Though I would like to have you for dinner sometime soon, Agent Brown." He licked his lips and walked away, disappearing inside the chamber.

Phillip shuddered and mumbled under his breath. "Fuckin' creepy-ass vampires." He made his way toward James, who was still controlling his anger at Tepes's constant comparisons to his father. "We need to talk."

James let out a slow, long breath. He forced his body to relax. It was Phillip. Phillip wasn't the one pushing to get him to join the council as their lapdog. He wasn't the one constantly comparing him to a psychopathic serial killer, either. "I didn't have time to call you before things got out of control," he said. "Clint led me directly to the wrestling match."

Phillip bristled and then shook his finger at James. "See, that shit? *That's* what we need to talk about. How the hell are you so certain Clint Gordon is a damn werewolf?"

"He appeared just after I lost Clifford in the arena," James said. "I saw him in the audience. He was set to open fire, but he hesitated when I entered the ring."

"They ended up in the same place?" Phillip said. "That's your evidence?"

"They were also in the same area as the Fillmore the other night," James said. "It's easy enough to determine that he shifted from one form to another."

"He'd have been naked as hell in that arena."

"Unless he kept backup clothing somewhere he could access quickly."

"Not that damn quick, James. Hell, *you* aren't even that fast."

"I ran into someone backstage and got delayed. It would've given him time."

Phillip stepped closer to James. "What's he smell like?"

James raised an eyebrow. "I've told you this before. Cedarwood."

"No," Phillip said, shaking his head. "Clint. What does *Clint* smell like?"

"Nothing," James said. "He has no scent. Though I doubt you are in the mood for another round of rhyming."

Phillip gave a bitter laugh. "Hey, you got something right for a change. Motherfucker, *you* smell like cedarwood whether you're tall-dark-and-ugly *or* Steroid Scooby-Doo."

"That is a new one. I like it."

His friend let out a long, slow breath as he turned away and rubbed his face. "God *damn*, you're a stubborn ass."

"I prefer to think of it as a healthy persistence."

"You and your damn one-liners," Phillip said, turning back to him. James could see the frustration still very present on his face, in his stance. There was something else in place, something James picked up on immediately and caused his temper to rise.

It solidified it for him when Phillip spoke again.

"I'm sorry about Molly, James."

"I don't need your pity," James snapped. "I need your help."

"With what?" Phillip snapped back. "Hunting down a human being like he's some goddamn supernatural?"

"He's not human."

"Oh, bullshit, James. You don't know that any more than anyone else. I've known him for years. Fuck, we went to the damn academy together. The man has a *family*, James. Wife. Kids. All of it."

James raised an eyebrow again. "I fail to see how his familial life has relevance in either of the hobbies that hold his current interest."

"That's why we have to *investigate*," Phillip fired back. "We go to his house. We ask questions. That's how this works. You're gonna cause him to panic. If he's lost his shit, he's liable to go on another shooting spree and blow his own head off to keep himself from facing the consequences."

The words were out of James's mouth before he could process what he was saying. "It would at least save me the effort."

Phillip blinked. "What?"

"We are not talking about two different fugitives," James said, staring hard at Phillip, his body tense and rigid as he fought to keep his temper under control. "And believe me when I say that I will not hesitate to take him down if given the chance. Regardless of what form he may be in at the time."

Phillip gave a bitter, frustrated shrug. "Oh, that's it, huh? Kill him. Great solution, James. Hell, you even got help with it from the suckhead in the other room *and* Smith now that you fucking sicced 'em on Clint. I'm sure that'll make Molly heal right the fuck up."

"What is that supposed to mean?"

"You know good and goddamn well what I mean," Phillip roared. "You're not doing this just to stop the murders. You got a boner for Clint because he shot Molly."

James nodded. "That does give me a certain motivation."

"James," Phillip said, pursing his lips as he put his fingers to his mouth, his hands together as if in prayer. "Mass shooters rarely get caught. They usually kill themselves or get themselves shot before they can be apprehended. We have a chance here to help a lot of people, including the shooter. I know Clint, and he wouldn't do what he did. Something made him snap. He's going to jail for the rest of his life. But at least we get answers."

"In the meantime, there is a werewolf running loose that has killed multiple witches for no apparent reason," James argued, his voice louder than he'd intended. "How do you expect to capture him? He's at least as powerful as I am, if not more so." He shook his head. "We can't risk him getting away from us while we're trying to take him alive. Regardless of what form he's in." He paused, consciously lowering his voice when he spoke again. "Even if he is Clint when we find him."

Phillip exploded. "You'd be after Clifford even if Clint never shot the place up the other night. Even if Molly was okay. But *hell* no: you've been obsessed with Clint since you got wind of Molly getting hurt. You've had it in your head off the *jump* that he's tied to that other damn werewolf, and you've got not a fuckin' *shred* of evidence to back it up." He shook his head. "No, instead you get all wound up and dumber than usual because this fuzzy fucker triggered *your* damn daddy issues."

James's vision yellowed as he clenched his fists. He growled, the noise his own. The wolf resisted him, stifling the growl as it sent him urges to stop, sent him memories of himself and Phillip laughing and cutting up. His thoughts were chaos, his body hot with anger. He saw no fear in

Phillip's eyes, no acknowledgement of his animalistic warning. Phillip looked angry, frustrated.

Disappointed.

"You're in this for vengeance, James," Phillip shouted, his tone still hard and angry. "Period, dot. So much so, you just sent a bunch of vampires and a deepfake black-ops organization out to kill a mentally ill human being. And, based on what you and that sketchy motherfucker in the other room said, that shit doesn't make you any better than David goddamn Coldstone!"

James spoke again, this time letting his anger speak for him. He let the words out with no effort to stop them from being said. The wolf mewled inside his head, lying down and putting its paws over its eyes. He felt his chest tighten, making it harder for him to breathe. He had enough for one last thing to say to his best friend.

His brother.

"Get out of my sight."

Phillip blinked in surprise, physically jarred as if he'd been slapped in the face. He scrunched his face in anger again and pointed his finger at James. "Fine. You get some sense, you know where to find me. Otherwise, fuck you. I'm out." He stalked off toward the elevator, muttering a torrent of profanity under his breath as the doors opened. He stepped inside the elevator, turned around to hit the button on the control panel, and gave James the middle finger until the doors closed.

He felt his throat tighten, shuddering as he took in a deep breath and exhaled slowly, letting the sudden wave of regret and loneliness weigh him down to the point where he could feel some strain in his back and knees. He kept his eyes locked on the elevator doors; his teeth clenched to fight back the urge to shout at the doors for Phillip to come back. To see reason. Clint was Clifford. He had to die. There was no way around it.

Right? he thought to the wolf. *Too much risk of him getting away, killing more people.*

The wolf groaned and turned away, showing its rear end to James as it settled down for a nap.

You're so much help, James thought to the animal. *I don't know what I would ever do without you. Besides live a normal life.*

The wolf lifted its tail and released a fart loud enough to drown out any other possible sound in his mind.

At least you carry yourself with a level of class.

The wolf sent him an image of Clint. The officer smiling and laughing as he and Phillip embraced in front of the Fillmore and caught up. Old friends who had trained together at the academy. Taken the oath to Protect and Serve. Clint had been friendly, jovial.

Had smelled like…what?

The wolf sent him another image. Clifford tore at Ginger's body, gored her chest open, and tore her heart free. James felt his blood boil, his rage consuming his body, his wolfen instinct driving him to kill.

Was it wolfen? Or was it him?

Clint had smelled like…what had he smelled like?

Nothing. Something.

The wolf showed him Phillip. It wasn't just anger he'd seen in Phillip's eyes. There was something else. All too familiar. He'd seen it before. He'd never wanted to see it again.

Pain was something he never wanted to cause anyone.

"Damn," James muttered. "*Damn.*"

Lacy nudged his elbow, startling him. "Hey," she said in a soft voice. "Come on, sweetie. I'll drive you home."

James looked down at her. "I believe I would like some fresh air first."

The streets of Uptown Charlotte were alive as if midnight had marked the beginning of Prime Time for the night goers. Lacy led James through a packed Epicenter and down to the street. He stopped when they reached the sidewalk, looking around at the swarms of people moving along on both sides of the busy street. The streetlights seemed wholly unnecessary, the digital signs on a few of the buildings casting a glow on the area would flicker and change hue depending on what advertisement was currently on display. The air was rich with the smells of the food cooking at the restaurants committed to staying open at least until two in the morning, if not later, depending on how busy they were. James checked his phone. The meeting with the council had barely lasted thirty minutes.

"Friday nights are always so busy," Lacy said from beside him. "I love the scene. Lots of people, lots to do. Lots to eat." James looked down at her, and she gave him a wry smile. "I said what I said."

He rolled his eyes and started walking up the sidewalk. She fell into step beside him, gently putting her hand in his. He gripped her hand instinctively, letting her interlace her fingers with his own. *Have to maintain the image,* he thought.

"I'm sorry you and Phillip had a falling out, Jimmy," she said.

"He is not seeing reality," James said as they crossed South College Street and continued toward South Tryon. "He's trying to save an old friend."

"Wouldn't you do the same thing?" Lacy asked. "What if it was Phillip who'd gone bug-nuts? Started shooting up places full of people? Moonlighted as a werewolf serial killer copycat?"

James hadn't thought about it in those terms. Phillip was more than a little high-strung. He took medication for his blood pressure, the hypertension not caused by anything other than stress. But he was principled, at times loyal to his own detriment. He'd lied to James about being part of the SCU when they'd gone to Westenra Island only because reading James in directly could have put all of them, including Mindy, in a bad situation. More than once, James had stood between Phillip and harm's way, both in their skirmishes with the supernatural and in normal situations, "Normal" being the operative term if one was referring to people being assholes of any given flavor.

But what if Phillip snapped? Lost his mind and started hurting people? He imagined a scenario where it was Phillip who had opened fire at the Fillmore. The wolf sat up in his mind and sent him a thrum of energy perfectly aligned with his own consciousness, the scenario playing out to completion. Phillip walked into the Fillmore, his face strained, covered in sweat. He pulled a fully automatic assault rifle and opened fire. Dozens of people dropped while the venue filled with the screams of panicked people trying to escape. The police broke through, opened fire on Phillip.

James was in wolf form, planted firmly between Phillip and retribution. The hailstorm of bullets that would have torn Phillip to pieces pelted into his thick, bluish-silver coat. The reaction was natural. Instinctual. James tried to recreate it again, but the idea of letting Phillip die caused his throat to close slightly, his chest tightening. He let it play out the same again so he could breathe.

"No," he said. "I could not."

"Then you know where Phillip is coming from on this," Lacy said as they approached the corner of Trade Street and Tryon. "So, stop being a dick. He could use some empathy, and you could use a kick to the ass."

The area was buzzing with people despite the events of the past few days, tourists and locals alike taking in the Charlotte nightlife. The brilliant streetlights and constantly moving car headlights clashing against the darkness made the place far more active, in James's opinion, than it could ever be during the daylight hours. Lacy let his hand go, sauntering ahead to the large disc sculpture installed in the middle of the corner square. She waited for the group of tourists taking photos with the statue to finish up and move on before she leaned against it casually. James stood in front of her, watching her as the cool city breeze made her long curls flow. Her usual short-sleeved pink Hello Kitty shirt and denim shorts made her stand out amongst a crowd dressed for the cooler weather.

One older woman looked at her and nudged her husband as they walked by. "The cold apparently doesn't bother the young and the working," she said to him, giving Lacy a disapproving glance.

Lacy shrugged. "Dead girls don't care about the cold, grandma." Her eyes suddenly glowed bright blue as she grinned, her fangs fully out. "Move on. Judgy leftovers are still edible."

The older couple both gasped, their eyes wide as they scurried away. Lacy laughed, her eyes returning to normal and her fangs retracting back into her mouth.

"Subtle," James said. "But entertaining."

"I do my best," Lacy said as he settled beside her against the disc. "You ready to stop being a dick?"

"That's the second time you've called me a dick. I'm not sure I follow."

"Jimmy, you've been a dick since the shooting." She stood and faced him. "Sweetie, I get it: highly traumatic event, someone you care about got hurt, major shit happening all at once. But you've been obsessed, and Agent Smith already warned you he might lock your asses up. I'm surprised he isn't already here to haul you off."

Her words hit him, caught him off guard, and filled him with instant remorse. He wanted to reflect on what she'd said, wanted to look back over the past few days. He wanted to apologize to her, to Phillip, for letting his anger get the better of him.

The sharp, ear-splitting sound of bullets pelting the opposite side of the disc sculpture in that moment took higher priority.

11

James and Lacy ducked out of instinct, huddling closer together to make sure they were both shielded by the disc sculpture as bullets sprayed the area, the sound of gunfire blending with panicked screams of terror as hundreds of people scattered to escape the assault. Cars slammed on brakes, crashing into each other, and some ran up onto the curb to get away. He shifted, his clothing falling away in tatters and shreds of fabric. The air was heavy with the scent of gunpowder as bodies dropped to the ground, some writhing in pools of blood forming from wounds where the rounds had torn into them.

Lacy shouted at James, making hand gestures indicating what she was saying. *"Get his attention, I'll take him down! Go!"*

He charged out from behind the disc as Clint paused to reload. The officer looked up at James as he slapped a new magazine into the rifle. Another scream rose above the cacophony, higher-pitched and set apart from the others; sharp enough for James's right ear to flick in the direction it came from.

He turned and saw the old judgy couple running away toward the road as traffic continued to pile up and police sirens wailed only a few blocks away. The grandpa shoved his wife aside, overextended, and fell to the ground as a car barreled at him, tires screeching on asphalt. He held his hand up as if to ward off the vehicle as it came to a halt inches from him.

James glanced at Clint, saw him aim at the old man. *Not tonight,* he thought as he took after the grandpa. He got to him and pulled him back as another car slammed into an SUV a few feet from where grandpa had been lying. James pulled the old man close to him as bullets slammed into his back, each one bringing searing pain and the stench of burning dog hair and flesh. His back tightened, the muscles fighting to work the bullets out as more peppered him. It was enough to hurt, maybe even to bleed, but whatever gun was being used didn't have the power to send the rounds through him as he held the senior close to his chest and took the full magazine to his hunched form. The gunfire paused again. James dragged grandpa over to where he and Lacy had been standing, placing the disc between them and Clint. He scanned the area as the gunfire resumed, the ear-splitting sound of the bullets slamming into the metal making his ears ring. He peered around the side of the statue to see Lacy charging Clint. She was only a few feet away from him when she was tackled by a group of younger men and women, their eyes wild and their mouths open with their fangs fully extended as they hissed and snarled at her, moving erratically with no real strategy to their attack.

Younglings, James thought. *What the fuck?*

Clint had to be stopped before he shifted and got away. James could smell the cedarwood in the air, faint but present. His back had already healed, the bullets popping onto the pavement covered in his drying blood, but he couldn't leave the old man alone. The grandpa moaned in terror and pain, his wrist bent wrong.

Suddenly, the air was rich with the stench of rotten blood, and James lashed out to his right with his claws as a youngling invaded his cover. The thing fell, gagging and gasping with what was left of its throat before turning into dust.

A cop car in front of him jumped the curb before it came to a halt. The officers jumped out, guns raised and pointed at James. "Freeze," the driver shouted before he blinked and followed it with *"What the fuck?!"* The old man shouted, and James looked up to see Clint step around from the other side of the statue and open fire on the officers. Both cops dove behind their unit, one of them shouting as a bullet clipped his leg.

James reacted instantly, lunging at the cop car with the old man tucked against him. He pushed grandpa into the backseat and slammed the door shut as Clint fired on him, the bullets embedding themselves in the bulletproof glass and in more parts of James's body. His flesh pushed the rounds back out as fast as they entered, some of them barely piercing his fur. He tucked and rolled away, got his feet under him, and launched at Clint. The shooter blinked, turned on his heel, and ran through the chaos of screaming, injured, and dead people and wrecked cars as more police showed up. James pursued.

Their chase effectively ended as Clint changed to a speed once clear of the crowd that James had only ever seen in vampires. He ran after him at wolfen speed, moving virtually unseen by human eyes as he tailed Clint through Uptown, the city now alive with cop cars and first responders making their way to the scene. James kept pace with him, relying on the occasional obstacle to slow Clint down enough for him to gain another foot or two as they ripped through town and onto 277. Before James knew it, they headed south back toward the state line, running alongside traffic. Clint never veered one way or another, never acted like he was trying to lose James as he darted down the exit ramp onto Carowinds Boulevard and zipped right toward the main entrance to the park. James did the same as his quarry ran up the hill next to the road and into the parking lot.

James paused when he had asphalt underneath him, looking around the brightly lit and empty lot. *Where had Clint gone?* He took the scents of the nighttime air in over the glands in his mouth. Asphalt, tire rubber, fried food. Gasoline.

Blood. Vanilla.

Lacy appeared next to him. "Saw you take off after I finished with the assholes that jumped me. Where is he?"

James shrugged.

"Shit," Lacy said. "This place is huge. If he got in, there's no telling where he is." She looked up at him. "Do you have a scent on him?"

James gave her a thumbs down.

"Right," she said. "No scent. Damn."

James looked around and realized they weren't far from the main entrance to the park. The giga coaster of the park's trademark skyline loomed over them. He followed the coaster tracks with his eyes, his wolfen vision making the darkness inconsequential, until he saw them disappear underneath the bridge leading to the front gates. He motioned for her to follow him, then darted in and hopped the fence as if it were nothing more than a step and he made his way down the slope and into the concrete ditch and tunnel underneath the bridge. The green tracks were larger up close, dominating a good portion of the underpass floor.

James shifted into human form. "I smelled cedarwood in Charlotte when he opened fire."

"But no Clifford?" Lacy asked.

James shook his head. "I may have missed his scent when I first met him." He paused. "Or he somehow covered it up."

"If he knows to cover it up, that means he knows about you," Lacy said. "Jimmy, that's not good."

"I've lost his scent," James said. "He was running as fast as most vampires I've seen."

"Okay, so he's a vampire?" Lacy shook her head. "I got close enough to him before the younglings jumped me. I didn't get the vibe from him."

"Vibe?"

"Vampires can clock other vampires pretty easily."

"I am still trying to figure out why there were younglings there," James said.

"It means some asshole is using them as grunts again." Lacy looked away from him and muttered. "Shit. I was right."

James raised an eyebrow. "About what?"

A gunshot sounded from somewhere inside the park; the report echoed, making it difficult to zero in on which direction it had come from. James shifted into wolf form, pulled the wolf even closer to the forefront of his mind. *You heard it too.*

The wolf barked, then shared its memory with him. He heard the gunshot again, this time a little more keenly. He got Lacy's attention, pointed at his ears, then motioned for her to follow him as he made his way out of the tunnel and up onto the concrete. They scaled the locked gates and were inside in less than a minute. The park was completely dark, the only light coming from the moon in the cloudless sky and the light pollution from the parking lot lights blending into the sky with the rest of the faint glow given off by the city center a few miles up the interstate. James sniffed the air, smelled the heavy collage of fried treats, motor grease, and asphalt. He could see the large first drops of some of the roller coasters, their forms monstrous and looming in the night with their motors running like titans snoozing in place. The fountain in the main area at the entrance was quiet, the water still and reflecting the night sky like a mirror. He tapped the wolf's memory again and moved past the fountain, over the bridge featuring the state line between North and South Carolina, then moved left into the park.

He was barely a hundred yards in when he saw Clint duck down a pathway underneath one of the roller coasters. He took off after the shooter, catching the scent of fresh blood and gun oil. Clint darted left off the walkway, moving at lightning speed as James followed. He saw Clint drop his gun as he took another turn and jumped the fence surrounding the carousel. James stopped, Lacy darting up next to him. She grunted. "Well, shit," she said, looking at the carousel. "I've seen way too many movies for this not to be a trope."

A radio squawked from somewhere inside the ride. "Henderson! Respond! We're headed your way! *Henderson!*"

She approached the ride, James close behind her as they made their way past the waist-high fence and onto the dark platform. She motioned at James to stay low and check in the opposite direction. She pointed down at the platform, indicating to meet back here. He nodded, then made his way through the rows of horses and carriages lining the old ride frozen in time, their mouths and eyes often open mid-whinny and their legs gathered and hooves raised as if charging through a circus parade.

James heard someone shout from the other side of the merry-go-round. "This is Henderson! I've got trespassers at the carousel!"

Two guards appeared at the platform within seconds. James ducked down and crawled on all fours until he was around to the other side, where Lacy stood with her hands up. A guard, Henderson by James's assumption, had his feet planted in a shooter's stance with his gun pointed directly at her chest.

Lacy sighed, sounding bored as she spoke. "Look, handsome: unless you're just itching to shoot me, you don't need the gun. I'm five-four and a hundred and fifteen pounds soaking wet."

Henderson glared at her, pulled the hammer back on the weapon. "Shut up."

"Sweetie, I've got great boobs. You don't want to mess those up, do you?"

James recognized her tone. She couldn't make slaves out of people, but she had the ability to make strong suggestions stick.

Henderson kept his aim and his glare locked on her. "I didn't notice."

I can distract him, James thought. *Draw his fire so she can knock him out.* The wolf growled inside, bracing for James to move.

"Henderson!"

Both James and the wolf froze in place as two more security guards stepped up onto the platform, their guns also drawn and pointed at Lacy. She turned to them and smiled. "Hey, boys. I was just asking Henderson here if he really wanted to shoot me." Her smile grew. "You don't want to shoot me, do you?" She stuck her lower lip out in a pout, her voice going slightly higher as if she were a small child. "Why does everyone want to hurt me?"

The two new guards put their guns away, the older of them approaching her. "No, honey, of course we don't," he said, his tone soft and caring as if a father speaking to his daughter. "It's dangerous this time of night."

"I wanted to see the park after it closed," Lacy said innocently. She glanced at Henderson. "He still wants to hurt me."

The older man rounded on Henderson and scowled. "Henderson! Stand down! You're scaring this poor thing."

The second of the newly arrived guards approached Henderson. "Seriously, man. She's not even armed."

Henderson kept his glare on Lacy as he lowered his weapon.

"You can put your hands down, sweet," the older guard said to Lacy. He looked at Henderson. "What the hell were you shooting at? Not this poor girl, I hope."

Henderson kept his eyes locked on Lacy, then looked past her and directly at James. "Stray dog." He stared hard at James, the corner of his mouth twitching slightly as if trying not to smile. "Scared the shit out of me."

He knows I'm here, James thought to the wolf. The beast growled at Henderson and gnashed its teeth. *I'm going to need you to calm down. The last thing we need is to create another headline.*

The wolf backed away, and James did the same, moving further back into the darkness.

"You gotta lay off the damn caffeine, man," the younger guard said to Henderson.

"You could've shot this poor girl," the older guard said, putting a protective arm around Lacy. "Good god, kid! Didn't you hear about the shooting that just happened in Uptown?"

"That's why I'm here," Lacy whimpered. "I was at the gas station when I heard about it, and I got scared and ran when they said the shooter was at large."

"I'll give you a ride back to your car, sweetheart," the older guard said. "Jake, Henderson, you two keep things under control." He turned and guided Lacy off the carousel. James went the other direction, sniffing the ground until he found the gun he'd seen Clint throw away.

Hoyt will want this, he thought. The wolf barked in agreement.

James leaned against the railing overlooking the tracks of the roller coaster running underneath the bridge. He'd stopped at a clothing shop on the way out of the park to grab something to wear so he could shift back into human form without drawing attention to himself. He'd found the basics: shirt, shorts, underwear. He'd worry about shoes later.

Clint's assault rifle was leaned up against the railing next to him, positioned where he could stand in front of it and keep it hidden when Lacy and the guard walked out. He replayed everything, slowed it down from light-speed to something more discernible. Was it him? Was Clint following James? Hunting him?

No, James thought. *He deliberately tried to kill that old man.* James felt the memory of the soreness in his back where Clint had emptied the magazine into him while he'd protected the elderly man. He remembered seeing Clint simply spraying the area, then randomly, almost casually shooting those running away. He wasn't picking and choosing targets specifically.

And his face was expressionless. During both shootings. He never showed emotion until James stepped in, until he was dealing with something other than a crowd of innocent people he saw as open game.

It didn't strike James as the kind of cool intent that he'd seen in other supernatural psychopaths he'd dealt with before. Younglings functioned on pure instinct and raw emotion. Mature vampires were far more calculating, often weaponizing emotions against their victims. Clint's face looked more like he was a tradesman focusing on a project. Like it was a job. James thought back to the times he'd seen Clint react to him showing up. It was less of a *"You!"* reaction and more like James had interrupted him, had broken his concentration while trying to do his work.

Utilitarian. That's the word he was looking for.

But why? What drove him? He'd seen so many articles about mass shootings. The shooter was usually stereotyped by the news as a "troubled individual with multiple mental disorders." Phillip was always able to find the receipts showing the alarming number of shootings by these "troubled individuals" were politically motivated. But Clint didn't seem the type. The police would have searched his house by now, would have released something. Phillip would have found it immediately, would have told James.

They would have dealt with it. Together. Like brothers.

James shook his head, the wolf giving a low mewl as it wagged its tail at him. *Trying to cheer me up? Since when?*

The animal lay down in his mind with another mewl, looking up at him with sorrowful eyes. James felt a tinge of instant guilt. *Lacy's right, I am a dick.*

The wolf sent him the sound of Phillip's voice. *"Mass shooters rarely get caught. They usually kill themselves or get themselves shot before they can be apprehended. We have a chance, here, to help a lot of people here, including the shooter."*

James followed Phillip's line of reasoning easily. They'd had the conversation before about what it could mean to gather more information on the shooter's mindset after one of the multitudes of attacks that happened on a regular basis. "There've been more shootings than days this year," Phillip had said a month or so ago when the topic had come up. "And most of them have ended with the shooter either getting shot by the police or doing himself in before they can get to him. And if they do a psych evaluation of the few they've caught, they sure as hell don't publish it. Imagine if we could figure out what a major part of this bug is?"

"It's the guns," James muttered under his breath. Even though it hadn't hurt him enough to matter, there was something chilling about Clint unloading a full clip from an assault rifle into his back while he was the only thing standing between a stream of gunfire and another person. He didn't know what kind of gun it was and wouldn't have been able to pick it out in a line-up if he tried. James never had to concern himself with guns. He didn't hunt outside of his wolf form, and he wasn't concerned about protecting himself from unseen enemies crouching in the shadows waiting to pounce on him and do whatever it was those who felt the need to constantly carry firearms on them out in public were trying to protect themselves from.

His mind shifted to tonight. Clint had taken off. Why had he dropped the rifle? And what was Henderson's deal? The security guard had seemed to resist Lacy's mindjob. He'd seen James but hadn't reacted to the large werewolf lurking in the shadows. Was he, himself, a supernatural? And, if so, what kind?

"Jimmy, what in the name of *fuck* are you wearing?"

James looked up to see Lacy walking toward him. "I had to make do with what I could find."

"Are you wearing anything that doesn't have the logo on it?"

"I believe I am fully decked out."

"You look like a tourist."

"At least my phone has a camera." He peered past her and saw the older security guard closing the gate and watching them. Lacy waved at him, and he smiled and waved back before turning and disappearing back into the park. "I see you've made a new friend."

"Yeah," Lacy said. "He said I reminded him of his kid. I may have also convinced him and his buddies that they never saw us. He should be a clean slate in about five minutes."

"Even Henderson? The one that caught you originally?"

Lacy shook her head. "Yeah, you noticed that too? He didn't even try to fake it. The mindjob had zero effect on him."

"I wonder if he might be a supernatural?"

Lacy shrugged. "Could be. I didn't get a vibe off him. I'm pretty certain you could tell if he was a werewolf or vampire as well." She stared down at the rifle behind James's legs. "Holy shit, is that it?"

James nodded. "I picked it up on the way out. I plan to give it to Hoyt to look at it."

"Good call." She glanced up at the night sky, then at her phone. "Shit, what a night. Gonna be daylight in a few hours, and I'm in the mood for a waffle. Wanna get breakfast on the way home?"

12

As much as James preferred pancakes, he couldn't deny a waffle with a side of bacon and eggs.

He and Lacy had to run back to where she'd parked her car in the parking deck adjacent to Epicenter. The run had taken maybe fifteen minutes; the drive back was a solid forty-five minutes between late-night Charlotte traffic and the constant speed checks on the interstate all the way back to Rock Hill. He and Lacy kept conversation to small talk, asking about movies either of them had seen, and James told Lacy a few of the wilder stories about his time at comic book conventions with Phillip.

"I don't know if I'll be able to watch *Star Wars* with a straight face," Lacy had said while laughing at one of James's stories about a late-night private party at a larger convention in Atlanta, Georgia.

James nodded. "Had I been told that I would see that much of a Wookie, I would likely have stayed in the hotel room."

"You poor thing."

"I may need counseling."

It was still over an hour until sunrise when they arrived at Coldstone Keep. James couldn't help but notice Phillip's car was missing from the garage. He also couldn't smell Phillip's scent in the house above what lingered in most everyone's home. The wolf whimpered and looked at his mind's eye with a sorrowful expression.

Part of James was indignant, wanting to feel a sense of relief and victory at Phillip's departure. His best friend had compared him to David Coldstone. James was nothing like his father.

His mother had told him the stories of David's killing spree and what they'd found in the basement of Coldstone Keep. She'd paid a fair amount of money to have it gutted and remodeled into an unused finished space. She was content to let it sit empty and forgotten rather than leave any indication that David had killed so many victims in the basement of their own home. When she'd died while James was in college, he decided to sell the Keep since he was now old enough to claim it as his inheritance from his father.

That was when he found out about a provision in David's will. The estate could never be sold off or developed.

He decided to live in a small apartment instead, only using the fortune when he needed to pay bills or buy necessities like food and clothing, since he was also unable to give it away. There were provisions in David's will locking the family funds in place. James couldn't offload the fortune in any way other than paying bills and swiping a debit card for his own personal expenses while Coldstone Keep stood. It was also a registered Historical Landmark, which meant it couldn't be torn down or remodeled outside of preservation and structural integrity. David Coldstone had managed to make sure his family was stuck with his legacy no matter what.

At least it paid the bills.

Lacy parked the car in the garage. Inside the house, James immediately noticed the empty docking station for one of Phillip's video game systems on the shelf underneath the TV.

"Huh," Lacy said. "Bacon must be at a hotel or something."

James shook his head. "His mother lives in the downtown area."

"Are you serious?" Lacy said with a laugh. "You two fought, and he went to stay at his mom's place?" She clasped her hands together and scrunched her nose. "You two are fucking adorable." She unslung the assault rifle from her shoulder and sat it down on the coffee table. "We need to get this to Hoyt soon. And you need sleep. You're wiped."

"I can contact Hoyt and take it to him later today." James picked it up and looked it over. "Though I'm not sure what he is supposed to find out from it." He turned it over in his hands. "Where is the button to take the bullets out?"

"Jimmy?"

"Yes?"

"Have you ever even *held* a gun before?"

"Phillip has one of those zap guns for his old Nintendo system."

"Oh my god."

"Those ducks had it coming."

Lacy stood. "Sweetie, please hand me the loaded semi-automatic assault rifle before you hurt yourself." James held it out to her, and she took it from him and sat back down. She did something with it, and the clip dropped out into her waiting palm. "Shit, he'd just reloaded. It's only missing one or two rounds." She pulled another piece out and held it up. "There. Now it's a paperweight."

"I can attest that the bullets are not silver," James said. "My back is fine, by the way."

"Yeah, I saw that," Lacy said. "Scary shit."

"And here you are in my living room handling a gun as if you've done this several times." James's anger rose slightly as he finally felt the adrenaline rush from earlier subside.

She gave him an annoyed glare. "Here we go again. Jimmy, I've already told you everything I can."

"How deep does this go?" he asked. "You said this was bigger than we thought."

"It is." Lacy sat the parts back down on the table and sighed. "There are some things that are just classified, Jimmy. And it's safer for everyone, including you and Molly, if I don't tell you."

James sat down in the high-backed armchair that Phillip jokingly referred to as his "throne" and stared at Lacy. She sat up straight. "What?"

"I'm waiting for you to explain things to me."

She sighed again. "Goddammit, Jimmy."

"What will it take?" James asked, keeping his tone even as he watched her face fall while he spoke. "How many more people need to die? How many children need to watch the adults around them get gunned down? Or get killed, themselves?" His gaze hardened. "A number would be perfectly fine. I prefer to work with clear goals."

Lacy's eyes looked heavy as if she were a mortal who hadn't slept in days. She stared at James, her expression the most tired and defeated he'd ever seen from her. "You are such an asshole sometimes. You know that?"

"I have a gift."

She inhaled deeply, then let it out in a long and slow exhale before she started talking. "When Marianne got taken, I insisted that

Smith put me on the hunt for her because she's family. He didn't want to do it at first because he felt like I was too close to it. Then he found out that you and Phillip were after what turned out to be the same group that we were after. When the council got wind of it, they ordered him to do anything he could think of to get you underfoot so they could convince you to become the Knightwolf. I got installed as a plant."

"I know all of this," James said, letting his boredom show in his tone. "I would like more current events, please."

"It's pertinent," Lacy said. "I was going to come back to Rock Hill with you after we left Westenra Island, but I got called away as soon as we got here."

"Why?"

"The same reason I got called away when we got to the place in Hilton Head."

James blinked. "I'm not sure I follow."

"We've been tracking illegal arms being bought and sold for a while now," Lacy said. "Once we figured out that supernaturals were involved, Smith had Tepes make the right phone calls to get the human authorities to back off and let the SCU have it."

"I'm not sure why I was never made aware of this during my brief employment with the SCU," James said.

"Because I've been undercover," Lacy said. "We've managed to narrow down the search."

"And?"

She looked at him, guarded. "James, I'm serious. You cannot repeat this. It could get us both killed. Phillip too."

James nodded.

"It's someone from the Council of Night."

"Which explains why there were younglings at the shooting," James said, unsurprised. "And why you were in Savannah. You weren't there because we were there. You were there to investigate Noble Jones."

"Oh no, I'd already ruled Noble out. I was totally there because you were there," Lacy said. "You two have a bad habit of stumbling into shit that is way bigger than you and fucking things up. I was there to make sure you didn't do that."

"And?"

"You did that when you arrested Noble Jones."

"We prefer to be consistent."

"Smith fired you two for optics. As soon as this is over, you two are back at the SCU."

"I decline."

"You don't get a choice, Jimmy," Lacy said. "If Smith makes good on his threat to dox you, you'll be forced out of here. You won't have anywhere to go. Your assets will be frozen by the council. He's giving you a choice."

James rolled his eyes and sighed. "Come quietly or be brought in kicking and screaming?"

Lacy shrugged. "Hey, it's a choice."

"I demand an option C." He stood and moved to the fireplace, leaned against the mantle, staring up at where the portrait of his parents had once hung. He'd burned it the day he moved back into Coldstone Keep. He had plenty of old photos of his mother, which didn't include David Coldstone, so burning the family portrait had not been an issue for him.

"Believe it or not, Jimmy, I've been keeping the Council away from you as best as I can," Lacy said from her spot on the couch. "It's why I convinced Smith to make me your handler full-time starting with Savannah and going after that necromancer."

"When did the new Wolf-Man Killings start?"

"They started before you went after Mindy Robertson, then ramped back up again while you guys were in Savannah," Lacy said. "It was why I got called back when we hit Hilton Head. And it's why I'm the one who brought you in."

The wolf paced in his mind, grunting as it gave him a sense of confusion. The animal wanted to trust her, wanted to accept her as an ally again. But the sense came with wariness. Could he really say she'd betrayed him? Her intentions, her motives, her actions, all were blanketed under lies. But they were lies meant to protect him. And, by proxy, Phillip, Molly, and anyone else he might get close to.

His mind flashed to Westenra Island again. Not to their kiss, but to the moment he'd held her on the front porch before the sun had begun to rise. He remembered his shirt becoming soaked through as her supernatural body began to sweat under the low, persistent light of dawn just before she let him go and darted inside to avoid being burned alive.

Well, as "alive" as a vampire can be.

James's thoughts formed more words than his mouth could handle as he stared at her. He managed to consolidate the wave of words into one. "Why?"

Lacy looked hurt for a split second before she stood and walked over to him. She moved into him, resting her forehead against his chest as her arms snaked around his waist. Her blood and vanilla scent made his pulse race, his chest tightening slightly against his lungs as he felt the cool touch of her against him. He put his arms around her out of instinct, held her close to him as the wolf inside his mind lay on its back and exposed its belly. The creature's influence heightened his senses enough for him to hear her whisper.

"Isn't it obvious?"

She looked up at him, her eyes meeting his. He stared into the deep, impossibly ice blue depths as he leaned closer to her. James pulled her tighter to him and felt her grip on his waist tighten in acceptance, her breath against his as his lips brushed hers.

The horrific scream, accompanied by the rapid grind of an electric guitar riff and frantic drums, caused both of them to step back from each other. Lacy picked her phone up and answered. "Hey, Hoyt. You're on speaker." She motioned at James. "Say hi, Jimmy."

James stared at her, trying to catch his breath. "Hi, Jimmy."

"Hey, James," Hoyt said, his canned voice coming from the phone in Lacy's hand. "Had to check on a few things. Saw your text, Lacy. You said you have something for me?"

"Yeah," Lacy said. "About an hour before sunrise. Good timing."

"A Medical Examiner is never late," Hoyt said, using his best impression of Gandalf the Grey from The Lord of the Rings. "Nor is he early. He arrives precisely when he means to." He dropped the impersonation. "I had to go research something I may have found. I'll fill you in on it once I have something concrete. And the lab doesn't have windows, so you can crash here. What do you have for me?"

<hr>

James and Lacy arrived at the lab about thirty minutes before daybreak. Lacy had joked about sleeping in the morgue along the way. "I kind of think about it like a hotel," she'd said. "But with way better A/C."

Hoyt looked up from his desk as James and Lacy entered. "Holy shit, are you guys okay? I heard about the shooting on the news." He motioned at the rifle in Lacy's hands. "If this is the gun our guy used, then you're holding what killed twelve people tonight. The whole city is locked down."

"We got it from the shooter when we chased him," Lacy said. "He tossed it aside and took off."

"Okay," Hoyt said, moving up to them and holding his hands out. "Gimme."

Lacy handed it over. Hoyt set the rifle down on the examination table and pulled the overhead exam light closer, which allowed James to finally get a clear look at the weapon. It was very much like an assault rifle carried by the military. Lacy handed the clip over to Hoyt as he put on a set of magnifiers and leaned in to get a closer look. "Standard AR-15 loaded with .22 caliber bullets. Nothing special about it other than the serial number being scraped off."

"I am to assume that it takes more than peeling off a sticker," James said.

"Yeah, you gotta grind and sand it off," Hoyt said. "Usually with a Dremel tool or even a side-grinder. Then you just smooth it out and repaint." He pointed to a spot on the rifle. "It's usually right here."

"I've never understood the point of removing the serial number," James said. "Though it does seem to happen frequently on television."

"Because it's the easiest thing to do," Hoyt said, still examining the AR-15. "All guns have a rifling pattern in the barrel that is unique to each serial number. You can get the pattern off the rounds and use it to track the registration, find out who owns it, and pretty much follow it every place it's been. Filing the number off doesn't make the gun completely untraceable, though." He looked up at James, his square magnifiers making his eyes dramatically larger as if he were a cartoon character. "That's usually done when whoever plans to do illegal shit with it sends a file down the barrel."

"I would imagine that would cause problems with the bullets," James said.

"Nah, just doesn't put the same spin on them," said Hoyt as he quickly disassembled the rifle. James was impressed at the proficiency he showed, his hands working seamlessly as he placed each part down on the table until he only held the detached barrel. He picked up a small, pen-sized flashlight and shone it down the barrel as he peered inside from behind the bright LED. "No obstructions, nothing obvious going on." He set the light down, opened a nearby drawer, and pulled out a coil of tubing with a cell-phone-like device on one end and a small camera scope on the other. He pressed something on the device and sent the scope down the barrel. "Yeah, that's better."

"What is it?"

"Your buddy, or whoever he got this from, sent a file down the barrel. The rifling is fucked, so there's no tracing this gun anywhere."

"Where would Clint have gotten a machine gun?" James asked.

"It's not a machine gun," Hoyt said. "This guy is a semi-automatic. Means you press the trigger one time; it fires one round." He indicated the stock of the gun. "It's got a bump stock, though."

"A what?"

"A *bump. Stock*," Hoyt said, emphasizing the two words as he pointed to the part of the rifle James knew rested against the shoulder. "It replaces the regular stock and uses the gun's recoil to bounce it back and forth between the shooter's shoulder and the trigger finger. So, you can basically hold down the trigger, and the gun does all the work. It's still considered a semi-automatic, but the work is being done by kinetic energy rather than a self-igniting propellant system."

James and Lacy looked at each other, then at him. Lacy nodded and pursed her lips before she spoke. "That was a lot of big words, Hoyt."

"Indeed," James said. "You sounded smart."

"Fuck you guys," Hoyt chuckled before he let it fade and stood up straight, pushing the magnifying visor up away from his eyes. "Funny as that was, this is bad." He motioned at the dismantled rifle on the table in front of him. "This gun is completely incognito. If I were on TV, I'd say that the way our bad guys filed the serial number and rifling is amateurish. Truth is, it's the best way to make a gun disappear off the radar. They could set up an assembly line with enough people using basic tools you can get from any store and crank out hundreds of rogue firearms a day."

"Shit," Lacy muttered, putting her face in her hands. "This just keeps getting better."

James leaned on the table, looking over the parts and sighing before he turned his attention back to Hoyt. "Is there a supernatural way to trace it?"

Hoyt grinned. "Now you're talking. Grandpa taught me a pretty neat trick when I was a kid. It'll take me some time, and it's not going to get super specific, but I can probably point you in the right direction." He glanced around. "Hey, where's Phillip? He finally give up this third shift bullshit?"

James's phone chimed mercifully in his pocket. He pulled it out and checked the text notification. His heart both leapt in his chest and almost stopped at the same time as he read the text message.

"What is it, Jimmy?" Lacy asked.
"Molly is awake. She would like to see me."

13

Molly had been moved to the Women's Tower at Piedmont Medical in Rock Hill, which was not only used for expecting mothers but also for patients in surgical recovery. The wolf kept James's senses at peak, and he could sense the quiet of rest permeating the air, adding a calmness to the typical scents of chemicals hospitals used to make sure every surface was as sanitized as possible. He could also smell the musk of fear in the air, some of the rooms giving off the warm, sweet smell of sweat and panic.

"They do that when they need the space," Hoyt explained before they left. "It's closer to her home, and they need the beds in the ICU for the new victims, and the recovery rooms are occupied. They wouldn't have done it unless she was stable enough to move. It's good news, James."

It was less than fifteen minutes before sunrise, but Lacy drove James to the hospital anyway since it was a five-minute drive from Hoyt's office. Visitation hours were still closed, but Lacy did her mindjob trick on the security guard at the front desk. He ended up waving them through while he preoccupied himself with his new obsession with Candy Crush on his cell phone after being convinced his purpose in life was to play the game until told otherwise.

Lacy walked calmly beside him as he made his way to the room where Officer Candy Crush had told them Molly was being kept. He stopped outside her closed door and breathed deeply as the wolf pulled back, dulling his senses to where he couldn't feel and smell every emotion and scent around him. *At least you have the capability of being considerate.*

The wolf chuffed at him and lay down to take a nap.

"I can wait for you here if you want," Lacy said. "There are no windows in the hallway, and I can head down to the morgue to crash if the sun comes up."

"No," James said. "You need to get somewhere safe. I can make my way back home after I'm done here." He paused, then looked at her. "Thank you."

"Sure," Lacy said, giving him a small smile. "Friends and stuff, right?"

Molly's voice came from inside the room, muffled because of the closed door but still audible. "James?"

He nodded to Lacy and opened the door and stepped in, leaving it open in case he would need to call for a nurse if something happened.

A long, thick privacy curtain hung from the ceiling and acted as a makeshift foyer partially opening into the rest of the room. The room itself was cold and unfeeling despite the cherrywood-colored shelving and drawer unit lining the wall on the right. The low warmth from the puck-light above the built-in sink area kept the room from being too dark to navigate. A built-in couch lined the opposite wall just under the windows, and a recliner sat in the far left-hand corner facing the television mounted inside the wooden shelving system. James followed the rhythmic beeping of the echocardiograph and saw Molly in the hospital bed. Her black hair was only slightly disheveled. Her olive-toned skin looked better than it had when he'd seen her in the ICU. Seeing her awake rather than lying there being kept alive by machines made his heart flutter with joy.

His chest tightened with guilt from the memory of himself and Lacy standing in his living room in the most intimate moment they'd had since Westenra Island.

"James," she said, her voice soft and sleepy. "What time is it?"

"Not quite five in the morning, if I'm not mistaken," James said. "Unless you're wanting to call your parents. I have no idea what time it is in Britain."

"It's nine in the morning at home, you wanker." she said, rolling her eyes and giving a weak smile. "My parents already called. They can't get a flight over here due to delays. How did you get in here? Visitation hasn't started yet."

"I have a friend who did me a favor."

"Is it Lacy?"

James blinked as the wolf made a curious noise inside. "Lacy?"

"I've heard you mention her before," Molly said. "Another friend of yours and Phillip's? Is she here?"

James smelled the blood and vanilla an instant before Lacy appeared next to him. She smiled and gave a small wave. "Hi," she said. "Lacy Faulkner. It's nice to meet you."

Molly smiled back. "Likewise." She glanced at James. "I'm sure you've had your hands full these past few days."

"James is a handful on most days," Lacy said. "But he's housebroken, so it's not so bad."

"Right," Molly said. "Like a dog." She gave a small laugh and looked at James. "At least she has you figured out."

"I try to remain an open book," James said.

Molly and Lacy spoke in unison. "Bullshit." The three of them shared a chuckle, though James stopped immediately when he saw Molly wince in pain. "Please, no more jokes," she said. "Laughing is painful."

James turned to Lacy and motioned at the clock on Molly's bedside table. "It's getting close."

"Right," Lacy said with a nod. She turned her attention back to Molly. "It was nice to meet you. I hope you recover soon. I'll let you two catch up." She turned back to James, and he couldn't help but notice the sadness in her eyes as she gave another nod before she left the room, closing the door quietly behind her.

"I believe she wants to be more than friends, James," Molly said. "Woman's Intuition and all that."

"It's complicated," James said. "And one-sided."

"I don't think it is," Molly said. "I saw how you looked at her. It's okay, I'm not upset or anything. I think it's adorable."

Under any other circumstances, James would have a joke lined up about a werewolf and a vampire finding a budding relationship while slaughtering things trying to kill them. The joke would have been in poor taste since Molly didn't know what he really was. He changed the subject instead. "How are you feeling?"

"Tired," Molly said. "A little weak. Like someone shot me in the bloody stomach or something."

"I am so sorry," James said, his throat clenching. "I didn't want any of this."

"How could you have known this would happen? No one really knows when something like this will happen. It just does."

"I feel some responsibility," James said. "You were there because of me."

"I was there because I wanted to be there," Molly said with a weak smile. She shook her head. "James, I know that this is not the appropriate time, but it can't wait any longer."

"What can't wait?"

She took a slow, deep breath. Her eyes were fixed on his. "I need time, James. I need to sort myself out. And it has nothing to do with being shot, of that I can assure you."

James cocked his head to the side slightly. "I'm not sure I follow."

Molly closed her eyes and took another slow breath, wincing in pain as she exhaled. "James, I don't understand what is going on. I'm lying in a hospital bed after having emergency surgery because I was fucking shot. Yet, the moment you walk into the room, the only thing stopping me from climbing you like a bloody tree is the pain, the equipment attached to me, and the drugs." She shook her head. "My god, what is wrong with me?"

"Nothing," James said. "I am simply that charming."

She looked back up at him. "No, you really aren't. And levity will not help me right now. Laughing hurts, remember?"

James was about to make another joke and thought better of it. The look in her eyes was telling. She was in pain. Not just physical pain. And he could sense the confusion coming from her. "I maintain that there is nothing wrong with you."

"I slept with you multiple times the first night I ever met you," she said. "Every time we've met up, we've had sex."

"I am aware," James said, stifling back another joke. "We're still new to our relationship. Most couples are the most sexually active in the beginning."

"James, I'm asexual."

James shook his head. "I'm not sure I know what you mean."

She gave him a confused blink. "You mean to tell me that you've never met someone who is ace before?"

He shrugged. "I don't get out much."

"I'm not typically interested in sex," she explained. "At all."

"That sounds difficult."

"Not really," she said with a shrug. "It just doesn't do it for me." She rubbed her forehead as if staving off a headache. "Yet, when I'm with you, I'm a completely different person. I can't get enough. And no matter how much I get, I want more." She pulled her hand down and gestured at him. "Yet, when I'm away from you, I feel normal."

James felt his chest tighten and his stomach knot. "I'm sorry," he said. "I still don't understand."

"I'm not me when you're around," Molly said. "I care about you, James. I do. But I need time to sort this out. I don't understand this side of myself, and now I'm a survivor of a gunshot wound. It's all too much to handle at once." She shook her head. "I can't do it all. I want to see you, I do. But I need time." She paused and sighed again, this time with a tear streaming down her cheek. "Right now, more than anything, I need a friend. Not a lover."

James slept fitfully, tossing and turning in his bed. It seemed as if he woke every fifteen minutes or so, what Molly had said to him echoing in his mind.

"I want you to come visit me," she had said before he left. "I need to try to interact with you without sleeping with you. According to my therapist, at least."

"Of course," James said. "You know, it was never an expectation."

"I know," Molly said. "It's one of the things I appreciate so much about you. That you never obligated me. That I could have said no." She'd paused. "But I could never say no. And that isn't normal. Not for me."

He'd called an Uber to take him home since the sun was up by the time he'd left Molly's room. Any level of sunlight would literally cook Lacy alive if she were exposed. He remembered their time in Charleston when they'd fought vampire younglings until daylight. Lacy had been burned so badly she was a charred, skinless husk by the time he'd gotten her back to the hotel room and shoved her under the bed and out of the sunlight. He'd exposed himself publicly, but he'd carried her all the way from the beach back to the hotel regardless. He'd saved her life.

And it was more than probable that the SCU had gone to great lengths to keep the event quiet and out of the media.

He looked at his phone and noted it was Saturday, and much later in the day than he thought. There was a food truck event happening in Downtown Rock Hill. The wolf licked its chops as it flashed images and memories of the smells of various forms of fried food, eventually focusing more on funnel cakes covered in powdered sugar.

I never figured you to be a proponent of deep-fried pastries, he thought to the animal.

The food truck event was one he and Phillip usually never missed. Phillip had a certain affection for funnel cakes and introduced James to their glorious existence years ago while they were in college.

There was also a likelihood that Phillip would be there.

James looked at his phone again, debating with himself. He wanted to call Phillip, ask for a meetup. Talk things out. But he also knew Phillip was likely spending all his energy trying to prove James wrong about Clint. James had seen it with his own eyes. It was impossible that Clint and Clifford were so consistently in the same places at the same time and not be one and the same. But what had caused him to snap? He seemed like a normal guy when they met him at the Fillmore. What kind of thing could cause someone to go to such lengths to do something as horrific as shooting up a crowd of innocent people?

That one was easy.

James remembered when he first discovered he was a werewolf. He was in high school the first time he shifted into wolf form. He'd been out in the pastures, wandering around and chatting with Phillip when it happened. It was nightfall, and a full moon.

Phillip had taken it well.

"Holy Merry Christmas shit!!" Phillip fell back on his rump as James stood over him, staring down at him from much higher than normal. His vision was yellowed, clear in the darkness as if he were wearing night vision goggles. Phillip backpedaled on the ground, trying to put more distance between himself and James. *"What the fuck?!"*

"I don't know," James said, panic welling inside him. "What just happened to me?!" At least, that was what it sounded like in his head. When he spoke, all he heard come from himself was a series of woofs and barks. He crouched down and mewled.

Phillip shook his head in disbelief. "James?"

James barked and wagged his tail.

Phillip stood up, still keeping his distance, his hand out as if warding off the potential for attack. "Holy shit," he said.

James barked again.

"Damn," Phillip said. His expression lifted, his eyes widening as his mouth broke into an excited grin. "*Dude!* Why didn't you tell me you were a werewolf?"

James shrugged.

"You didn't know," Phillip said. "This is a first for you?" He paused. "Bark once for yes, twice for no."

"*Roof!*"

"It makes sense," Phillip said. "Hell, we both know about your pops." He rubbed his chin. "I guess lycanthropy can be genetic."

James had not been nearly as accepting of his own condition as Phillip had been. He told his mother, showed her. She hadn't been surprised at all, had even told him he had to keep the new discovery his most closely guarded secret. The loneliness began to set in shortly after. Even with Phillip around, James felt confined. Caged. His freshman year in college was when his mother died in a car accident, which understandably added to his depression. He thought about opting out, ending it all. He thought about running away, hiding. Never coming back.

He'd never once thought about hurting people in retaliation for his own misery. Not like Clint. The wolf inside him was likely different from James's wolf. It wanted to kill, wanted chaos and destruction. It was highly possible that the animal was driving Clint insane, pushing him to kill in both human and wolf forms.

And Phillip was hell-bent on capturing Clint, treating him like a normal human criminal.

He saw the wolf sit down in his mind. It kicked one of its legs up, reared down, and began licking its scrotum.

You're doing this, why?

The beast looked up at his mind's eye and chuffed at him as it sent him a mental image of a shower.

Right, James thought. *I do need a shower.* He imagined what Phillip would say if he knew about the wolf. He could even hear it in Phillip's voice.

"Why am I not surprised that it takes your imaginary friend cleaning his beans in your face to remind you to take a shower?"

He had to get to downtown Rock Hill. Phillip would already be there. He and James never missed the food trucks.

James scheduled a ride on his phone. The wolf sent him an image of both him and Phillip at the food truck festival, laughing as they ate funnel cakes and watched some of the local performances going on. If nothing else, Phillip was a creature of habit. *I can't think of a better chance to talk to him,* James thought to the wolf. *He will likely be more receptive to reason while eating a funnel cake.*

The wolf sent him a sense of skepticism, following it with a grunt as it cocked its head to the side.

Who wouldn't be more receptive to reason while eating a funnel cake? James asked the creature. *After all, it is a funnel cake.*

The wolf chuffed at him, then wagged its tail and barked. James sensed hope. *That's better.*

The sun had just set, which was usually the best time to go to the festival. James was waiting on his Uber when he got the emergency alert from his phone, screeching, ear-splitting even from inside his pocket. James pulled it back out to check the bulletin. He saw the contact tag for the SCU ahead of the rest of the message. He read it twice before running out the front door in a full sprint, his body already shifting, his clothing falling to shreds as he blasted down the driveway at wolfen speed, shot past the car coming down the drive. He didn't pay attention to the driver's reaction of pulling off to the side and putting the car into the ditch. He didn't pay any more attention than necessary to the traffic on the highway, avoiding the cars and trucks easily as he ran. The cool air did nothing to ease him, the wolf pressing harder in his mind, making him go even faster.

He had to get to Phillip, had to hope it wasn't too late. Despite the fire inside his veins, the words from the banner on his phone gave him a chill.

> Active shooter in Downtown Rock Hill. Police on
> the scene.

14

James covered the twenty-minute drive from Coldstone Keep to Downtown Rock Hill in less than five. His heart pounded in his chest, his blood running hot through his veins as he gnashed his teeth and prepared for battle. He would end this tonight. He would take Clint apart, even if Clint was in wolf form. He didn't care anymore. No one else was going to get hurt or killed. No more shootings. No more murders.

He slowed as he neared Main Street. The crowds milled about, shopping at vendors and standing in clusters chatting up friends and family. The streetlights were at full brightness, the warm glow making the shadows on the ground as busy as the people casting them. A train had parked on the tracks between the railroad stops. James hid behind the main engine, peering around and listening, his sight and hearing fully enhanced and wolfen. People laughing, mixed conversation. Someone said something ignorant, and someone else called the man a dumbass. But it wasn't Phillip. It didn't have the same ring to it. The screams and laughter of playing children mixed in with the rest of the sounds floating over the hum of a dozen food truck generators. He sniffed the air, the stench of engine grease and coal burning his nostrils. He pulled it in over the glands in his mouth, detecting the smells of fried foods and asphalt mixed with gasoline from the generators.

He smelled blood and vanilla an instant before Lacy spoke behind him. "What the hell?"

James glanced at her over his shoulder and huffed.

"I'm guessing you got the text too?" she asked, holding up her phone and showing it to him. "I woke up to this bullshit."

James read the screen.

Active shooting in downtown. Get there and eliminate the shooter.

The contact banner read "SCU Emergency Dispatch." He shifted into human form and turned fully to Lacy. "I also received a text." He raised an eyebrow at her. "Why do you have a backpack with you?"

Lacy gave him a look as she unshouldered the pink backpack and handed it to him. "Figured you probably heard something and freaked out. Because I've met you."

James accepted the backpack and opened it to find a change of clothes along with a pair of shoes. "Thanks," he said as he began to dress. "I was concerned Phillip would be out here."

"He probably is," Lacy said. "You two can't keep away from food trucks. It's actually kind of disturbing."

"I was going to try to talk to him."

"You think he'd listen?"

"Funnel cakes make everything better."

"Pancake batter dropped into fryer grease and covered in powdered sugar," Lacy said, shaking her head. "Doesn't take much, I guess."

"Not pancake batter," James explained. "Far different texture and consistency. There is also a notable difference in the level of sugar and butter."

"You have a problem."

"I have a passion."

"Wow, Jimmy."

James peered around the train again, looking over downtown with his human eyes. The wolf growled inside him, sending him a sense of caution. *You're right,* he thought to it. *This could be a setup.*

The theme from "Mr. Belvedere" blared from Lacy's phone. She answered it and held the phone out. "You're on speaker. You two play nice."

Smith's voice carried his typical edge of irritation and smugness. "I'm gathering that Mr. Coldstone is with you?"

"Good evening," James said, mimicking Bela Lugosi's accent from *Dracula.*

"Charming," Smith said. "Agent Kimble is also with me."

"And I'm here to tell you that we didn't send out any all-calls," Kimble said in the background. "I've got Sanchez on it now with the rest of IT, but the bottom line is someone decided to be cute and sent out a false alarm." Something chimed in the background, and Kimble spoke again. "Just got a text from Sanchez. Looks like Faulkner and Coldstone are the only ones who got the message."

"That's a little weird," Lacy said. "James and I are already here. We'll check it out."

"Very good," Smith said. "We cannot risk this being more than a distraction. Kimble, keep me updated on the findings from IT. Agent Faulkner, ensure that the area is secure."

"What about me?" James asked.

"Find somewhere that is not in the way," Smith said. Three beeps later, the screen was blank.

Lacy put her phone back in her pocket and looked at James. "He's going to shoot you one day. You know that, right?"

James nodded. "I can only hope that he will display a modicum of personality before firing."

Lacy rolled her eyes. "You're impossible."

"Does that mean charming?"

"You think you're so cute."

"I can even do tricks."

She slugged him. "Shut up." She took the backpack back from him and slung it over her shoulder before she nudged her chin in the direction of the crowds. "Ready?"

"Date night?"

"Thought you'd never ask." Lacy put her hand in his, interlacing her fingers with his. "Let's go, handsome."

James led her away from the train and up the hill to the festival. The streets were closed to through traffic, allowing people to cross and congregate without the worry of cars driving up and down the festival area. The ticket tent's line stretched at least thirty people, though the process moved quickly, and those waiting weren't pressed since the tickets were for purchasing food and drinks rather than admission. A group of teenagers congregated on the steps of the courthouse, all of them on their phones. One of them gave a cheer, and the others groaned while the champ bragged about his kill streak and trophies. Another cluster of people made their way down a flight of stone stairs to the local "barcade," which had moved a few of the smaller machines outside for the festival. There was a local author, a steampunk accessories dealer, and a booth where a local comic book shop had set up a large table with long boxes full of comics and a second table full of rare toys from fandoms like Ghostbusters and Star Wars.

And not one of the dozens of people perusing their nerdy interests while drinking a beer was Phillip.

"You good, Jimmy?" Lacy asked.

"Why do you ask?"

"You're moping a little more than usual. Molly broke up with you or something?"

James nodded. "As a matter of fact, she did." He told her what Molly had said to him.

"Damn, I'm sorry," Lacy said. "Makes sense, though."

"Why is that?"

"Humans can't resist us," Lacy said. "Not on a pheromonal level. If you were putting off the pheromones of being attracted to her, she didn't really have much of a choice in it. We're all animals, at the end of the day."

"Meaning?"

"Meaning that even Phillip would probably jump your bones if you decided to get horny for him." Lacy laughed. "That would be funny as hell."

James felt a tightness in his chest along with a pang of hurt. Had everything with Molly been a lie?

He pushed it down. He couldn't focus on that right now. "Phillip isn't here," James said, his tone matter-of-fact.

"You don't smell him?"

"I don't have to," James said. "Whenever we come here, we immediately go to the ticket tent and get what we need to get our funnel cakes. We then go to the barcade so that he can play video games and look for comic books while we have a beer."

"Maybe he's still in line for his funnel cake?" Lacy said. "It's possible."

James shook his head. "No, it isn't. This festival begins just before sundown. He likes to come early enough to beat the lines and get a fresh funnel cake before there is a risk of getting one that's been sitting for a bit. It's also the best time to make sure he gets first look at the comic books in case he finds something rare."

"Maybe he's already in the barcade?"

"If he is, that would be the only place he could be. And that would also mean he finished his funnel cake twice as fast as he normally does."

Lacy looked at him and grinned. "Wow, Jimmy, that's impressive. You know your bestie."

"He is a creature of habit," James said. The wolf stepped forward in his mind and pressed on his sense of smell again. Pizza, fried food, body odor, asphalt, soil from the places where the city had planted flowers and such during the beautification project a few years back. Blood and vanilla, which was unsurprising since Lacy was standing next to him.

Cedarwood. The wolf made a noise inside his head, and he saw his vision yellow.

"Jimmy, easy on the eyes," Lacy said beside him. "Not real subtle when they turn yellow as all hell."

"I seriously doubt Clifford is here for a funnel cake," James said, still scanning the area.

Lacy's tone hardened to all business. "Where?"

"I can't narrow it down," James said. "He's brushed up against too many people. Left some of his scent."

"He's gotta be in human form," Lacy said. She let go of his hand and pushed her hair out of her face. "Shit, Jimmy. There's gotta be over a thousand people here."

"I can't pinpoint him," James said. "I would need to shift to follow the scent trail."

"Yeah, there are leash laws," Lacy said. "We'll split up. Where's the rest of the party?"

"Food trucks," James said. "Other side of the church."

"Which church? There's one on every corner."

He took her hand. "This way." He led her down the street, moving past the ticket tent and into the large fountain park that consumed the city block between an older church and an even older apartment building. The fountains were in full performance, the water shooting high into the air from multiple spigots and arcing to form a pattern enhanced by the ever-changing up-lights from the water below, moving gently from color to color. The food trucks encircled the park, each one catering to lines of people eager to try new treats or partake in favorites. A high school marching band played down near the fountain while the cheerleaders performed to the spirited and bombastic music, all of them decked out in school colors and doing choreographed dance moves to the band's cover of whatever pop song was popular with the kids at the moment. Someone was dressed as a clown and was twisting long balloons into various shapes for the kids, mostly swords and dogs.

"Why does every small-town festival have a balloon animal clown?" Lacy asked. "Kinda cliché."

"I believe there may be a law," James said, distracted and still looking around. He heard the clown announce that he would be back in a few minutes as Lacy spoke again.

"Oh, *shit.* You have *got* to be kidding me."

James stared directly at the clown and took a double-take as the clown waved back at him. "James! Holy shit, didn't think I'd see you out here!"

Lacy squeezed James's hand. "It's him."

"I am aware," James said.

"Doesn't Phillip call him something?"

"Cooter Critter."

"Ew."

Chuck Creighton walked up to James and Lacy wearing a large grin, his clown makeup making his smile seem even larger and more stupid. "Good to see you, man! How've you been?"

"Keeping out of trouble," James said.

"Right," Chuck said with a snort. "I've met you." He looked at Lacy. "Haven't met you. Chuck." He held his hand out to her.

"Agent Faulkner," Lacy said. "Officially grossed out."

"Agent?" Chuck said, blinking. His eyes widened with the realization. "Oh, you're with the SCU." He glanced around before leaning in. "I've been behaving myself; I promise. No more running up skirts for me." He beamed proudly.

James and Phillip met Chuck when they first joined the SCU. Chuck earned the moniker of "Cooter Critter" from Phillip due to his habit of turning into a mouse and running up the skirts of unsuspecting women. He became a regular target for James and Phillip and had, in a way, formed a somewhat awkward friendship with them. Initially, James was disgusted by Creighton. He had no tolerance for anyone who committed sexual assault of any kind. However, things came to light after a few arrests. Chuck did not do it for sexual gratification. He had a love of getting a reaction out of people, and nothing made someone react more wildly than a small mammal scurrying around downstairs.

"Oh?" Lacy said to him. "Why the change of heart?"

"Besides being informed that I was technically committing sexual assault?" Chuck eyed James. "Well, the last time I got caught I got chased into an escape room, wound up inside Coldstone's mouth, and he almost swallowed me like a multivitamin."

Lacy gave James a look. He shrugged. "I was in wolf form." He turned his attention back to Chuck. "Have you seen Phillip around?"

"Nope," Chuck said. "Sure haven't. I know you guys come out here for about every one of these, so I was gonna apologize for the whole biting his nipple thing last time we hung out."

Lacy looked at James again. "Wow, Jimmy."

"It isn't what it sounds like."

"It sounds like you three are into some freaky shit."

Chuck piped in, grinning like a buffoon. "You should've seen the people who saw us on the elevator. It looked like the start of a joke." He chucked James on the arm. "Hey, James! A black guy, a white guy, and a naked dude are on an elevator—"

Lacy pursed her lips, her normally pale complexion reddening slightly as she held back an obvious burst of laughter. James spoke before she could let it go, cutting Chuck off at the same time. "Chuck, I need you to be serious for a minute."

"Right, sorry," Chuck said, letting his own laughter fade.

"I need you to tell Phillip that I need to speak to him if you see him. It's important."

"Yeah, sure. Number the same?"

James realized his phone remained somewhere on the front lawn at Coldstone Keep. Lacy stepped in and gave Chuck her number along with a warning never to use it unless it was either an emergency or he had made the conscious decision to become paraplegic. Another high school marching band started up a catchy, bombastic version of a pop song. A group of children screamed excitedly as the water fountain in the center of the park reached the peak height of its cycle, shooting water at least twenty feet into the air. The smells of fried food intensified as the funnel cake truck nearby saw a surge of patrons seeking a sweet treat. Another truck specializing in corn dogs sat next to it, also sporting a rather impressive line.

Cedarwood. There was cedarwood.

James let the wolf step forward until his vision was just at the cusp of turning yellow. He could smell everything now, could tell what direction it was coming from. He found the cedarwood again, focusing on that and ignoring the rest of the scents around. He traced it easily to a man standing in line at the food truck with the fried strawberries and barbecue. The man was tall, broad-shouldered, with a baseball cap and sunglasses on.

Not Clint, but he reeked of cedarwood nonetheless.

The man broke out of line abruptly, walking away James took after him, not at a run, but his pace urgent. Lacy called out behind him. "Hey, Jimmy! Wait up!"

The guy was nimble, moving among the sea of people deftly and without shoving into anyone as he made his way toward the festival entrance. James kept his distance despite his quarry obviously knowing he was being pursued. They were back on Main Street in seconds, and James saw the figure dart left at the corner leading to the barcade. He saw his prey duck inside and immediately disappear into the crowd.

"Fuck," James muttered under his breath. The wolf chuffed, agitated. The smells and noises of the barcade would be overwhelming unless he shifted fully and took on the height of his wolfen senses.

But Phillip might be in there, he thought. The barcade was one place he was sure he would find Phillip, who was probably inside pumping quarters into the Teenage Mutant Ninja Turtles pinball machine and completely unaware of the possible danger.

James descended the concrete stairs to the patio and entered the barcade. The air went from cool to cold, the vents inside pumping air furiously to combat the radiant heat from the multitude of people combined with the dozens of arcade cabinets lining the walls. There was no seating at the bar, each stool occupied by people having drinks while they played one of the many console game systems the barcade offered for those who wanted to game while they enjoyed a beer and pizza. The chorus of people chatting mixed with the chaos of the machines booping and beeping, some of them blaring computerized music while others rattled with badly simulated gunfire.

And no Phillip in sight. Nor was the man who smelled like Clifford. Like Clint.

Phillip's voice sounded in James's mind. *"You said Clint had no scent."* Would he be able to hide it? The man he was chasing was not Clint. Clint was black and was still wearing his Charlotte/Mecklenburg Police uniform. This guy was white, wearing a blue button-down shirt and faded blue jeans.

James walked up to the bar. The barkeep, a girl in her twenties and covered in tattoos, saw him and made a motion to let him know she would be with him in just a minute. He nodded at her, then looked around the crowded arcade area again.

That was when he saw Clint duck out through the front door.

James went after him, sniffing the air to pick up the cedarwood scent. It was nearby, but not in the direction Clint was headed. He saw the uniformed cop jog up the stairs, seemingly oblivious that he was being followed. James took the steps two at a time, keeping Clint in his sight until he found himself back in the crowded streets of Downtown Rock Hill with no idea where the shooter had gone. People tended to move away from uniformed police officers, giving them plenty of space even in crowds. Clint should have been obvious.

He pulled the wolf as far forward as he dared, opened his mouth slightly as he took the scents in through both his nose and mouth.

Cedarwood. To the right. Down the alleyway.

He took after it, tried to put eyes on Clint again, but found nothing. He was on Black Street now, behind the bars and restaurants lining East Main Street. More people were in those back lots, the bouncy houses shaking and dancing as small children jumped and screamed excitedly inside, running in and out from one bounce house to the next.

Seeing the kids playing, having the time of their lives as their parents chatted with each other and looked on, was what made James's heart drop into his stomach when the staccato of gunfire shattered the joyous sounds of the festival.

15

No one reacted at first. A few people asked if the fireworks were about to start. Maybe someone was setting off firecrackers or poppers? James heard a small child ask their mommy where the pretty colors in the sky were.

In seconds, confusion gave way to panic and chaos as the air filled with screams. People scattered in terror. The wolf braced inside his mind as James stood his ground, listening for the direction of the gunfire. More popping, metal slapping against metal. Glass broke, the noise not dissimilar to gravel being kicked.

The new parking deck in University Center.

It was less than a second for James to realize he couldn't shift. Not out here. The last thing these people needed was him adding a werewolf to the list of things they were running from.

He ran down behind the alternative bar next to the barcade. Fewer people were in the area because the crowds had escaped in the opposite direction. James stepped behind a large dumpster in the back parking lot of the apartment building he'd lived in what seemed like ages ago and stripped. He set the clothes aside, shifted, and made for the parking deck as the gunfire continued in earnest.

You die tonight, he thought, gnashing his teeth.

James leapt into the parking deck with ease, landing in a parking spot occupied by a single motorcycle. He made his way deeper, listening for another round of shots. The lights on the deck flickered, the strobing effect disorienting him for a second before the entire building went black. He always marveled at how no one realized how loud electricity is. He stood there for a moment, listened in the absolute quiet for movement, the sound of a gun reloading, anything that would give away his quarry's location as he looked around the parking area. Dozens of cars had been shot into oblivion; their exteriors riddled with bullet holes, and most of the windows shot out. He could smell gasoline from where more than one tank had been shot open and was pouring fuel onto the concrete. He felt his muscles tense at the thought of fire, then remembered a conversation he and Phillip had had only a month ago.

"Cars do not do that on impact," Phillip had said, rolling his eyes at the movie they'd been watching. "You know what it takes to make a car explode?"

"I've seen movies where they shoot the gas tank," James had said.

"Yeah, that won't even do it most of the time."

"It did at Noble Jones's place."

"Yeah, they were using fucking .50 caliber Brownings. And thank you for the reminder of my tragic loss."

Phillip, of course, had been talking about his own car being destroyed and the Corvette he'd borrowed from Noble Jones to help them make their escape from the SCU during the kill order they'd been under.

James sat up on his haunches and sniffed the air, his hackles raising at the cedarwood scent wafting through with the night breeze. It wasn't as strong as if Clifford was on the same level as him, but it was potent enough to tell Clifford was on the deck somewhere. He saw Lacy drop in through a window on the other side of the deck, her bloody vanilla scent slightly stronger than the cedarwood. Her eyes glowed bright ice blue, and James could see her fangs fully out.

He looked upwards and sniffed again, then waved to get Lacy's attention. He pointed up at the ceiling. She nodded, pointed at him, and then at the end of the deck where the ramp continued to the next floor. She pointed at herself and then in the opposite direction. James nodded and chuffed, and Lacy was gone in a blur. He moved toward the stairwell, then up the ramp. He kept low to the concrete, moving carefully. Larger than Lacy, he knew he couldn't move as fast as her and maintain his stealth. The cedarwood grew stronger, and he also caught the telltale tinge of burning gunpowder.

Clint was here.

He stopped at the top of the ramp, keeping in the shadows as he looked down the row of parked cars with his wolfen vision. He stayed low, peering around the corner to get a better view of the area. Cries and screams of the crowds below now mixed with approaching sirens.

Fantastic, he thought bitterly to himself. *I believe our timeframe has just become drastically shorter.*

The wolf huffed in agreement.

Another sound sent chills down his spine. He ducked away from the corner into the darkest part of the ramp as the stairwell door opened. A man peered out, looking around the dark parking deck with wide eyes. James could smell his sweat, could almost taste the sweetness of tobacco mixing with the salty perspiration only true terror could cause. The guy was large, his round face drawn in panicked caution as he whispered over his shoulder in a thick Southern accent. "It's clear. I don't see nothin'."

"That man was firing right at us," a woman's voice said, her accent equally as thick. "I don't like this, Clive."

The small, tinny voice of a little child sounded as well. James felt his stomach turn. What were these people doing here? "Mommy, I'm scared."

"Me too, baby," the mother said.

"Why was that man following us?"

"Wasn't the same guy who shot at us," Clive said. "We get to the truck, we're gone."

"But the police just showed up."

"And they can deal with it without us here," Clive said, cutting her off. "Now keep quiet and stay low. The truck is right over there. Heather, you got wards up?"

Wards? James thought, the wolf also making a curious sound inside his head. *She's a witch. Makes sense why that guy smelled like cedarwood. But he wasn't Clint.*

James watched the three of them move from the stairwell, ducking behind cars as they made their way toward a large beat-up pickup truck. He saw Clive open the back door to the truck to let the little boy in, the wife helping the child into the car seat as Clive opened the driver's side door, pulled a hunting rifle from behind the backseat, and checked to make sure it was loaded.

"Excuse me, sir?"

The family froze, Clive took aim, and James stared hard at the source of the voice. A young man stepped out from behind a car a few spots down. He was short, had brown hair, and wore a college jersey. He held his hand over his side, blood leaking through his fingers. His other hand was tucked behind his back.

James tensed at the sight of the free hand holding an assault rifle like the one at Hoyt's office: AR-15. The wolf urged him to attack. *It could cause a panic,* James thought. *The little boy could get hurt if we move too soon.*

The wolf braced, keeping tense as it sent James the urge to protect the child as if he were its own pup.

"Holy shit," Clive said, lowering the rifle. "You okay, kid?"

"I've been shot," the kid said, his voice weak. "Can you…help me?"

Clive started toward the kid. "Hang in there, buddy. My wife's a medic."

He can't see the gun, James thought. The wolf barked inside as he watched Clive move away from his truck and toward the kid. *He can't see the gun!*

James leapt from his vantage point as the kid raised the gun to point it at Clive, the movement seeming slow as if the world was underwater. The assault rifle thundered, belching fire and bullets in the same split second Clive's facial expression showed the realization that he was going to die in front of his family. James felt the impacts hit him in the ribcage, his thick wolfen skin and fur stopping the lead rounds from piercing his flesh. He snarled, swiped at the kid, and smacked him into the trunk of a car before flinging him across the parking lot. James heard a much larger report, took the blow to his back as he rounded on Clive and saw him yank back on the bolt-action rifle and take aim again. James swatted the gun out of Clive's hand and shoved him toward the truck and his screaming wife and child. More gunshots echoed in the parking lot, more rounds smacking into James as he spun back around to see the college kid marching toward him, the assault weapon blazing as he went. James leapt out of the way as Clive's pickup roared to life. The tires spun on the smooth concrete as he yanked the vehicle out of the parking spot, shifted gears again, and sped down the row of cars before turning the corner near the Exit sign.

The sound of gunfire ceased abruptly, replaced by the telltale clicking of an empty clip. James drew his jowls back into a toothy, hungry grin. *I will not kill him,* James thought to the animal. *But I'm not quite sure he'll survive being a chew toy.*

That was when the kid tossed the gun aside and rushed in. The wind left his lungs too fast for them to recover as James was lifted off his feet and slammed into a nearby SUV, the force of the impact caving the vehicle in. James gasped for air, struggled to make his lungs respond, but the kid was on him again, pummeling him just as he felt glorious air fill his body. Another blow landed squarely under his eye, knocking his head to the side.

Instinct took over, his blood boiling as he grabbed the kid by the head and slammed him against a column. Concrete chunks and dust blew out over the area, large cracks working their way up to the ceiling. The kid's body became limp in James's hand. He dropped it, staring down at the body.

No injuries. None.

The kid's eyes flicked open, and James's jaws clacked together from the force of the kick Shooter McGee landed to his chin. He staggered back, and the kid was up too fast for James to process how he'd gotten to his feet. James shook it off and growled.

The kid grinned. "Wow, you really are a stubborn fucker, aren't you?" His skin began to ripple and darken, his hair receding into his scalp until it was a short, paper-thin layer on his head. It was only a few seconds before James was staring at Clint.

What...? James thought, his mind racing for some kind of explanation. It was Clint in front of him. But…shapeshifters could turn into humans? It made sense. Why not? But he'd never seen it before. Did Phillip know? Considering how protective of Clint he'd been, James guessed not. But here was the man they'd been chasing for days, standing right in front of him, freshly turned from a young college-aged white kid to a fit, muscled black man. The jersey, once loose on the shooter, was now fitted over Clint's broad chest and shoulders, and had no hole from being shot and no blood from the wound.

And no scent.

"Wrong again," Clint said, grinning as he wagged his finger at James.

It was then that James heard a werewolf's howl from the levels below.

Clint gave a nonchalant salute and took off at what looked like vampiric speed. James gnashed his teeth in frustration as a woman's scream sounded from the same area as the howl had come from. He hit his wolfen speed and shot down the ramp to the level below, where he saw Clive's truck parked in the driving lane. The headlights shone on Clifford just before the werewolf clasped his hands together and brought them down on top of the hood. The back end of the truck lifted from the force, the hood caving in and the headlights shattering. Clifford punched the windshield, but the glass only wavered and rippled with a blue glow as if it had a force field surrounding it. Lacy zipped past him and lunged at Clifford. She slammed her fist into his jowl, sent him staggering back. He recovered and took a swipe at her. She ducked it, then leapt as he took a follow-up swipe at her legs.

James barreled down the row as Clifford managed to grab Lacy by the throat and lift her off her feet. Clifford dropped Lacy and snarled at James as they collided, James tackling him to the ground and unleashing his own snarls and barks as they rolled in a feral entanglement of claws and teeth. He felt Clifford's teeth nip his cheek, tasted blood as he closed his jaws on his enemy's arm. Clifford bucked, caught James off guard long enough to clamp his hands around James's mouth and force it shut. James saw stars as Clifford bashed his head into the hood of a nearby car, and was too disoriented to stop Clifford as the werewolf picked him up and threw him at the row of cars on his left. James hit one car and rolled over the tops of a few others before he hit the concrete. The human family screamed in panic as Clifford continued his assault on the truck. James got to his feet, saw Clifford trying to tear his way in, his claws raking against the blue energy field protecting the thin glass windows. Lacy hurled herself at Clifford and knocked him away from the vehicle again.

The wolf sent him an urge to howl. He pushed against it at first, only hesitating when the wolf put his attention on the wife, Heather, inside the truck. He felt something else from the beast, an urge to howl. A word came to mind that he couldn't shake.

Kin.

He grunted. *I believe Phillip would call that a "Hail Mary."* He barked at Lacy, moved to the center of the lane, and pulled the wolf forward.

Then Lacy looked at Wolf, her eyes widening as she turned and shouted to the human female in the car, the Kindred. "Get down! Protect your hearing!" Wolf sent a pulse of energy to the Kindred in the backseat of the truck, felt her acknowledge it. Her song changed, asking now for silence and peace, protection from the sounds of war as wolf stood to full height, reaching its arms out and rearing its head back to call to Fenrir for strength and fury. The call shook the man-made ground beneath wolf's feet, set off a chaotic harmony of screaming from the cars all over as wolf pushed the call harder to rise above the noise and reach the ear of the Wolf God.

Fenrir. Hróðvitnir.

The other *vargulfr*, the *hyski*, staggered backwards and clamped its hands over its ears as it yelped in pain. Wolf felt a jolt of force from the cars in the building. The air was full of glass in an instant, thick as the snow at Winter's Gate on the shores of Hy-Brasil. It released the call, letting it fade as it sent its love and devotion to Hróðvitnir. The James moved forward, and wolf submitted.

James fell to his knees, his body racked with exhaustion as he fell forward, catching himself on his hands before he could faceplant. The glass gravel on the deck was an inch thick, the only vehicle in the place with the windows still intact being the truck with Clive and his family. A large blue orb surrounded it, fading slowly as Heather opened her eyes and looked at James. She nodded, then told Clive to "get us the hell out of here." The engine sputtered and clunked as Clive started the truck and drove past where Clifford had collapsed. Lacy moved to James and knelt down next to him. "Damn, Jimmy. Good one."

He glanced up at her and chuffed, then turned his gaze to Clifford. The werewolf stirred, sitting up and getting to his feet as if he'd just gone nine rounds straight with Mike Tyson. He shook it off, turned to James, and growled low. Lacy's eyes glowed blue again, her fangs whipping into place, and her nails growing as she stood and planted herself firmly between him and James. "Let's go, handsome. I can do this all night."

Clifford hesitated, looking at James again. James stared back at him, his gaze hard as Clifford cocked his head to the side, leaned forward slightly as if he were about to attack again, then hesitated. James forced himself to stand, clenching his fists as he growled at Clifford.

Clifford chuffed at him, the sound derisive as he turned on his heels and shot into the night with wolfen speed. James started to go after him, only stopping when he heard the sirens heralding the appearance of a legion of police cars and SWAT trucks. The deck was surrounded in seconds, SWAT members in full riot gear holding the line with their shields raised while the army of law enforcement took cover and aimed firearms of varying degrees of caliber at James and Lacy. *"Freeze!" "Don't move!"*

And, of course, the one James was most used to. *"What the fuck is that?!"*

Lacy sighed next to him. "Well. Shit."

"Dude, that's the wrestler from the other night," one of the officers said from somewhere in the crowd. "What the hell did he do?"

We may be okay, James thought to the wolf, keeping his tone level and reassuring. The beast was braced for attack, with James using every bit of his mental fortitude to keep it from pushing him forward into yet another bad decision. *We can get out of this. Maybe sign some autographs.*

"Looks like he shot the fuckin' place up," another voice said. "Look at all the cars in there."

We are not okay, James thought to the wolf, his tone unchanging. *We are likely not going to get out of this without a certain amount of chaos.*

The wolf grunted at him and sent him an image of Phillip beating him with a newspaper.

"Down on the ground, hands behind your head," an officer shouted over the loudspeaker.

Lacy sighed. "Okay, this sucks."

James chuffed and licked his chops. Neither of them would be killed by the weapons being aimed at them. It was highly unlikely that the department had adopted the use of pure silver for its ammunition. But it would sting like a bitch.

And worse, someone who *could* be killed by a bullet would likely get caught in the crossfire. Even though there wasn't a single cop who would hesitate to open fire on him, James also couldn't help knowing every man and woman there had a family to go home to, or at least people out there who cared about them and didn't want to see their loved one take friendly fire.

The loudspeaker sounded again. *"Follow instructions now, or we* will *kill you!"*

Lacy shouted back to him. "Give us a second, buddy! And stop shouting into that thing, you're scaring my dog!" She rolled her eyes and muttered. "Jerk." She glanced up at James. "We need to get out of this without causing even more of a problem."

James looked around the garage again. Every car he saw was surrounded by broken glass from his sonic howl. The witch and her family had escaped the garage, but was there anyone else there? He saw more police taping the area off. A few news vans had rolled up, and reporters were already talking into microphones while their cameramen filmed every second. A helicopter flew overhead.

The wolf stepped forward in James's mind to the point where it had only slightly more control over his body than he did. Wolf sniffed the air, took in all scents, and ignored the odors coming from the guard. No other scents in the building than the cars. No pheromones. No fear other than one or two of the humans who were shouting at the James and the Lacy. James pushed the wolf back into place. *That was helpful,* he thought to the beast. He gave Lacy a low *"woof!"* She blinked, and he made a running motion with his fingers while pointing in the other direction.

"What if there's someone else in here?" Lacy asked.

James shook his head and woofed again.

"Place is empty?"

He gave a thumbs-up.

"Awesome. Now, how the fuck are we gonna take advantage of that, sweetie?" She motioned at the SWAT team. "I don't think we're gonna be able to distract them."

Something else mixed into the scents in the air, blended with the smells of gasoline and oil from the cars, blood and vanilla from Lacy. A burning sweetness, his mind instantly showing him an image of an old man on a porch smoking a pipe, another image of a noir detective with a giant cigar in his mouth.

No. Not those. Someone else popped into his memory as the dull scent of cocoa butter and sage. The tobacco smell grew stronger, and the police started to talk to each other back and forth as a cloud of smoke rose up around them. Their voices turned into alarmed shouts as the smoke thickened, growing dense enough that it was getting harder to see outside the parking deck.

"What in the *actual* fuck is going on?" Lacy said.

James felt her tense next to him. He put his hand on her shoulder and woofed. He knew those scents.

A familiar, grandmotherly voice spoke from inside the fog. "There's a gap straight ahead. You two gonna get the hell out of there, or keep standing there like a couple of dumbasses?"

James motioned for Lacy to follow him, then shot forward into the cloud hiding the police from view. He blew by shapes of cars and coughing people, smelled Lacy close behind him as he bolted down East Main Street, climbed to the top of the courthouse, and made his way across the rooftops. It was less than a minute before they stood on top of his old apartment building on the opposite end of the street from the parking deck. The fire department sirens blared in the night as two fire engines sped toward the parking deck to put out the non-existent fire.

James saw Ruby standing on the roof with them just before he caught her scent, the last of the tobacco smoke that cloaked her wafting away in the breeze. She took a long pull of her cigarillo and breathed out the smoke rings as she nodded toward the parking deck. "I might need to cut back."

James shifted into human form. "Lacy, this is Ruby."

"I know who she is," Lacy said. "You're the head of the Daughters of Baba Yaga."

Ruby smiled. "I see the SCU is still keeping tabs on an innocent old woman?" She fluttered her eyes in mock innocence. "Whatever did I do to deserve such surveillance?"

"Where do I start?" Lacy said. "And thanks for the rescue."

Ruby laughed and took another puff of her cigarillo. "My pleasure, sweetie." She turned her attention to James. "You, Mr. Coldstone, should be the one I'm thanking. The woman you saved tonight is one of my top apprentices."

"Clifford showed back up," James said. "And so did Clint."

"Which means your theory of them being the same person just got tossed in the shitter," Lacy said as her phone started ringing. She pulled it out of her pocket and answered. "Hey, Hoyt. Yeah, he's here with me. We also have the head of the witch council here in case you're interested." Her expression turned serious. "What? When? Okay, yeah. I get it. No, we'll be there in a few minutes." She hung up and looked at James. "Let's go grab your clothes. We need to go see Hoyt. Like right now." She turned to Ruby. "You too."

Ruby laughed. "Am I in trouble?"

James knew the expression on Lacy's face. Whatever Hoyt had said to her, it wasn't good. "I believe we may all be in trouble."

16

They found Hoyt in the lab, standing over a gurney with a covered body on top. Another few had been pulled out of their drawers, each of them also covered with a sheet. He motioned James to the set of lockers near his desk before saying, "Looks like y'all had an eventful night. Clint again?"

"And Clifford," James said.

"Two for one special," Lacy said. "Doesn't get much better than that."

Hoyt nodded, then nodded at Ruby. "Hey, Ruby."

"Hey, Hoyt," Ruby said. "How's your grandfather?"

"Still dead," Hoyt said with a shrug. "But he manages to catch the game on the weekends."

"You two know each other, I see," James said as he finished putting on the scrubs.

"All a community, man," Hoyt said. "We're waiting on one more person."

"Oh?" James said.

The lab doors opened, drawing James's attention as Phillip entered, his expression both annoyed and exhausted. "Hoyt, this better be good. I had a lead about Clint's—" He stopped talking when he saw James, and his eyes flashed. He looked back at Hoyt. "I don't have time for this."

"Likewise," James said, feeling the mix of sadness and anger welling up

138

in his gut. He wanted to talk to Phillip, and now he had the chance. But the memory of him comparing James to David Coldstone lingered.

Lacy rolled her eyes. "You two are worse than a couple of girls."

Ruby gave both James and Phillip a disapproving look. "You got that right, sugar."

"We'll figure it out," Phillip said, glaring at James. "Until then, go bury a bone in someone's yard."

"At least I listen to other people," James said back, keeping his tone even.

"Oh, bullshit," Phillip spat. "You're stubborn as hell, and you don't listen to me worth a shit. Otherwise, we'd already be done with this bullshit."

"I was listening," James fired back. "You were just incorrect."

Phillip threw his arms up. "Oh, but I gotta agree with you based on a hunch and no evidence?"

"I trust my instincts," James said. "Things would be easier if you did as well."

"Says the guy who identified a suspect by sniffing his crotch."

"And I was correct."

Lacy put her fingers to her mouth and let out a shrill whistle, which filled the lab. Both of them stopped and looked at her. "*Christ*, you two," she snapped, shaking her head. "Get a goddamn room and fuck about it, already."

"You two thought about marriage counseling?" Ruby asked.

James and Phillip both spoke in unison. "It's not like that!"

Lacy reached into her backpack and pulled out a spray bottle. James started to speak, at which point she aimed it and shot a mist in his face, accompanied by a sharp and loud *"Bad!"*. He snorted as the water filled his nose and dampened the stubble on his face.

Phillip cackled. "See what you get?"

Lacy turned the spray bottle on Phillip. *"Bad!"*

"Hey!"

James wiped his face off and glared at her. "I don't see how this—"

Lacy sprayed him again. He sputtered and stepped backwards as she pointed the spray bottle at Phillip. "Anything else?"

Phillip held his hands up and shook his head.

She pointed at James. "Jimmy?"

James held his hands up as well. "I yield."

"Good." She put the bottle away. "Don't make me take this out again."

Hoyt spoke up, his tone both urgent and irritated. "Look, I don't know what the hell happened between you two, but we got bigger problems going on here. Now both of you shut the fuck up and listen."

James and Phillip looked at each other again, then back at Hoyt. "Very well," James said. He turned his attention to Phillip. "There was an incident in Downtown Rock Hill this evening."

"Yeah, I heard," Phillip said. "What happened?"

"James's theory of Clint and Clifford being the same person got knocked down," Lacy said, stepping in. "Both were in the same place at the same time."

Phillip gave an indignant grunt. "Told you."

"Clint may not be an issue anymore," Hoyt said. "That's why I called you guys here. You too, Ruby."

"He got away," James said. "But he wasn't Clint at first. He was some college student I've never seen before."

"You're saying he changed?" Ruby said.

"Indeed," James said. "That was before Clifford showed up."

"But then he ran off," Lacy said. "Guy was moving almost as fast as a vampire. We don't know where he is. That was after he picked James up and flung him around like a rag doll."

"Yeah," Hoyt said as he moved over to the gurney where he'd been standing. "He's here." He pulled the sheet back, and James heard Phillip make a noise of revulsion at the sight of Clint on the table. He was nude. The Y-stitching on his chest indicated an autopsy had already been performed. His dark skin was pale, bruised, and covered in deep scratches.

And his face was missing. It'd been taken off, torn away with jagged edges left behind.

James watched Phillip, who had gone dead silent, staring hard at Clint. His eyes watered slightly. He wiped them, glanced at James, and fixed his composure. The wolf nudged James's senses a little, and he could smell the pheromones Phillip gave off, dull and sweet from his heart racing and his body reacting in upset and sorrow.

But not shock.

"What the fuck?" Lacy said.

"This doesn't make sense," James said. "How did he end up here? He was just Downtown at least twenty minutes ago."

Hoyt looked at Phillip. "Phillip brought him in. Found him earlier today."

James turned to Phillip. "Why didn't you call me?"

"You ain't the only one who's busy," Phillip said. "I'm a civilian now, remember? I was up to my ass in cops and interrogations all day. Then, when I finally got a chance, you don't answer."

"There was an emergency," James said. "I had to shift. My phone is at home." James paused. "You said he had a family."

Phillip nodded to the other closed lockers in the morgue, his eyes watering. "His wife and kids are here too."

James felt a pang of guilt. He shouldn't have gotten so angry at Phillip. Had he listened to him, taken a moment, then he could have been there when Phillip found Clint's body.

"I went to the house to talk to his family," Phillip continued. "Wanted to get some insight on what was going on. Why the hell does a cop go nuts and start shooting places up?" He shook his head. "Found them all in the living room."

"And they weren't fresh," Hoyt said as he folded the blanket back. "Time of death puts them all at least four hours before the Fillmore shooting." He pointed a gloved finger at the exposed skull that had once been Clint's face. "The face was pretty much sawed off and peeled away." He looked back up at James. "He was dead when this happened. Multiple wounds, and the bruising on his neck indicates strangulation. But it was quick. His trachea is crushed, and the discs in his neck look like they were strained to the limit. Whatever did this had huge hands with enough power to strangle a grown man to the point of almost breaking his neck." He pulled the cover back over Clint and moved to another body. He pulled the sheet back to reveal a young man's body in the same condition. "Victim is in his early twenties, college-aged. Again: face torn off and neck showing signs of extreme strangulation."

James looked the body up and down. "That appears to be the same kid I saw at the parking deck."

"The same thing happened to those agents on Westenra Island," Lacy said.

He moved to a third gurney, and James recognized Ginger. Ruby gave a small gasp and put her hand over her mouth, as Hoyt shared the details. "Jennifer Watson, face still intact, chest torn open. Which means Clifford definitely isn't your face-ripper."

"Poor, poor thing," Ruby breathed under her hand. James saw a tear roll down her cheek. "She was so young. So sweet."

"Wait, her name was Jennifer? Oh, right, never give out your name." James sighed before asking. "What about Clint's family?"

Hoyt shook his head. "Nope. Wife and both kids were still intact. Torn up, but their faces were left alone. Whatever did this has an agenda, and it needed Clint."

"Makes sense," Phillip said. "A cop can get access to a lot of places civilians can't."

"You have two different cases going on here," Hoyt said as he covered Ginger-Jennifer back up. "They may be related; they might not be. I don't know, honestly."

"Fuck," Phillip muttered. "We're right back at square one."

Hoyt nodded to James. "You telling me that you saw Clint change seals the deal on that case. We may have a skinwalker on our hands."

"A skinwalker?" James said.

"It's an old Native American legend," Ruby explained, pulling her hand away from her mouth and wiping her eyes. She gave Hoyt a stern look. "Navajo. Properly *naaldlooshii*. And not something to take so casually."

"It's a shapeshifter," Lacy said. "Same thing."

"Not even a little bit," Hoyt said. "Shapeshifters usually can't shift into copies of their native species. So, a human shapeshifter can't shift into another human. That's why you see them turn into animals, and they usually have a preference. In Wade Anderson's case, he liked being a werewolf."

"That's not far off from being a human being," James said.

"No, but shifters can train themselves to have complete control over their transformations," Hoyt said. "He probably figured out how to stop the shift into a gorilla and do the parts that mattered as a dog."

James remembered Anderson's wolfen form appearing remarkably apish. "Then what is the difference?" James asked.

"Skinwalkers literally take on the form of whoever or whatever they kill," Hoyt said. "They take the face because that's the window into the victim's soul." He shrugged. "At least that's what grandfather always thought."

"What about Clifford?"

"Clifford is a straight-up werewolf," Hoyt said. "I've seen some of the security footage. I don't know why he's taking the hearts other than he's also a serial killer." He indicated Clint's faceless body. "This changes the whole game. If we're dealing with a skinwalker, that means he can blend in with no problem. Anyone could be the unsub."

"Unless we have photos of his victims," James said. "We could identify him…or her with that."

"Sure," Hoyt said. "As long as you have the identity of every single victim he's ever killed. They don't run out of forms they can take. A skinwalker can carry as many skins as they want. All they need is the face."

"Like that movie with John Travolta and Nicholas Cage," Phillip said.

James said, nodding at Phillip. "Decent film."

"Typical nineties action romp," Phillip said. "Can't deny John Woo."

"Doves," James said.

Phillip nodded. "Yup. Doves."

James looked back to find Lacy, Ruby, and Hoyt staring at both of them like they'd lost their minds. James pursed his lips and cleared his throat. "Apologies, continue please."

"They also take on the memories of their victims," Hoyt said, shaking his head and getting back on track. "Remember that whole 'window to the soul' thing? So, imagine a dude walking around killing people, nabbing their faces, and taking on the memories of each victim as he goes. If he's killed fifteen people, that's fifteen lifetimes he's got rolling around in his head."

"That would drive someone crazy," Lacy said, turning to James. "Like *really* crazy."

"No one's seen or heard of skinwalkers in ages," Hoyt said. "It's an old Navajo legend, and not many Natives really believe it anymore because of how few sightings there've been, if any."

"That is because they are just that," Ruby said. Her tone caught James's attention, her haunted expression matching her voice. "Legends. A natural-born skinwalker has not existed for hundreds of years."

The moment was broken by the sound of music coming from Lacy's pocket. James placed it as the theme to *NCIS* as she pulled it out of her pocket and answered. "Faulkner." Her eyes widened, and she gave James an alarmed expression. "Hang on, Kimble, let me put you on speaker." She pressed an icon on the screen and held the phone out. "Okay, say it again."

"Who else is there?" Kimble asked from the phone. "Why the hell am I on speaker?"

"Ruby with the Daughters of Baba Yaga," Ruby said. "How are you, Darlene?"

"And us, Agent Kimble," Phillip said. "Me and James. We're here to help."

James gave Phillip a perplexed look as Kimble's muttered reply came from the phone. "Oh hell, anyone but you two." She cleared her throat. "No time. I got with Sanchez in IT, and that text message definitely came from the SCU. Just not from me."

"Then from who?" James asked.

"No idea," Kimble said. "They apparently used a military-grade application to block anyone from seeing what they were doing."

"I promise it wasn't me," Hoyt said. "I've been up to my eyeballs in bodies here, and the most I would do is order pizza on Smith's credit card."

Phillip covered his face with his palm. "That's just as illegal."

Hoyt shrugged. "He offered; he just keeps forgetting."

Phillip pinched the bridge of his nose, his eyes closed as he muttered. "*Dumbest* smart person I know."

"You've already been cleared, Hoyt," Kimble said. "And we've also cleared Agent Brown since he also has a working knowledge of computers."

"And me?" James asked.

Lacy, Hoyt, and Phillip all snorted.

"We were looking for people who at least know how to send an email," Kimble said. "Last I remember, you're doing good to open the web browser."

James set his jaw. "I know how to send an email."

"With attachments?"

"Now you are just being difficult."

Kimble gave an exasperated sigh as Lacy mouthed *"Stop!"* to James. "The only way those texts could've been sent is if whoever sent them was here in the SCU office."

"We were just talking about skinwalkers," James said. "Have you ever heard of them?"

"A little," Kimble said. "Mostly internet creepy-pasta bullshit."

The wolf sent James a memory, one that caused his chest to constrict instantly. He and Lacy were on the pier of the rental cottage in Jacksonville, Florida, when the yacht came at them. They'd barely escaped as the large boat crashed into the pier and took out the house.

It was a simple inconvenience compared to finding Mindy Robertson's yellow dress covered in blood on board the vessel.

"Not her blood," Phillip had said.

But it smelled like her. Hadn't it?

The vampire he'd chased on Westenra Island. Had he had a scent? The guy had just disappeared. Nothing ever came of the SCU agents on the island who'd been killed, their faces torn off and their bodies torn to pieces.

All of them.

"But not Clint," James said out loud, staring hard at Clint's faceless body under the sheet as things began to add up in his head.

"You okay, Jimmy?" Lacy asked.

"Every victim on Westenra Island was torn apart," James said, turning his attention to the group. "Their faces were gone, and their bodies were torn apart. And their cabins were demolished." He motioned to the body. "Why not Clint?"

Ruby shrugged. "Every skinwalker is different. Even though they are what they are, they're still human beings at their core."

"So, we're dealing with *two*?" Phillip asked.

Ruby shook her head. "I wouldn't think so. Creating a skinwalker takes years. And they are territorial creatures. A skinwalker meets a skinwalker, it's on sight. Someone is going to die."

"That means something distracted our unsub," Phillip said. "Bad enough to run him off before he could do to the family what he did to Clint."

"Clifford is part of this somehow," James said. "His showing up at almost every shooting cannot be coincidental."

"I looked over what was left of those agents from Westenra," Hoyt said. "Exact same injuries and claw patterns. If it *is* a skinwalker, it's the same one we're dealing with now."

"You people have had more run-ins with the skinwalker than we have, and we may have a lead on Clifford," Kimble said before anyone else could respond. "It makes the most sense if we work together on this."

James nodded. "Indeed. Ruby, would you be willing to help us?"

"Whatever saves my girls," Ruby said. "There aren't many of us left now."

"I'm leading this operation now," Kimble said. "We're gonna have to keep it on the quiet. I don't even know if we can trust Smith."

"Or you," Phillip said. "How do we know you're not the skinwalker?"

"How do I know you don't drink out of the toilet like your boyfriend?"

Phillip nodded to the others. "It's her."

"Now that we've settled that bullshit," Kimble said. "I need you three to go to the airport in Rock Hill."

"Another shooting?" James asked.

"Nope. Arms shipment, but Clint was spotted in the area."

"Arms shipment?" James raised an eyebrow. "Rock Hill Airport is a private airport where people keep their personal planes. It's not a place where cargo shipments come in and out."

"Which makes it the perfect place for a plane full of bullshit to show up in the middle of the night," Kimble said. "Show up, take over the tower, land a plane, get out."

"Vampires could do it pretty quietly," Lacy said. "A place that small? Show up and mindjob whoever you need to, it would go down with almost no trouble."

James raised his eyebrow. "I still do not see the correlation between an arms shipment coming into a small airport in the middle of the night and a skinwalker causing a mass shooting almost every night this week."

"Neither did we," Kimble said. "The arms shipment is a completely different case, but seeing Clint around the area that just happens to be where the drop is going to take place is making us think there's something bigger at play here. You three go check it out, but do *not* engage. That clear?"

"If Clint is there, then he means to cause more chaos," James said.

"If that happens, you know what to do," Kimble said. "Otherwise, you're just observing."

"And Clifford?"

"We'll handle Clifford," Ruby said. "I've already told my girls to go into hiding and prepare. We'll be ready for him."

"Okay," Phillip said. He looked at James. "We need to talk."

Phillip and James stepped outside into the hallway. James's nerves were on edge, not only about the revelation they'd gotten in Hoyt's lab, but about the prospect of talking to Phillip about things. It had to happen, he knew it did. It didn't make it any easier.

"We need to fix this shit," Phillip said as the doors closed. He motioned between the two of them as he said it. "Look, I ain't sayin' I told you so. That's being a dick. And yeah, I should've called you—"

"I'm sorry," James said, cutting him off. Phillip stopped talking and stared at James, blinking as if caught off guard. "You were right. I should've listened to you. I was angry. I wanted vengeance for Ginger." He nodded. "I should have been there with you when you went to Clint's home."

Phillip swallowed hard before he spoke. "I shouldn't have compared you to your dad. That was fucked up. I'm sorry."

James shrugged. "Brothers fight."

Phillip laughed. "Yeah, we do."

"You did tell me that you told me, however."

"Yeah, about Clint not being Clifford," Phillip said. "I knew this bullshit was out of character for Clint. That there was a chance it wasn't him." He paused. "Well, not *all* him."

The doors opened again, and Lacy stepped out into the hallway. "Now that you two have made up, I need to read you in before we head to the airport so you know what you're looking at."

17

Just before I sidetracked myself to save my niece, I was part of a case the SCU was working on, looking into illegal arms sales and shipments," she'd said. "The first time I split was because we'd gotten some intel on a shipment that came in, but it was gone before we could manage to get anywhere near the plane. These guys move *fast.*"

They had all agreed to take one car out to the airport. It made the most sense for Lacy to drive since the SCU could track her car and send backup if they needed it.

"And the second time?" Phillip asked from the backseat.

"The Wolf-Man Murder copycat put a few more victims down. At the same time, there was a massive influx of guns on the black market."

"Any idea who might be behind it?" Phillip asked.

"We think it's internal," Lacy said. "Someone close to the Council of Night."

"My money's on Bathory," Phillip said.

James looked over his shoulder. "And what do you base this theory on?"

Phillip shuddered. "Woman gives me the creeps."

James nodded. "She does have an air about her."

"She's scary as shit."

"Indeed."

"And why the hell did she keep looking at me like I'm a snack?"

Lacy spoke up. "Because she was hungry and you're food." Phillip sucked his teeth at her. "Sorry, Bacon. That's the reality. And we have to be super careful about who we accuse. So far, we've been able to rule out the council members themselves. But the trail has been leading in that direction, which has us thinking it's a subordinate."

Phillip shook his head. "And you think they're shipping weapons in and out of the Rock Hill-York County Airport?"

"It does seem unlikely," James said, turning his attention to Lacy. "That airport doesn't typically cater to commercial flights."

"Yeah," Phillip said from the backseat. "It's all privately owned aircraft."

"Who says they're using commercial aircraft?" Lacy said as she turned down Airport Road. "Think sneaky, guys. What is the least likely plane to draw suspicion if you wanna import shit you shouldn't be importing? Everyone else will be looking for a cargo plane."

"Huh," Phillip said with a grunt. "And we're looking for a jackass with a bi-plane and too much time and money on his hands."

"Yup."

"Bad news for you, sweetie," Phillip said, mimicking Lacy's typical tone when she used the word. "Just because it's a small airport doesn't mean they don't have guards on duty. And it doesn't mean they don't have a lifeline to the Feds."

"Which is why we're gonna be *careful*," Lacy said, stretching out the last word. "The tower over there is tiny, but there's still someone there watching things. We get in, we verify the plane and take pictures, we get out. Simple."

"Sure," Phillip said. "So easy. Why didn't I think to do this before?"

"I'm not sure I agree with your assessment on this being easy," James said to Lacy. The wolf mewled inside his mind, shifted nervously in place before sitting down and giving him a sense of worry and concern. "Phillip is right. This airport is going to be under surveillance."

"I've got Hoyt scrambling their camera feed," Lacy said. "They're seeing a loop of the same shit that's been going on for the past hour. Still, we need to be sneaky. Now, where do I park?"

Phillip guided Lacy to a small, wooded area that the airport often used for public events. The annual Come See Me Spring Festival included an air show where families could tour the facility and take rides on planes, helicopters, and even a hot air balloon. James stayed quiet as he worked to rein in his thoughts while the wolf paced back and forth nervously in his mind. He wasn't surprised that being at the airport, even the private small one in town, reminded him of Molly. Her rejection hurt, though she hadn't been cruel. It was more of what Lacy had said about humans and supernaturals.

It meant her attraction to him, all of their intimate moments; all of it was a lie driven by pheromones he couldn't help putting off. Had it always been the case? James was no stranger to being in relationships. He'd dated a few girls in college, one of them for over six months before she transferred to another school hundreds of miles away.

It explained why he'd never had problems finding a date.

He turned his thoughts to the shooting in Uptown moments before he and Lacy had chased Clint down the interstate and into Carowinds. Well, *not* Clint. Something else. A skinwalker. And why had younglings shown up? The last time he'd seen any was when Count Wangenheim had been using them to keep James and Phillip a step behind him while he'd trafficked Mindy Robertson down to Westenra Island. They weren't exactly rampant. They had to be freshly made. Every vampire went through that stage. But how were these being controlled? It would have to be a powerful vampire, which meant an *old* vampire. Like werewolves, a vampire's strength increased with age. And not just their physical powers. Lacy's ability to control the minds of humans was powerful, but he could imagine if she were as old as Elizabeth Bathory, or even Vlad Tepes.

Or Dracula.

And Clifford being on a rampage against witches was connected somehow. It had to be. Clifford had been at every shooting. There'd been a witch at two of the three. Were they working together?

Lacy turned in her seat to address both James and Phillip. "Okay, guys. Need you to remember we are just taking a look. We aren't here to stop anything; we aren't here to interfere. We go in, and I take some pictures with my phone. Phillip, you do the same." She looked at James. "You'll be wolfed out. Phillip is the only one here who can't see in the dark."

They got out of the car, and James pulled the wolf forward enough to sniff the air. He smelled the asphalt from the tarmac, smelled the distinct odor of airplane fuel and engine oil. His mother had taken him out to the airport many times as a child to let him look around at the planes. He'd been to a few air shows, had watched the Air Force show off their fighter jets for the crowds while vendors hocked their wares and food trucks served the finest deep-fried everything. He could almost taste the deep-fried strawberries.

The wolf sent him an image of a ra\\bit eating in a garden. James shifted his memory to eating a large turkey leg he'd gotten from a tent where a local restaurant had set up a smoker. The wolf panted happily in his mind and gave a satisfied woof.

Strawberries are good, James thought to the animal.

The wolf chuffed and put the image of the rabbit back up.

"Most airports have a contract with the FAA," Phillip said as they made their way across the lot and toward the tall fence separating them from the airport. "The Federal Aviation Administration. They have a spot for Federal aircraft to operate, which means that national and international shipments via the U.S. Postal Service are checked through here as well as any military craft."

"I thought this airport didn't cater to commercial flights?" James said.

"It's just a check," Phillip replied. "They don't typically drop off shipments here. And it only really happens when there's a reason."

"Would an investigation into illegal arms shipments count?"

Phillip nodded. "Yeah, I'd say that falls on the list."

"Which means security is insane," Lacy said. "Armed guards, video surveillance, you name it."

"That may prove to be a challenge," James said.

"The FAA doesn't usually have werewolves and vampires on their watchlist."

"Fair point."

"And they don't operate here," Lacy said. "They can, but not on the regular."

"Doesn't mean there won't be beefed-up security," Phillip said. "If we got shady shit going on here, whoever is behind that shady shit will definitely have security of some kind working for them. And we might as well assume they have someone on the inside working the com tower and watching the cameras."

"There are a few blind areas," Lacy said. "But not many. Even though Hoyt is fucking with their cameras, we still need to be careful. Once we cross the fence, it's time to be stealthy or get shot at." She motioned at her shirt. "This is my favorite shirt; I'd really like to not have it shot up and bloodied."

"It's the same damn shirt you wear all the time," Phillip said.

"I know, but this one's special."

"How many pink Hello Kitty shirts do you have?"

"How many comic books do you have?"

Phillip paused, then mumbled. "We ain't talkin' about me."

Lacy tucked her phone away into the pocket of her shorts. "Okay, that plane should be hitting the tarmac soon. Jimmy, shift and follow me."

"How the hell am I supposed to keep up with you?" Phillip asked.

James had already stripped and shifted. He pointed to his back and gave a large doggy grin, panting with his tongue out.

Phillip shook his head and muttered. "I hate this shit." James crouched down onto all fours as Phillip climbed onto his back. James heard him sigh and felt him wring his hands into the fur between his shoulder blades. "Here we go again," he said, still muttering. "Hi-Yo, Dumbass. Away."

James followed Lacy as she made her way to the fence. It stood at least ten feet tall, the top lined with razor wire. The lot in front of them was filled with small planes of every variety, as if they were at an aircraft sales lot. "We're not gonna see anything from here," Lacy said as they came to a stop. The area was flat, the planes in the lot obstructing any view beyond. James could see the tops of the small hangars in the airport, but nothing stood out. "The fence is to keep people from wandering in, and it's not like you can see shit anyway."

"Yeah," Phillip said with a nod. "I used to come here with my mom to watch the planes land and take off. This is the spot where we'd come. Can't see the runway but for the last little bit when the plane's taking off."

"Our plane is due to land soon," Lacy said as she checked her phone. "Kimble sent me an update. It's on approach."

"What's the plan?" Phillip asked.

"We need to get shots of the cargo," Lacy said. "And anyone around so we can try and ID some people."

"You aren't thinking we'd sneak aboard before they unload it, are you?"

Lacy looked at Phillip and blinked, her expression a little stunned and perplexed. "And risk getting caught and already trapped inside a nice, neat little box for them? Why the hell would I wanna do that?"

Phillip snorted. "I've met you."

Lacy grinned at him. "Aw, Bacon. Did you just take a dig at me?"

"I want to know what level of stupidity we're about to sink to."

Lacy snickered and replied in a sing-song voice. *"You really liiike me! You really liiike me!"*

James's ears perked up as the wolf set off alarms in his mind. He heard something clank in the dark, like a tool hitting the concrete. Someone shouted an order. It was faint, too far away to pick up exact details. But he could tell the direction. His eyes fell on a small hangar on the opposite side of the airport from where they stood. He gave Lacy a low *"Woof!"*

"Sorry, Jimmy," Lacy said. "We'll get serious."

"That ain't it," Phillip said. "Something's up. We need to get over that fence right now."

Lacy nodded and kicked off the ground, launching herself at least fifteen feet into the air. She cleared the fence easily, landing on her feet on the other side with no sound whatsoever. She turned to James and motioned for him to follow as she whispered to him. "Your turn, Jimmy."

James felt Phillip wrap his legs tighter around him and shift his weight. "Be gentle with me, James."

James snorted. *Oh, the jokes,* he thought as the wolf panted wildly in its own way of laughing in hysterics.

"Phrasing, Bacon," Lacy said from the other side.

Phillip had just started saying something to the effect of what Lacy could do with her phrasing when James kicked off, launching himself into the air. Phillip's comeback to Lacy blended from a sharp retort to a high-pitched Wilhelm scream.

"Shove your 'phrasing' up you're a-*aaaaaahahahaass!!*"

James hit the ground solidly on the other side of the fence and took a few steps to maintain his balance before he let Phillip climb off. Lacy stood there with her eyes wide and her lips pursed, obviously stifling a burst of laughter. "You okay?" she said, her voice small and shaking in her struggle.

"I haven't ridden a horse since I was a kid," Phillip said as he bent over and braced his hands on his knees. "Fuck, that was scarier than a damn horse."

James stayed in wolf form as Lacy made the joke that had also been rolling around in his mind.

"Trail rides on Mr. Ed don't prepare anyone for doggy style, Bacon."

He stood up and glared at her as she burst into laughter, covering her mouth to stifle the sound. Phillip stuck his chin out at her in indignation. "Fuck you." It wasn't until Phillip turned his glare on James that James realized he was panting with a large grin on his face. Phillip narrowed his eyes at James. "You too, Goofy."

"You're the only one of us who screams like Goofy, sweetie," Lacy said.

Phillip rolled his eyes. "I get it. 'Ha-ha. Phillip almost shit his pants.' Can we please continue with the stupid-dumbass thing we're here to do?"

Lacy wiped the tears from her eyes. "Christ, that was funny as hell." She cleared her throat and spoke to James. "Okay, which way?"

James snapped into position, bracing himself as if ready to take off running. He lifted one arm and curled it under himself and jabbed his nose in the direction of the hangar. The wolf panted inside with laughter as James imagined the sound of a tight spring whipping into position.

He saw Phillip nod out of the corner of his eye. "Pretty sure it's that way."

"How'd you guess?" Lacy asked with some sarcasm.

"I think he's got some pointer breed in him."

Lacy rolled her eyes. "You're both morons. Let's go."

James crouched back down onto all fours and moved across the lot, keeping low and using the planes as cover as he led them toward the hangar. The voices and activity started to become clearer as they approached. James paused, held up a fist to tell Lacy and Phillip to hold up. He sniffed the air, could smell the scent of fresh fuel and a recently scrapped tire.

The plane is already here, he thought. The wolf chuffed in his mind, giving a sense of caution. *Lacy's intelligence was off. Kimble is no idiot. If she was given bad information, that means it's someone on the inside of the SCU.* He decided to keep his determinations filed away for later. Now wasn't the time to speculate about what was going on. They needed to get into that hangar.

"Damn plane's already here," Phillip whispered behind him. "I thought you said it wasn't yet?"

James looked over his shoulder and saw the perplexed expression on Lacy's face a split second before it was gone.

"You two move on up and see if you can get a better look," Phillip said. He pointed ahead. "I'll take cover behind that red Cessna."

James and Lacy nodded. James motioned for her to take the left flank. She nodded again, and he started toward the hangar, heading to the right. He stopped when he could hear what was being said from inside the hangar. There were only a few voices. He crouched down lower, peered out from the underside of the plane at the open hangar doors a few hundred yards ahead. There was another small plane, though it was slightly larger than the other planes at the airport. It was white, and he barely saw the faint outline where someone had removed the FedEx decals. He counted at least five people in black mechanic's jumpsuits, one of them using a forklift to unload a large crate from the plane's cargo hold. The other four were working on the plane, two of them checking the engines while a third was inspecting the tire pressure on the wheels. The fourth carried a tablet with him and was marking things off as he spoke to the others.

"How much longer?"

One of the men at the engines spoke up. "Almost done here. Bad fuel line, but it's already replaced." He stepped back and wiped his blackened hands off with an equally blackened rag. "Just need to tighten this down and we're set."

"Well, hurry the fuck up," the supervisor snapped. "We're still on schedule, and I wanna stay that way."

The mechanic nodded and walked off to get whatever he needed to get, while the supervisor turned away and went to bark at the people managing the cargo hold.

James kept watching the unloading process continue, moving quickly as if under a tight schedule. It was only a few seconds before he realized they weren't unloading the plane at all.

They were loading it.

His ears perked as he heard Lacy make a noise at him. He turned his attention to her, saw her motion to herself, then to the hanger. She pointed at him, then to Phillip, and motioned for them to stay put. Lacy zipped to the hangar in vampiric speed, clearing the distance from her hiding place to the front corner of the building in a second, peered inside, then was gone again.

James heard Phillip mutter under his breath. "Well, so much for no contact."

He turned away and saw the plane where Phillip was hiding. Phillip pulled his phone out of his pocket and looked at it, his eyes widening in both surprise and disbelief. He glanced back at James and mouthed *"Holy shit,"* then motioned for James to move up. James started to move, then stopped when a figure moved in the darkness. It stepped out from behind another plane, the shadows doing nothing to hide who it was from James's yellowed wolfen vision.

Clint had his police sidearm pulled and aimed at Phillip. His eyes flashed like a couple of diamonds as James heard the telltale click of the safety being unlocked.

18

The click of the safety releasing. That was what did it. That was what set him off.

The wolf filled his consciousness almost to the point of taking over, making every muscle in his body twitch with raw power as he launched in Phillip's direction, releasing a series of barks and snarls at Clint. Phillip cursed and rolled out of the way just before James plowed into a small airplane nearby. The aircraft buckled under the force of the impact, tires screeching as it slid across the asphalt and crushed Clint into the plane where Phillip had been crouched. He continued to push for a few seconds even though the wrecked planes weren't moving under his weight. He felt his wide-eyed fury turn into determination.

"James," Phillip said behind him. He sounded out of breath. "He's a fucking souffle, man."

James stepped back, the pain in his shoulder where he'd hit the airplane already subsiding. The wolf sent James a mental image of Clifford. *Indeed,* James thought. *Time to shift our focus.*

"Thanks," Phillip said as he checked his gun. "Hope no one noticed that."

Shouts erupted from the hangar followed by a series of gunfire. A human figure flew from the open bay doors, sailing high into the air as he screamed and flailed his arms and legs. James registered the full combat gear before the man smacked down on top of a nearby plane and rolled to the ground where he lay still.

Lacy shouted from inside the hangar. *"A little help here would be great!"*

I believe they noticed, James thought. The wolf barked in agreement as James made for the hangar, dodging two more flying men in combat gear as he barged into the hangar and caught sight of a man climbing into the cockpit of the plane. The man saw James, shrieked, and closed the door behind him. James heard the engine make a noise, chugging as the two-bladed propeller turned a slow cycle. He grabbed the blades before they could go any faster. The blades bent and warped, pushing against his grip as the engine choked and sputtered. A cloud of black smoke belched out from behind the propeller before the blades gave in to James's grip, bending forward. James let go and stood tall as the pilot inside the plane shrieked in horror, his eyes wide and panicked at the sight of the were-wolf that trashed his airplane.

I've always wanted to do that, James thought.

The wolf gave him a derisive chuff.

Let me have my moments, James thought to the creature.

"James!"

Phillip's voice startled him back to attention. He wheeled around and saw two of the SWAT guards grappling with his friend, holding him by the arms while a third one approached him with a handgun aimed at Phillip's face. The guy was screaming at Phillip to stand down and stop resisting. One of the captors buried his fist in Phillip's gut, sending him to the ground.

It felt like a lifetime. It was a few seconds.

James reacted, barreling down on the group with a savage snarl. He grabbed the first officer by the helmet and slung him out through the open hangar doors. One of the SWAT guys holding onto Phillip let go and opened fire. James ducked the bullets out of instinct, darted to the side as more rounds flew his way. He changed course, zigzagging as he charged the firing officer. He reached out to slap the gun away, his massive, clawed right hand connecting with the weapon just as the cop fired again. James blinked at the searing pain in his upper bicep but followed through with his attack. The gun went flying, and James put the guard down for the count with a solid left swing. He noticed the insignia for the Rock Hill Police Department on the SWAT gear immediately. *Interesting,* he thought.

His adrenaline was short-lived as searing agony spread over his arm, causing his hand to seize, his muscles to tense. James dropped to one knee and put his hand over the wound, the pain radiating throughout his arm.

Familiar pain. *Silver? Oh shit.*

He squeezed the wound slightly, the pain dulling as his flesh healed slowly. The bullet had only grazed him. He sighed in relief but still felt a little shaken.

And pissed.

There were three left. He rushed the first one as the man turned to fire on him with an automatic assault rifle of some kind. James grabbed the gun from him, broke it in half, and smacked him in the helmet with the stock. The guard went down, and two more came rushing in. Lacy zipped in front of them, grabbed them both by the head, and clapped their heads together so hard their helmets cracked. She dropped the two unconscious men to the ground and brushed her hands off as if she'd just finished a hard day's work. "Damn, those concussions are gonna *suck.*"

His ears perked at the sound of Phillip's shout. "All clear!"

James stood and moved over to the plane, stepping over unconscious guards and workers. Lacy was close behind him as Phillip ran up to join them. "What the hell happened to 'be sneaky'?"

"I fucked up, I guess," Lacy said with a shrug as she looked down at her now bloody shirt. The red was dark against the pink, where Hello Kitty waved from her position on Lacy's chest despite the spatters of blood across her printed white face. "God damn it. This shit's never gonna come out."

"Like your whole closet isn't full of the same exact damn t-shirt," Phillip said.

James ignored them as they continued to banter back and forth. He made his way to the back of the plane, his arm now healed and only tender where the bullet had grazed him. He gently touched the spot where the fur was growing back. The skin was warm underneath. He couldn't shift back to human form yet. Not with an injury slowing his healing like that in wolf form. It would be a few minutes.

"None of these assholes are cops," Phillip said as he knelt down next to one of the knocked-out SWAT members. He reached down, pulled a badge wallet from the guy's vest, and opened it. "Badge numbers aren't even right. ID is fake as hell."

"How can you tell?" Lacy asked.

"I still know most of the guys at RHPD," Phillip said. "Enough of them that recognizing none of these motherfuckers ain't happening. The badges aren't right. RHPD uses a similar shield, but there's one too many numbers. And the identification card is all wrong. Whoever is heading this up isn't doing their homework."

James saw the forklift parked behind the plane; a large wooden crate was suspended off the floor on the forks where the loading process had been interrupted. He could already smell the gun oil mixed in with whatever packing they were using to throw off non-supernatural K-9 dogs. Just like the massive cocaine shipment they'd discovered when they'd tracked Mindy Robertson to Jacksonville, Florida. He saw a small insignia on the side of the crate.

The same one he'd seen on Agatha's neck in Savannah, Georgia.

He pulled the top off the crate and looked down at the neatly packed assault rifles inside. He saw the spots on each one where someone had removed the serial numbers. He figured likely the rifling was also altered. Lacy walked over and stood on the opposite side of the crate, peering in as she gave a low whistle. "What the *shit?*" she said. "Pretty sure this didn't come in from Amazon."

James nodded, then scanned the area for Phillip. He paused; his muscles tensed immediately as his heartbeat began to speed up. He saw the unconscious people littered about, saw the mess they'd made of the hangar.

He didn't see Phillip.

Phillip isn't one to wander, James thought to the wolf as he urged the beast back to its feet. His arm was almost fully healed, the tenderness mostly gone, and the spot just barely warm now.

He felt his blood run cold as he heard Phillip's voice from the front end of the hangar. "James, stay where the hell you are."

James moved from the back of the plane around to the front, facing the large open hangar doors. He clenched his fists at the sight of Clint standing next to Phillip with a handgun pressed to Phillip's temple.

Not even a mark, he thought to the wolf. *We crushed him between two airplanes. How?*

"Gotta do better than that, Fido," Clint said, his voice lower and gravelly, a stark contrast from the friendly and jovial man they'd met at the Fillmore. "Takes more than a little pinch to put me down."

"Cute little operation you've got here," Lacy said as she moved up next to James.

Clint shrugged. James could hear the sirens in the distance, still far enough away to not be heard by human ears but growing closer by the second. "Serves its purpose. You three are a pain in the ass, though. Gotta go." He looked at Phillip and grinned. "You first."

James was in motion, charging Clint at wolfen speed as the slide on the handgun moved. Phillip slapped the gun to the side. Clint fired wild, and Phillip used the opportunity to knock Clint off balance with a jab to the face. Lacy knocked Phillip backwards as James swung at his target, his claws out and ready.

Something crashed into him, knocking him to the side and away from Clint. James felt the air forced from his lungs, his ribs straining from the impact. Claws raked at his body, savage snarling mixed with the sound of gnashing teeth as he reacted out of instinct, grabbing his assailant and rolling to put his enemy underneath him. His senses flooded with cedarwood as he and Clifford hit the concrete and continued to roll. Clifford bucked, and James flew off him and into the cargo plane. He recovered and shot back at Clifford, his yellowed vision hot with feral rage. He caught a glimpse of Lacy as she zipped over at vampiric speed. Going low, she clipped him on the back of one knee. James put his arm out as Clifford started to go down and clotheslined him to the ground. Clifford tried to recover, but James was on him. He sank his teeth deep into Clifford's shoulder, blood hot and coppery filling his mouth instantly as Clifford yelped in pain and fought to buck James off. He slammed his open hand into the side of James's head and sent him sideways with a chunk of meat in his mouth.

James shook the dizziness off and stood, glaring at Clifford, his body hot with fury. He dropped the piece of meat from his mouth, the blood warm and tacky on his furred jaw, neck, and chest. Clifford kept his hand pressed over the wound, dark blood flowing between his fingers, his arm soaked in crimson. He glared at James, breathing heavily.

We knocked the wind out of him, James thought, the fury swelling inside of him as the wolf growled deep within his mind, the sound rattling in his throat and escaping his own jaws as he bared his teeth at Clifford. He felt a swell of hatred and loathing as he spread his arms in challenge, his eyes locked on his enemy. He caught Lacy's scent as she moved up beside him, her ice blue eyes wild and glowing, her fangs fully out, and her fingernails extended into wicked claws. "You owe me a shirt, asshole," she said, her words slightly distorted from working around her fangs.

Clifford barked once at James, his eyes flashing like two yellow lights just before he turned and bolted out of the hangar on all fours and into the night. James started to chase after him, then stopped himself. The cedarwood scent was already gone. His arm was healed up, and he shifted into human form. "Damn it."

"I'm okay," Phillip called from behind the forklift. James saw him rise up from his hiding spot, one of the assault rifles clutched in his hands. "I'm good."

"Officer McShooty took off too," Lacy said, retracting her fangs. She glanced in the direction of the open hangar doors that led out into the rest of the airport. James's ear twitched at the sounds of the sirens getting closer by the second. "We gotta get the hell out of here."

"We gotta ditch the car," Phillip said. "That's gonna be right in the middle of where they're coming in."

"Damn," Lacy said. "I liked that car."

"Your rich-ass boyfriend can buy you another one." Phillip handed her the assault rifle. "We need to take this to Hoyt. Take a look at what's stamped on it."

Lacy turned it over as James moved closer to her. "Holy shit," she breathed. "Smith needs to see this." She held the gun up to James with the stock up. He saw something etched into the material.

He didn't have time to process what he was seeing before he heard the crash of the airport gate being plowed down by the armored SWAT van, the wailing sirens loud in the night as dozens of cruisers drove into the airport alongside the SWAT vehicle. More flooded in on foot, all of them wearing riot gear and all of them armed with firearms of every type.

James shifted back into wolf form and crouched so Phillip could climb on. Lacy was already gone, zipping to the back of the building and sending the locked door flying off its hinges. "This way!"

Phillip already had a solid grip on James's fur as James took to all fours and ran through the opening, crouching low to avoid catching Phillip on the door frame. A few police officers had already gotten into position. They opened fire immediately, with surprised shouts followed by wild shots into the air. Lacy ran ahead with James close behind her as they crossed the entirety of the airport in seconds, stopping at the tall perimeter fence separating them from the woods on the other side. Lacy jumped it easily, landing on the other side with the assault rifle still in her hands. Gunfire was followed by the telltale sparks of bullets grazing steel next to him. James ran along the fence, ammunition grazing the wire mesh behind him as he stayed ahead of the onslaught. Phillip shouted in his ear as the gunfire roared behind them. "Chopper!"

James's yellowed vision flooded with light as the helicopter hovered above, its spotlight aimed directly at them. Someone over the loudspeaker was shouting at them to stop, warning about shooting if they kept resisting. James pushed harder, banked to his right as more gunfire sounded. He began to feel himself running blindly, fought back the panic welling up in him. The wolf stood firm in his mind, pressed hard against him, stopping shy of completely taking over. *We have to get Phillip out of here,* James thought to the beast. It barked in agreement, stood firm in its place in his mind. James felt his body warm with the raw power the wolf gave him as he started down the runway, the lights on either side of the tarmac blinking in a wave pattern indicating the direction incoming and outgoing airplanes would use to take off or land. It had to be a certain length to give the planes time to build up speed for take-off. The wolf pressed him again. He knew what it was trying to do.

It would be long enough.

"What the hell are you doing?!" Phillip shouted from on his back. "We're sitting goddamn ducks!"

Hang on, James thought as if Phillip could hear him. Phillip's grip tightened on the locks of fur, legs squeezing harder around James's midsection. The wolf made one more step forward, and James stood alone in the darkness, still able to feel and see what was going on around him.

Wolf saw the flimsy wall at the end of the long road, saw the humans with their guns and their black armor already converging. The loud storm of the flying vehicle, the thing the James called "helicopter" was close behind them, its bright light watching Wolf. The James barked at Wolf to run, to get out of there. To get the Phillip to safety. Wolf pushed harder, picking up speed as it tore down the road, the steel birds the James called "airplanes" blurring by along with the barking people and hateful guns. It felt the Phillip on its back, felt the grip on its fur.

Brother. Had to protect brother.

We haven't gone this fast with him before, the James shouted from inside. *Slow the hell down, you're going to lose him!*

The Phillip screamed in Wolf's ear. *"James! Slow down! I can't hang on!"*

Almost there. The fence with the bladed coils. Wolf needed the Phillip to hang on longer. Legs squeezed tighter around Wolf's ribs, hands buried deeper into fur.

Do it, the James called. *He's got a good grip!*

The Phillip screamed, but Wolf sensed no fear from its passenger as it kicked off the ground, reaching for the night sky beyond the top of the razor wire fence. The blades would pass below them with ease. They would lose the helicopter in the trees and the night.

Wolf was blind, seeing nothing but hideous and painful white before the loud thunderclap silenced the roar of the aircraft behind them, the shouting from the Phillip, the gunfire, left nothing but a high-pitched whine in its wake. Wolf yelped in pain, the James crying out from inside as well, as it covered its eyes and fell backwards in Wolf's mind. It charged forward, pulled Wolf back into the dark recesses as the ground came at them.

James felt the full impact of hitting the hard, rocky ground with his shoulder, his body rolling over top of him, bending his neck at an awkward, painful angle as his momentum flung him into the trees beyond the runway fence. The air left his lungs the instant he slammed against a large pine tree hard enough to crack the bark and rain pinecones down around him.

He blinked multiple times as the wolf yelped and growled in blind panic. His injuries were already healing, the tinnitus calming down, and the pain in his eyes subsiding as his vision cleared. He got to his feet and saw they'd made the jump.

His chest clenched as he saw Phillip's crumpled form stir on the runway on the other side of the fence. A SWAT officer was already standing over him, assault rifle pointed as he shouted orders. The helicopter had ascended, keeping its searchlight on Phillip as more SWAT vehicles pulled up. The searchlight panned the woods, barely missing the werewolf standing in the trees watching as the army of police officers converged on Phillip.

James snarled, baring his teeth as he moved forward. The wolf urged him and pressed its will with its feral rage, matching his own determined anger. He wouldn't let them take Phillip. He would tear them all apart if the handcuffs so much as *bruised* Phillip's wrists. They wouldn't have silver bullets. They wouldn't be able to hurt him enough to stop him. He saw it in his mind, his massive form landing over top of Phillip, protecting him as he fought off the SWAT team.

Gunfire. It wouldn't harm him. But Phillip...

James gnashed his teeth in frustration. He couldn't risk them panicking and accidentally shooting Phillip. He stepped back deeper into the woods, making sure he was out of sight as he watched them help Phillip to his feet and start reading him the Miranda rights. His anger faded to helplessness and frustration. There was no choice. Not if he wanted to make sure that Phillip would live through the night. There was nothing he could do.

He kept his jaw clenched as he turned and tore through the woods, tears soaking the fur around his eyes as he put more and more distance between him and the one brother he'd ever known.

19

It was four in the morning when James found himself on the balcony outside his bedroom. He stared out over the dark pastures of Coldstone Keep, the air carrying the warning bite of fall on the horizon. It meant the days would only cool off marginally if at all, but the nights would become cooler and brisk. It meant his favorite scents of the woods, the sweet, mildewed smell of the flora and fauna soaking in the evening dew, would permeate the air more strongly. It meant the year was on its way out, that a new year would be on the horizon after a year carrying more life-changing events for him than he'd experienced over the course of his entire previous lifetime.

He'd signed up to help Phillip solve cases the Rock Hill Police Department could never solve. Cases involving vampires, zombies, and whatever else bumped in the night. Phillip would determine whether the crime was supernatural; he would call James in to "wreck shit," and then Phillip would run interference and cover up the creepy side of things while James stayed a recluse. It was supposed to be easy. He helped Phillip, helped people, and was able to remain isolated away from the stigma of being the son of the most notorious urban legend the city had ever had to cover up to keep the façade of "Small Town America."

Then his life exploded at the beginning of summer. And now it was November.

The wolf sighed deeply in his mind as it lay down in its dark home, resting its chin on its crossed paws. James still hadn't told anyone about the beast inside of him, about their symbiotic relationship. The wolf was its own being, carried its own consciousness and will. But it was also part of him and worked with him instead of against him. When they'd first separated, the creature had panicked, had taken over James's body in an effort to fight and escape. It'd almost eaten Phillip, an animal cornered and seeing no other option but to fight its way out. But it listened to James, saw him as a part of itself. He figured the creature was likely male, given its insatiable sexual appetite, but he found it easier to refer to it as "it." And it had revealed what he considered a superpower to him, his Sonic Howl.

What the wolf called "The Call to Fenrir," though James had no real idea why that was relevant.

Phillip would know.

The wolf sent him a sorrowful mewl, meeting his mind's eye with its own forlorn expression. *I don't blame you for what happened,* James thought to it. Neither of them had seen the SWAT officer at the end of the runway, nor had they noticed the flash-bang grenade before it went off. There was no way to notice. They'd been going too fast, had been focused on getting out of there. Getting Phillip to safety. Now Phillip was in a holding cell.

He blinked at the ringing coming from the lawn below. It kept up, the loud and generic digital ringing mimicking the old-style telephones of the eighties and nineties screaming from his iPhone somewhere in the grass. He hadn't thought about reclaiming it when he'd gotten back. The night had been too manic. There were very few people who had his number, and all of them would likely call him at this hour if it were important. He pulled his robe off and kept it in his hand as he shifted and jumped down into the yard. James followed the ringing to the spot near the driveway where he'd dropped his phone when he'd shifted and taken off for the festival downtown. He shifted back to human form, picked the phone up from the pile of ripped clothing, and saw Lacy's contact on the screen. He pulled the robe back on and answered. "Hello."

"Hey, nice of you to ditch a girl just when the date was getting hot," Lacy said. It was a joke, but he could hear the tension in her voice alongside the sound of the car in the background. "I'm headed your way. You okay?"

"I'm fine," James said. "What happened to you?" He could hear his own empty tone as he spoke.

"I got sidetracked," she said. "Saw you had Bacon covered and decided to try and lure some of the local military off your back so you could get out of there with the least amount of airborne ammunition as possible. *Jeezus*, these guys are armed to the *teeth*."

"They got Phillip."

"How?" Lacy asked. James could hear the genuine surprise in her voice. "I saw you haul ass down the runway with him on your back. There's no way they could've caught up to you two."

James sighed. "Well, despite being fairly immune to mortal non-silver weaponry, flash-bang grenades can still be effective against anything with eyes and ears."

"Shit," Lacy said. "Yeah, those damn things hurt like hell." She paused. "So, they arrested him?"

"Yes." James turned and started walking back toward the house.

"Shit," she muttered again. "Okay, I'll get on the horn with Hoyt and see if he can find out what's going on. Maybe he can dick with things and set up a release that looks legit. I'll be there in about five minutes. Just sit tight."

James made it to the front door as she talked. He opened it, stepped inside, and closed it behind him. He stared into the dark, quiet main hall. The air was dusty, claustrophobic.

Cold.

"See you soon," he said. He ended the call and stood in place, staring into the darkness without seeing the room around him as his mind continued to spin. He fought down the urge to hurl his phone against the wall, his gut filling with anger and frustration. Not just those things. Something else. Something wicked he was all too familiar with.

James had moved to the study and was sitting in the dark, staring out the window, when Lacy walked into the house. A human might not have noticed him, the only light in the room being the moonlight coming in through the windows. But she came directly in. She sat down on the opposite side of the desk. He could feel her looking at him, could smell her scent clearly, but he didn't acknowledge her in the long stretch of seconds before she finally spoke.

"Hey, Jimmy. How're you holding up?"

James remained stationary; his eyes locked on the outside. "I have been better."

"I'll bet."

"Were you able to contact Hoyt?"

"Yeah, I called him right after I called you. He said he'd be at the lab in thirty. Figured I'd give you a break and drive us both there."

"I appreciate it."

He heard her stand and move around the room. "Damn, Jimmy. Lot of books in here. Are the walls behind these shelves painted? You can't even see them."

"The shelves are built in," James said, still staring out the window. He heard her pull a book from one of the shelves and leaf through the pages.

"You ever read any of them?"

"I've read all of them." He stood and turned to her. "They aren't mine."

Lacy stared at him in awe. "Holy fuck, look at the brain on Jimmy. There's gotta be a least a thousand books in here."

"I was never one for television until I met Phillip."

Lacy nodded solemnly as if taking in new and impactful information. "Wow. And here I thought you weren't all that bright."

He raised an eyebrow. "Only when it comes to computers. Otherwise, I like to think I am quite literate."

Lacy nodded again. "I see," she said in a serious tone. "So, what you're telling me is…you're a dork." Her serious expression softened into a humored grin. "It's kinda hot."

James stared at her for a few seconds. Under normal circumstances, he would've been amused. He started toward the study door, moving past her as he spoke. "I'll get dressed."

Her face fell slightly. "Come on, Jimmy," she said as he reached for the door handle. "Where's the smartass? Didn't you say making jokes was a defense mechanism?"

His response was gruff. "I am not in the mood for jokes." James jerked the door open and moved out into the corridor leading to the main staircase. He wanted to be left alone. He had to figure out how to get Phillip out of jail and had to figure out where Clint and Clifford ran off to. His body was warm with anger, his heart beating fast. It took everything in him not to shift, blow through the front entrance doors, and rampage to the police department to break Phillip out. But he also knew doing so would cause more problems for everyone.

"James!"

Her shout stopped him, but he didn't turn around to face her. He clenched his fists by his sides. Her tone was sharp, but not angry. The wolf lay dormant inside, keeping its head down with its chin resting on its paws. He clenched his jaw, and the wolf sat up long enough to give a long and dramatic yawn before lying its head back down. James braced himself for another argument with Lacy pointing out why he was being a dick.

"I'm sorry about Phillip," she said, her voice gentle and quiet. "We'll get him out of there."

James turned his head, eyed her sidelong over his shoulder. "He's likely injured."

"Then he'll need to stay put until he gets cleared for transport," Lacy said. "He'll need the medical attention." She started walking toward him, her footfalls muted by the thick carpet on the wood floors. "That's why I called Hoyt first instead of Smith or Kimble."

James nodded.

"You need to get some sleep," she said as she stopped a few feet from him, looking up at him in the dark. "You've been grumpy."

"I have a lot to be grumpy about."

"Yeah, that's fair." She bit her lower lip. "I'll listen if you wanna talk."

"Phillip saw something on that rifle," James said, avoiding Lacy's offer to facilitate his emotional offload.

"Yeah," Lacy said. "It was Tepes's house crest."

"It doesn't make sense. If Tepes is the one behind this, why emblaze his emblem all over everything that incriminates him?"

Lacy shrugged. "I agree with that."

"And Clifford has been at almost every incident that Clint has started." He paused as something lit up in his mind. The wolf raised its head quickly, its ears perked. "Clifford is tracking Clint."

"I thought Clifford was killing witches."

"He's possibly doing both," James said, staring past her into the dark as he pieced his thoughts together. "He's never aided Clint during a massacre, and Clint runs off as soon as Clifford shows up. But he's also a serial killer. He can't help himself. So, he's been killing witches off left and right." He focused on her again. "Clifford is playing both sides of the coin."

Lacy furrowed her brow in thought as she nodded slowly. "Makes sense. Counterpoint: Clifford picks a witch to kill and tracks her down, but Clint keeps showing up and fucking up his plans. Clint is tracking Clifford."

James shook his head. "Counterpoint: Not every shooting has had a witch present."

"That you know of," Lacy countered, taking a step closer to him. "There were thousands of people at the wrestling match, and hundreds around Uptown. Any of them could have been witches."

"Indeed," James said, taking a step closer to her. "But I chased Clifford to the coliseum. He hadn't planned on going there."

She stepped closer again. "Counterpoint: he led you there. Clint was in the audience, which means he was there before we got there."

"Which alludes back to my previous point. Clifford is tracking Clint, *and* he is a serial killer." He didn't realize he'd taken another step closer to her until he noticed she was inches from him. "And Clint is working for someone on the council who wants to make sure everything points to Tepes."

Lacy nodded, then closed her eyes and shook her head with a defeated sigh. "Damn."

James blinked. "What?"

"Brains make you even sexier."

James didn't have time to respond before her lips were planted on his, her skin and mouth cool to the touch. He returned the kiss, wrapping his arms around her and pulling her closer to him. The wolf was wide awake, writhing on its back in his mind and panting happily. The urge grew inside him, welled in his gut and chest as the wolf rolled forward. He felt his strength build, his heart pounding as his body grew warm. He ran his fingers through her long, chocolate curls before placing his hand on her neck and pulling her into a deeper kiss. His canines grew as she ran her tongue over them. He returned the gesture, felt her fangs grow against his own tongue. James gripped her shoulders and pushed her against the wall, breaking the kiss. He stared into her eyes, her bright blues even brighter as they began to glow. He tasted the blood in his mouth where her teeth had cut his tongue, saw some of his blood on her lips just before she licked it away. Lacy gave a small moan, her eyes rolling in ecstasy. "Jesus, your blood tastes so good." She pushed back at him, forcing him to the other side of the corridor easily before yanking the front of his robe open. She ran her fingernails over his chest, a trail of blood left in their wake. "I want more," she said, looking up at him, her fangs elongated and her eyes fully glowing.

His vision was yellowed, his muscles swelling as his strength grew. Her pelvis was pressed against his, her denim shorts the only barrier between them. His urge was animalistic, feral. This was what he wanted. What he'd always wanted. It was different than the other times she'd kissed him. He'd felt something was missing, something held back both by her and himself.

Not now. Not ever again.

She pushed him back gently, her glowing eyes fixed on him as he sat back on the desk and watched her undress. She was nude in seconds, every motion she made in her undress sensuous, delicate. His robe had fallen off his shoulders into a heap on the floor at some point before she'd made him sit. He stared at her small, silhouetted form in front of the window. The curve of her pert breasts and her hips, the way her hair hid so much of her face save for the bright sapphires glowing through the locks, all of it perfection to him. But none of it compared to the whisper from her as she moved closer to him, pressed her nude form against him, nuzzling her face against his neck.

"James..."

He grabbed her around the waist and rolled, pinning her down on the desk. She gave a delighted, hungry snarl and smiled at him as he leaned down and put his mouth on hers again. He felt himself touch her, the surprising and sudden warmth and wetness from her body waking up every primal fiber in him.

He wanted her, needed her.

He also wished she'd put her phone on Do Not Disturb as it blared *Secret Agent Man* from the shorts on the floor nearby.

She stiffened underneath him, then released as she smacked her fist down on the desk. "God *damn* it, Hoyt!"

Everything flooded back into his mind as he moved off of her and stood next to the desk where she lay. The wolf barked and cried inside his mind, his body aching and yearning to ignore the phone call, to continue what he and Lacy had started.

Two insane supernaturals were on the loose. People were dying. And Phillip was in jail.

James reached down, picked up Lacy's shorts, and pulled her phone out of the pocket as Johnny Rivers continued his performance. He saw Hoyt's contact on the screen.

"Just answer it," Lacy said, grumbling. "I might scream at him if I do."

James answered the call and put it on the loudspeaker. "Hoyt, you're on speaker."

"Hey, James," Hoyt replied. "Is Lacy busy?"

James looked back at Lacy, who rolled her eyes and sat up as she muttered, "I *was*," under her breath. They'd stopped glowing, and her fangs had retracted. "What is it, Hoyt?" she snapped.

"I thought you said they arrested Phillip at the airport?"

"They did," James said. "I watched them cuff him. They read him his rights."

"Okay," Hoyt said. "But I'm looking in the records for both the city and county, and there's nothing about it."

James's chest constricted immediately, the urge and fire in his blood from just a moment ago now calm and cool.

"What do you mean there's nothing about it?" Lacy asked.

"There is the likelihood it simply hasn't been filed yet," James said, keeping his tone even. It was a denial. He knew it was. He'd been around Phillip long enough to know better. But he had to reach, had to chance the reality he was faced with was not reality at all.

"Not likely at all, man," Hoyt said. "We live in the digital age. Cops have laptops in their cars that could probably play current-gen video games if they wanted to. Their vehicles are tracked via GPS, and even their body gear has a blip on the radar. Something goes down, they have to call it in right then and there. They make an arrest, they call it in, and do the field report before they even leave the scene. And there's a time deadline. They miss that deadline, it's a bad day at work for them. And that's even *with* dispatch noting down every damn thing they hear on the radio."

Lacy stood up from the desk and moved closer to James, looking at him as she spoke. "The entire Rock Hill SWAT team was there."

"Negative on that too," Hoyt said. "No reports of any dispatch out to the Rock Hill Airport. They got a lot of calls asking about the sirens and gunfire, and they notified the York County Sheriff's Office to respond."

"That doesn't make sense," James said. "The airport is in Rock Hill."

"But it falls under York County jurisdiction," Hoyt said without missing a beat. "It's weird, man. The city and county lines here look like a toddler got into the candy and went nuts with his crayons on the map. RHPD can show up as support, which they did, but only at the request of the county. And all they found when they got there was millions of dollars in damages."

"The guns," Lacy said. "We found a crate full of unmarked assault rifles that they were loading out of a cargo plane."

"Nothing about that," Hoyt said. "Trust me, that would already be in the headlines. Right now, the only headline you'll find is a suspected terrorist attack on an empty private airport."

James remembered Phillip commenting on one of the people he'd knocked out during their impromptu raid on the hangar. *"I still know most of the guys at RHPD,"* Phillip had said. *"Enough of them not to recognize not one of these motherfuckers. The badges aren't right. RHPD uses a similar shield, but there's one too many numbers. And the identification card is all wrong. Whoever is heading this up isn't doing their homework."*

Lacy looked up at James. "Then who the hell has Phillip?"

"Good question," Hoyt said. James heard something make a sound in the background, like a notification. He heard rapid-fire typing, then a pause before Hoyt spoke again. "Oh…oh, *fuck.*" He dragged out the last word for a second before he continued. "Uh, guys? Get the hell out of there. Like right now."

"What is it?" James asked.

"Yeah, Smith just detained Kimble, and the SCU is on their way to arrest you both."

James looked at Lacy, and could tell she also heard multiple vehicles speeding down the driveway, tires grinding to a halt on gravel, and doors slamming accompanied by people shouting commands.

"Oh, my bad," Hoyt said. "They're already there."

20

At the window, Lacy's phone in his hand, James pulled the wolf forward in his mind. He saw several people in tactical gear moving around in the yard in his wolfen vision, saw the armored van with the FBI logo on it with no other designator underneath, though everyone out there had the letters "SCU" on their uniforms.

"They're supposed to bring you in alive, if that helps," Hoyt said over the phone speaker.

"That's nice of them," Lacy said, her tone dripping with sarcasm. "Heavily armed, *non*-lethal cock-blocking."

"What?"

"Don't worry about it," James said as he watched the SCU tactical squad get into position. He saw a few of them duck around out of sight, likely covering the other possible exits the mansion had. A large, familiar man in a black suit stepped out of one of the black SUVs. "I believe Agent Squeaky Toy is with them."

Lacy joined him at the window. "Fuck." She turned away and started toward the clothes she'd left lying on the floor next to the desk. "I need to get dressed."

James's ear twitched, the wolf already in place. He could hear the house settling, years-old timber creaking under the heavy plaster and lathe walls as the air outside began to change from the cold night to a brisk autumn morning. The HVAC system was running, trying to keep the mansion temperature a comfortable sixty-eight degrees, the air from the vents warm enough to fight off the cold but not so warm to be uncomfortable.

Boots on hardwood floors, the telltale creaking of leather belts supporting gear, the click of a gun safety being released, followed by a few more. A whisper. Orders.

James moved to Lacy and grabbed her arm as she was picking up her clothes. She started to protest, but he held a finger up to his mouth and shook his head. He leaned close to her ear and whispered. "They're already inside." She stopped resisting immediately, her eyes flashing bright blue as she tilted her head.

The wolf paced back and forth in his mind, growling and nervous. Why the sudden assault? Smith hated him. But Smith was also far more creative than sending in a brute squad. The fracas at Epicenter had involved agents, none of whom had been wearing tactical gear. Why the sudden need for a siege on his home? "Something is off. We need to leave."

Lacy looked at him as if to argue, then stopped as she also heard the footfalls on the other side of the closed study door. There was a clicking sound as the door opened and a cylinder rolled in, belching smoke from either side. The thick, acrid cloud filled the room. Lacy reacted quickly, grabbing her pink, bloodied Hello Kitty shirt and shoving it in James's face over his mouth and nose. He could still smell the smoke from the grenade, but his senses were now overwhelmed with her scent. Not enough of the toxic cloud could break through the makeshift filter of cloth saturated in Lacy's blood and vanilla. His eyes burned, but the wolf was already forward, ready to fight the damage back with his wolfen healing.

The agents on the other side kicked the door the rest of the way open, all three in the room in a second's breath with their assault rifles up. It was even less time before the three red lasers from the scopes found James and Lacy standing in front of the window. Lacy moved in front of James, standing fully nude between him and three men armed to the teeth with fully automatic weapons. All three men wore full armor, head to toe, including full face gas masks.

"Stand down, Agent Faulkner," the one in the middle said, his canned voice on the mask's speaker reminding James of one of the stormtroopers from Star Wars. "You're both coming with us."

Lacy started to speak, but something else caught James's attention, distracting him from what she was saying, other than demanding to know why the hell they were being taken in. The two men behind the one speaking kept their guns aimed. One of them stood firm, the red laser on his rifle squarely placed in the center of James's chest. James could smell the man's sweat, could smell the distinctive scent of the Kevlar vest he wore. He breathed slowly; his focus unbroken in the seconds Lacy argued with the squad leader.

The man on the other side of the squad leader kept his aim as well, but his scent was drastically different. Coppery-laced rot mixed with the Kevlar; the scent was recognizable under the offensive amount of cheap cologne he wore.

Phillip's cologne.

James heard the click of the trigger from Stinky's rifle before the shot went off. He shifted, moved at wolfen speed, swept Lacy's ankles out from underneath her as the bullet passed through where her head would've been and grazed his shoulder. The pain was the hot, angry, and hateful pain that only came with silver. He rushed the other two while they were still caught by surprise, the leader in the midst of shouting *"Hold your fire!"* when James plowed into him and swept him aside as he took a wide swing and slapped the shooter's rifle away, sending it through the window behind the desk. The other human turned to fire, but the bullets pelted against his coat and barely broke his skin. He swung his right hand out, backhanded the agent on the side of the head, and dropped him like a sack of bricks. Stinky darted past James and had Lacy on her feet with one arm wrapped around her, his hand on her neck. He held a long, wicked-looking military knife against her ribcage. She raised her leg and brought her heel down on his boot hard enough to cave in the steel toe before she elbowed him in the gut and broke his grip on her. James pounced, grabbed him by the head, and tore it from his shoulders before tossing it aside. It smacked against the wall and exploded into dust, the rest of the body following suit until all that was left was an empty uniform on the floor.

"We gotta get the fuck out of here," Lacy said as she dove for her clothes. "This is bad. None of the tactical agents are supposed to be supernaturals."

James's ears perked up; his attention drawn to the now open window. Some movement. Whispers. A small metallic click. A memory from earlier when they'd taken Phillip. Just before he'd leapt the fence.

He grabbed Lacy by the waist and scooped her up into his arms, ignoring her protests and shouts as he made for the door. They were barely in the hallway before the room filled with light. Lacy's cursing and shouting turned to screams. James smelled the sweet stench of burning meat, his heartbeat speeding up even more as she howled in agony. He charged down the hallway, stopping a few doors down as he heard commotion in the dining room on his left. He moved to his right, shouldered the door open, and ducked into the music room, his attention immediately on the grand piano in the center of the studio. He shifted his foot behind him, kicking the door shut before he moved around to the opposite side of the piano. He held Lacy close to him, tried to tune out her groans of pain as he put his back against the piano and shoved it over to the door.

The wolf grunted in his mind, sent him an image of a toddler pushing around a toy dump truck with large plastic wheels. *For us, yes,* James thought to it. *For the average human, moving a thousand-pound piano is more of an endeavor.*

The wolf chuffed at him but stopped complaining.

Lacy shifted in his arms. He walked over to the bar and laid her out on the top. She'd taken most of the blast on one side of her body, the skin blackened and charred in places, some of it peeling back to expose slightly cooked muscle and sinew. Half of her face was burned, and some of her hair had fallen out or burned away. The flesh on her wrist and arm, in particular, was cooked until it was dried, reminding James of chicken left on the grill for too long. The meat was shrinking away from the bone in places, the bone itself blackened and brittle.

More commotion in the house, shouts of "Shots fired!" and orders to flank the hallway sounded. Someone had seen them duck into the music room. They didn't have time for her to take cover and heal. It would take at least a day, maybe longer.

The wolf sent him the memory of the time on Westenra Island when she'd fought with a suspect. The guy almost killed her. James had fed her some of his blood to help her heal despite the sound of Phillip's voice in his head screaming at him about tired movie tropes. The wolf whined, and James sensed the shared apprehension along with the determination to help her.

"J...James," she said, her breathing becoming ragged. Her eyes were closed; her face screwed into a pained grimace as pieces of burned flesh flaked off the side that had caught some of the blast. Her good eye opened slightly, but the other had liquified and was running out of the socket and down her mangled cheek. The muscles on that side were slackened, only one side of her mouth working as she formed words. "It...hurts..."

He held his arm out over her mouth and gave a low whine. She shook her head, but he chuffed at her and moved it closer to her mouth.

"I...can't..." she said, shaking her head weakly. "Hurt you."

His body tensed when he heard the boots on the floor in the hallway. The wolf growled inside. He pulled his arm away and bit down into the forearm close to the crook of his elbow, hot blood gushing into his mouth and pain radiating up and down the tendons and nerves. He held it out over Lacy again and squeezed his fist. Blood poured from the wound into Lacy's open mouth. Her skin began to heal immediately, and she gripped his arm and buried her face into the wound, drinking hungrily as she covered herself in his blood. He felt his knees weaken, dizziness causing him to waver as he tried to pull away from her. She held fast, her strength suddenly greater than he realized. Her eyes snapped open, her pupils glowing bright ice blue as her hair finished growing back to its original luster. He stopped fighting, the wolf pacing back and forth in his mind, mewling as it began to limp. *She won't hurt me*, he thought, trying to convince both himself and his symbiote. His knees weakened more as his mind started to fog, his vision blurring. The wolf stepped forward again, but he pushed it back with what will he had left, put his free hand on the back of Lacy's head, and held her against his arm. Her eyes were wide, wild, and feral, her face gaunt as the last vestiges of burned flesh disappeared into perfect, smooth, healed skin. He dropped to one knee, his own weight too much for him to handle anymore. He blinked slowly, his vision blurry. He didn't know when he'd hit the floor. All he could feel was his strength leaving his body through his arm, where Lacy's cold lips were locked onto his wound.

She was taking far more blood than she had on Westenra Island. And James couldn't stop her.

A muffled shout. Something like a warning. The door to the music room exploded inwards, taking the piano with it as the room filled with fire, splintered wood, and shrapnel.

She jerked and pulled away from him. He saw her snap to attention, her wild-eyed predator gaze laser-focused on the tactical agents moving into the room, all of them shouting at her to stand down as they pointed their weapons at her. Her mouth was open, her fangs fully out, her breathing harsh and heavy. Her face, neck, chest, and hands were covered in his blood. He saw the corners of her mouth turn up in a rictus grin.

"Agent Faulkner," one of the agents said, his gun aimed. "Stand down!"

"She's feral," another shouted. "We gotta put her down!"

He heard the click of a trigger; the telltale sound the average human wouldn't hear heralding the oncoming bullet.

Lacy rushed them in a blur, moving so fast James could barely make out her shape. Gunfire ran wild as tactical agents flew in all directions, some smacking into walls while others cracked the windows. Shouts turned into screams as blood sprayed the walls and floor. James felt strength in his legs again, warmth in his body as the blood replenished itself. The healing sped up, and James was well enough to stand again. He pushed himself up off the floor, gathering his legs underneath him as Lacy continued her onslaught. He ducked as a large mass flew at him and smacked the wall next to him, the wet tearing of meat and the splatter of blood and gore followed immediately by the stench of bile and shit. James saw the freshly disemboweled agent starting to fall just as Lacy grabbed him and tore his head off his shoulders.

It took her less time to put down ten armed men and women than it did for James to get to his feet, the wound on his arm almost completely closed. The room was strewn with what was left of the tactical agents, some of them in various stages of dismemberment and evisceration.

None of them had turned to dust.

James's strength had returned. The wolf kept itself in the forefront of his mind, barely close enough to fully take over. He braced himself as Lacy turned to him, her eyes glowing, her face drawn in primal hunger. Her nude body covered in pieces of meat and blood, some of it his. The glowing faded, her psychotic expression melting away to shock. "Holy shit," she breathed, raising her hands and staring at them in horror before looking down at the rest of her body. She looked up at James, her lower lip trembling. "James, what just happened?"

James shook his head and growled, pointing at the window. *Time to go.*

She stood in place, staring at the carnage she'd caused with what James could only assume was shock and confusion.

Thirteen. They'd taken out thirteen tactical agents. Two unconscious. The other eleven dead, one of them vampire dust, so the dead part could be debated. James knew that the SCU would've sent more than thirteen agents.

He rushed Lacy, grabbed her up in a bridal carry as he turned on his heel and leapt through the window in an explosion of thick glass and wood. Agent Squeaky Toy's voice sounded over the bullhorn, the high-pitched voice ordering him to stand down. James held Lacy closer to him as he did his best to run at his wolfen speed on two legs, blowing by Agent Squeaky Toy with enough force to send him flying backwards with a loud two-toned squeak as if he were being chewed on. More gunshots rang out in the night air, the rounds pelting his coat and falling away harmlessly as he moved over the front pasture toward the woods. Squeaky Toy shouted into the bullhorn for the agents to cease fire. James entered the woods, the clear, open field now replaced with dense foliage. He let his mouth open slightly, drew in the scents of wet foliage and mildew over the glands in his mouth. He kept up his pace, working off his memory of the countless times he'd hunted in these woods and following the scents. His chest and arms became soaked; Lacy's sweat matted his fur against his skin. Her normally cold body was getting uncomfortably warm. She clutched at the fur on his chest as she curled into more of a ball in his arms as if to hide. The wolf sent him an image of the sunrise just as the sky took on the purple hue that heralded dawn.

He picked up a different scent. Plastic, old vinyl. Moldy sheet rock.

The trailer.

James darted to his left, leapt over a felled tree as he made his way down toward the creek. He'd seen the place a few times during his full moon hunts. It wasn't far. He hoped the SCU didn't know about it, but he also knew Lacy didn't have time for him to second-guess himself as the first rays of sunlight spread across the sky above the trees. He heard the creek water running and saw the trailer ahead. It sat up on the embankment across the creek from him. He leapt across the eight-foot chasm easily, shouldered the rotted door open, and looked around. The side of the trailer with the kitchen and master bedroom had collapsed completely, but the living room floor was mostly intact. He eased Lacy down into a nearby corner, then pulled up the rotted plywood to reveal what was left of the crawl space beneath, the steel supports rusted and only about two feet from wet, black earth. He glanced back at her. She lay on the floor;her body covered in blood and now soaked in sweat as if she'd been caught in the rain. She started shivering as smoke began to slowly rise from her nude form. He picked her back up and gently lowered her into the hole, settling her onto the damp earth. She stared up at him as he picked up the sheet of plywood he'd removed, watching him as he placed it back over the hole, covering her up just as the sunlight began to shine in through the windows.

He barely heard her speaking from below.

"I'm sorry, Jimmy. I'm so sorry."

He squatted on top of the board, staring intently at the door as he growled. They would be there any second. They would realize he had only used the trailer to keep Lacy from burning up in the morning sun.

He wasn't trapping himself inside.

He was holding his ground. He would take as many of them down with him as he could before he let them get to Lacy.

He braced for combat, his eyes wild and muscles tense as he waited for the inevitable fight he likely would not win.

21

The late afternoon sun sent rays through the trees to sneak through the broken, mildewed windows of the dilapidated trailer in shafts of orange light. James didn't know how much time had passed since he'd tucked Lacy away into the crawl space, how long ago he'd come to the realization the final stand he was prepared to make wasn't going to happen, and the world disappeared into black the instant his adrenaline faded. He sat still on the floor just above where Lacy lay, carefully keeping his weight focused on where the steel joists would be as his senses searched the world. He berated himself for becoming a sitting duck and leaving Lacy unprotected.

Compounding the issue, without them, the SCU might decide Phillip was no longer useful. He had fought his eyes closing as wave after wave of exhaustion crashed against him, and he still had failed.

He stared through the disintegrated, half-open front door, watching the sun firing through the tree leaves, bathing the sky in pink hues, flickering into deep orange that would soon turn purple before fading to black. He smelled the heavy scent of mold, rotting wood and sheetrock, and dust from the trailer as well as the fresh scents wafting in from the outdoors. Nothing to cause him alarm.

Unable to stop it, he let his mind replay the raid on his home. The flash-bang grenade they'd used hurt Lacy to the point of almost killing her. How had they managed to weaponize literal *sunlight?* He hadn't thought twice about giving her some of his blood, remembering how quickly it had healed her on Westenra Island. She'd reacted with surprise when she'd had his blood, acting like she'd just taken a shot of some kind of energy drink or drug. She'd taken enough of his blood to stagger him, but it was nothing compared to what she'd taken today. She'd rendered him so weak that even the wolf had been blindsided and unable to step in.

Then she went feral and killed at least ten people that James could think of. Maybe less, maybe more. All the parts made it hard to count. He'd been too weak to pay much attention during the rush. All he knew was that the SCU would be after them both with a vengeance.

He didn't blame her, nor did he blame himself. She would've died if he hadn't let her feed. And they both may have died had she not killed those agents. Hoyt had said the SCU had ordered them to be taken alive. Yet the agents had fired at them with silver bullets and used a flash-bang grenade loaded with sunlight.

Why had Smith arrested Kimble? And why did he want James and Lacy dead? Who were the fake cops at the airport guarding the weapons shipment?

And how did Clifford factor into everything?

None of it made sense.

He stayed in wolf form as he stood, listening to the sounds around him and taking note of the scents in the air again. The wolf gave a low mewl and sent him an image of Lacy lying in the dirt below.

They don't know we're here, he thought to it. *They would have been here long before now.*

The wolf gave another worried whine. James couldn't blame his animal companion. He had run to the trailer as a last resort. He'd been ready to hide Lacy from the sun and make a last stand against the SCU, had waited at the ready for at least an hour. But there was nothing. No one had followed him. It was as if they'd *allowed* him and Lacy to escape.

More things making no sense.

He decided to take a look outside to make sure the area was secure. Lacy would be up soon. He had to keep low since the ceiling in the trailer was just seven feet tall, with some of it collapsing in. Moving, he saw an area in the living room close to the pile of rubble he had missed last night where the floor had caved completely in solidarity with the kitchen and master bedroom.

I'm surprised I didn't fall through the floor last night, he thought to himself. *Luck, I suppose.*

The wolf sent him an image of a morbidly obese dog lapping up beef gravy out of a water dish. James rolled his eyes. *You are aware that not every thought I have is open to or in need of interpretation or response from you, right?*

The animal gave him a big goofy grin as it panted its laughter at him.

James moved to all fours as he made his way through the front door and directly down to the damp, leaf-covered ground. The front steps had rotted away a long time ago, but the trailer was also sagging down enough that the drop was only about two feet. Nothing for a creature of his size, but a human being would have to put in more effort than if there were a proper set of stairs. He could hear the air as it moved through the trees overhead, the multi-colored leaves stubbornly hanging on to their branches, shaking, the noise musical and soothing. Autumn was his favorite time of year. It was the one time when the world had color, felt vibrant and alive. It soothed him, brought him memories of playing in huge piles of leaves and trick-or-treating when Halloween came around.

And, like most things in his life, it was fleeting. Summer tended to take too long to fade, and winter came quicker than it had any right to.

He moved to the center of the front clearing and straightened his arms, lowering his haunches into a sitting position, his ears perked as he took in his surroundings with his wolfen senses. His vision was only tinged with yellow, the sun still too high for his natural dark vision to be necessary. The scents were rich and vibrant as the yellows, oranges, browns, and reds saturated the world around him. Flora and fauna, mildew of damp earth and tree bark, the subtle smell of vanilla and blood from underneath the trailer where Lacy slept.

No cologne. No nylon or gun powder. No boots or gear squeaking against body armor. No whispered coordination and orders. Just the serenity of the woods at twilight as the sun stubbornly held onto its last, lowest point in the sky moments before it would be forced to surrender to dusk, fading away and taking its warm orange glow with it.

From mass shootings to a wrestling match, he'd managed to catch far more attention than he liked having. Things had been simpler for him before Wade Anderson had started up the murder spree that led to James galivanting all the way down the East Coast to take down a vampire-run crime empire. He'd lived alone, spent most of his time hanging out with Phillip or reading and keeping to himself whenever Phillip wasn't around. He didn't go out much, didn't even live in his childhood home, and his inheritance from his father was substantial enough to cover his bills for the rest of his life. He occasionally helped Phillip if a crime in the city was being committed by a supernatural being. It'd never been more than a blip on the radar, certainly not a network of criminals and politicians.

And yet, reflecting back on things, he realized the feeling he was having, the loneliness and boredom tugging at him, was all too familiar. Like he'd always felt as if he were standing outside looking in while the world burned in front of him.

James breathed out a long, heavy sigh accompanied by a low growl from deep within. He wasn't doing any good sitting there dwelling on his own shame. He needed a distraction, needed to function. He moved around the area on all fours as he searched for any sign of trouble. He picked up a few extra scents as he sniffed the ground, small woodland animals that searched for the last vestiges of food to hold them for the winter. A few deer had even wandered through, the scent causing the wolf to send him images of it tearing into a freshly hunted meal. He started to argue with it, but the sudden audible growling in his stomach stopped him.

You're right, he thought. *I need to eat. It won't do either of us any good to be malnourished. Especially after all the healing last night.*

The wolf yawned wide, causing James to do the same. He needed an energy boost.

Something moved in the brush, the crunch of leaves under hoof barely audible.

The hackles on his neck stood on end, his body tense as he froze in place, pushed aside everything in his mind as he focused on the spot where the noise had come from. Every muscle in his body was at the ready, held perfectly in place by his will. He could sense caution, even a little fear. He slowed his breathing, hunched down lower to both make himself less obvious and to ready himself for attack.

The buck peered out from behind the trailer, careful to survey the area. It was easily larger than most of the deer around, though not as big as it could be. South Carolina's overpopulation of deer resulted in smaller animals and an extended hunting season, as well as plenty of loopholes in hunting laws allowing for some population control. It sniffed the air, paused for a second, then stepped out fully and began to sniff the ground for food. James felt the hunger grow inside him. He stared hard at the buck as he calculated the right attack to take down his dinner. He could move in right now. His wolfen speed would allow him to put the buck down before it knew what hit it. It would be alive when he started to devour it, ripping meat from bone and letting the blood pour down his throat. It also meant he wouldn't have to hunt the creature, wouldn't have to leave Lacy completely unguarded.

The buck froze again, its head jerking up and its ears perked in full alert as it stared right at him. It shuddered, turned, and took off into the woods. The hunger intensified, causing him pain. He couldn't remember when he'd eaten last, either as a human *or* a wolf. The wolf sent him an image of himself in wolf form sitting at a table in a fancy restaurant while waiters dressed in tuxedos brought him platters of raw meat and filled his wine glass with a deep red merlot.

James licked his chops. *Then again, there is something to be said for fast food.*

The wolf gave an enthusiastic bark inside his mind, the scene changing to him riding on top of the Corvette Phillip had borrowed from Noble Jones while they were in Savannah as they sat next to the burger menu at a drive-thru.

He shot after the buck, banked right, and hit his wolfen speed to flank it. The buck made a panicked snort as it redirected, weaving in and out of the trees as it headed deeper into the thick woods. James did the maneuver again, this time guiding his prey back toward the trailer. The animal conceded, its hooves kicking up leaves and soil as it bolted in the direction James chose for it. He kept his pace slower on purpose, just enough to see the creature's movements and predict what it would do next as it attempted to zigzag through the woods, a prey's natural instinctive method of escape from a predator. He kept after his quarry easily, his mouth partly open as he took in the sweet pheromones of delirium caused by primal fear emanating from the animal. James and the wolf operated as one, the sensible and human awareness of time and caution blending with the feral yearning of the hunt. His blood flowed freely, fueling his muscles, the adrenaline recharging his exhausted body. He faked right again, the buck dodging him exactly as he'd planned as he guided the animal. It leapt over a fallen tree and landed squarely in the leaf-covered clearing in front of the dilapidated home. James sensed the small, fleeting sense of relief from the creature stymied by the overwhelming panic and wild terror consuming the animal's every breath and movement.

The instant of ease was all he needed to make it his prey's downfall.

He lunged, reached out, and landed on the buck with his hand on its back. He felt its spine snap as its body collapsed under his weight. The buck's pained bleating noise turned into a gurgling rattle as James locked his jaws onto the animal's neck, more bones and cartilage cracking and popping, muscle snapping and unraveling under his bite as blood, hot and sweet, splashed over the inside of his mouth, coated his tongue, and matted the fur on his face and neck. He kept his jaws locked as he yanked back. The sound of tearing meat and sinew sickened his human side, but caused his wolfen side's mouth to water more as he swallowed the blood flowing from the animal while he chewed hungrily on the hunk of flesh. The buck twitched and shivered on the ground as it bled out, the blood flow from the arteries in its open neck slowing as shock and blood loss worked to stop the creature's heartbeat. He knelt back down and tore a piece of the shoulder off with his jaws, chewing hungrily and going in for more, his stomach growling from hunger despite the meal he was taking in. The prey's struggles grew weaker by the second as James continued to eat. He held the buck down as he took another bite, his teeth grazing its spine, the body giving a slight jerk. Other than the small, automatic, mechanical reaction, his prey was dead and oblivious to the fact it had been reduced to being a meal.

He rolled the animal onto its back and tore the chest open, revealing the heart. The wolf panted hungrily inside, licked its own chops as its yearning caused James's own mouth to salivate as he pulled the heart free. He held it up, studied the motionless organ resting in his hand.

Werewolves didn't eat the heart for any kind of ritualistic reason. As he had explained, it was the most flavorful part of the prey. He'd eaten the hearts of deer plenty of times. It wasn't this uncontrollable urge. The wolf wanted it, but it wasn't a desperate need. He didn't sense a life-or-death urgency from his counterpart.

Yet Clifford has a thing for taking the hearts, he thought. *I don't get it. It's tasty. But so are pancakes.*

A quiet, feminine voice caught his attention. "Hey, can I get in on that?"

James looked up from his meal to see Lacy standing in the doorway of the trailer. He blinked, surprised at how he'd missed the sun setting while he'd been eating. *I guess I was that hungry.*

She was still nude, but the wounds she'd sustained the night before were healed. Her skin was perfect, showing no traces of the splashed blood or the soil that would've stuck to it while she slept in the dirt under the floor. But something about her was off. She was paler than usual, her eyes sunken and her features sallow. She was gaunt, her eyes focused on the deer, glowing blue with primal hunger.

James stood and moved toward her. He held the heart out to her and gave a small growl mixed with a low mewl in his throat. She smiled at him, put her hand over her chest. "Oh, Jimmy. I was wondering when you'd give me your heart."

He chuffed at her.

"You're right," she said. "Bad timing for that joke I guess." She took the heart from him, having to grab the large organ with both of her small hands. "Oh, it's warm! Good." She bit into it, smearing blood on her face and pouring it down her chest as she ate hungrily. She spoke around a mouthful of raw, bloody meat. "Oh my god, so *good!*"

James shifted to human form. "I believe this may be the first time I've seen you feed on something besides me."

She shrugged as she chewed. "I have a couple of sources around if I want human blood. But I love deer meat." Paused and pointed at herself. "Country girl." Her complexion was already starting to come back, the color returning to her skin and the dark circles fading from around her blue eyes already glowing more brilliantly than they had before. He watched her eat for a moment. She nodded at the trailer as she chewed. "Okay, I gotta know: Why the fuck is there an old trailer so close to your house?"

"We're right at the edge of the property," James said. "Probably a quarter mile or more from the house. My father put the trailer in when he first expanded as a place for the contractors to use as an office, however, it was abandoned shortly after he died. And, well, it is the Carolinas, so it stayed."

"Convenient," Lacy said.

James shrugged. "My mother let us use it as a fort when we were children."

"We?"

"Phillip and me."

"Ah, got it."

The memory of her going insane flashed in his mind, the people she tore apart, and the ecstasy on her face while she'd done it. "I believe we should talk about last night."

Lacy stopped eating, wiped her face with her forearm, blood smearing over her skin. She looked up at him, the glow fading from her eyes, her fangs retracting. Her tone was forlorn, sad. "I'm sorry, James," she said. "I didn't mean to go nuts. Your blood…"

He remembered when she'd drunk from him the first time, that evening on Westenra Island. She hadn't taken nearly as much. *"I said God damn,"* she breathed in his memory. *"I've never...holy* shit."

"You were dying," James said. "We'll deal with it."

She opened her mouth as if to speak, then closed it and turned away as she nodded. "Right. Yeah." She stood, dropped the last piece of the shared meal back into what was now an unrecognizable carcass. "Jimmy, we're in deep shit. The SCU is going to be all over us."

"They haven't so far," he said as he stood. "We aren't far from the Keep. If they were going to come after us, they would have already."

"Huh," Lacy said. "That *is* weird."

"Did you know any of them?"

"No," Lacy said. "Now that I think about it. I don't think so. But it's not unusual not to know everyone who works there. Especially if they're in a different department."

James sighed. "That is a fair point." He glanced around the area, listening for any sounds out of place. "We should get moving."

"Good idea," Lacy said. "Only one small problem: I'm naked."

"As am I."

"Right, but you can fix that by turning into Lassie and Donkey Kong's love child. Wanna take a guess what people will see when I'm all vamped out? Spoiler: a petite naked chick with fangs and a blood fetish. Not everyone is into that."

"I never thought you to be so modest."

"We have to be able to blend into a crowd on the fly just in case," she continued. "Which means you need clothes too. And our phones, unless the SCU took them." She stood and stretched her body, reaching her arms high above her head before letting them relax by her sides. She cocked her head to one side until James could hear a series of pops and clicks, then did the same on the other. "Not the comfiest place. Think I slept on my neck funny." She looked up at him. "When's the last time you slept?"

"Define the difference between sleep, being knocked out, and blacking out, and maybe I can answer you. Why?"

"You look like hell."

"I appreciate the compliment."

She waved off his sarcasm. "I'll go to the house and see what's up. You stay here and get some sleep."

He shook his head. "Phillip is out there, and Clint and Clifford both are still at large. We can't afford to rest right now. Especially with the SCU hunting us."

Lacy smiled and patted his head. "Sweetie, you look like you could sleep standing there. And a couple of hours isn't going to make or break anything." She turned away from him and made her way to the trailer, talking over her shoulder. "I can get in and out a lot easier than you, so get some rest."

The wolf barked in his mind, and filled him with a sense of warning as she entered the trailer. He blinked, tried to warn her to wait, then reached out to stop her just as the flooring gave way underneath her. She managed a shout as she disappeared back into the crawl space.

"*Fuck!*"

2 2

Sleep came quickly and unexpectedly. A full stomach after so long without food would do that. James couldn't remember when he'd curled up in the branches of the fallen tree he'd found nearby, the colored leaves mostly attached. He'd shifted, slept in wolf form in case of an ambush. He could feel the warmth of his thick, silvered fur keeping the night's chill at bay, and hear his own deep breathing accompanied by the occasional involuntary growl. The wolf was forward, present in his mind, keeping his senses alert. It hadn't been a deep slumber, not enough to make him unaware of his surroundings.

He hadn't dreamed, hadn't moved at all from the position he'd fallen asleep in. He wanted to go back to sleep, but his mind was already screaming at him about precious lost time. He had to get up, had to find Phillip. Had to make a plan on how they were going to bring down Clint and Clifford, how they were going to find out what the hell was going on with the SCU.

The to-do list kept growing longer and making him more tired despite the rest his body had forced on him.

He opened his eyes and peered out through the canopy of leaves and branches surrounding him. How long had he been out? Lacy had said she would be gone for half an hour, that she would be back by the time he woke. He didn't smell her around, however. Had he only dozed for a few minutes?

Realizations started hitting him like a punch in the gut. His home had been wrecked and was now a crime scene. He'd been forced into combat in public. It was a safe bet that the footage of a werewolf fighting vampires in the open during a mass shooting was all over the news. His home was compromised. His secret was out. Not even Hoyt could make something like that disappear. The Council of Night would probably also be looking for him. The last time they'd offered him his father's old position: the Knightwolf. He'd turned them down because he didn't want to be under anyone's control. With the recent events, they were likely not going to give him a choice. And then what?

Would it really be so bad? To have the protection of the Council of Night?

The wolf growled at him, giving him a sense of distrust toward the council.

I don't trust them, either, he thought to the beast. *But they would also have the resources we could use to find Phillip and end all of this.*

The wolf chuffed at him. He couldn't help but agree with it on a certain level. It meant giving up his freedom, his ability to choose whether or not to fight. Then again, had he ever had a choice? He couldn't think of any alternative to going after Mindy when she'd been taken by the traffickers, stopping Agatha from using an army of the dead to take down the Council of Night, starting with Noble Jones. And the idea of walking away from Clint and Clifford seemed as far-fetched as expecting Phillip to give up his comic book collection and video games.

The wolf growled in his mind, forced a low growl in his own throat. His musings silenced themselves instantly as the scent of rot and blood mixed in with the mildew and soil smells of the woods. He glanced up at the sky, saw the clouds in his yellowed vision. If there were any humans nearby, they wouldn't be able to see anything at all. They were too far out from the city to see much light pollution, and the clouds were too heavy to allow any moonlight.

They would be easy fodder for the vampire that emerged from the trees on the other side of the clearing from him.

He steadied his glare at the youngling as it sniffed, its eyes glowing red and its mouth open to reveal its fangs. The woman crawled on the ground toward the remains of the buck he'd killed earlier, pausing every so often to look up at her surroundings and sniff the air before continuing forward. She appeared middle-aged, her body clothed in a torn skirt and a tattered blouse stained with blood. She sniffed at the dead animal, her feral grimace turning up in disgust as she moved past it and toward the trailer.

Younglings were freshly turned vampires, their human side still too shocked to take back any control over their feral urges. A youngling would typically be held by the vampire who turned them until they could regain their senses, locked away and fed like a pet until they were able to control themselves. It was why the human population outnumbered the vampire population so substantially. James remembered Lacy telling him that in Charleston.

He also remembered they had been used as foot soldiers to cause chaos to help cover up a vampire-operated crime syndicate.

The wolf sent him an image of the youngling he was watching breaking into a home and going after a family. He clenched his teeth together. Regardless of why the youngling was there, he couldn't let it go free. There was too much risk that it would do exactly what the wolf was imagining.

He thought back to the youngling he'd fought in Hilton Head before heading to Charleston. He remembered interrogating the thing, remembered it responding to him.

Depending on her state, she may be somewhat coherent, he thought to the wolf. *She may have information. Only one way to find out.*

He waited until the youngling had stepped up inside the trailer before slowly emerging from his hiding spot. He kept low, moved on all fours to the back side of the place, and hid in the shadows behind an old abandoned pickup truck ten feet or so from the back door. James could hear her moving around, her footsteps so quiet that human ears wouldn't detect the sound. She spoke, her voice rasped and guttural.

"I can smell you," she hissed. "I can hear your heartbeat, little doggy."

James growled low. *Then you should be able to hear this.* He pulled the wolf forward, leapt over the truck at wolfen speed, launching himself through the trailer's living room windows at the youngling. He plowed into her, grabbing her by the head and slamming her down through the rotten floorboards easily. She screamed as she sprang back at him from the new hole he'd made, her claws out and aimed for his throat. He grabbed her again, used her own momentum to put her through the wall behind him. He charged at her, went through the hole he'd made with her, and made it even larger as he pounced. She was on her feet, braced and ready as he closed in. She tried to grapple with him again, but he slammed his open palm into the side of her head and sent her flying off into the night. The body dropped to the ground seconds before it turned into dust. James stood over the pile, staring down at it in frustration.

Shit, he thought. *I need to pull my punches better.*

The wolf chuffed in agreement.

His hackles stood on end as the air filled with the stench of vampire again. He heard movement behind him, heard the wet and rasping breaths as he turned around to see four people standing on top of and around the trailer. A few more shuffled around inside, came to the hole, windows, and doorway. All of them were dressed in various styles of normal, human clothing. All of them had glowing red eyes, elongated fangs, and fingernails stretched out into claws.

All of them stared at him with predatory hunger.

James snarled back at them, baring his teeth in a vicious grin. *Oh looky,* he thought to the wolf, the beast also ready to attack. *Lots more to practice with. Shall we?*

The wolf licked its chops as if it were about to dine on a fresh kill.

The vampires on the roof descended on him, all of them rushing at once. He darted left, hit the ground, and rolled onto all fours as he moved out of the way to put some distance between himself and his attackers. They moved faster, slamming into him from different directions and holding on like parasites as they clambered and clawed at him, trying to get through his fur. He staggered under the force of six vampires on him, each of them wielding more strength than a normal human being as they held onto his arms, legs, waist, and shoulders.

He swung wildly, the vampires on his arms hanging on with everything they could muster as he smacked the one on his left into a nearby tree, the sound of its spine cracking mixed with a surprised yowl before it dusted. He swung his other arm and shook that vampire off. The vampire on his shoulders tried to bite him, his fur stopping the teeth, the thing's breath frenzied and rasped. He grabbed the vampire by the head and slammed it to the ground, the force embedding the undead thing into the dirt by several inches. It flinched one last time when James pulled the head free, tore it off, and tossed it into the trees.

He twisted his body, letting the weight of the vampires on his lower half pull him down. He curled his body forward into a roll, then extended out once his legs were over top of him. He let his lower body drop, the weight crushing vampire limbs and ribcages. One of the vampires underneath him dusted when his hip crushed its skull. The ones on his legs crawled up his body, their injuries healing quickly. One of them was male, looked like he was in his early twenties. The other was female and probably around the same age.

I did not consent to a threesome, he thought. He bucked, the movement catching both of them off guard, then rolled over and grabbed each by the head. He slammed them together, their skulls turning to jelly in his palms. Brain matter, blood, and pieces of skull shot from between his fingers and into dust before he could drop the two bodies to the dirt. He stood in place, braced and ready for another onslaught in case there were more, his breathing deep and steady as he took in the air through his nostrils and the sensory glands in his mouth. He could still smell the vampire scent. He began to count on his fingers as he tallied up the numbers in his head. *The one on my shoulders, the two on my legs, the one on my waist...arms?*

He looked up from his hand at the sound of rustling in the brush. An older man stumbled out, his arm hanging loose where it had been dislocated from the shoulder, his hair caked in dirt, leaves in blood. It was only a second for James to realize the arm was held on by a few tendrils of muscle. It fell free, hit the ground with a wet thud, but the vampire didn't flinch as it made its way toward James, walking with a hobble indicating a broken leg.

They aren't particularly bright, James mused as the wolf growled inside. *At least they're determined.*

He readied himself for another attack, this time to take the hissing and rasping youngling's legs out. Once he made sure it couldn't escape, he'd see if it was lucid enough to answer questions. He bared his teeth, extended his claws. One good swipe would do it, snap a leg at the knee. He made ready to attack, but something held him up. He couldn't make himself move, couldn't attack. Even the wolf hesitated, urging him to hold his attack. Why wasn't the vamp healing? He had to have been turned recently. James remembered Lacy telling him once that newly turned vampires healed much more slowly at first, so it made some sense. He looked the thing up and down. The security guard uniform it wore was splashed with blood, but James could still make out the logo for the security firm, the name badge...

And the hospital ID.

He replayed the memories in his head before the wolf could get a chance, saw himself walk by the man who waved him and Lacy in to see Molly without looking up from his phone, the telltale sounds of Candy Crush breaking the quiet of the hospital lobby.

The security guard made to lunge at James, acting more like a zombie than a newly turned vampire. It stumbled, hobbling forward as it reached out with its still-attached arm. James didn't move, images of Molly in her hospital bed surging through his mind as his blood chilled, his skin broken out in gooseflesh under his fur.

The youngling took one more step before Lacy rushed in from behind, grabbed him by the head, and twisted. The head came free easily, and the body dropped to the ground and turned into dust. Lacy stepped back and brushed her hands off. "Damn, that was a fresh one. What the hell are younglings doing out here?" She paused, eyeing him. "Jimmy? You good? You look spooked."

James darted off into the woods, ignored her shouts at him to "hold up" and "what the hell!" Trees blurred by, soon giving way to the road as he tore down the empty highway toward town.

Toward the hospital.

The Women's Tower at Piedmont Medical stood tall, the lone beacon in the night, the low lighting in the parking lot and on the exterior giving an intentional sense of calm. Being at a hospital was stressful enough. Better to try to ease people before they even enter the building.

James's heart pounded, his chest tight and his shoulders tense, as he crouched in the small cemetery next to the tiny chapel sitting on hospital grounds. He pulled the wolf forward in his mind to the point of almost relinquishing control. His vision was enhanced, sharp as he scanned the tower from the ground up. Molly had been in a room facing the street. What floor?

He stopped trying to recall the small detail when he saw Agent Smith step into view in one of the windows.

James waited until Smith turned away, then darted from the cemetery at wolfen speed, moved through the parking lot, and leapt up onto the breezeway covering the patient drop-off loop in front. He pushed off again as soon as he hit the rooftop and hit the outer wall, using a nearby window as a handhold and kicking off again, catching the next one as he went. He did it over and over again until he reached the window he'd seen Smith at. He hung from the small handhold he'd found, his fingers aching at the strain but holding. The thick glass made it difficult; the voices inside were barely audible enough to hear them.

"I must say that I am not impressed, Agent Jackson," Smith was saying in his cool, arrogant tone. "You were placed here for a reason."

"I don't get it," Jackson said. "I literally just got here. She was gone before I even came in for my shift."

"Did you check the security logs?"

"Yeah," Jackson said. "The logs showed that she just walked out of here. Checked out and everything."

"But she did not, in fact, check out," Smith said. "According to the records at the nurse station, Miss Akter should be in here recovering from what was quite an extensive surgery."

"Yup," Jackson said. "And the security guard is missing too."

James peered around the edge of the window, saw Smith and Jackson standing at the foot of Molly's bed. It was empty, the covers casually folded over to the side. The rolling stand for her IV and EKG was still next to the bed and neatly packed up as if she'd been released. Nothing in the room looked out of place. Smith held an open folder in his hands, reading it over as he spoke to Jackson. "According to this report, she should not be up and around at all due to possible complications with her internal stitches."

"I tried to call it in to Kimble, but she isn't answering," Jackson said. "That's why I called you directly."

James saw Smith look up from the folder and raise an eyebrow. "I see." He closed the folder and handed it to Jackson. "I will have Dr. Blue check the security footage to see if we can determine exactly what happened here."

"Checked earlier," Jackson said. "Right before I called. Someone wiped it."

Smith nodded, his jaw muscles working as he clenched in frustration. "Very well. I will ask Dr. Blue to see what he can find out. He may be able to access something we cannot." He turned back at Jackson. "You will stay here in case Mr. Coldstone and Agent Faulkner show up." Smith started out the door.

"Want me to engage, or just call you?"

Smith stopped and spoke over his shoulder. "I'm sorry?"

"They're on our shit list, aren't they?" Jackson asked. "We're supposed to bring them in?"

Smith gave him a thoughtful look. "Just observe and report. Do not engage."

"Yes, sir."

Smith left the room. Jackson's cheeks puffed out as he let out a visible sigh, the sound too low for James to hear through the thick glass. He pulled his phone out of his pocket. James couldn't see what was on the screen before Jackson held it up to his ear. "Hey, we need to talk about something real quick." He turned and left the room, leaving James out of earshot and distracted.

Molly. They got Molly.

23

James made his way back down the tower, using the effort to keep himself more focused on not losing his grip and less focused on Molly being taken. He kicked off and dropped the last fifteen feet, landing easily. He headed back toward the small church, his mind racing as he went.

They took Phillip; now they had Molly. There was no doubt in his mind that they were targeting him, jerking him around. Was that what all of this was about? Some kind of vendetta against him? What had he done? And to whom?

The wolf made a derisive noise in his mind.

That's fair, he thought back to the wolf. The list of people and things he'd pissed off in the past few months was long enough to fill a phonebook. Even though he'd killed a good many of them, there were others out there who probably wanted him dead by any means necessary.

But would they cause a series of mass shootings on top of a series of copycat murders to stir up Wolf-Man hysteria? It seemed like something Wile E. Coyote would do to catch the Roadrunner rather than the simplicity of just hiring someone to shoot him with a silver bullet.

It didn't make sense.

It would make more sense that they aren't happy with me snooping around, he thought to the wolf as he continued toward the church. Clint knew who he was, and so did Clifford. It was possible they *were* coordinating against him, trying to stop him. They hadn't expected James and his friends to show up at the airport.

Stopping in front of the church, James felt a knot in his stomach like a gut punch and sat down, shifting into human form and moving into the darkest corner of the front stoop to hide. His heart pounded, his breathing made more laborious by the tightening in his chest as his memories of every encounter with Clint resurfaced and ran like a montage on loop.

He'd never wondered where his family's wealth had come from. He'd never cared enough to worry about it other than knowing it hadn't been good. He stayed as detached from it as possible. There were provisions in David's will prohibiting James and his mother from doing anything with the fortune. They couldn't donate it to charities, gift large sums to individuals, nothing. They could spend it on whatever they wanted, but only up to the specific monthly amount deposited in the bank account. Any violation of those terms would result in access being cut off completely, the money retrieved from the out-of-terms party via massive lawsuits intended to do nothing more than destroy whatever charity or organization the money went to, and that was where the landslide would start.

As long as Coldstone Keep stood, David Coldstone's billions would be the chains keeping his family under his control, even after death.

All built on a mountain of victims in a sea of blood.

The idea that David Coldstone had possibly amassed his wealth in the illegal arms trade made James physically nauseous.

The growing fury forced a tear down his cheek, his body reacting to the disgust at his own bloodline. He was the last Coldstone. If he died, the bloodline would end. There would be nothing left of his father's legacy. The estate would be handed over to the state for auction. No one would have a Coldstone to pursue for one reason or another. The Council wouldn't have a potential Knightwolf. The people who had Phillip and Molly wouldn't need them anymore.

And likely kill them.

And then what? It wasn't about him. The arms traders weren't killing people because of him. Clifford wasn't murdering witches and whoever else got in his way because of him. He would die, and they would be back in operation with no one even close to stopping them.

In that moment, James Coldstone wanted to die. The bitterness he felt wasn't from feeling hopeless and tired, but because he knew he had to live.

He let out a long, slow breath as he heard Lacy's voice whisper to him from out in the cemetery.

"Jimmy? You okay?"

James pushed his thoughts aside and looked out from his hiding spot in the doorway. "Outside of being nude in fairly cold weather, I'm fine." He saw her emerge from behind one of the larger headstones and make her way toward the building. She wore a new Hello Kitty shirt and denim shorts, and she had a backpack slung over one shoulder. Her sneakers barely made any sound as she approached.

"I was wondering," she said as she unshouldered the backpack and tossed it to him. "You kinda took off there. Figured you came this way when you recognized the guy I took out back at our hidey-hole."

James caught the backpack easily, opened it, and began to dress. "They have Molly."

"Shit," Lacy said. "You're sure?"

"Smith was just up there." James finished dressing and handed the empty satchel back to her. He explained to her what he'd seen and heard through the window.

"Damn," Lacy said with a sigh. "Okay, now what?"

"Were you able to retrieve our phones?"

"Yeah." She motioned at her clothes. "And I took a shower. Felt gross. The Keep was completely empty, which is weird because they didn't leave someone there to guard the place." She pulled her phone out. "Hoyt sent me a few texts. Said to come see him as soon as we can."

<hr>

Lacy had managed to retrieve her car from the airport as well, the vehicle surprisingly left untouched despite the airport being closed due to the heavy police presence while they investigated the fracas from the night before. They drove to Hoyt's and parked around behind the buildings, hiding the car behind a dumpster before they went inside the back entrance he'd left unlocked for them.

Hoyt looked up from his laptop and grinned. "I'm glad to see you guys," he said. "How're you holding up?"

"Molly has been taken," James said.

Hoyt nodded. "Yeah, I just got the report. Smith was on the scene personally, which is weird."

"Where is Ruby?"

"Got a call from one of the girls in her coven and left to go check on her."

"They also opened fire on us at Jimmy's place," Lacy said. "I thought you said they weren't there to kill us."

"They weren't," Hoyt said. "I've got the rosters of who was deployed out there, and they were all SCU agents."

"I killed twelve of them," Lacy said.

Hoyt nodded again. "I heard you raised a little hell, but no one saw exactly what happened since nobody from the SCU entered the house."

James raised an eyebrow. "I have several broken windows and a fair amount of damaged woodwork that would argue with you."

Hoyt typed rapidly on the keyboard. "Not according to the report. But they did say someone entered. Operation went from a capture to a rescue."

"Bullshit," Lacy said. "Hoyt, I saw them. They were wearing SCU uniforms and carrying SCU standard issue weapons. You can't exactly buy that shit off Amazon."

"And they used grenades loaded with sunlight," James said. "Which I would think is impossible."

Hoyt shrugged. "Nah. Flashbangs emit UV radiation, which is what causes vampires to burn." He typed on his keyboard. "Check this out."

The television screens on the wall lit up, all of them showing different documents. James walked over to the nearest one displaying a group of photos with names beside them. Everyone looked stoic, disciplined. Each had a pin on their collars with the FBI logo. James studied them, replayed the events in his mind. The wolf stepped in with its own memories to help sharpen his mental images.

James shook his head. "None of these people were in my house last night."

"Exactly," Hoyt said. "According to the report, the SCU showed up just as *another* group was breaking in. They called in reinforcements right away, but all they found was your handiwork. Ruby went to warn the rest of the witch covens in the area to get scarce, and she ran into a little bit of trouble with people dressed in SCU tactical gear as well."

Lacy slumped down onto a nearby stool, rubbed her face, then ran her hands through her hair. "What the *fuck* is going on?"

"Pretty simple," Hoyt said. "The SCU has been compromised. Smith cleared Kimble and released her. They called an all-hands-on-deck meeting, took attendance, and then locked down the office. No one in, no one out. Ruby left right before the order came through."

"Did they find anything?" James asked.

Hoyt nodded. "Yup. One guy there identified himself the instant Smith and Kimble made the announcement."

"He turned himself in?"

"Not really." Hoyt stood and walked over to the Meat Locker. He opened up one of the lockers and rolled the table out, the body on it still covered in a sheet. James could already smell the stench of burned meat and vinegar barely contained by the cover. Hoyt pulled a small jar of Vicks VapoRub out of his pocket, opened it, and used his finger to spread some on his upper lip before he handed it to James. "Helps with the smell."

"No, thank you," James said as he took it and passed it on to Lacy.

Hoyt shrugged. "Suit yourself, dude." He pulled the sheet back, and James had to swallow down a rush of bile as the stench intensified. The stench of burned human flesh was pungent, sweet and acrid at the same time, and mixed with the vinegar sourness. It was as if someone had used vomit to douse the flames on a burning animal. The body on the table was male, maybe the same age as James, if slightly younger.

It was the man's face that James couldn't look away from.

The mouth and cheeks were entirely gone, the meat blackened and melted away to expose decomposed teeth and jawbone. The throat was also burned and melted open to the point where the neckbones were exposed. The skin leading down his chest was discolored but not nearly as damaged as the face. The guy's stomach was a different story. James could see where the skin had opened into a hole, the flesh inside looking like it had been cooked.

Lacy audibly gagged behind him, her cursing muffled by what James assumed was her hand covering her mouth and nose.

"Holy *fuck*, Hoyt!"

"Guy up and drank a full bottle of fluoroantimonic acid," Hoyt said. "Watched the footage during the meeting. Craziest shit I've ever seen." He reached over to a nearby worktable and retrieved his tablet. He tapped on the screen a few times, then read from the report he'd pulled up on the screen. "This stuff can only be stored in either a Teflon-coated container or a bottle made out of PFA."

James stared at him. "I am not sure what that is."

"Oh," Hoyt said. "Sorry. Perfluoroalkoxy alkanes."

"I am still not sure what that is."

"Ah, no problem," Hoyt said, looking up from the tablet. "They're copolymers of tetrafluoroethylene and perfluroethers, pretty similar... to..." He trailed off as James just stared at him. "I'm not helping."

"I am going to need you to explain this to me as if you are explaining it to a small child."

Lacy moved up beside him. "Use smaller words, sweetie. We've had a rough week."

"Heard," Hoyt said. "The stuff our friend the Incredible Melting Man drank can't be stored in any old plastic or glass container because the acid is strong enough to eat through all of that. The bottle he had was made out of the PFA I told you about, which is a type of plastic." He motioned to the body. "Our guy here took down an eight-ounce bottle of the shit right there in the main office of the SCU." Hoyt shuddered. "I'm glad the security footage doesn't have audio. I can only imagine the noises he made."

"I can assure you they were quite unpleasant."

James and Lacy both wheeled around and glared at Agent Smith, who stood in the doorway of the lab smiling with his hands in his pockets. Kimble stood next to him, holding her finger to her nose. She looked at Lacy and motioned at the Vicks container in Lacy's hands. "You mind?"

Lacy tossed her the container as James clenched his fists. "I'm guessing this is the part where you try to arrest me?"

Smith's expression didn't falter. "What is it they say in the movies?" His accent changed from his usual British purr to a barking Transatlantic. "You'll neveh take me alive, coppah!" He chuckled before he spoke again, returning to his normal tone and accent. "I wanted to bring you in for questioning after your little stunt at the airport, but I was delayed by orders to have Agent Kimble arrested and detained." His eyes narrowed. "Orders that I did not give."

"It came down the chain from somewhere," Kimble said. She gave Smith what Phillip liked to call "side-eye."

Smith ignored her. "Still, I believe it is safe to assume that the SCU—"

"Has been compromised," James said, cutting him off. "As usual, we are ahead of you."

Smith's mouth twitched, but the smirk remained. "Do tell."

"I've smelled cedarwood at every single shooting," James said. "And Clifford showed up every time Clint was busy shooting the place up except for the one in the middle of Charlotte."

"Yes," Smith said. "Your antics in the middle of an extremely busy intersection in Uptown Charlotte have been documented." His eyes narrowed at James. "Widely."

"I'm still trying to figure out how no one got a clear shot of you when the shit hit the fan." Hoyt pointed at the largest of the televisions on the wall. James watched it silently replay the evening Clint shot up the block in front of the sculpture in the middle of the city. People ran in terror, scattered. He saw a blur shoot by the screen. The person taking the video spun, but all they managed to catch was James's hunched back as he protected an old man from the torrent of bullets that slammed into his fur, sending blood and bits of meat flying, the flesh healing as fast as it was damaged.

"It's ended up on some conspiracy theory sites, and I've managed to—"

"*Enough!*"

Hoyt and Lacy startled at Smith's loud, sharp tone. Kimble stepped back from him, her eyes wide. His expression had changed, his lips pursed in an angry frown, his eyes wide with anger. He moved closer to James, shouting as he went. "I'm curious, Mr. Coldstone: what part of the word 'secret' are you utterly incapable of understanding?" He stopped when he was face-to-face with James, their noses almost touching despite James being at least a solid inch taller. Smith lowered his voice from a shout, but his tone dripped with disgust. "You show up on my doorstep as it were, and you and your idiot best friend manage to fuck things up so spectacularly that I cannot even *begin* to cover for your sorry asses to the council."

"You threatened to expose me, then you fired us," James reminded him, his jaw set and his tone cool and clipped. "You also tried to kill us. And I would advise you to watch your mouth."

"Or what?" Smith raged, his face reddening. "You have no idea what you are dealing with, little *pup.*"

Lacy stepped in between them with her hands out. "Okay, dial back the testosterone, you two." She looked up at James. "Down, boy." She turned her attention to Smith. "With all due respect, sir: You sent me to Savannah to babysit those two. Then you showed up there when they arrested Noble Jones."

James kept his glare locked on Smith, who returned the stare with the same amount of venom. "Then terminated an employment that was forced on me under the threat of doxing."

Smith didn't break his stance, his expression, or his stare as he spoke.

"Mr. Coldstone, I did not meet you until the Fillmore shooting. I learned of your employment through an email, and I was told that you both were hired directly by the council."

The only sound in the room was the low thrum of the coolers where Hoyt kept the bodies and the occasional beep from the laptop signaling a new email's arrival. He kept glaring at Smith, searching for any indication that the agent was joking. Smith had never been the type to rib or trade banter. In fact, Phillip often joked he planned on buying Agent Smith a personality for Christmas.

"Shit," Hoyt said, rubbing his forehead. "Okay, that explains a lot." He turned away and went over to his laptop, where he began typing furiously. The screens on the wall changed, each one pulling up different articles. It didn't take James long to notice the common word they all shared.

"What are we looking at, Dr. Blue?" Smith said.

"I explained it to James earlier, but what you just told me makes it way worse."

"In a situation where the darkest department of the FBI has been infiltrated by persons unknown and the one person who was caught decided to drink the most corrosive acid in the world rather than face incarceration, I find it highly unlikely that things could be any worse."

Hoyt looked up from the laptop. "Based on what you just told me, I know exactly what we're dealing with."

"A skinwalker," James said. "You've already explained this."

"Then you'll remember that skinwalkers take the form of whoever they kill by eating the face."

"Right," James said. "Yet Smith is still alive."

"Which means we're dealing with a skinwalker someone created."

"I am going to need clarification."

"Okay," Hoyt said, stepping away from the laptop and holding his hands up. "So, there are two types of copycats out there. You know about skinwalkers, the other is the *Winyan Nupa.*"

"Bless you."

"It's Sioux for Two-Face." Hoyt returned to his laptop, blowing up an image on one of the screens. The pic was a crude sketch of a Native woman in rags with two faces, one on the front of her head and the other on the back. Her stomach was distended as if she were somewhere between pregnant and obese, and her arms and legs were muscular and twisted. "In lore, it's a cannibalistic ogress the elders would tell stories about to scare the kids into acting right."

"Of course," Lacy said, rolling her eyes. "Why wouldn't it be yet *another* myth that turned out to be real?"

"I'm not sure I follow," James said.

"It's the same word the Lakota used for a doppelganger," Hoyt said. "It's something that can mirror you almost to perfection."

"But it doesn't need to kill its victim?"

"Nah," Hoyt said. "Think of the Winyun Nupa as the best mimic ever. All they have to do is see you, and it's a done deal. They hear you talk, bonus. But they're limited to one at a time. Their ability to copy you only goes for as long as their memory."

"Meaning that our unsub would have to have been in the SCU for an extended period," Smith said.

James turned his attention to Smith. "Have you had any newcomers recently besides myself and Phillip?"

"Not that I am fully aware of," Smith said. "I sent Agent Faulkner to Charleston once she made it clear to me that she would go to her great-grand-niece's rescue regardless of orders to stay away. I saw an opportunity to track down and make our case against Wangenheim."

"Give me a minute, and I can check the database," Kimble said as she pulled her tablet out of her handbag. "I'm pretty sure the BAU brought on someone new that week."

"BAU?" James asked.

"Behavioral Analysis Unit," Lacy said.

"Ah, right. I remember now."

"Here we go," Kimble said. "Looks like the BAU got a guy two days before Agent Faulkner deployed to Charleston. Intern, Robert Booth. Graduated from the University of North Carolina with a degree in Criminal Psychology and Law Enforcement." She turned to Hoyt. "Just sent it to you so you can put it up on the big screen."

Hoyt nodded and typed on his laptop. The largest screen on the wall suddenly displayed a dossier with a photo of a guy James had never seen before. He had long hair pulled back behind his ears, which made his clean-shaven face appear even more round.

"I remember him," Smith said, crossing his arms and giving the young man in the photo his reptilian glare. "He had a particular interest in our division."

James raised an eyebrow. "I thought the SCU was top secret?"

"According to the FBI, we are an elite division dealing in White Collar crimes, primarily fraud and embezzlement on the corporate and Federal levels." Smith took a few steps closer to the monitor. "Mr. Booth was more interested in our work despite his initial placement with the BAU."

"Interns are just there for the credits," Kimble said. "The directors don't usually hand-pick interns since all the kids do is shadow and take notes so they can get credit hours toward their field experience. And they are *heavily* monitored. It's not like on TV where these kids end up in serious situations. Usually, they're sitting around the office taking notes and asking questions."

"So why does he stand out?" James asked.

"Because he became interested in us when we had a case overlapping with the BAU," Smith said. "A CEO killed his own wife after she found out he was embezzling money. As it turns out, he was one of Wangenheim's regular customers."

"Gross," Lacy said.

"Well, what's even more gross is what he probably is now," Hoyt said. "A doppelganger can become a skinwalker via the Wendigo."

"Cannibalism," Smith said. He looked at James. "For the slower ones in class."

"Cannibalism fucks up your mind," Hoyt continued. "And it alters your body chemistry because of the damage it does to your spirit. Once the Wendigo takes hold, it transforms you. That's what the Navajo warned the other tribes about back in the day, whenever it came to mimicry. Go too far, and you end up past the point of no return."

"Could he still change into other people?" Lacy asked. "Since he was a doppelganger before?"

Hoyt shrugged. "Possible, but limited. Maybe for a few minutes at the most."

Kimble cursed under her breath. "Long enough to impersonate someone who can send out orders via text message. Great."

James rubbed the stubble on his chin as he glared at Booth's photo. Clint was at the hangar that night at the airport, working with the people who were handling the shipment of weapons. There was no doubt he was part of the operation. And it made sense that he and Booth were one and the same.

And he'd sent his group along with the SCU to kill James at his own home. Booth wouldn't have done so if James and his friends weren't too close for comfort. What could happen if the whistle got blown? It had to be worth something major for one of them to actually kill himself in the most horrible way imaginable after being caught.

And they had to know James and Lacy had escaped. That was why they'd taken Molly.

To get his attention.

"Pretty safe to say they've got the inside scoop," Hoyt was saying as James let his thoughts swirl.

"Not for long," Smith said. "We should have the rest of them identified in the next hour." His phone chimed in his pocket. He pulled it out, his brow knitting as he stared at the screen with what James could only describe as a mix of confusion and surprise. He quickly returned to his usual stoic, pompous expression as he looked up at James. "Interesting."

"Are they still concerned about the extended warranty on your vehicle?"

Lacy snorted at the joke, but Smith didn't react at all other than speaking in his formal, professional tone.

"The Council of Night would like a word."

24

The wolf paced back and forth in James's mind, growling and whining, its anxiety emanating out into James's own consciousness and causing his body to react. His chest was heavy, his shoulders tense and rigid.

Something was off.

"That's random," Kimble said.

"Indeed," Smith said as he put the phone back into his suit pocket. "The council has been on lockdown ever since we discovered the breach at the SCU."

"I'm sure last night's bullshit is already on record," Lacy said, turning her attention to James. "We did a lot of damage at the airport."

"It is not," Smith said. "The local law enforcement already sent us the reports, and we have worked with our usual contacts to keep the story contained."

"Even the bad guys know to keep shit that goes bump in the night quiet," Hoyt said. "They don't wanna deal with public scrutiny any more than we do." He did some typing on his laptop and pulled up security footage from multiple cameras on the different screens in the lab. The chambers were empty, though the fires in the sconces and braziers around the chambers and main hall burned bright in the darkness. "Not seeing anything."

"Yet the fires are burning," James said.

"Always," Lacy said. "Kinda like security lighting."

"Fair enough."

"Dr. Blue," Smith said. "Are you able to investigate via astral projection?"

"Nope," Hoyt said. "Never been there, so I don't have a focal point."

Kimble took a step closer to the screen wall. "Speaking of security: where are they?"

James moved closer to the screens, studying each one as the others did the same. None of the doors were guarded, and the front desk where Lacy and he had checked in during their last visit to the council was also empty.

"I called in a full lockdown as soon as we figured out we were compromised," Kimble said. "There should be at least two people in full tactical gear at every damn door in that building."

"Would that not be a moot point if you were compromised?" James asked.

Kimble scowled. "We have contacts with the Charlotte-Meck police. Unless they were infiltrated as well, all they know is that they're to keep that building secure." She paused and pulled her phone out of her pocket. She cursed, slammed the device down onto the concrete floor, and stamped on it until the screen went blank. A small tendril of smoke emanated from the cracks.

James stared at her with a raised eyebrow. "I'm assuming the newer model is out?"

"Destroy your phones," Kimble said, ignoring him. "Right now."

Lacy pulled hers out of her pocket and snapped it in half with ease. She held her hand out to the others. "Gimme." James, Hoyt, and Smith handed her their phones. She snapped the devices in half one at a time, then threw the pieces into the garbage can.

"Smart," Hoyt said. "Hack the phones. These guys aren't kidding around."

James looked at the main screen again, staring at the camera footage of the main council chamber. The wolf bristled inside him, stood up in his mind, and began to pace around as it growled and licked its chops. It sent him images of Phillip and Molly alongside images of the members of the Council.

Of Ruby. And Clifford.

Lacy told him the SCU had traced things back to someone involved with the council. But not a member. *Never* a member. But what if it *was* a member? Tepes seemed the most likely. He ran the Council of Night, ran the largest and most powerful vampire house in the country. Of all the others, it would make the most sense that he would have the means to pull something off. The more James thought about it, the more it made sense. Tying it all to Tepes would be easy.

That was what bothered him the most.

Tepes didn't strike him as the type to have or want anything to do with chaos. Mass shootings were the definition of chaos. He couldn't see Tepes having much patience for a lack of planning and organization. In fact, Tepes struck James as the type of person who wouldn't even want *planned* and *organized* chaos. The risk of drawing attention was far too high, and the shootings were already hitting the news.

Noble Jones was a friend. As was Montoya. The wolf had stopped growling at the mere thought or mention of those two a while back. The wolf did *not* like Tepes.

Or…

"What can you tell me about Bathory?" James asked.

"She is an esteemed member of the Council of Night," Smith said immediately. "She is second in command to Master Tepes. Why?"

James turned to him. "And?"

Smith bristled. "And that is all you need. She, like the others, is a protected member of the Council of Night." He narrowed his eyes at James, scrutinizing him. "You are more human than canine, are you not?"

James clenched his jaw, pushed the wolf down as it growled at Smith, and started forward in his mind. He glared hard at Smith and spoke through gritted teeth. "If you are going to call my intelligence into question, I would ask that you not do so while protecting a politician for no other reason than their spot in the pecking order."

Hoyt spoke up from behind his laptop. "And Bathory is also known as 'The Blood Countess.'"

Smith closed his eyes, pursed his lips, and blew out a long sigh. "Thank you, Dr. Blue."

Hoyt nodded and winked at James. "No problem." He cleared his throat. "But that's just the surface. Keep digging, and the problems start to set in."

"Such as?" James asked.

"These vampires all have backgrounds from hell," Hoyt said. "But it's all documented through stories and anecdotes, which means lots of inconsistencies."

"Which means there's no real way to know their actual background," Lacy said, chiming in. "Depending on who tells the story, a vampire could be a wild animal or a pillar of the community. Or both."

James stared at the camera footage, watching the image shift as the camera moved back and forth, surveying the chamber. Something moved in the shadows. He stepped closer, staring hard in the darkest corner on the opposite side of the room where the camera was pointed as Phillip stepped out of the shadows. He looked around, then helped Molly out into the open and into one of the high-backed chairs at the table. She was still in her hospital gown, and her expression was both terrified and confused. Phillip said something to her, then walked around the room to the doors and tried pushing and pulling on them, only to find them locked. He cursed, then headed back over to Molly.

James looked over his shoulder at Smith. "I believe I know what my plans are this evening."

"It is a trap," Smith said. "Even you cannot be so idiotic that you can't see that."

"Don't underestimate my idiocy," James said, turning back to the screen. "I'm not seeing an alternative choice here."

"They have to know there are cameras in that space," Lacy said, moving up beside him. "They're luring you."

James kept his eyes on the screen. "It's working."

"You will not have support from the SCU," Smith said. James turned away from the monitor and faced him. "The unit has been compromised. We will have no way to reliably back you up."

"It could take hours to secure the agency," Kimble added. "Maybe even days."

"Besides," Smith said, his tone serious. "I am not certain you will do well without adult supervision."

Lacy stepped forward. "I'll go with him." She turned to James. "What's the plan?"

James spoke without pause. "We go in, break the doors down, get Phillip and Molly out of there, and kill anything in our way that tries to stop us."

Smith sighed and rubbed his brow. "Brilliant," he muttered. "I wish I could formulate such an intricate, effective strategy."

Lacy just stared at James. "That the best you got?"

"Simplicity can be a key to success."

"Oversimplification can get you killed."

"At least we won't be bored."

"Cappuccino?"

"I'll buy."

"I'll get the car."

Lacy decided it would be best to park her car at the Arrowood Road station and take the train in. "Parking is going to make things more complicated," she'd said as she guided the Mini Cooper off the interstate and down the exit ramp. "We'll get there a lot faster by train." The light rail train was on its late-night transit, and James found himself and Lacy the only other passengers on board besides a group of three college-aged girls wearing expensive-looking cocktail dresses and heavy makeup, plus a man sitting a few seats down from them, dressed in an old trench coat and staring into his cell phone.

The wolf displayed the memory of seeing Phillip and Molly locked in the chamber, along with an uneasy feeling. *I am aware of the danger*, he thought back. *I don't care. I'm getting them out of there.*

Kimble's voice sounded over the earpiece he wore. "Checking in."

"We're here," Lacy said next to him in a low voice.

"Good," Kimble said. "Looks like Hoyt's got you on the GPS as well."

Smith had insisted they be in contact, and Hoyt hadn't helped by brandishing two earpieces from his desk drawer. "As I said before," Smith had said as James had given the earpiece a look of disgust. "You require adult supervision."

"These are on my own personal radio frequency," Hoyt said. "Just in case something like this comes up. Can't be too careful."

"I thought you said you wouldn't be able to provide support," James argued as he begrudgingly put the earbud in place.

"We cannot," Smith said with a grin. "But I do enjoy a train wreck when I have the opportunity to watch one."

"Looks like you're three stops away from Epicenter," Hoyt said over the com as the train blew through a small tunnel and shot down the tracks toward the NoDa area.

"Got anything for us on the building?" Lacy asked.

"Yup," Hoyt said. "Place is empty, all doors are locked. Someone triggered the alarm there, but the signal to the authorities is cut. This is definitely a setup."

"Can you get in?"

"Maybe. There's a firewall that isn't supposed to be there that's keeping it from phoning out. Whoever's dicking around with it is almost as good as me." He paused. "Almost."

James sighed as he started pondering back and forth, picturing a variety of scenarios that involved breaking through the doors or windows and forcing their way to the top floor. Glass rained down over the lobby area as he crashed through the entryway in wolf form, his muscles larger than usual, rippling under his dense fur. He went over to the elevator and forced the doors open, stepped inside, and climbed up through the maintenance hatch to the top of the elevator car. He grabbed the steel cables with one hand and pulled Lacy close to him with the other. She looked up into his eyes and kissed his nose. "For luck," she said just before she grabbed onto him, buried her face into his chest, pressing herself close to him as if seeking comfort. He leaned out, bit the steel cable apart in one chomp, and held on tight as they shot up the elevator shaft.

The wolf gave him a derisive chuff that somehow drowned out the sound of the floors blurring by him and Lacy as the cable flung them upwards. The scenario melted away into the animal sitting alone in the dark, staring at James with its mouth closed and its head cocked to the side.

Yes, James thought. *I watch too many movies. But it could work.*

The wolf grunted at him and replayed the scenario up to the point where James bit the cable. Instead of it giving easily, the imaginary James let out a pained yelp as blood and broken teeth fell from his mouth onto the top of the cab, the cable unharmed.

Now you're just killing the fun.

The wolf grunted at him again, turned around, sat with its back to him, and lifted its tail slightly. He heard a loud fart echo in his mind.

I appreciate the effort, James thought to the beast. *It's just not the same.*

The wolf sent him an image of Phillip screaming at him. "You are just. Fucking…*stupid!*"

James smiled a little. *Much better.*

The train came to a stop at the bus station at Epicenter. He and Lacy disembarked, making their way into the bustling area. One of the bars had a live performance going, the song a cover of a classic rock tune he hadn't heard in years. The bassline was loud enough that James could feel it under his feet despite the unusually low number of people milling about. The tension in the air was tangible, heavy, and oppressive. People were afraid, and James couldn't blame them. Three mass shootings in as many nights and all within the same relative area was nothing to take lightly.

"Ladies," the singer bellowed over the PA system. "Let's give your gents a kiss!" He broke into another song as the couples around began to kiss and cheer. Lacy latched onto James and began to do the same, reaching up and kissing him passionately before moving to the side and speaking into his ear.

"Gotta blend in, Jimmy," she said. "This way." She pulled away, grabbed his hand, and tugged him in the direction of the escalator. They went past it, turned a corner, and made their way toward the glass entryway across the dark courtyard. Clusters of people huddled around on corners. James could see most of them smiling and laughing, though the sound was less joyful than it was manic and the smiles were forced and sometimes wavering. Eyes darted around, bodies were rigid, and the air reeked of panic and discomfort. The weight in the air made the music uncomfortable rather than uplifting.

James heard Lacy in his earpiece. "Hoyt, we're about ten feet away. What's up?"

"Oh, I'm in," Hoyt said.

"I'm guessing the other guy was not as good after all," James said.

"Hey, I said *almost*," Hoyt said. "I've got your route set up. Front doors, elevator, straight to the top."

"The place is empty, right?" Lacy asked.

"Supposedly," Hoyt said. "I'd probably still keep my eyes open."

James reached out, grasped the handle, and pushed the large glass door open. He let Lacy move past him, then followed her into the vast lobby. The lights were on, the marble bright in the room. James pulled the wolf forward to heighten his senses as they moved past the front kiosk, where there should have been a security guard. Lacy continued to the elevator, but James paused as the scent of blood caught his attention. He stepped closer to the kiosk, looked over the polished wood at the blood-spattered screen positioned below the countertop. He followed the trail of spray down to the pool of blood on the floor. He saw the source of the pool, the teeth behind the lower lip, the skin on the sides tattered and torn.

"Whatcha got?" Lacy asked as she stepped up next to him. "Oh *shit*."

"I believe that is someone's jaw."

Lacy glanced up and around. "Hoyt, do you have the security cameras still?"

"Yeah," Hoyt said over the com. "I don't know how I had them before, but yeah."

"They want us to see," James said, talking to Lacy over his shoulder. "It's part of the trap."

"Someone got their jaw torn off down here at the security desk," Lacy said. "Can you back up? See what happened?"

James heard Hoyt type on the other end. "No. It won't let me go back to anything before what we got on the feed earlier."

The wolf growled, sending James a sense of caution. "They're letting us know we're expected," he said to Lacy. "Reminding us that we're walking into a trap."

"And that we don't have a choice," Lacy said, looking back at him.

"Yeah," Hoyt said. "Or it could be that someone corrupted the shit out of all of the files on the drive your buddy Hoyt is logged into except for the ones we're watching like reruns on the Asshole Network."

James had a sinking feeling. It was too easy. He looked around at the brightly lit lobby. "Hoyt, can you turn the lights off, please?"

"You got it." The lobby went to darkness instantly, the lighting from outside barely enough to see by. James dug the earpiece out, handed it to Lacy, and shifted to wolf form.

The scent of cedarwood hit him before he was done changing.

He crouched down, sniffed around the security desk, then followed the scent to the elevator. Lacy was close behind him, her scent mixing in. He pushed the vanilla aside in his mind and focused hard on the cedarwood.

Clifford was here. Why?

Lacy spoke from behind. "Hoyt, we're at the elevator. Open, sesame. May as well use it while we can."

James could hear the tinny sound of Hoyt's voice coming from the earpiece he'd handed Lacy. The doors opened, and the dim lighting inside the elevator cab bright compared to the dark lobby. James stayed low and crept into the car with Lacy right behind him. He stood and shifted to human form as the doors closed behind them. Lacy held her hand to her ear and spoke. "Hoyt, I don't have a key fob. Can you get us moving?" The elevator began to move upwards on its own.

James spoke to Lacy. "Clifford is here."

Lacy's eyes widened slightly in alarm. "Well, shit. You sure?" She handed him his earpiece. He took it and put it back into his ear.

"Yes. His scent is all over the security desk." He paused. "And this elevator cab."

"Not seeing anything on the cameras," Hoyt said through the com.

"Why the hell would he be here?" Lacy asked.

"I have no idea," James said. "Other than it has something to do with Booth."

Hoyt spoke again. "Guys, I've searched all over the building, and I don't see shit. Phillip and Molly are still holed up in the council chambers, and I got Booth in one of the back offices just outside the chamber, but that's it." He paused. "Looks like he's on the phone."

"Clifford would be fairly difficult to miss," James said. He pulled the wolf back forward to enhance his sense of smell again. The cedarwood was strong, unmistakable. But where…

He looked up at the ceiling, his jaw set as his eyes stopped at the maintenance hatch. Lacy looked up as well, then put her hand to her ear and spoke. "Hoyt. Stop the elevator."

"You're already at the top floor," Hoyt said as the elevator came to a stop.

James took the earpiece back out, shifted to wolf form and moved slowly, his massive form taking up most of the space inside the cab. Lacy pressed against the back wall as he stared up at the hatch.

It wasn't latched.

He reached up and pushed it open. He could see upwards into the dark shaft, could see where the cables looped around the pullies at the top of the shaft, the anchorage point small from thirty feet away. *There's no way we're going through that hatch,* James thought to the wolf. *I'll have to do it as a human.* He shifted to human form and turned to Lacy. "Help me get up?"

She gave him a wry smile as she opened her mouth to speak. It was the last thing James saw before a massive, furry, clawed hand clamped down over his face.

25

The wolf was forward in his mind before he could think about calling on it. The hand slipped away when his face changed shape. He grabbed the wrist and yanked Clifford down through the ceiling and into the small elevator car. Clifford grappled onto James on the way and pulled him down with him, causing the cab to jar and shake. James swung blindly and yelped when claws raked across his chest and face. Clifford clamped his jaws down on James's shoulder, the pain of canine teeth scraping against wet bone nauseating. James yelped again, bucked, and rolled Clifford into the back wall just as Lacy leapt up out of the way. She shouted down to him from the top of the elevator car. "Get the doors open!"

He tried to stand and turn, but Clifford grabbed him and held him down. James drove his elbow into Clifford's face again and again, the last blow sending blood into the air along with a few teeth. James rolled onto his front, shook off Clifford's already weakened grip and made for the doors. He pulled them apart until there was enough of a gap for him to put his hands through and spread them. The doors caught and continued to open automatically as Clifford slammed into him from behind and rolled him into the lobby until James was on his back. James had his feet ready as Clifford positioned himself on top. He pushed Clifford off him, sending his enemy back into the elevator car in a heap. He was still flailing, trying to get to his feet, when the elevator dropped down the shaft in a free fall, the roar of the car speeding downwards shaking the floors. James heard screeching steel before it all stopped in what didn't quite sound like an impact.

He got to his feet as Lacy swung down from above and through the jammed doors into the lobby. She was breathing heavily, but otherwise she was unharmed. She looked down the shaft. James stepped up beside her and shifted into human form. "I don't think it hit the bottom."

"It didn't," she said. "Hoyt just told me. Emergency safety feature in case the braking system fails. But I'm sure that shit hurt like hell either way. Buys us time."

James turned away from the elevator door and made his way through the lobby toward the council chamber doors. The candelabras on the wall were lit, the flames casting shadows around the room, though the lighting was dimmer than they were during James's last visit. The doors were closed ahead, the carvings appearing more demonic in the low dancing light. He shifted back into wolf form, looking up at the ceiling with his wolfen vision at the mural of Dracula attacking the armies of humans, vampires, and werewolves with his own army of vampires and werewolves.

Something on Dracula's hand had caught his eye, but the ceiling was too far away to really make it out.

"What is it, Jimmy?" Lacy asked as she stepped up next to him. "Did Bacon fall down the well again?"

James ignored her as he stared harder at Dracula's hand.

At the gold ring on his finger.

"Jimmy," Lacy said, tugging at his arm. "Look."

He followed her stare and saw one of the large chamber doors open slightly. He could feel her tense up next to him as they both braced for another fight. The bite on his shoulder wasn't fully healed, but the pain wasn't terrible. He stood in place, waiting for whatever fight to come next.

He had to make himself not rush in when Phillip's voice called out from inside the dark chamber.

"Who's out there?"

James shifted into human form. "It's James and Lacy. Are you okay?"

"James?" Molly answered from the same direction Phillip's had come from. "What the hell is going on?!"

"Hey, we need some proof of life here, Bacon," Lacy said. "How do we know you're not the skinwalker?"

"Skinwalker?" Molly said.

"Come to the door," James said. "Let me see you."

"No problem, let me uncuff myself from this chair first," Phillip spat back. "Get your dumb ass in here!"

James turned to Lacy and nodded. "It's him." He walked up to the door, opened it wider, and entered the chamber. The torches on each column were lit, the warm orange light just enough for James to see Phillip and Molly sitting in chairs at the table. Their hands were cuffed behind the chairbacks, the position holding them in place. Molly's eyes widened as James approached. She blinked in confusion. "James, what is happening? And why are you nude?"

Lacy looked at him. "She doesn't know?"

"Hasn't come up," James said over his shoulder as he made his way to Phillip. "You have your keys?"

"Right side pocket," Phillip said. "Next to my car key."

James reached into Phillip's jacket and pulled out the keys, fiddling with them until he found a small handcuff key. He freed Phillip, then moved over to Molly and did the same. She jumped up and wrapped her arms around him, sobbing loudly. He pulled back from her. "Are you okay?"

She shook her head. "I'm fine. I mean, I'm healed. It's like the gunshot never happened."

The wolf raised alarms in his mind as he heard Lacy speak to Phillip.

"You just keep handcuff keys on you?"

"Yeah," Phillip said. "I was a cop. You tend to forget it's there after a while."

Lacy motioned at him. "*And* they let you keep your gun?"

Phillip shrugged. "I was knocked out up until about an hour ago, the room is solid concrete with oak doors reinforced with steel. Not like a gun's gonna do me much good anyway," he said. "I was just as surprised as you when I woke up with it still on me." He looked at James. "And you *had* to know this shit was a trap."

"Indeed," James said, moving away from Molly.

Phillip blinked. "Then what the hell are you doing barging in?"

James's ears twitched, the wolf standing tall on all fours in his mind as Clint's voice came from one of the dark corners of the chamber. "He didn't have a choice."

Phillip pulled his gun and took aim in the direction Clint's voice had come from. Lacy's eyes glowed bright blue, and James maneuvered himself to put Molly behind him as the wolf stepped forward in his mind. He pushed back against the creature, keeping it on the brink of causing him to shift. "Come out," he said, unable to keep the growl out of his voice. "This ends now."

Booth slowly emerged from the back corner opposite the room from them. He kept an assault rifle aimed at James as he grinned with Clint's face. "Hi."

James kept his demeanor calm and cool despite his urge to rush the skinwalker and try to tear him to pieces. "I'm guessing that rifle is loaded with silver bullets?"

Booth shrugged. "One or two. Just enough to put down a dumb mutt." He glanced past James. "Now that the gang is all here, we can settle this up."

"Us meddlin' kids aren't gonna go down easy," Phillip said as he released the safety on his gun.

"Why?" James asked, taking a step forward. "What is this all about?"

Booth shrugged. "Nothing personal. At least not on my end."

"So, you *are* working with someone."

Booth's smile widened. "Plead the fifth."

"Who?"

Booth held up a finger. "No, no, no," he said as if gently scolding an impatient child. "Not there yet."

"Why did you bring us here?" Lacy asked.

"My employer would like a word before you're not a problem for us anymore. Wants to feel you out." His gaze settled on Molly. "And meet the new blood."

James heard Molly speak behind him. "What does he mean? James, who are these people?"

"I'll fill you in later," James said over his shoulder.

Booth snorted. "Are you serious? She doesn't know?"

"Know what?" Molly asked.

"She doesn't need to know," James said to Booth. "She is not part of this."

"Oh, she's totally a part of this," Booth said. "Is now anyway. She's already taken the first step."

"First step in what?" Molly asked, her tone sharper. "All I know is that I was sleeping in my hospital room and woke up in the backseat of your car, you bastard." She moved up beside James and put her hand on her stomach. "And my injury is gone. How is that possible?"

Clint's skin lost its dark tone, fading into a much paler hue as the police uniform turned into a white coat. His hair grew out and turned shaggy, white, and sparse. Glasses appeared on his face, the lenses making his eyes seem much larger. It happened quickly, not unlike how James could shift into wolf form. He guessed it was less than a second before Clint was gone, and an older, gentle-looking doctor stood in his place, aiming an assault rifle at them. He gave a grin that would have been friendly, warm, and comforting under different circumstances.

Like if one were lying in a hospital bed healing from a gunshot wound, James thought.

"Oh," Molly said, the sound escaping her in a long, low groan. "Oh my god."

"Don't worry, Miss Akter," Booth said, his voice now higher in tone and cracking as if he'd been smoking for a while. He sounded less like a cop and more like a caring grandfather. "An infusion of vampire blood, and your injury will heal up before you know it." He shifted again, this time into the intern James saw in the photos at Hoyt's lab. He was small in stature, his collared shirt and blue jeans hanging off his lithe frame.

"Meet Robert Booth," James said. "Skinwalker."

"That's what you actually look like?" Phillip asked as he moved up next to James, his gun still aimed. "Hell, I'd wanna change into someone else too."

James saw Booth's eye twitch, his grin falter. He set his jaw as an idea hit him. "Indeed."

Phillip snorted. "Remember the one kid? Billy Conner?"

"The name is familiar."

"We called him Elmer."

Lacy stepped up to the opposite side of James from Phillip and next to Molly. "Please tell me you called him Elmer because he ate glue."

"By the bottle."

"That's amazing," Lacy said with a laugh. "Dude, your name is Elmer from now on."

"That's enough," Booth said in a sharp, frustrated tone like a young college student at his wits' end. He made a motion with the rifle as if to remind them he still had it aimed at them.

Interesting, James thought. The wolf chuffed and started panting as it sent a familiar, mischievous urge to him. James hated bullies. He'd been known to be the kid on the playground who would come running to the aid of someone being picked on or beaten up by bullies. He could tell

Booth had been the kid on the playground James would have rescued from painful wedgies and being ganged up on because he liked "nerdy" things.

He couldn't find any sympathy for Booth. He tried. He dug deep, thought about what Booth's childhood might have been like. But his thoughts quickly turned to memories of Molly in her hospital bed, to the old man he'd guarded while Booth had emptied a full magazine of ammunition into his back. What would drive someone to do such a thing?

James's chest tightened as the wolf growled, his body warm from the anger boiling inside. He didn't care about Booth. He couldn't find a way to wonder what drove him to madness. The screaming people, the deafening gunfire, the blood running from the victims on the ground in rivers.

Molly.

All she'd done was show up for her date with James. She hadn't even entered the building, and her decision to meet James had almost cost her life. He gritted his teeth, the smile fading as the wolf urged him to attack, urged him to kill in hatred.

He knew what made Booth tick. He knew how to get to him. It wasn't a matter of appealing to him, showing sympathy, or gaining trust.

James felt no regret at his conscious decision to tear his enemy down in every way.

"Ah, now I remember. Of course." He looked at Phillip. "Not the most well-put-together individual, considering his diet."

Phillip grinned, winked, and turned his attention back to Booth. "You do that shit, too, Booth? Eat glue?"

"He looks the type," Lacy said. "I'll bet he could suck a bottle dry in less than a minute."

"He's got the lips for it," Phillip said. "High-Speed GSLs."

"GSLs?"

"Glue-Suckin' Lips."

"Nice."

James watched as Booth's face started to redden, his jaw working as he shook with anger, the gun wavering but still pointed at them.

"Shut up," Booth snapped. "All three of you keep your damned mouths shut!" He waved the rifle at them again. "This thing is loaded, remember?"

James felt Molly trembling behind him, heard her pleading with him. "Please stop. He's going to shoot us."

"No," James said. "He won't."

"Fucking try me," Booth said with a slight waver in his voice.

"You would have already," James said, stepping forward out of Molly's grasp. "You've been instructed not to harm us."

Booth stammered, then closed his mouth and adjusted his aim, holding the rifle up and staring down the iron sights. "Says who?"

"Says your pattern," Phillip said. "You show up, shoot the place up without targeting anyone specific, then bolt out of there. Ain't nothin' stopping you from putting us down right here and now and walking away."

"But you'll do what you're told," James said, taking another step forward. "You always have."

Booth pointed the rifle specifically at him. "Shut the fuck up." He clicked the safety off on the rifle. "Motherfucker, I will *end* you!"

"I don't think you will. You wouldn't want to face the wrath of whoever is pulling your leash."

Booth's eyes were wide with rage and hatred. James took another step forward. "That's been your entire life, hasn't it?" James said. "Too afraid to stand up, bullied by those who recognized how weak you are. Of course, you could never let on that you are a doppelganger. It would add 'freak' to the long list of labels I am sure you carried."

Booth stared at him, his breathing growing quicker.

"That is why becoming a skinwalker was so appealing," James continued. "You could be someone else for a while. Not just look like them but also have their memories. *Be* them."

"Someone with a set of balls," Phillip said. "Hell, you even fucked that up. Clint actually had a spine."

James took one more step forward, the rifle only a few feet from his head. "Imagine how nice it would have been if the person who gave you the gift you have would have included some testicular fortitude."

Lacy piped up from behind him. "Means 'No Balls,' Elmer."

Booth lowered the rifle, turned his eyes down at the floor with a frown. He looked back up at James and grinned. "Well, you're half right. I'm not supposed to kill you." He shrugged. "I'm sure she won't mind you missing a kneecap."

James couldn't react fast enough. Booth moved with supernatural speed as he aimed, the motion so quick he might not have seen it had the wolf not been enhancing his senses.

It clicked in James's mind as soon as he saw the flash from the barrel, the ear-splitting gunshot inside the tall open chamber lasting a split second before agony sent him down to the floor, gripping his mangled knee.

The bullet had gone through, but he could still feel the fiery burn of silver, the wolf howling and wailing in pain as it also went down, its right knee matching James's. It felt it as well, the creature weak and maimed as it licked at the bloody mass where its kneecap had once been. He'd only ever been shot with silver when he was in wolfen form. The pain in his human form was nauseating, his arms seeming too heavy to move as he lay facing up at the ceiling. He heard Phillip shout his name alongside Molly's screaming. Booth was standing over him, the barrel of the rifle pressed against James's forehead.

"Son of a bitch," Lacy snarled at him.

"One move and I finish it," Booth said. "Got one more silver round in here, and it's got his fucking name on it." James saw him look up. "Means drop the fucking gun, asshole. As if it'll do you any good anyway."

James heard Phillip curse just before the clatter of a gun hitting the floor. He could hear Molly crying, sobs muffled as if she had her hand over her mouth. He couldn't turn his head. Too weak, too much pain. The silver didn't feel like it was spreading, but even the slightest movement sent new waves of pain radiating from what was left of his knee out to the rest of his body.

Lacy moved in a blur, crashing into Booth and tackling him to the floor. The attack caused him to fire, but the bullet went wide and buried itself in a column somewhere near the ceiling. Pieces of plaster and stone rained down, but all James could do was close his eyes as the debris fell and peppered his face and body. He heard Lacy grunt, heard Booth curse before Lacy let out a sharp yelp. The scuffling stopped, and James opened his eyes in time to see Lacy drop down onto the floor next to him, her eyes closed and her face slackened. A large bruise formed at her temple. Phillip shouted at Molly to get behind him, but James couldn't pinpoint what direction they were in.

He closed his eyes, tried to move only to be met with another wave of pain. A weight pressed down on his chest, hot breath on his face. No scent, no odor, just pressure. He opened his eyes to Booth sitting on top of him, straddling him. Booth was leaning down, his face inches from James's.

"You got me wrong," he said. "I spent a lot of time in trouble because I don't do what I'm told. But it's amazing what I'll do for a metric *shitload* of money." He grinned. "*And* power? I'll be anyone's bitch for what I'm getting off of this."

The wolf struggled inside, started dragging itself forward. James saw a greenish glow in Booth's eyes, saw the skin on his face ripple. He noticed the scars on either side of Booth's face, stretching from the corners of his mouth up his face like a permanent smile. Booth's teeth were sharp, jagged like rows of shark's teeth.

The wolf struggled forward, stopping when the pain became too much for both of them. His human body couldn't get rid of the silver like his wolfen form could, despite the bullet passing through. The wolf started to move forward again. He could feel its influence take him; his muscles slowly began to work. He pushed it back down to keep himself from shifting. The wolf radiated with panic and surprise. He sent his own urge back at it.

Trust.

James opened his eyes and focused them on Booth as he forced his voice to work, forced his mouth to form the words.

"You…are still a coward."

He punctuated the statement by spitting in Booth's face.

Booth didn't react, didn't flinch at the weak insult. There was barely any of James's saliva on his face. He grunted and moved his face another inch closer to James's. "She wants you alive long enough to make sure she watches you die." His grin stretched further, the scars on his cheeks splitting apart. Black fluid poured down his jaw and neck instead of blood, staining his shark-toothed grin that stretched literally from ear to ear. "I think I have a better way to prove I killed you. Always wanted to be rich." He paused. "I wonder if I'd be a werewolf, too?"

"Not how that works," James said.

Booth shrugged. "One way to find out."

26

Darkness has different levels, which most people don't understand and yet realize at the same time. There's darkness that your eyes can adjust to, the type where you can get around a room with minimal amounts of tripping and bumping into things. Then there's the blackness where a person literally holds their hand up to their face and still can't see it, no matter how long they've let their eyes "adjust." It's the perfect environment to give a person that brief instance of feeling helpless, lost, without any sense of direction. It is as close to being in the void as a person can get without actually being in the void. Other senses heighten quickly, particularly the sense of hearing.

Neither of those darknesses really mattered to James. Most supernaturals, werewolves and vampires included, could see in the dark. Granted, it was all saturated in a deep yellow in his particular case, but he could see just fine. It was helpful when he was hunting at night, or in those instances where a bad guy might try to get the drop on him, not realizing what they're dealing with. Not even night vision goggles had as much clarity.

It wasn't particularly helpful in his current situation. He hoped the other victims weren't alive for this, hoped that they didn't feel or see what was happening to them. It would've been horrific seeing Booth's maw open wide, the jaws expanding out far beyond his face as he lunged in. James felt the hot, black fluid drip onto his face and burn his skin before the inhumanly-sized mouth closed on him. The jagged teeth sank into the meat, tearing at the skin as the creature worked its teeth through, ripping flesh from the bone. James saw the inside of the skinwalker's mouth, the uvula in the back moving with every hot, rancid breath it took as the muscles worked to pull his face free. The tongue lapped over his mouth and eyes, taking in the blood flooding from the wound. The wolf struggled to move forward, mewling as it pleaded with James to release it.

He didn't let it go. He couldn't. Not yet. He couldn't let it retreat, either. It needed to stay right where it was.

Booth pulled back, and James felt his facial muscles slacken as they were torn free from his skull, heard the sick and wet tearing of meat as Booth pulled James's face off. James shivered, his body cold from the pain as Booth chewed hungrily, tendrils of bloody meat and skin hanging from his mouth. As he stood over James, his form grew even taller, skinnier, more skeletal than before. His clothing molded into his skin, blended in as if he hadn't been wearing any.

Blood filled James's eyes, burned. He tried to blink, but no eyelids came down to clear his vision. He tried to speak, but his lips would not work, would not form words. He tried again before he realized no lips covered his teeth. He felt his body grow even weaker, felt the wound from the silver bullet begin to numb as his face began to burn.

Booth was just a shape standing over him now, inhumanly tall and lithe, pale and featureless.

"I don't need guns," it rasped, its voice serpentine and wet. "I like them. But the taste of flesh, the chaos of fear," It made a gurgling noise, its shape swooning in James's blurred vision. "This is what I crave."

The wolf mewled weakly inside, its paws scraping at the surface it lay on as it tried to move forward. It sent dread to James, anger and betrayal. It blamed him, swore vengeance against him for his betrayal.

Trust me, he thought as his own body began to lock up and tremble from shock. *I won't let us die.*

The wolf sent him waves of doubt and disbelief. It mewled again, and James felt its cry to Fenrir, its plea for aid and protection.

The blood in his eyes was starting to dry, but he could still make out the skinwalker as it looked down at him. It shrank down slightly, its shoulders broadened, its arms and legs filled out. Dark hair grew on its head, its face changing and growing features as it went from the willowed form to a muscular, lean shape. He couldn't make out its facial features completely, couldn't tell the color of the eyes or how much stubble grew on its chin. He didn't need to.

He'd seen himself in the mirror enough times to know what he was looking at.

He felt his heart slow. His chest became heavier, making it harder to breathe. He pulled at the wolf in his mind, urged the creature forward. *Now! Do it now!*

The wolf's ears perked. It tried to get up, but its legs failed. It inched its way forward, its anger and hurt turning into relief and determination. He kept at it, refused to let up as he pulled at his companion. He couldn't close his eyes, couldn't shut away what he was seeing as his double stared down at him from above. Yet, his vision darkened. He heard Lacy next to him, felt movement as she moved, heard her scream his name. He heard Booth hit her again. He heard Phillip calling to him as well, cursing and pleading with him as gunshots sounded, bullets slamming into Booth with no effect.

James opened his eyes. Everything around him was dark. The floor beneath him was cold, black like solid onyx. He moved his head, glancing around wildly. Why wasn't his vision yellow? Where was he?

His eyes fell on the heap of silvered blue and gray fur nearby.

The wolf was huge, larger than any dog he'd ever seen. But it was frail, weak. It lay still, its breathing slow. He tried to speak to it but couldn't make words. He went to move but his body was too heavy, the pain too much.

Not like this, he thought.

The wolf moved its head slightly, its ears perking up as it faced him.

We're not done, James thought. It was everything in him to move his arm toward the wolf, reaching for it. The tips of his fingers brushed soft, thick fur. It blinked and gave off a small, confused whine. *The call*, James thought.

Fenrir. Hróðvitnir.

The Wolf God.

James made his body work, made himself shift closer as the wolf did the same. He ran his fingers into fur, buried them in until he could grab a handful and pull. He cried and the wolf cried out at the same time as he pulled the animal close to him and used all of his will to send it an urge. A command.

Do it!

Wolf felt the James pull it close, felt the James's heartbeat with its own, the steady thump slowing as its body clenched and cooled from the pain and loss of blood. But the James fought the darkness, the pain, and pushed it to call. It thought of Fenrir, thought of its days lost and locked away in the cage of Hróðvitnir's making. Not out of hatred for his son but for protection from the vengeance being wrought by Odin's army.

The wolf drew its will, felt the James doing the same as it let its voice come forward in its cry for help, for the grace of its father. The sound was weak, breathless. It felt the James do the same with a small, weakened groan. It pushed again, drug the call forward as it felt warmth slowly move in its body, fill its veins with new life, its muscles with renewed strength. It felt something grab it by the scruff and pull, dragging it forward just past the James. It felt the James's spirit entwining with its own, felt control come back as it rose to its feet. The James stood behind the Wolf and called to it to push harder, to save the Phillip and the Lacy, to think of the Kindred they protected from the *naaldlooshii* and its ally, what seemed like eons ago.

The James's body twitched, the muscles moving and shaping only slightly. The Wolf couldn't do it. Not alone. It turned to the James and barked. The James nodded without speaking, stepping forward until it stood with Wolf on even ground.

James felt the creature's heart beating with his own, the two organs seeming to beat as one in his own chest. Wolf pushed harder with its will, rearing its head back. James did likewise, his own heart beginning to race as he felt the bones in his physical form shift and move around, the agony lasting a brief second as the flesh on his face stretched over exposed bone that shaped and formed itself, teeth growing and sharpening, the warmth of thick fur pushing back the shock and cold. He felt his legs regain strength, felt his form grow as the call reached his throat. The wolf stayed its ground in his mind, stayed by his side as he rolled, shoved Booth away as he stood tall and reared his head back. The Sonic Howl was louder than he'd ever heard, the sound causing the stone accents and columns in the room to crack.

He let the howl go as he turned his eyes down at where Booth had fallen. The skinwalker stood and glared at him.

The other James was nude, just as James had been before he'd shifted. Blood ran freely from the skinwalker's ears. He swayed on his feet as he stared at James in disbelief. *"No,"* the other James, Booth, screamed at him. "You—"

James rushed him before he could finish the sentence. He grabbed

Booth by the head and slung him across the room. The *naaldlooshii* hit a column hard enough to smash in one side and hit the floor as chunks of concrete fell away. It recovered and snarled at him. James saw his own human face twist in feral rage, the fingernails on what resembled his own hands grow into talons. The visage rippled, wavered, an ill-fitted outfit on Booth's frame.

He can't shift, James thought. He pulled his mouth up into a canine grin. *Good to know.*

Booth rushed him, the move clumsy and drunken, but James ducked and swiped out with his own claws. Booth screamed in pain as he dropped, and James caught a glimpse of the gouges he'd raked into Booth's side, exposing his rib bones. James snatched Booth up by the head again, gripped it as he made ready to tear it off.

Something hit him hard, knocking him sideways, causing him to let go of Booth. He rolled over the kindling that had once been the conference table and stopped when he hit the large chair that Tepes had sat in the last time he was here. He rallied quickly, prepared to attack, then stopped as he watched Clifford lift Booth up by his neck. Booth's face shifted, blurred from James's face to someone else he'd never seen before. It changed to Booth's normal face, then Clint's before it blurred again, shapeless and featureless.

Clifford jerked him, slung him like a rag doll. James heard a distinctive, sickening crack before Booth went limp. Clifford smashed the body into the floor, leaned down, and tore Booth's chest open like a set of French doors. He buried his face into the chest cavity, slurping and chewing as blood sprayed up from the open ribcage. Clifford stood, soaked in blood, as he ran his tongue over his teeth and grinned at James. James stared back at him, taking in the powerful scent of cedarwood. He snarled at Clifford, challenged him. The other werewolf stood motionless, staring back at James without responding. James saw Lacy stir in the corner where Booth had tossed her, then she was quiet again. She was out cold.

"James," Phillip called out from the shadows. *"James!"*

The world was a blur as Clifford rushed in. The collision knocked the wind out of James, but he grappled his enemy anyway and twisted his body, using Clifford's own momentum to send him to the floor. James let go and rolled away to give himself a split second to catch his breath. Clifford recovered and pounced, rolling James over again. James braced his arms against the onslaught of jaws snapping in his face, and nipped at his cheek just under his eye. He retaliated, pounding his closed fist against his attacker's ribs until they gave with a loud cracking sound. Clifford yelped and reared back, giving James time to put his arm up as Clifford lunged back in for his throat. He felt the sharp teeth puncturing through fur and flesh before raking against bone. He reacted without thinking, jerking his arm upwards despite the pain. Clifford held on, his head forced upwards, and James sank his teeth into Clifford's neck and shoulder until hot, coppery blood filled his mouth. Clifford howled and yanked free, leaving tendrils of meat in James's mouth as he backpedaled away, his hand clamped over the wound.

James got to his feet, blood running freely from the wound in his arm. His hand was weak, the tendons and muscles torn and twitching as they slowly began to mend. The fur on his chin, neck, and chest was sticky and tacky from Clifford's drying blood. He clenched his fists, his injured right arm making it more of an effort to curl his fingers into a ball. He growled low, locked in on his opponent as he prepared to attack again.

Clifford slumped against the wall, one hand over the wound as he held the other up in defense, gesturing to James as if telling him to hold off. The wolf growled inside his mind. *No quarter*, James thought as he drew his mouth back and exposed his teeth.

Clifford was human in less than a second, the man nude and still holding the same pose he'd had before as blood continued to run from his wound. He was tall, had dark hair and chiseled features, though his hair was streaked with the silver that came with age. He was lean and muscular for an older man.

Familiar.

"James, wait! Stop!"

The air caught in his chest, his lungs locked up as his heart pounded. He took a step backward, caught off guard. He had heard Clifford speak, had understood the words, but he couldn't process them. His mind was a blur, memories flashing in front of him, times he'd spent with his mother while she showed him photos and told him stories of what had happened before he was born.

It wasn't possible. He was dead. She'd shot him with a silver bullet, had ended it. It was a trick. It had to be a trick. What now? More witches? Another necromancer?

He just stared, tried to comprehend what his eyes were seeing as David Coldstone stared back at him.

27

As a child, James often wondered what it would have been like to meet his father. What life would have been like had his mother not killed her husband when she'd found out what he really was.

As he'd grown older, he'd settled on what his reaction would be. His hatred had matured with the rest of him, made it easier to imagine himself shifting and tearing his father to pieces in revenge for the lives he'd taken, revenge for the legacy he'd saddled his own son with. He wouldn't care whether or not David held back, shifted into wolf form, or remained human. The end result would be the same: attacks fueled by blind rage until the body of David Coldstone lay on the floor of Coldstone Keep. And then James would burn the house to the ground with his father's remains inside. There would be nothing left.

Those words. Hatred. Rage. It was the two he kept close, kept hidden away from others in some weak attempt to keep his own bitterness from destroying him, from destroying his relationships.

He never realized those two words, those emotions, fueled him. Made him get out of bed when it was time. Drove him to protect innocent people from things like David Coldstone, Robert Booth.

Hatred. Rage.

It was when he'd been betrayed by those two words that he realized what had been driving him. Now they were pushed aside. He had questions swimming in the sea of emotions storming his consciousness. Uncertainty. Bewilderment. Shock. Grief. They overwhelmed him, overwhelmed the hatred and rage so familiar, yet those two familiar emotions rolled effortlessly with the rest of it. Not having them by themselves was different, leaving him feeling lost and confused as to what to do. His teeth clenched as the sound of his mother's voice in his mind brought forth a powerful emotion he could not push away. It settled in front of everything else, though the storm raged behind it, deafening and lonely.

Betrayal.

The wolf snarled, but James held it in place. He kept his thoughts to the animal simple.

Mine.

James growled as he took a step forward. He only stopped when another urge hit him. Not from the wolf, but from his own conscious.

Don't let on. Don't tell anyone. Never tell.

David stood firm, staring back at James as he spoke again. "Last warning, son. I don't want to have to hurt you." He paused, then glanced away for just a second before speaking again. "Or your friends."

Phillip stepped in front of James, stopping him. His gun was aimed at David. "Give it a shot, asshole." He clicked the safety off. "You're gonna start talking, or I let Scooby have his snack." He glanced up at James. "Turned around and something ran off with Molly. She was there and then she was fuckin' gone."

"You must be Phillip," David said.

"Good guess," Phillip said. "And you're Clifford the Big Furry Asshole. You got questions to answer."

David shook his head. "No time. Things are about to start, and I'm already behind."

"*What* is about to start?" Phillip asked. "Where did that thing take Molly?"

"My place," David said. "Big mixer. Meet you there?" He shifted and rushed in. James swept Phillip to the side, causing him to fire wildly, and took the blow as David tackled him to the floor. He tried to hang on, but David was off him and out the door. James got his feet under him and chased him into the lobby, but David had already gone down the elevator shaft.

"Fuck," Phillip shouted from inside the council chamber. "What the hell did he mean?"

James ignored the question and returned to the chamber to check on

Lacy. She was sitting up, rubbing her head and blinking. "Son of a bitch, that shit hurt. I haven't been knocked out cold in a while."

"Skinwalkers don't play," Phillip said as he stepped up next to them.

"What'd I miss?" Lacy asked.

"Booth is dead," James said.

"And something took off with Molly," Phillip added. "Straight up yanked her away and was gone so fast I couldn't even tell who or what it was. Clifford just ran off too."

James helped Lacy to her feet as she spoke. "Any idea where? We need to catch up to them now."

My place. That is what David had said. James knew where they'd taken Molly. He could smell something, the faint scent of rotted blood and…

It came together in his mind. He knew who was behind it. He mentally kicked himself for not seeing it before. They all smelled like that. But this one…

"He's going to Coldstone Keep."

Lacy looked up at him and nodded. "That's what he told you?"

"No," Phillip said, eyeing James. "He just said, 'My place.' What makes you so sure he's going there?"

"I can explain in detail later."

"Sweet," she said. "Road trip! Meet you at the car." She was gone before James could argue.

Phillip eyed the smashed elevator doors leading into the open shaft. "You took the stairs, right?"

***

As much as James wanted to run all the way to Rock Hill, he couldn't argue with Lacy's logic for taking her car. They needed to call Hoyt, Smith, and Kimble and let them know what was going on. There was no telling what was waiting for them at Coldstone Keep, and even if the SCU wasn't done vetting their people, any backup available would be handy. She was doing well over a hundred when they passed the Carowinds exit in Fort Mill, which was only possible due to the light traffic on I-77 at two in the morning. James hadn't bothered dressing, knowing he would just have to shift again when they got to the Keep. Lacy's tinted windows helped.

Hoyt had also made advance arrangements with the highway patrol to make sure no one bothered a certain Mini Cooper driving well over the speed limit.

"I can't believe you killed a skinwalker," Hoyt said over the speakers. Lacy had called him via a spare burner phone she kept in the glove box. "That's not an easy thing to do and live to tell about it."

"It was Clifford who killed him," James said. "I merely gave him the opportunity."

"You 'merely' let him chew your face off and damn near kill you," Phillip said from the backseat. "I thought you were dead."

"That makes sense," Hoyt said. "If he was still alive when the skinwalker ate his face, then shifting probably made it unstable for Booth."

"Glad to know there's a science to this shit," Phillip muttered.

"Nah," Hoyt said. "Totally 'woo-woo' stuff."

"It doesn't matter now," James said. "What matters is stopping whatever it is Clifford and company are planning."

"Well," Hoyt said. "If James is right, we'll be blind the minute you get to Coldstone Keep. There's no surveillance set up there. I'll be able to see your earbud locations and Lacy's car. Period."

"Where are Smith and Kimble?" Lacy asked.

"Back at the SCU, trying to finish up the vetting as fast as possible. They've found six more assholes in the mix. Two of them were able to opt out before they could be taken, but the rest were detained and locked up in holding cells. All of them had vials of fluoroantimonic acid on them."

"Anyone they can send for backup would be helpful," Lacy said. "We don't know what we're walking into."

Phillip tapped James on the shoulder. "Clifford acted like he knew you. You recognize him at all?"

James hadn't told Phillip and Lacy who Clifford really was. He'd never shown either of them a picture of David Coldstone and had only ever seen pictures his mother had shown him when he was a child. He'd burned everything once she'd died as part of his effort to delete his father from his life, short of burning the house down, which he hadn't been able to bring himself to do. Even though he hated the place, it was his childhood home.

There was no denying that his father was alive. As much as the revelation had rocked him, he had to keep it suppressed. Molly was in danger. The people responsible for half of the carnage over the past week were still above ground. He'd process it later.

Or just let it go. David Coldstone did not deserve his attention.

"He was likely tracking us the entire time," he said. "And our names are not exactly unique or hard to remember."

"I'll hit Smith up and see where they're at," Hoyt said. "If they can send you anyone, I'll let you know. In the meantime: don't do anything stupid."

"I believe that request was thrown out of the window when we knowingly walked into an obvious trap," James said.

"And when you crashed a televised pro-wrestling event," Phillip said.

James nodded. "Then there was the altercation we had with the SCU at Epicenter."

Phillip chuckled from the backseat. "Agent Squeaky Toy."

"Indeed," James said, also nodding. "Agent Squeaky Toy."

"Hoyt, you've met us before, right?" Lacy chimed in. "Tall ask, sweetie."

Hoyt laughed. "At least I can say I tried." The line went dead.

"By the way," Phillip asked, leaning forward from the backseat. "What the hell was that shit with Clint? Booth. Whatever."

James spoke over his shoulder. "As in?"

"As in I watched him chew your damn face off, and you damn near died on us." Phillip's voice had a somber tone behind the usual high-strung cadence.

"I remembered Hoyt saying that the skinwalker shifted into people who were dead," James said.

"And you took a chance that it was a law of the supernatural world and not a cause-and-effect result of the face-eating," Lacy said. "Big risk there, Jimmy. I'm glad it worked out."

"Me too," Phillip said, clapping James on the shoulder. "Just don't ever do that shit again."

Lacy laughed. "Aw, you two are so cute!" She pulled the car off the interstate onto the exit ramp and was speeding down Celenese in seconds and passing the few cars out as if they were standing still. One or two honked at them as they blew through red lights and intersections. James glanced at her and saw her eyes glowing slightly, a telltale sign she was using her vampiric reflexes to keep them from ending up in a wreck or ditch. "What's the plan?"

James stared out the window, recognizing the far end of Celenese as they headed into Newport. The wolf paced inside, eager and frantic.

David Coldstone. Alive. Stronger than he was simply because of his age and experience.

But Phillip and Lacy would also find out about David. They would want to help. The wolf sent back resistance to the idea. They could handle getting Molly. James wanted answers, and he couldn't do that if all three of them were there at once, all trying to fight the same fight.

He would handle his father himself.

He unbuckled his seatbelt.

"Jimmy?" Lacy asked as the car's seatbelt alarm sounded. "What the hell are you doing?"

"Get Molly," James said. "I will move ahead and keep Clifford busy."

"We don't even know who has her," Phillip said.

"Bathory," James said immediately. "I picked up her scent in the council chambers."

"Oh, *shit*," Lacy breathed at the same time Phillip clapped his hands and said, "Fucking. *Called* it!" James looked at Lacy, saw her rubbing her temple as if staving off a headache.

"I *told* you that bitch was evil," Phillip continued.

"Little bit more than that," Lacy said. "Story time: She's the one we've been looking at for our case at the SCU. Lots of weird money transfers to her accounts, but nothing that we could make a move on. We've been waiting on something to come along that we could pin on her, but her status makes her damn near immune."

"Why the hell would she take Molly?" Phillip asked.

"That I don't know," Lacy said. "The whole thing has been a cluster-fuck from day one between the shootings, the murders, and the arms shipments. But if she's the one behind the arms shipments, then that means she's connected to the shootings."

"Which means that Booth was working for her," James said.

"Still doesn't connect Clifford," Phillip said. "Seems like he's been acting on his own with the murders. But then he also knows what's going on with Molly, and that shit doesn't really add up with the whole arms dealing thing."

James grabbed his door handle. "There is one way to find out."

"Wait a damn minute," Phillip snapped, grabbing James by the shoul-der. "What the hell are you doing?"

James kept his tone casual. "I plan to jump from a moving vehicle, shift before I hit the ground at a roll, then sprint to the Keep ahead of you to barge in recklessly and keep the bad guys distracted while you two show up to rescue Molly and assist me if need be."

"Nice plan," Lacy said, not hiding the sarcasm. "I'll bet that took some effort."

James glanced over his shoulder at Phillip. Phillip stared back at him, then his expression softened a bit. "I know that look. Something you aren't telling us."

"And?"

"And there's no way we can stop you."

"Precisely."

Phillip let go of him and sat back. "Just don't forget to say Parkour."

"Excuse me?"

"Parkour," Phillip said as he pulled his gun and ejected the clip to check the rounds. "You're about to do some ninja shit. When you do stupid shit on an acrobatic level, you gotta say Parkour. Otherwise, it doesn't count. We've had this conversation before."

"Have we?"

"Yup."

"Then I will take your word for it and follow protocol." He glanced at Lacy, who was shaking her head. "He does have a point."

Lacy sighed. "You two are *so* fucking stupid."

He breathed, pushed the door open, and shouted, "Parkour!" as he dove from the car. He shifted before he hit the ground in a roll. Once he got his feet under him, he took off down the highway toward the Keep. He blew by the car easily, barely registering Phillip and Lacy's shouts as he passed. His focus was ahead, the wolf inside him panting and hungry as it pushed him harder, his speed increasing as he sped into the night.

He figured he had at least ten minutes before Lacy and Phillip caught up to him as he stopped at the end of the driveway where it turned into the garage. It would be enough time if he focused on one thing. Part of him felt guilty for being so willing and quick to push Molly to the back burner in terms of his priorities. But Bathory was using Molly to lure him in. She needed her captive alive until he showed up. Lacy and Phillip would be able to handle it while James went after his father.

Then it would all be over. And he would have some explaining to do.

He grunted, his wolfen way of chuckling, as the image of Ricky Ricardo played in his mind. *"Luuu-cyyyy! You got some 'splainin' to do!"*

Lacy would understand keeping secrets. She'd kept so many, and he still didn't know who she was, which made his feelings for her all the more complicated. Phillip would be a different story. His family life hadn't been an episode of whatever overly-complicated drama series was popular at the moment. Phillip wouldn't understand why James didn't tell him about David right away. He wouldn't understand why James had to face his father alone. He would accuse James of over-complicating things, of spiraling.

But it wasn't complicated. Not at all. His father was supposed to be dead. He wasn't. James would fix that. End of story, end of chaos.

Vengeance.

James had heard the warnings before, between therapists and Phillip. Vengeance was poison. It added fuel to the fire, which could make things worse for everyone involved. And it would leave a person hollow, without a sense of purpose, once it was all said and done.

He wanted to let the revelation of his father being alive give him pause, stop him in his tracks. He wanted it to confuse him, make him rethink his feelings, and how he would handle things. By all standards, it should have disrupted his entire life. It would make him feel normal. And it had at first, but briefly. The need to kill his father, take vengeance for a lifetime of pain and imprisonment, overtook everything. He would make David pay with his life.

And then what?

James shoved that question away. He had no answer for it. He didn't care to find one.

The wolf licked its chops in his mind as it pressed harder on him. It radiated hatred as it showed him an image of David standing in front of him. It flashed a photograph that Layla Coldstone had shown him when he was a child. Anger flared at the sight of her, fueling the white-hot rage for his father even more. If she had lied to him, it was because she had been forced to. James couldn't think of any other reason why she would have kept it a secret.

Another lock on the door to the cage built by his own father.

He heard something moving inside the house. The windows were still blown out from the raid. He moved around the garage toward the front of the house, keeping low as he crept up to the nearest window. He listened as Elizabet Bathory's Hungarian accent purred out from the dark interior.

"The hour is almost here."

Molly's tear-filled voice answered back. "What are you talking about?"

James sucked in a quick breath as he heard Ruby's cold, angry tone. "Three in the morning, sweet."

"The mockery of the Holy Trinity," Bathory explained. "When the dark has the most sway."

"I've told you already," Ruby said. "This ain't gonna go the way you think it is."

"I didn't ask your opinion," Bathory replied as if explaining a simple concept to a small child. "I told you that I would have the rest of the Daughters of Baba Yaga eliminated if you do not. Should I also explain the political ramifications of wiping the witch council off the map?"

I have to see what's going on, James thought to the wolf. He moved gently, slowly sitting up until he could just see over the windowsill and broken glass. A work light had been set up in the room next to where Molly sat in a wheelchair, her arms and legs tied to the chair and the wheels locked in place. She'd been stripped to her bra and panties. Ruby stood next to her, glaring at Bathory before dipping her finger in what looked like a mason jar of blood and drawing a symbol on Molly's chest resembling the others already covering her body. Bathory stood with her back to him, her arms crossed in front of her. She wore a blood red, form-fitting evening dress over her delicate figure. Her impossibly white skin glowed in the moonlight, contrasting against the deep red fabric.

Ruby spoke in a low voice to Molly. "I'm so sorry, honey."

"Then stop," Molly begged, tearing up again. "Please stop."

"I can't," Ruby said, shaking her head. "I want to, but I can't." She dipped her fingers in the blood again and finished the symbol on Molly's chest before moving down to add more to her thighs.

"How soon?" Bathory demanded.

"This takes time, hon," Ruby said in a sharp tone. "They gotta go on in a certain order in certain places."

"At least silence her. I tire of her sniveling."

Ruby apologized to Molly again, closed her eyes, and whispered something under her breath as she covered Molly's mouth with her hand. She pulled it away and continued painting the runes on her. Molly tried to speak, but no sound came out.

James sniffed the air. Cedarwood. David was around somewhere. Lacy and Phillip still hadn't pulled into the driveway. The wolf sent him a strong sense of alarm and warning, the message coming off as panicked and surprised. The cedarwood scent grew stronger. Molly sobbed again as Ruby stepped back from her. "It's done." She turned to Bathory, her expression furious and defiant. "Do whatever the hell you want. Either way, you'll burn in hell."

Bathory stepped toward Molly. "Thank you for your sacrifice."

Molly spat at her.

Bathory laughed and began to chant in Latin.

Phillip and Lacy would not make it in time. It hit James that time was up only a split second before he leapt through the window and charged at Bathory. She stopped and turned to face him.

She was smiling.

28

Bathory's smile barely registered in James's mind before David grappled him from behind and yanked him backwards, slamming him against the floor hard enough to split hardwood floors but not break through. James rolled himself out of David's grasp and kicked out, sending the other wolf across the room and through the double doors into the main hall. James got up and charged as David stood and readied for another attack.

His chin hit the floor mid-charge before he registered the pain from the blow to his head right above his eye. The room spun around him, his vision blurring in and out as a small hand gripped him by the jaw and lifted his head easily. He blinked a few times as he stared into Elizabet Bathory's deep red eyes.

"I was wondering when you would be here," she purred. "I was growing impatient." She swung her free hand around and slammed it into his muzzle. He felt a tooth dislodge as he fell sideways out of her grip, his mouth filling with blood. "I am over four hundred years old," she spat. "Did you *really* think I would be bested by some trust-fund mongrel with daddy issues?"

She delivered a savage kick to his stomach, causing him to buckle under the pain as his muscles knotted and his previous meals threatened to come back up. She grabbed him by the shoulder and jerked, the sound of his arm breaking free of the orbital socket his only warning of the new and white-hot agony over taking the blows she'd already delivered. The pain went all the way down his arm, across his shoulders, down his back. She dropped his arm, letting it fall limp as he snarled in pain. "I am stronger than you, little puppy. Stronger than your father. Stronger than your little vampire bitch who, I am certain, is close behind you." She leaned down to him, putting her mouth close to his ear as she whispered. "I am looking forward to her screams as I tear her apart. I will feast on your human friend. And you will watch." She stood and stepped back from him, smiling down at him as David Coldstone moved up beside her. He shifted into human form and stared down at James with a blank expression.

"I'm sorry, son," he said. "I don't have a choice on this." He knelt and placed his hand on his injured shoulder. "I need to think about a bigger picture than us."

The wolf lay on its side in his mind, its own injuries mimicking his. Healing would be slow. Injuries from another supernatural took longer. Even if he shifted to human form and back, the healing would only be half done.

But he needed answers. And he needed to stall.

James shifted into human form despite the wolf's protests. His arm remained dislocated, his head spinning. He could feel the bloody gap in his mouth where the tooth had once been. "Good to see you too, Dad," he said, his voice croaking from the pain and the air being kicked out of him. "And you are still an asshole."

David nodded and stood. "Not gonna try to make you understand, son."

"May I attempt?" Bathory said, stepping forward and standing over James. "After all, he is necessary for us to move forward."

"See, Dad?" James said. "It's easy to make your kid feel important. Maybe she and Mom could've given you notes."

Bathory gave a low chuckle and a small smile. "It's admirable that you find yourself able to make jokes when you are staring at death's door, Mr. Coldstone. I wonder if your wit will serve you upon my lord's return?"

James felt his stomach knot. The wolf flashed him a mental image of the mural from the Council of Night's outer chambers. He put his good arm underneath him and pushed until he was able to sit up and lie back against the wall underneath the window he'd jumped through. "I've never been one for religion. I may need you to speak in simpler terms."

"Of course," Bathory said. She moved over to where Molly sat, stepping past Ruby until she stood behind the wheelchair. "House Tepes has ruled our world with its wealth and power for ages, even before my time. No one has ever dared to defy him, challenge his authority." She ran her fingers gently over Molly's cheek. "Until now."

"Agatha," James said. "She worked for you?"

"For a time," Bathory said. "She was one of Ruby's witches before." She paused, leaning forward to Ruby, her tone condescending. "Am I correct, Ruby?" She reached out and placed a hand on Ruby's shoulder.

Ruby jerked away and spun on her. "She was," she said, her voice bitter and angry. "Until you corrupted her, turned her to necromancy."

"An art form that made her much more useful than before," Bathory said. "If it helps; I merely spoke with her on the matter. She did not need the coercion you believe was required for her to turn to dark magic."

"She was angry," Ruby said. "Her family had been killed by vampires."

"It wasn't Dracula's brand on her neck," James said, piecing it together. "Or Tepes's. It was yours."

Bathory nodded. "Indeed, our crests are similar. I can assure you that it is quite intentional. My family was tied with House Tepes for generations as allies. Until I saw them for what they really were, our houses were bonded."

"Which explains why you are part of the Council of Night," James said. "And now you want control of it?"

Bathory laughed. "Heavens, no! I do not wish to replace Tepes and rule the council. It is so much simpler than that. I am not interested in politics." She stood over Molly and rested her hands on her shoulders. Tears streamed down Molly's face from wide, frightened eyes staring sideways at long red nails resting against her bare skin. "I plan to destroy them. All of them."

Savannah suddenly made more sense. "Agatha wasn't sent to steal land. She was sent to kill Noble Jones."

"Very good," Bathory said. "I have another paying a visit to Montoya in Florida as we speak. But I will need something more if I am to face Vlad Tepes. He is over six hundred years old. Virtually invincible. And no one else would possess the strength even close to his." She grinned. "Except one."

"She plans to bring Dracula back," Ruby said as she pulled a cigarillo from inside her shawl. She lit it and took a drag. She turned her attention to Bathory, gesturing with her cigarillo and exhaling smoke as she spoke. "And good luck with that one, hon. Been tried, failed over and over again.

Most you'll get is that poor girl killed and a pissed off dark spirit you can't control."

"Not if I have a gift to give him," Bathory said.

Ruby shot her a look of skepticism. "What in the Sam Hell could you possibly give the Lord of Darkness?"

"Money," James said before Bathory could answer. "She is behind the arms dealing that we uncovered at the airport."

"I've made millions already," Bathory explained. "But it isn't enough. Not for what I mean to accomplish." She motioned at David. "Which is why I also have an alternative source."

James turned his eyes to his father. "You plan to hand her the family fortune?"

David nodded. "Billions, James. Have you ever actually looked at the accounts? Hundreds of billions of dollars just sitting there. The collected interest alone is worth more than she's made in arms dealing over the past year."

"And as I am still alive," James said. "And you are allegedly not; it cannot be touched."

"Ding," David said in a monotone calm. "We have a winner."

"Then why have Booth shoot up most of Charlotte?" James asked. "I would think you'd be more careful, considering how long this has been in the making."

"That one I can answer," Ruby said, glaring at Bathory and David as she puffed on her cigarillo again. "Skinwalkers are made, like I told you. She let me in on that shit before you got here. Had Agatha make Booth one, then sent him to Westenra Island to cause chaos and keep the SCU too preoccupied to worry about looking at her since they've been onto her for months." She turned and faced Bathory directly. "What you didn't count on was Booth losin' his damned mind, which Agatha would've warned you about before she even started. You thought you had control over him, and he went on a damn spree instead."

"At first, the shootings were a sufficient distraction," Bathory said. "But they became excessive, and we had to act."

"So, you sent dear-old-dad to handle him," James said, glaring at David. "And you couldn't help yourself. Which is why the killings started up again."

"Not at all," David said. "None of the people I have ever killed were random."

Ruby stamped her foot and shouted at David, her eyes wide with anger. "Every one of those witches you killed was one of my girls, you bastard!" She took an angry draw on the cigarillo and blew a massive cloud of smoke into the air. "Right from the start!"

What did that mean? James started to piece it all out. Every one of David Coldstone's victims had been witches. Most of them had dabbled in necromancy. How far back did it all go? Witches and vampires had been at war for generations. He remembered Alma from House Abercorn in Savannah, how offended and horrified she'd been at the suggestion of necromancy. Ruby had confirmed that it was a dark art that most witches avoided. Dark magic was poison to the soul.

Supernaturals were different from mortals, but they still shared one absolute commonality with humans: they were people. They had feelings, desires, motives. They were driven, resourceful, flawed. Human history was rife with people willing to put aside their own values if it meant survival, preservation of their kind and culture. The age-old question always lingered, regardless of whether a person was human or supernatural. Where was the line? How far would a person be willing to go to protect their world, their kind?

Themselves?

"The witch covens found a way to fight back against you," James said, looking up at Bathory. "They had a weapon you couldn't defend yourselves against, and they were willing to set aside their morals." He turned his gaze to David. "And you set out to stop them like a good dog."

Ruby grunted. "Like a treacherous piece of shit."

"The trap set for you at the council chambers had many purposes," Bathory continued. "To kill Booth and to make sure that my message is clear. Once the chamber is discovered in ruins, all will know that the Council of Night has fallen."

"And to lure me here," James said, not taking his eyes off his father. "To kill me."

"You got too close," David said. "You drew too much attention to Elizabet."

"Elizabet?" James replied. "Am I to assume that you are more involved than just a pet?" He turned back to Bathory, who suddenly seemed weaker than before. Her shoulders slumped slightly; her eyes sunken. David moved to her quickly, shifting into wolf form before offering his arm. She bit into him, drinking hungrily as she stared at James over her meal. "I see," he said.

"The blood on your girl is hers," Ruby said. "She had to use it for the ritual. It made her weak."

Bathory pulled away from David, who staggered and leaned against the wall while he waited for his strength to come back. "Werewolf blood is strongest," she said as she stood tall again, her color returning and her posture confident. "As it did with Agent Faulkner, too much of it can lead to Bloodrage. But just enough can make us stronger and more formidable instantly."

The wolf stood in his mind, shook itself off. It stretched and yawned, giving him a sense of refreshed energy. All he would need to do is shift, and all his wounds would be healed. It padded around a bit, then licked its chops and growled as it sprang forward to force a shift. He pushed it back. *Not yet,* he thought. *Lacy and Phillip should be here by now.* He looked over to Molly, saw her quietly screaming, her tears making the runes Ruby had drawn on her face run. Bathory waved Ruby aside and stood in front of the wheelchair. "Now," she said, interlacing her fingers and stretching her arms out to make her knuckles pop. "Where was I?"

"About to make a stupid-assed decision that'll get us all killed," Ruby said with a derisive grunt. "Including *your* skinny ass."

"I'm sure Lord Dracula will show the witches kindness once I explain your part in his coming," Bathory said. She shrugged. "Or not. What do they say? One way to find out!"

James caught a scent in the air. Blood and vanilla. Cologne.

"You've forgotten a small detail," he said loudly to get Bathory's attention.

She snarled at him over her shoulder. "Enough talk, mongrel."

"It *is* important."

"Be quiet."

"You probably will want to hear what I have to say."

She rounded on him. "*What!*"

James grinned at her. "Where there is darkness and injustice, he will be there."

Bathory blinked and looked at David. "What on earth is he talking about?"

David shook his head. "I have no idea."

He kept going. "He seeks out wrongs and protects the innocent."

David stared at him. "Please, son. For your own sake: shut the fuck up."

Ruby snorted. "Good luck with that one."

Bathory stormed over to James, reached down, and gripped him by the throat. She lifted him easily, her claws digging into his skin. "I can make him stop."

James felt her hand squeeze, his throat starting to close as he tried to take in air. The injuries in his human form still made it difficult for him to struggle. He heard David and Ruby both shout something, but his heartbeat in his ears was too loud to make it out. Bathory kissed his cheek and put her mouth close to his ear. "One less dumb dog to worry about."

The wolf rushed forward, his hearing enhanced the instant Phillip's shout sounded from the window. "Go, Team Super Wolf!" Gunshots rang out, and James was in wolf form just as Bathory took a round to the shoulder and one to the skull. She released James and staggered away only to be tackled to the floor by Lacy.

James rushed David, who had shifted back and was already coming at him. They collided, and James grabbed him and swung him to the floor as David held on, his jaws clamped on James's neck, and his head jerked at the meat. James yelped in pain and clawed blindly, his hands raking over David's face and causing more loud yelps and barks as his enemy released him and rolled away. James rushed again, this time going for his father's throat. David countered him, rolled him again, pinning him down and slashing at his face and shoulders with his claws before going in for another bite. James caught one of his arms and bit down on David's wrist, blood splashing over his tongue and bone cracking and splintering as his teeth met again. David howled in pain and pushed James off of him, holding the stump where his hand used to be as he fell backwards and slumped against the wall next to the fireplace. James readied to rush him again, the wolf's savage barking inside matching his own. *I'm going to take you apart.*

The gunshot rang out a split second before the back of David's skull blew open, spraying pieces of gore on the wall behind him. David blinked, but one of his eyes was a smoking hole where an eyeball had once been. He slumped down to the floor, his body shifting to human form as he fell to the side and lay still. The hand James held on to had also shrunk in size, now human in his large wolfen grip.

"Go help Lacy," Phillip shouted at him. "Go!"

James tossed the hand aside and charged Bathory as she held Lacy up by the throat the same way she'd tried to strangle him before. She looked at him and hissed, baring her fangs before she threw Lacy at him. He readjusted his charge and caught Lacy, letting the force knock him over so she landed on top of him. She rolled off and hit the floor.

He got to his feet and charged Bathory again, stopped at the sight of Ruby lying on the floor. Bathory was gone.

The wheelchair sat empty next to Ruby's still form.

James shifted to human form and went to Ruby. She moaned as he rolled her over onto her back, her eyes partially closed, blood running from her temple. "What happened?"

"She took the girl," Ruby said. "One last part, and we're in deep shit."

"Where?"

She shook her head. "I don't know. Somewhere in the house."

Phillip spoke up from behind James. "That narrows it down. Shit, there's rooms in this place even James hasn't been in since he was a kid."

He saw Phillip helping Lacy to her feet. She looked over at David's slumped form, speaking between coughs. "At least we got…*ugh*…one of them." She patted Phillip on the shoulder. "Nice paint job." She shook her head and rubbed her throat. "Bitch almost broke my damn neck."

Phillip spoke to James. "Saw Bathory knock Ruby the fuck out. Where'd she go?" He saw the wheelchair. "Oh, *shit*."

"You two get Ruby out of here," James said, standing. "I'm going after Bathory and Molly."

"I'll be fine," Ruby said as Phillip helped her to her feet.

"Pretty sure you got a concussion," Phillip said. He looked up at James. "We can't leave her alone."

"We can't let Bathory finish what she's started, either," Ruby said.

Phillip shook his head. "Finish what?"

"No time," James said.

"And no place for humans," Lacy chimed in, turning to Phillip. "I'm sticking with Jimmy. This place is too big for him to search alone."

Phillip nodded. "Right. I'll get her out of here. You two go waste that scary heifer and save the girl." He pointed at James and spoke in his best Ricky Ricardo voice. "You got some 'splainin' to do."

"Of course," James said.

"I mean it," Phillip shot back. "I saw that shit in the garage on the way in. My damn Warhammer figures are everywhere, and the table is smashed all to hell."

James felt relief at Phillip's attempt at levity.

Lacy nudged him on the arm. "Hey, let's go kill an evil bitch and save the girl. It'll be just like our first date."

29

James returned to wolf form while Phillip escorted Ruby through the nearest broken doorway. He hit all fours, put his nose to the floor, sniffing to pick up either Bathory's or Molly's scent. He focused more on Bathory's, taking into account Molly being covered in the vampire's blood would make the scent harder to differentiate.

Not that he needed to tell them apart.

"Where the hell do we even start?" Lacy asked. "This place is huge."

James ignored her and kept searching. He smelled Bathory all over the place, smelled the cedarwood from Davd's corpse. He set aside Lacy's scent in his mind. The blood side of her was different from Bathory's; sweeter and richer with the coppery scent blood usually had. Bathory's carried more rot, but hers was also paired with the scent of roses.

He couldn't smell Molly at all. Not even when he inspected the wheelchair.

Where are they? The wolf chuffed at his thoughts and gave a loud whine. His mind was running in overdrive, trying to sort out what had happened in such a short time. His home had been invaded and wasn't safe anymore. The Council of Night chambers were in ruin. The SCU was in disarray.

His father was alive. At least up until just minutes ago. Phillip had seen to that. Part of him carried a small resentment. It should've been him, not Phillip.

But would he have been able to kill his own father?

James moved into the main hall, sniffing around the giant staircase. The cedarwood had faded, but Bathory's scent remained strong and moved upstairs.

The sound of something heavy hitting the floor from upstairs was all he needed.

He bounded up the steps and tore right, Lacy behind him as he burst into the dark corridor and down the hall toward where the noise had come from. He heard Molly cry out, heard Bathory say something in what he assumed was Hungarian. Every door was closed, the dust in the corridor thick and undisturbed. He'd never been down this way, not since he and Phillip had moved in. They hadn't gotten to this part of the renovation yet.

He turned left and stopped. Lacy came to a halt behind him as he stood and sniffed the air, listened for more noises. A few display cases lined the walls, old Victorian-looking lamps on top of each one and the interiors lined with different types of books, baubles, and whatever other trinkets and trash David had managed to acquire during his travels. Each display case had a deer head mounted above it, the various antler types all covered in thick cobwebs and grime from years of neglect. He remembered his mother telling him to stay away from this area of the house when he was what some called a "rambunctious grade schoolboy."

Of course, as was expected, he snuck in at every opportunity.

The museum, he thought to himself. *I called this wing the museum when I was a kid.*

He'd been able to break into one or two of the rooms as a child. The one nearest to him on the right was an armory, the weapons and gear from different eras in countries like Japan, Mongolia, and multiple European territories. A room across from it contained a multitude of pottery going back to ancient Greece. The only room he never was able to get into was at the far end of the hall. The door had a different kind of lock on it, one that none of the skeleton keys on the keyring he'd swiped from his mother's closet would fit. She'd told him once the key had been lost, that she would have to have someone come and drill the lock for them to get into the room.

It was the one door in the hallway standing slightly open. A reddish glow came from inside, flickering and shaking as if it were candlelight. He smelled something...*off* emanating from the room, a combination of Bathory's scent and the mold that grew on dead animals.

"Well, *that's* not at all obvious," Lacy said. "How should we approach?"

James barreled down the hallway on all fours as Lacy shouted behind him. "How about some communication next time?!"

He hit the partially open, heavy door with his shoulder as he charged in. The door swung around as if it weighed nothing and slammed into the wall, the knob buried in the plaster and lathe. He paused at the sight before him, felt as if someone had slapped him across the face. Lacy entered behind him, running into him before she stopped and sucked in a breath.

"What. The. *Actual* fuck?"

The hardwood floors in the room were perfectly polished, the dark wood making the deep red walls stand out more in the dim light. It was furnished like the cigar lounges he'd seen in movies, particularly the ones about the Titanic. Chairs and sofas sat near a fireplace, the fire adding to the candlelight in the room. A large chandelier hung from the ceiling and was adorned with hundreds of candles.

It wasn't the furniture and décor stopping him in his tracks, making his chest freeze and his stomach knot.

It was what it was all made from.

The chairs and sofa were constructed of bones, possibly human, possibly a variety of other animals. He could tell from the stitches, scars, and blemishes that the upholstery was skin, dried and leathered. The chandelier was nothing but bones of all sizes, the candles held by hands of varying sizes and shapes. The centerpiece of the light fixture was a cluster of four skulls, each one facing out with the mouth open in a silent scream. Lampshades were obviously made of leather, more than likely human. The lamps themselves were human spines, four of them placed on small round glass-topped tables, the glass held by three animal spines bent to the point of looking like a macabre flower to support the glass at the top and act as a foot for the table on the bottom. A full human skeleton hung upside down on a cross above the fireplace, and matching ones hung from the walls on either side of the room, also inverted.

Was this what his mother had been hiding from him? That his father's insanity knew no depths? He didn't doubt the remains he saw were victims of the Wolf-Man Killer, but it didn't play to what he'd seen previously. David Coldstone had mauled his victims and eaten their hearts. James hadn't seen anything over the years to indicate the kind of meticulousness this room would have taken to set up. It was all deliberate, all of it done with the kind of care one would expect from a house in a magazine. Despite its horror, everything in the room was neatly made and precisely placed as if it were a functional part of the house.

James didn't recognize the symbol on the floor, a circle lined with runes and a triangle in the center. Molly stood in the middle, her eyes closed and her hands down by her side as if she were sleeping standing up. Her body remained covered in bloody runes, her head listing to the side.

He heard Lacy speak in a low voice next to him. "It's like Martha Stewart hooked up with Ed Gein."

Bathory stood behind Molly on the outside of the circle, facing the fireplace with her arms out to the sides as if greeting a long-lost lover. She spoke without turning to face James and Lacy. "Welcome to this most glorious night, James Coldstone."

"Oh, never mind me," Lacy said back to her, kicking up the sarcasm. "I'm just the eye candy."

That was when James noticed the long, elegant knife in Bathory's hand. The vampire master turned around at the sound of Lacy's voice and smiled. "Ah, Agent Faulkner. Come to arrest me?"

"Nah," Lacy said. "I'm here to watch Jimmy tear you in half."

James growled at Bathory and started forward. Bathory moved quickly, wrapping her arm around Molly's shoulders and lifting the knife to her throat. "Be careful, Mr. Coldstone," she said, pressing the point of the blade into Molly's skin until blood ran down the blade. "She cannot feel pain, but it does not mean she cannot die."

James held his ground and shifted to human form. "Drop the knife. She has nothing to do with this."

"She is special to you," Bathory said. "That makes her part of this."

"You need her alive," Lacy said. "Isn't that right?"

"Relatively speaking," Bathory said. "It does not mean that two possible replacements aren't standing before me. Back up."

"You wouldn't be able to start over," Lacy said. "Ruby's gone, and the SCU is on their way. Already shot a text to Agent Smith about getting cover to the rest of the witches in the coven."

Bathory tossed her head back and gave a throaty laugh. "None of it will matter. The SCU is in too much disarray. The Daughters of Baba Yaga have almost been completely wiped out. The Council of Night is finished. No one will come in time."

"You're crazy as hell," Lacy said, dropping her sarcastic tone. "Why the fuck would you want to bring Dracula back?" She put her hands on her hips. "As if that's even a thing."

"Vlad Tepes is pathetic," Bathory said. "He does not understand where humans stand in relation to us in the order of things. They are our *food*." She leaned over and ran her tongue from Molly's neck all the way up her cheek before pulling away and inhaling as if in ecstasy.

"Okay, that's a little much," Lacy said. "And Dracula is a myth. No one knows who killed him, and even if it wasn't a myth, you'd need his ashes."

Bathory shrugged. "Semantics."

"Nuts," Lacy corrected.

James glanced around the room. The windows were covered by dark curtains, but he could see some of the moonlight from outside. He could shift into wolf form and get Molly out that way. He needed to get Bathory away from her. Rushing in wouldn't work. Bathory was too fast, and Molly would die. "What is this room? Why is it in my house?"

"Your father set it up," Bathory said. "With my help, of course. It took us several months of work. We finished just before your return, which was admittedly unexpected. Death is all around, Mr. Coldstone. And necessary. The warmth of life has no place here." Her eyes narrowed at him. "You are no exception. Your home is cursed, James Coldstone. Because of this room and the purpose it serves. Once I have killed you, I will use your bones to fortify this space. Your skull will hang above the mantle."

"You need me if you plan to take my money," James said.

Bathory shook her head. "A beneficiary does not have to be a Coldstone by blood."

What does she mean by that? James thought.

"The SCU has been onto you for months," Lacy continued. "You really think we're gonna just lie down?"

"How will you call for help from Agent Smith if your communications have been intercepted?" Bathory asked. "There is no one coming."

James saw his opportunity. "I can think of plenty of ways."

Bathory looked at him. "Oh?"

"There are billboards."

Lacy blinked, glanced up at him, then smirked as she turned back to Bathory. "True. I might know a guy who can fly an airplane. We could get one of those big banners."

"Morse Code."

"Smoke signals."

"Interpretive dance."

"Oh, I like that one!"

Bathory stared at them. "I am over four hundred years old, and yet I have never known greater stupidity than what I am seeing in front of me."

James shrugged. "I'm an overachiever."

"Welp," Lacy said, clapping her hands together. "As much fun as this has been, it's time for me to put my foot up your ass."

"Enjoy this night," Bathory said, grinning. "It will be your last." She laughed and stepped away from Molly, who still stood motionless but now with blood running from the fresh cut on her neck. She hadn't reacted at all to Bathory sticking her with the knife or jostling her. Bathory stepped outside of the circle and held her hands up in a fighter's pose, holding the knife at the ready. "I'm going to bathe in your blood." She paused and eyed Lacy, then James. "It should not be difficult to guess which of you is a virgin."

Lacy nudged James. "Hey, bitch has a sense of humor." She zipped away at vampiric speed and charged Bathory, swinging and kicking as her opponent ducked and weaved. Lacy spun and brought her heel around in a roundhouse kick, but Bathory blocked it and slashed out with her knife, forcing Lacy to backpedal from her as the blade came within inches of slicing her throat open. James charged in as Bathory came around for another swipe, grabbed her wrist, and opened his mouth to clamp down on her skull. She kicked him hard in the stomach, knocking the wind out of him, and jerked her hand free from his weakened grip. She kicked Lacy in the face, knocked her backwards into one of the skeletal tables, then slashed James with the blade. The pain spread across his chest, through his torso and back. He put his hand to his blood-soaked fur as he dropped down to one knee, the familiar sting making his muscles weaken. His strength started coming back quickly as Bathory chuckled and stood over him.

"Silver blade," she said. "Never leave home without it." She raised the knife, turning it over, and went to drive it into his face before Lacy crashed into her and tackled her to the floor. Bathory yowled as Lacy pinned her down on her back.

"Jimmy, get Molly," Lacy shouted. "I've got Madam Sucks-A-Lot."

James rushed in to grab Molly and slammed into something hard enough to stop him dead in his tracks. He reached out for her again, but his hand was stopped by an invisible barrier. He turned to Lacy and barked.

Lacy rolled her eyes. "Okay, lady. What gives?"

Bathory laughed and bucked Lacy off of her. James rushed in, but the vampire master was on her feet again. She slashed out with the knife, but he caught her wrist and squeezed until it broke, causing her to drop the blade. Her pained scream mixed with her laughter. *I'm done with this*, he thought.

Something about her scent stopped him.

Ash. He smelled ash. It had a different tinge to it. Not burning wood. His eyes moved down her cleavage, the scent stronger from there. He barked at Lacy, who walked over and reached down into Bathory's top. "Don't read too much into this, sweetie. You aren't my type." She pulled out a small leather pouch and held it up. "What the hell?"

Bathory smiled. "A family heirloom."

James saw the insignia on the pouch as Lacy held it up in the low light. He knew it well by now.

Dracula's crest.

"Ashes passed down through generations of my family line," Bathory said. "Our devotion to the Dark Lord is eternal." She looked at James, still smiling. "A smudge on a knife can be so effective."

Lacy's eyes widened. "Oh, *shit*."

James turned back to Molly, at the wound on her neck. The bleeding had stopped. He let go of Bathory and moved closer, making sure he was seeing what he was seeing, that he wasn't losing his mind.

The trickle of blood coming from the cut on Molly's neck was traveling back up into the wound.

Her eyes opened. She relaxed, standing straight, and gazed around the room with a bewildered expression. Her eyes rested on James, her expression hardening as she spoke. "Where am I?"

W ho has disturbed me?" Molly gritted her teeth and shouted at James. Her voice was different, lower and guttural. "*Speak, Knightwolf!*"

James stared at her eyes, the wolf inside growling with warnings and panic. His heart sank, a lump of fear clawing at his throat; he could not find Molly in those eyes.

"My lord," Bathory said, moving up to the circle. "It was I who summoned thee."

James stepped back as Lacy moved up beside him. "Jimmy, we are *fucked.*"

Molly focused her glare on Bathory. "For what purpose?"

"To make this world in your vision," Bathory said. "To serve at your side as your most devoted follower."

Molly gave her a derisive grunt and stared down at her body. "Yet, I am covered in an incantation written in your blood." She looked down at the floor. "And bound in a circle surrounded by death."

"Merely a failsafe, my lord," Bathory said.

Molly's eyes flicked up at her. "I see."

"I would not want any unfortunate mistakes to be made," Bathory continued.

'Unfortunate mistakes?" Molly's mouth turned up into a sinister grin

James had never seen on her face before. "I must appreciate your efforts, Elizabet Bathory."

Bathory bowed her head. "Thank you, my lord."

"A circle of binding fueled by the air of death, and incantations written in the blood of the one who would control the summoned." Molly wiped away one of the runes on her arm and licked the blood from her hand. "It must have taken great effort to invent such a trite way to explain your efforts to enslave me."

Bathory's head snapped back up, her eyes wide with horror.

Lacy tugged on James's arm. "We need to leave. Like now." She started pulling him in the direction of the door.

Molly raised her hand, and the door slammed shut, shaking the bones on the walls.

Lacy sighed. "I guess we'll hang out since she insists."

Standing tall, Bathory swallowed hard and clenched her fists by her side. "I do not deny that there is a means to an end, my lord. There are needs that must be met."

"Needs?" Molly asked, cocking her head to one side, her expression going blank. "*Your* needs?"

"The needs of many," Bathory said. "And mine above those if I am to rule at your side."

"Money," Molly said, curling her lip in disgust. "Wealth. I can smell the greed on you like trash in a hovel."

"It is a new world," Bathory said. "A world that demands wealth and rewards it with power. And you will have it in spades." She motioned at James. "I will have a fortune thanks to his father's gullibility. Limitless and expansive."

"And then what?" Molly asked. "You will simply relinquish control? Allow me my freedom? In exchange for what?" Her tone shifted, grew angrier. "Power? *My* power? You seek to wield me like some weapon? Against whom? What have you to gain but more wealth and power? I seek to rule all living things. You seek *money*." She spat on the floor. "That is what I think of your greed, Elizabet Bathory."

Bathory laughed. James could hear the nervousness in it. "Very well. Say what you will. You are trapped in a frail little girl's body inside a circle of binding and surrounded by the remains of those who would oppose you. Your words may be beyond my control, but your actions belong to me."

Molly's grin widened. "Do they?" She stepped forward, moving toward the edge of the circle. "You control my autonomy? Because you gave me a body? Brought me back into a world that has forgotten me?" She took another step, now standing on the edge. "To what end? You would keep me here, use my power and influence to gain control of a world that would love nothing more than to see you and yours dead? All in the name of your own greed." One more step, slow and deliberate, as Molly came to a stop.

And stood outside the circle.

Lacy spoke in a low, soft, shaky voice. "Oh, *that's* bad."

Bathory backed away, any trace of confidence gone as she cowered. Molly kept moving toward her, still grinning. Bathory slumped against the wall, trapped as Molly stepped up to her. "I carry the girl's memories. She was infused with your blood to heal her wounds. You were warned by the witch that your plan was flawed."

"I beg your mercy," Bathory said, falling to her knees and clasping her hands together. "I was foolish, my lord. I allowed my arrogance to cloud my mind." She bowed her head, this time sincerely as tears rolled down her face. "Please forgive me and my ignorance. I will serve you, my lord. I swear my soul to you." She looked up at Molly. "I beg for your forgiveness."

Molly smiled and gently cupped Bathory's face in her hands. "I forgive you, my child," she said. "And your husband."

Husband? James thought.

Bathory smiled, sobbing as she spoke. "Thank you, my lord."

Molly jerked Bathory to her feet by her head. Bathory sputtered, flailing her arms as she tried to fight back. She screamed as Molly dug her fingers into her face, blood running from each wound. She slapped at Molly's arms and hands with no effect.

"You forgave me," she screeched.

"I did," Molly said, her tone calm. "Therefore, your punishment will be swift." She pulled Bathory close until their noses were almost touching. "I am Drakul. I am Lord of Night. And I will be controlled by no one."

She slung Bathory across the room and into the fireplace. The fire enveloped the vampiress instantly, covering her from head to toe as she crawled back out. James moved to rush in despite Lacy's protests, but Molly shoved him backwards hard enough to send him down onto his rump. Bathory wailed as she crawled toward Molly, reaching for her. Molly simply stared at her until the arm fell limp to the floor.

"James," Lacy shouted. "Take cover!" She ran past him and kicked

Bathory's body back into the fireplace. Flames belched out into the room and roared up the chimney. James saw the wall above the fireplace smoke and discolor. The fire blew out from the fireplace, hitting the curtains at a nearby window; the dust in the air was glowing embers as flames flowed out over the ceiling like water.

Molly grabbed Lacy by the hair and drove a foot into the back of Lacy's knees, sending her down to the floor. James rushed them and grabbed Molly, lifting her and tossing her aside. She hit one of the glass-topped tables and shattered it, hitting the floor as the fire spread across the wood toward her. He helped Lacy to her feet. "I'm okay," she said. "We gotta get out of here. Vampires aren't real big on fire."

Molly, James thought. The wolf protested, but he ignored it and rushed over to where she'd landed. He knelt to pick her up, but she rolled over and raked her nails across his face. He yelped from the pain and surprise and went for her again, but she was already on her feet. She held out her hand, and the fire swirled around her, engulfing her. James watched as the flames encircled her without burning her. She rounded on him and snarled. "You will learn your place, Knightwolf."

Why does she keep calling me that?

The wolf barked in his mind, urged him to run. He looked around the burning room. The fire consumed the crucified skeletons on the walls, the heat growing more intense by the second. The windows were blocked by burning curtains. Lacy wouldn't make it through the fire, even if he covered her. His eyes fell back onto Molly just as she pointed at Lacy. The fire around her shot out at Lacy like a striking snake. He yanked Lacy out of the way and backpedaled as it struck where she'd been standing and burned a hole in the floor in seconds. Molly pulled it back as if it were a whip in her hand and reared back to strike again.

He had to move. No more time to think.

James pulled Lacy close to him and barreled at the door as another tendril of fire shot out from Molly's hand. He plowed through the door and into the corridor at a run, the cold air gone in a second as fire billowed out from the room behind him and ignited the dust and old carpet. Molly screamed over the roar of fire as he turned the corner and headed toward the main hall. He tucked and rolled through the doorway, shielding Lacy from the fire licking his back as he burst through and into the main hall. James released her, and they made their way down the stairs. They stopped at the bottom, and James looked up to see the fire spreading over the walls and railing like napalm.

It was a split second before Molly stood at the top of the stairs, fire encircling her and igniting everything it came close to. She started down the steps slowly, leaving a burning footprint on each step as she went. Her eyes glowed a deep red, her mouth drawn into a bitter smirk as she kept her gaze leveled with his. "She is still here, Knightwolf," she said. "In pain. Screaming. Suffering." She stopped midway on the steps.

James shifted to human form. "Molly, fight back! This isn't you!"

Her eyes closed as she swooned. "She can hear you." Her eyes opened as she grinned. "And she is afraid of you, Knightwolf."

"Why do you keep calling me that?" James asked.

"Why do you deny what is in your blood?" Molly replied. "I can sense it flowing through your veins. You carry the blood of the Hell Hound."

"David Coldstone is dead," James said, standing his ground. He pulled the wolf forward, kept it at the ready to shift at a second's notice. "And I must decline your generous offer to be your bitch."

Molly nodded. "Then you will join your father and his bride." She pointed at him and sent a column of fire his way. He shifted, and he and Lacy dove in opposite directions as the flames hit the floor. The stone cracked from the heat as the blaze spread over the marbled floor to the walls, engulfing the area in seconds. Debris fell from above as the ceiling started collapsing. James lunged through the fire at Lacy and pulled her out of the way as the upstairs landing came down. He made for the front doors and stopped when he saw burning rubble blocking his exit.

"This way," Lacy shouted as she darted into the living room. "Out the windows!"

James turned to Molly. She glared at him; her face twisted in hatred. *I have to try*, James thought. The wolf protested, barking in his mind as he made for her again. More of the upstairs landing came down, blocking his way. He backed away from the burning rubble, watching her as she stared at him, the fire around her body moving and swirling. He looked around, desperate to find a way to get to her. *I can jump it*, he thought, studying the pile of burning debris in front of him.

The chandelier dropped along with the rest of the ceiling, raining down on Molly in a torrent of burning wood, plaster, and brass. James stood for a moment in shock as the fire grew even more, and the area filled with the stench of smoke and burning rubble.

And propane.

James could hear the popping as the smell hit him. He turned, bolted into the living room as the popping noises grew louder and faster. He kicked off the floor and leapt through the window into the cold night air. He hit the ground running, heard Lacy and Phillip shouting from somewhere in the dark. He made his way across the driveway and into the front pasture, stopping and turning back to the house once he was a few hundred yards out.

The force from the blast pounded at him, shook the ground underneath him, even from so far away as the explosion disintegrated the mansion. A cloud of fire and smoke mushroomed into the sky. Trees and bushes around the manor burned away instantly. James could feel the heat from the blast on his facial fur, could smell the stench of burning plaster and insulation. His ears rang from the noise, drowning out the muffled sounds of Phillip and Lacy coming toward him. His childhood played in his mind, the memories he had of growing up in the Keep with his mother, exploring the pastures and woods around. The fight with Wade Anderson at the pavilion. All of the evenings spent with Phillip watching television or watching Phillip play video games.

The nights with Molly.

None of it mattered anymore. He shifted to human form as he continued to watch debris rain down into the bonfire that had once been his home. He didn't flinch when Phillip wrapped his arms around him in a fierce hug, laughing and crying at the same time. Lacy did the same, and James wrapped his arms around them out of instinct, his mind struggling to process what he'd seen.

Phillip and Lacy pulled away. Phillip clapped him on the shoulder. "Goddamn, I thought you were dead. Are you hurt?"

James shook his head. "Nothing that won't heal."

"James," Lacy said. "I'm so sorry."

"Where's Ruby?" he asked.

"She's in the car at the top of the hill," Phillip said. "Calling around and checking on the other witches in the area."

"I got a text from Smith a minute ago saying that the SCU is on the way here," Lacy said. She shrugged. "Better late than never, I guess."

Phillip counted heads and asked, "Where's Molly?"

31

Mostly dark, the conference room was silent save for the sound of the AC pumping air through the vent in the ceiling. The large monitor on the wall at the front of the room displayed the FBI seal against a black background, the logo fading in and out as a screensaver. The windows looking out over the outer FBI offices were covered by long, heavy black drapes. The air was cool, though stuffy. James stared at the table, working things over in his mind. He'd explained things to everyone once they'd gotten to the SCU offices, told them about what Bathory had said before Phillip and Lacy had shown up.

He'd told them about his father being alive.

That one ruffled feathers. There was no trace of David Coldstone once the house fire had been put out. Hoyt explained there was no way they would find remains of anyone. The heat from the explosion would have incinerated David's body instantly. James wouldn't have been surprised if no one believed him.

What caught him off guard was everyone believing him.

"You have no reason to lie about something like this," Smith had said. "And it makes sense if you look at his behavior prior to the incident at Coldstone Keep." He paused, cleared his throat before continuing. "I am sorry for your loss, Mr. Coldstone."

James wasn't sorry. Not at all. If anything, he wished he had been the one to do the job.

Lacy and Phillip sat in the room with him, neither of them speaking. All three of them were covered in soot, though Lacy and James were healed up for the most part. James still had a long scar across his chest from Bathory's silver knife, though it was now covered with an oversized SCU t-shirt.

Lacy broke the silence. "Jimmy, I'm sorry about the paint job joke. I wouldn't have made it if I'd have known."

"I found it rather funny," James said, staring at the table.

"Yeah," Phillip said, sitting up in his chair and facing James. "About your little secret."

"I didn't tell you because I didn't want to acknowledge him being alive," James said, his tone sharper than he'd intended. "I didn't want to give him anything."

"How would telling me your pops was alive change anything?"

James looked up at him. "Would you have killed him?"

Phillip stared back at him. "And you were going to?"

"I'd considered it."

"Bullshit," Phillip said. "And fuck you for keeping that shit to yourself."

"What was I supposed to do?" James asked, raising his voice. "Please, by all means, educate me on how I could have handled my presumably dead, serial-killing father showing back up alive and well more to your liking."

"You could've told *me*, motherfucker," Phillip shot back. "I'm your *brother*." He slapped the table. "Ride or die, bitch. We don't *have* secrets. That's Bro Code 101."

James glanced over at Lacy. She held her hands up and shook her head. "It's Bro Code, Jimmy. I can't help you."

James sighed. "You're right," he said, turning his attention back to Phillip. "I should have told you. But I didn't. And now he's dead."

Phillip sat back in his chair. "We've been tight too long for that shit. Shape up."

The door to the room opened as Smith walked in with Kimble close behind him. Ruby entered as well and sat down next to Lacy. Smith sat down at the far end of the table opposite James. "Out of respect, I will leave the lights off to maintain your preferred dreariness."

"You are too kind," James said, not holding back the sarcasm.

"I would like to clear up a few things," Smith said as Kimble opened her tablet and pulled out her touchscreen pencil. "First, by informing you that Elizabet Bathory was not your stepmother, but she was listed recently as a beneficiary to the Coldstone fortune."

"How?" Lacy asked. "David Coldstone was legally dead for years."

Smith nodded. "He was *reported* dead. There are no records of his internment, no documentation of his autopsy, nothing filed with the State of South Carolina other than 'Status Unknown.'" He turned his attention back to James. "She was added with your signature, Mr. Coldstone. Though we have already ruled it as a forgery."

"That explains how she planned to get her hands on your money," Phillip said.

"And why my father referred to her by her first name," James said. "Molly said I would join my father and his wife. Now it makes sense."

"She was using the mass shootings as a distraction," Lacy said, turning to Smith. "The arms dealing was how she amassed her fortune, and she turned Booth into a skinwalker early on to use him as her gopher. He was the one on Westenra Island offing agents left and right."

"Mortals who become skinwalkers do not stay sane for long," Ruby added. "That boy lost his mind, and Miss Bathory lost control of him."

"That's when she sent Clifford after him," Phillip said. He glanced at James. "I mean David. Sorry."

"I prefer Clifford," James said immediately.

"We also have her financials," Kimble said. "It shows large sums of money to political campaigns lobbying against any type of gun reform."

Phillip grunted. "Terrorize the shit out of the public, flood the market with guns, and watch people kill each other. As a distraction." He shook his head. "Damn, what an evil bitch."

"That woman messed up when she thought she could bring back someone like Dracula and control him," Ruby said. "Her original plan was to have Agatha control him once she was done with the rest of the council, and that was her first mistake."

"Why is that?" Smith asked.

"Dracula isn't a vampire," Ruby said, glancing at each of them as she spoke. "Never has been. Hell, the name 'Dracula' is just what everyone called him because of the books."

Lacy blinked. "Wait, that's not right. We've always been told that he was the original Lord of the Vampires. He almost conquered the world."

Ruby chuckled and nodded. "Oh, you're not wrong about what we were told, hon." She leaned forward, speaking directly to Lacy. "We were also told that Santa Claus would bring us presents if we were good little boys and girls." She addressed the rest of them. "Anyone else here wake up one night to pee and find mom and dad in the living room setting out presents?"

"I believe someone wrote a song about it," James said, jumping at the opportunity to lighten things up. "Though I'm fairly certain mommy was doing more than kissing Santa."

Phillip snorted. Lacy looked at him and stifled a laugh. "Okay, Jimmy, that was a good one."

Smith glared at him, unentertained. "I'm glad to see that you maintain your wit despite the recent events."

James smiled at him. "Are you?"

"No."

"Thank you for at least pretending for a bit."

Smith closed his eyes, took a deep breath, then opened them and resumed his formal demeanor. Phillip grinned at James. "You made that man woo-sah." He held his fist out. James gave him the fist bump.

"As for Elizabet Bathory," Smith continued, ignoring them. "Though her arms trade has been shut down and her assets frozen, the fact remains that there were multiple mass shootings between Rock Hill and Charlotte over the span of just a few days. The SCU cannot possibly keep that kind of thing out of the headlines, but we have been able to work the narrative that the shooter was killed. It is a nightmare. I do not envy the politicians, but we are in the clear.

"The Council of Night chambers were destroyed during your battle with the skinwalker. And they are now down a member. This will have ramifications. Not on you, but on the political relationships between the human world and the supernatural world." He turned to Ruby. "You were about to tell us about Dracula?"

"Drakul," Ruby said, correcting him. She pronounced it "Dra-cool." "Not the same thing. Dracula was a character created for a book. A vampire. Drakul was a warlock back in the earliest part of the first century who decided to take up necromancy. It's one of the reasons why it's considered a forbidden magic in the witch community."

"Until recently," Lacy said. "Hoyt managed to figure out that every one of David Coldstone's victims had practiced necromancy to some level."

Ruby regarded her with a raised eyebrow. "Sometimes you gotta do what you gotta do to protect you and yours."

Lacy nodded. "That's fair."

Ruby continued. "Drakul ended up becoming something else. I think the word some people like to use is 'Eldritch.'"

"As in Eldritch Horror?" Phillip said. "Like Cthulhu?"

Ruby shook her head. "Cthulhu is another work of fiction. Drakul is very real, as are the Eldritch beings that walk the earth."

"He became a god," Phillip said. "That's what you're telling us. Drakul started off as a witch and became a god."

"Not quite a god," Ruby said. "But a powerful entity. The only limitation is his need for a body. That's how your Molly survived that explosion, I assure you."

"Can Molly be saved?" James asked before Phillip could comment again.

Ruby looked at him, her expression saddened. "That isn't so easy a question to answer, sugar."

"Try me."

She sighed. "Drakul can be extracted from her body. Once he's out, he would have to be contained, either in another body or in some sort of prison."

"Where was he before?" Lacy asked.

"Purgatory," Ruby said. "His soul is too cursed to move on. That's how he became an Eldritch. Before he ended up in Miss Molly's body, he was roaming the earth as a shade. Still dangerous but more limited."

"Where?" James asked, leaning forward.

"The Eldritch spirits mostly congregate in the Appalachians," Ruby said. "It's a major ley line. It keeps the area sensitive to them, which gives them the ability to roam without being a problem anywhere else."

"Like the containment unit from Ghostbusters?" Phillip asked.

Ruby smiled at him. "That's right." Phillip blinked, causing her to chuckle. "You ain't the only one here that likes movies, young man."

Kimble spoke up. "We don't have any resources up in the Western North Carolina region, which supposedly has the highest concentration of Eldritch energy."

"Oh, sugar," Ruby said as if speaking to a grandchild. "I didn't say the ley line was *in* the Appalachians. The Appalachians *are* a ley line, in fact, *the* ley line from one end to the other. Think of it like the central nervous system, where all the other ley lines stem from."

"How do you know all of this?" Smith said.

"The spirit world talks," Ruby said, turning her attention to him. "And it gave me this information at a price."

"And that would be?"

She crossed her arms in front of her and gave him a defiant look. "Personal."

Smith nodded. "Very well."

"Did the spirit world tell you where Drakul went?" James asked. "What his next move is?"

Ruby shook her head at him, her expression falling slightly. "I'm sorry, sugar. My price was already too great. Only person who knows that is Drakul."

"How do we extract him from Molly's body?"

Ruby sat back in her chair, staring at James, her eyes sad and distant. "I'll tell you, James Coldstone. But I can make one promise to you."

"Go on."

"You aren't gonna like what I'm about to tell you."

James still had access to his bank accounts, so new clothes and toiletries for the trip were just a matter of going on a shopping spree. Lacy and Phillip were also in need and ended up tagging along with the SCU, escorting them to wherever they needed to go. James wasn't concerned with fully replacing everything he'd lost in the fire, nor was he interested in taking Lacy up on her offer to procure the prints for Coldstone Keep.

He didn't see the point in putting so much effort into a place he would never be going back to.

The destruction of the estate meant James now had full access to the fortune, billions of dollars that David Coldstone had made over the years doing the bidding of both the Council of Night and Elizabet Bathory as the Knightwolf.

Why had Drakul kept calling him Knightwolf? What had he meant when he'd said that James carried the blood of the Hell Hound?

"I didn't get anything on that, either," Ruby had said after telling him what it would take to free Molly. "I only asked what I saw was important. Who is Dracula, and how do we free that sweet girl? Nothin' else."

He'd even tried to talk to the wolf about it, bringing up its reaction to Drakul calling him Knightwolf.

The beast just yawned at him and cocked its head to the side.

"The Knightwolf is a position of importance to the council," Noble Jones said over the phone. Lacy had called him while they were on the way to the store to buy clothing and toiletries. She had him on speaker so James and Phillip could also hear. "Come to think of it, it was Bathory who came up with the name and position." He grunted. "Well, Tepes is gonna *love* this."

"You may inform him that I still decline the offer," James said.

"Yeah, I don't blame you," Jones replied. "In fact, once he finds out about this, he'll probably kill the job."

"Any leads on who's gonna replace Bathory on the council?" Lacy asked.

"Nope," Jones said. "Not yet. We're starting that search after the chambers have been repaired and Montoya stops cursing in Spanish about what Bathory sent after him."

Two nights later, James found himself sitting on the balcony of the apartment in downtown Rock Hill he'd lived in when all of this had started, staring off into the sunset as the sky turned different shades of orange and purple before the sun vanished over the horizon, leaving only the night. Smith wanted them close by, and the tenant scheduled to move in had canceled last minute. A phone call and a generous financial arrangement in favor of the landlord later, and James found himself sleeping in the comfort of irony on the SCU's dime.

As comfortable as he could be. Sleep wasn't easy to come by.

He kept seeing Molly's face, her body encircled in fire as Drakul used her to try to kill him and Lacy. He also kept seeing his father. Having David show up again in his life was starting to rattle him despite his best efforts at indifference. From what James could see, David was nothing more than a servant to a megalomaniacal vampire. He wanted to share in the power she scrambled for.

And it had gotten both of them killed.

Now he had to make peace with what he would have to do to save Molly from Drakul.

He heard Phillip's voice behind him. "Hey, want some company?"

"Sure."

Phillip sat down in the camping chair next to him and handed him a beer bottle. James popped the top off, clinked bottles with Phillip, and took a swig. The cold, rich, dark beer felt good going down his throat.

"Look man," Phillip said. "In all seriousness. I'm sorry. I know you hated the motherfucker, and I know you say you don't give a shit. But I've met you, and I've known you too long to be fooled by that."

James grunted. "If you are attempting to comfort me in my time of grief, I can assure you that I would much rather play in traffic than discuss my father." He turned to Phillip. "If anything, you've done me a favor."

"You really that cold?" Phillip asked. He took a drink of his beer and sat it down on the small table next to him. "You actually don't give a shit about your dad showing back up?"

"Should I?"

"I'd think you would at least have questions."

James shrugged. "Nothing that would keep me up at night. I don't care where he got the money. I have access to all of it now to do with it what I like, and at least half of it is going to charity. I don't care that he married Bathory just so she would have access to it once I was out of the picture. It was likely that Bathory was going to kill him anyway if she had been able to control Drakul." He gave a tight-lipped smile and raised his bottle. "If anything, I should thank you for saving me the trouble."

"Notice you didn't say you didn't care that he faked his death," Phillip said. "I wonder if your mom knew."

"I don't know," James said, staring back off into the night sky. "Drop it."

"I'm here if you decide to pick it back up."

James almost snapped at him but stopped himself. Phillip was trying to help. They had been through a lot together, especially over the past few months.

And there was no way Phillip could have known who David was. As far as he knew, he'd shot Clifford in the head with a silver bullet.

"Thank you," James said. "Will Lacy be joining us?"

"Nah," Phillip said. "This is Bro Time. She's on the phone with Hoyt about something. I wasn't listening. Figured she'd tell us if it was important." He sat up and turned to James. "What's up with you two anyway?"

"I'm not sure what you mean."

"Look. I know you dated Molly for a bit, but you still got all mopey whenever Lacy came up in conversation. And you two seem a little tighter these past couple of days."

James took a swig of his beer. "It's complicated."

"She's been an agent this whole time."

"Indeed."

"She lied about what she was doing in Charleston, and why she showed up in Savannah."

"Also valid."

"She can't be trusted."

"I did say it was complicated."

Phillip shook his head. "Goddamn, you are *hard*-headed." He looked over his shoulder, then back at James. "Just be careful. She's gonna have to do some real shit to get on my good side again."

"Like what, Bacon?" Lacy asked, startling Phillip as she stepped out onto the balcony. "Got any ideas?"

"You could do trust exercises," James said to Phillip.

Lacy nodded. "Yeah, that's a good idea, Jimmy!"

Phillip grumbled under his breath.

"You could do that one where you fall backwards and she has to catch you," James said.

"I promise, I won't bite," Lacy said, nudging Phillip's shoulder. "I'll eat beforehand."

Phillip muttered under his breath again, this time more audibly. "Both y'all can eat a dick."

James and Lacy laughed, and Phillip rolled his eyes before he joined in. Lacy leaned up against the railing next to James. "Just got done chatting with Hoyt. Ruby and the remaining witches are working with the Council of Night to try and track down Drakul. Ruby thinks she might be able to pull him out of Molly with minimal damage."

"That's good news," Phillip said. "They got a lead on where he might be?"

"Nope."

"That news is not as good," James said.

"Well, I said there wasn't a lead on Drakul," Lacy said. "That doesn't mean they don't have a lead on some hinky shit going on."

James raised an eyebrow. "Go on."

"Some wild shit is happening up in the Appalachians. Wanna take a stab where?"

"Kimble said Western North Carolina was a hot spot," Phillip said.

Lacy made a gun with her hand and pretended to shoot at Phillip as she made a clicking noise with her tongue. "Look at the big brain on Bacon! Turns out the shit that goes bump in the night up there got way more active over the past couple of nights."

"Victims?" Phillip asked.

"Nah, people up there know the rules on keeping that shit out of their homes. But it doesn't mean it won't come to a head at some point. Even the locals are starting to get nervous."

"I believe we may be taking a road trip."

"Hold up," Phillip said. "Let the SCU handle that shit. James, we almost died. *Again.* Hell, you came close to it a *few* times!"

"Molly is our friend," James said. "She doesn't deserve what happened to her. If we can save her, then we should try."

"I like your spirit, Jimmy," Lacy said. "Smith already said he'd probably send me up there. And I could use a hand since he's reinstated you two into the SCU." She looked at James. "This time, *without* the threat of doxing you. He's figured out you two work better without being micromanaged."

Phillip shook his head. "I don't like this shit, man. This last one was too much. You lost your damn house."

James turned to him. "I need you. We can't do this without you."

Phillip shook his head. "You need to have your head examined if you think I'm gonna be part of some damned rescue mission involving a fuckin' Eldritch horror."

James leaned closer. "Ride or die, bitch."

Phillip eyed him sidelong, sighed, then picked his beer up and chugged the rest of the bottle.

James pushed again. "Team Super Wolf forever?"

Phillip sputtered and stood up. He started toward the balcony door as he spoke. "I gotta piss. Y'all tell me when we're leaving."

James laughed for the first time in days. It felt good.

Lacy sat down next to him in Phillip's chair. "You two are adorable." She paused. "He's in, right?"

"He's in," James said. "He likes to complain. It's his therapy."

"Makes sense." She tapped his shoulder. "One more thing I wanna talk about, if that's okay? Don't worry, it's not about your dad or Molly. Figured you need a break from work for a night."

James turned to her. "A peaceful evening would be nice. What do you have in mind?"

She leaned over and kissed him; her lips gently pressed on his as she put her hand on his arm. He reached for her, his hand resting on the back of her head as he returned the kiss. His heart fluttered, the wolf inside barking and turning circles while wagging its tail furiously. He closed his eyes, losing himself in the kiss and her scent, savoring the taste of her lips.

His eyes were still closed when he heard Phillip's sarcastic tone from the doorway.

"Ain't that sweet. Gimme my seat back."

ACKNOWLEDGMENTS

It has been one of the more eventful years of my life. Hurricanes, floods, a broken spine, surgery recovery, etcetera, etcetera.

2025 can eat a dick.

This book would not have happened without the constant support of Nirvana Jane Briarwood, Cupid Gilbert, Lyni Gilbert, my readers, and my friends and family in the convention community who have stuck with me through it all. From my highest highs to my lowest lows, you all have been so patient with me and so supportive. I could never have imagined the outpouring that I've gotten through all of this, and it's just humbling to experience. Thanks to everyone who has pushed me, given me grace, and encouraged me not to give up even when it would have made things easier. I don't deserve any of you guys.

ABOUT THE AUTHOR

Jason Gilbert is an author and film critic best known for his action-packed and often irreverent *Coldstone Case Files* series and his dark Urban Fantasy/Alternate History *Clockworks of War* series. Jason streams on Twitch as Failflix with O Hai Mark and The Grey Cat on *Terrible Movies with Wonderful People.* His influences include horror cinema, bloody video games, dark beer, and heavy metal music.

The Coldstone Case Files

One with the Wolf
The Dog with Two Tails

Clockworks of War
Gaslit Insurrection
Gaslit Armageddon
Gaslit Revolution

Other Works
The Rifle Chronicles

FRIENDS OF FALSTAFF

Thank You to All our Falstaff Books Patrons, who get extra digital content each month! To be featured here and see what other great rewards we offer, go to www.patreon.com/falstaffbooks.

PATRONS

Dino Hicks
John Hooks
John Kilgallon
Larissa Lichty
Travis & Casey Schilling
Staci-Leigh Santore
Sheryl R. Hayes
Scott Norris
Samuel Montgomery-Blinn
Junkle
Vickie DeSantos
Quincy J. Allen
Allison Charlesworth

Thank You for Supporting Independent Publishing!

We believe that you should be able
to read your books, your way.
That's why this Falstaff Books
print edition includes a digital copy
at no additional cost!

Just scan the QR code with your device,
follow the directions on Prolific Works,
and enjoy!
You can also join our newsletter when prompted,
and never miss an awesome Falstaff Release!